Will heard Tess moving about the cart, the sound of her wet clothing dropping. "I am glad you were not hurt," he said, still smiling at the thought of her thrashing in the waist-deep water.

Tess's voice came to him from within. "You did not ask me if I was hurt — until now. You were laughing too loudly."

He was about to deny it, when she pushed aside the worn rug and then stepped back, running a comb through her wet hair. She had donned a monstrously large chemise, and it hung from her slight form in folds.

Will lifted himself into the gloomy interior of the cart. "You do not look too badly hurt. You seem to be as I recall," he teased. "Two arms, two legs . . ."

"The hurt was not a part you see."

"Shall I look for it?" he offered.

She gave him a sour face and turned away.

He wadded his wet shirt into a ball and thrust it into her hand. "Here, take my heart and step on it."

"I do not want your heart!" she exclaimed, though she could not keep from smiling.

Will smoothed her hair aside with gentle fingers and caressed her shoulders. "I thought I'd lost you to the beck," he murmured. "I'd sooner die than live without you." It was the truth, for at that moment, spurred on by the sharp pangs of desire, he wanted her above all else.

As much as she wanted to, Tess did not believe his pretty words. But the gentle touch of his marauding fingers sent a delicious chill racing through her limbs. She felt suddenly weak, helpless to resist his nearness, the warm scent of his skin, the broad shoulders, and the strong arms that so skillfully drew her to him.

He lowered his head to bring their lips together . . .

CAPTURE THE GLOW OF
ZEBRA'S *HEARTFIRES!*

CARNIVAL OF LOVE

PAIGE BRANTLEY

ZEBRA BOOKS
KENSINGTON PUBLISHING CORP.

ZEBRA BOOKS are published by

Kensington Publishing Corp.
475 Park Avenue South
New York, NY 10016

First Printing: October, 1993

Printed in the United States of America

Chapter One

"Milord, milord." The voice came to him from the swirling darkness of the tent. John Croaker, sheriff of St. Albans and justiciar to Edward IV, shifted on his cot and, raising his head, blinked into the haloed glow of a candle. The face framed in the haze of yellow light was that of his trusted lieutenant, Damon Swift.

"A boy has wandered into camp," he said in a breathless undertone. "A horseboy or the like who swears to have knowledge of Henry Lancaster."

The words and their implication cleared the grogginess from the sheriff's sleep-drugged brain. He sat up abruptly and called for his page. In the blackness of the tent he had not noticed the boy standing at the foot of the cot with his tunic and boots at the ready. The sheriff directed his words at Swift. "You say he walked into camp of his own accord?" In the fluttering light, John Croaker awkwardly struggled into his tunic and pulled on one boot.

"Yes, milord Sheriff. At first I, too, thought it a ruse, that the boy had been sent to deceive us, but there is more. He claims Henry Lancaster has sent a messenger south." Damon paused, handed him the other boot, then continued. "Langly was utterly convinced. He has gone to wake the king and ordered the boy brought to Edward's tent."

The mention of Langly's name brought a sour twist to the sheriff's lips, and he said, "It seems I must once again remind Sire Langly that I am King Edward's justiciar." The inflection of his voice left no doubt as to his intense dislike of the young lord who had so effortlessly wormed his way into Edward's inner circle. Frankly, John Croaker mistrusted Langly. He was ambitious and, moreover, he was Norfolk's man.

"Tell me all you know," Croaker demanded of his lieutenant as they stepped from the tent into the early morning darkness and quickly made their way past the smoldering fire beds and lines of tethered horses. They passed several boys carrying bundles of sticks for the fires. Here and there they passed a tent illuminated from within by a lamp or candle.

Langly and half a dozen other knights, King Edward's younger brother, the duke of Gloucester, as well as the earl of Norfolk and Lords Herbert and Hastings, were crowded into the king's tent. Edward, bleary-eyed, was wrapped in a fur-lined robe and sat on a leather-cushioned stool. On the far side of the tent, the heavy damask draperies surrounding Edward's bed rippled with movement. John Croaker noticed but thought little of it. Edward's love of bed sport was well known, and it was common for his favorites to accompany him on his travels.

At twenty-two, Edward had been king for three apprehensive years. He, with the support of his mentor, the earl of Warwick, had easily usurped the throne from the pious but feeble Henry Lancaster. Yet Henry still remained, like a ghost, to haunt him.

The object of all attention was the boy. He appeared dwarfed by the guards. At Norfolk's harsh command, he recited again the tale of his adventures. However, he wearily denied any knowledge of the old king's whereabouts. "They took him away. I saw them go, but I know not where."

"Who took him away?" Norfolk growled.

"The Percy's knights. There was a Frenchman with them, but I do not know his name."

Norfolk ground out an oath and made a menacing move toward the boy.

But Edward raised his hand. "Let him talk," he said. And addressing the boy, he asked, "What of the message? Did you actually see Henry Lancaster pass this missive to a knight?"

The boy nodded furiously. "He sealed it with wax, sire. It was red wax; I saw him tip the candle. I saw his lips moving, but there were too many voices between and I could make out but a word now and again." The boy's face brightened and he looked up hopefully. "London, I heard him say. London and the name of our heavenly Lord, but no more." His voice trailed off into silence, and he looked down at his hands as if he had just discovered them and did not now know what to do with them.

Edward was tempted to believe the boy. How like Henry, he thought, with all his piety and prayers. Perhaps it was Henry's meekness, his godliness, that Edward despised most and, yes, feared — for how does one kill a saint? "What is this knight's name?" Edward asked.

The boy hedged, wearing an expression of abject misery.

Norfolk, notoriously short-tempered, saw it as a ploy to extort payment and loudly threatened to crush the boy's skull.

Edward's swift look of displeasure did not go unnoticed by John Croaker. He stepped forward, quick to seize the opportunity, remarking, "We shall never know, milord Norfolk, if you relieve the lad of his faculties."

Norfolk responded with a hostile stare; but, censured by the ripple of laughter that passed through the tent, he said no more. He merely glared at the sheriff, whom he considered no more than a self-aggrandized peasant, and an upstart, common as dirt.

Common though he may have been, John Croaker was a good judge of human nature. He prided himself on being able to read men as easily as a priest reads Scripture. Norfolk was his enemy; he knew this and wasted no further thought on it. Rather, he turned his attention to the boy and asked, "Why have you turned against your lord?"

The boy, sensing the man with the pock-scarred

face might be his only salvation, answered eagerly. "My lord is dead, rotting on the moor, an' we was all turned out to fend for ourselves. I had no way to go, so I came here, hoping a knight would take me on as a groom, for 'tis all I've ever done."

A smile flitted over the sheriff's thin lips. "You expected no reward?" he pressed, observing the boy. His face was not yet a man's. He could have been no more than fifteen or sixteen—perhaps less, for there was something childish about his features, something almost feminine.

The boy shook his head vigorously. He had, of course, desired payment. In truth, it had been his only aim; but his cheekiness had turned to fear, and now it seemed he would be fortunate to be rewarded with his life.

"Boy," the sheriff continued, "this knight to whom Henry Lancaster gave the message, do you know what he was called?"

"No, sire, only that he was one of the Percy's knights. 'Twas because of the emblem on his tunic, the blue lion. I saw him take it off and put on a leather jerkin given him by a squire." When prompted, the boy told of the events following the battle, of the confusion, and of the abbey where Henry had taken refuge among the dead and wounded.

The fact that the sheriff had gotten more from the boy in a matter of moments than Norfolk had in an hour's time thoroughly annoyed the earl. He turned roundly and, catching John Croaker's eye, swept his gaze toward the king. "We're wasting time," he declared. "We still have not one whit of useful information. My methods get results."

Croaker's gaze remained on the boy, who had blanched white as whey.

"I know about the horse the messenger rode," the boy cried. " 'Tis a white horse and was the queen's favorite afore she went away to France. Its name is Turnip."

Laughter echoed through the tent, Norfolk's the loudest.

The boy's eyes roved frantically over the crowd, desperation rising in his voice. " 'Tis true!" the lad screeched. "The horse master said so!" He was nearly in tears. " 'Tis true! Oh, she called it something foreign and sweet-sounding, something I can't recall."

"Navet," Philippe de Commines offered.

"Aye, that's it, Navet," he repeated in his crude, broad accent.

"How truly enlightening," Norfolk mocked. "Now at least we know the horse's name."

Another round of laughter filled the tent, and one of the earls—perhaps it was Lord Herbert—said, "What sort of fool would choose a white horse? He'd rid himself of it at the first opportunity."

The sheriff, John Croaker, a squat, square-shouldered man with a mouth too large for his face, smiled slyly and remarked, "Lancastrians have never been known for their astuteness." Another ripple of laughter filtered amongst the assembled men.

Croaker paused a moment, for effect, then turning to the boy, queried, "You say you saw this knight. Describe him to us."

"He was young, no older than His Majesty, and tall like him. But his hair was dark an' cropped short for his helmet." The boy fell silent for an instant, as if he were thinking, then raised his head, beaming. "He was hurt," he went on. " 'Twas his leg. This one . . . hacked it was, an' deep, so that he limped when he walked."

"Then if you were to see this knight again, you would recognize him at once?"

The boy's shoulders sagged with relief. "Yes, milord sheriff. I would know his face among a thousand others!"

It was more than John Croaker had hoped for, and he approached the king with an assured air. "Place the boy under my protection, sire," he requested, "and I shall soon find this messenger."

Norfolk raised his voice in surly protest. Herbert took his side, but Edward, as he was apt to do, put them off, cajoling. "Take the boy," he said to John Croaker. "Find this messenger, for he will surely know of Henry's hiding place." The draperies rippled again with movement, momentarily capturing Edward's attention. He was smiling when he turned back to address the sheriff. "I expect results. Do not fail me."

The battlefields were far removed from the peaceful countryside that bordered the River Wharfe. Regardless of who emerged victorious, life would go on; the cotter's crops would grow; the sheep would graze, and the villagers' shops would prosper.

Only the landed gentry had cause to concern themselves over the outcome of the bloody feud between the houses of York and Lancaster. In all the valley, there were but two families who could claim noble ties. The de Traffords, though only remotely and by marriage, and the Hartleys.

After the disastrous Lancastrian defeat at the battle of Towton, the de Traffords had thrown in their lot with the Yorkists and sworn loyalty to King Edward. But Thurstan Hartley, the old earl of Devrel—who had lost his brother at the first battle of St. Albans, and lost two of his three nephews at Towton—had withdrawn from the struggle, disillusioned. What he had first seen as his duty—to uphold the rights of his anointed king, Henry VI—had involved him in a disastrous war of attrition that would not end until the flower of England's youth lay stone-cold dead on the battlefield. Like Pontius Pilate, he had publicly—though with words, not water—washed his hands of the struggle and stubbornly refused to pledge his loyalty to either side. However, his sole surviving nephew, the brash and youthful William, hell-bent on revenge, had quarreled with his uncle and gone off—in open defiance of his wishes—to serve the Lancastrian cause beneath the Percy banner.

* * *

Brother Osmond awoke with a start, lurched up from his bed linen, and sat blinking like an owl in the moonlit chamber. If a sound had disturbed his sleep, it was there no more. He muttered a prayer, but even holy words were unable to dispel the disquieting humor that had settled over him. After a time, he pried himself from the embrace of the down mattress and made his way unsteadily to the narrow slit of a window. Below, in the bailey, he saw only moonlight and shadows. Befuddled, he was about to turn away and set the blame for his sleeplessness on the tragic events of the day, when his ears caught a distant rumbling.

A mutter of thunder? A coming storm on such a cloudless night? Even his sleep-addled brain could not come to terms with such an explanation, and he stood staring into the shadowy June night. He was still there at the embrasure when the sound of heavy footsteps from the hall spun him round. Hamo, the steward, flung wide the door to his chamber.

Hamo, no wastrel of words, said only, "Horsemen are coming. I go to wake the lord."

"Yorkists?" Brother Osmond asked, but he had scarcely gotten the words from his lips before Hamo and his lantern had vanished into the swirling blackness of the hall. As Brother Osmond hovered at the door arch, two young kitchen boys topped the stairs with a lantern swaying before them. In the darkness of the house, an infant squalled. From the bailey below, the dogs sent up a noisy chorus.

Brother Osmond struggled into his robes and stumbled after the boys, taking Hamo's route to the lord's chamber.

By now, the entire household was awake. Servants converged in the lower hall. Disorder reigned amid a babel of voices and frenzied activity. In the apartments above, the bawling infant, having gained a second wind, wailed with renewed fury. Halfway down the hall, a stableboy raced past Brother Osmond. "Horsemen at the gate," he shouted. In another stride, the curate was confronted by the inquisitive and clearly fearful faces of Lady Maud and her serving woman framed in the glow of a single candle clutched between them.

In the earl of Devrel's garishly lit chamber, smoke poured from the guttering oil lanterns, and shadows leapt across the walls. Thurstan Hartley waved aside his squire's attempts to help him into his clothing. Hamo, his steward, was insisting loudly in a most ardent tone that the lord arm himself.

"No, Satan be damned," the old earl swore. "Let them murder me in my robe if that is their intent. Then all England will know what skulking cowards have seized the crown." And snatching up his robe, he fought his way into the fur-lined garment, motioning to the boy to light his path.

"Sire," Brother Osmond called, hurrying after his lord. "Might it have to do with young Will's return?" He bounded from the chamber, following the bouncing swath of light, past the anxious faces.

If the old earl heard, he made no reply. His fifty-four years weighed heavily upon him that night. There was the chronic stiffness in his hip and the occasional fluttering in his chest to remind him of the many battles he had survived. He would survive this, too, he told himself and strode on, weaving a path through those now gathered in the hall.

"Return to your chambers," he said. "Go back to your beds." He reached out his hand and gently touched his sister's shoulder as he passed, murmuring "It is nothing, Maud. What is left for them to take from us?" His eldest nephew's widowed wife stood by her door, with a colicky child in her arms. She looked terrified.

"There is nothing to fear, Elayne. It is only more Yorkist threats," he added, his voice trailing after him. "They cannot force my allegiance," he grumbled. "And they dare not murder me before Parliament convenes this Christ-tide. What is there left for them but to torment me to death?"

Down through the hall they went, past the knots of frightened servants, the ghostly glow of their lanterns casting fantastic shapes before them. The gates were opened, and the air of the soft, warm night was rent by the baying of dogs and the sound of jostling horsemen. Thurstan Hartley, clad only in his robe and slippers, stood before the thick oaken doors of Devrel Hall. He was a large man, both tall and broad; in his youth he had been formidable. His voice was still, and his words boomed above the clatter of mail and harness. "By whose authority do you disturb the peaceful sleep of decent men?" he called.

15

"By the highest authority, that of King Edward." The voice resounded from the mass of riders, who surely numbered thirty or more. From their midst, a squat, square-shouldered man urged his horse forward. In the moonlight and the wash of light from the lanterns, he appeared little more than a darkened form. "Thurstan Hartley, Earl of Devrel?" he inquired, peering into the haze of lamplight.

"I am the earl of Devrel. By what name are you known, and what business brings you to my door at this ungodly hour?"

"I am John Croaker, sheriff of St. Albans, justiciar of the Crown. I seek the person of William Hartley, a son of this house."

The old earl stood his ground, demanding, "To what purpose?"

"That is mine to judge," the sheriff pronounced, signaling to his troop to dismount. "Stand aside, sire, or suffer the consequences."

"My nephew is not within these walls," he assured him, almost affably, his tone altering.

The sheriff, sensing some trickery, spoke more sharply. "Where is your nephew? You cannot hope to defend him against my force. Turn him over to me. I have no wish to slaughter you and those of your house. Make no mistake, all will die. I will spare neither women nor children, nor even servants."

Brother Osmond said not a word. He looked on with a pale face and trembling lips. He did not doubt for a moment the sheriff's intent. He saw the future with a terrible clarity, for he knew as surely as he knew his paternoster where the earl was leading with his words. It was in his eyes and lurked in the tone of his deep, full voice. The earl was taking his revenge—a small revenge, perhaps, though Brother Osmond wondered what view the justiciar might take of being made the butt of an infernal joke.

"Softly, good sheriff," Thurstan Hartley advised in an all-too-calm voice. "There is no need to rant."

"I do not make idle threats!"

"I am certain you do not. Neither do I utter falsehoods. My nephew is not within these walls. He is there," Thurstan Hartley conceded, "in the chapel."

Alighting from his horse, John Croaker passed the reins to one of his guards. By nature he was suspicious. He feared duplicity, though he would not be deceived, for he had with him the young groom who had served at Henry's camp. With an impatient gesture, he had the boy hustled from where he stood by the restlessly stamping horses. A guard was posted on the house and gate, and the sheriff with the groom in tow, a dozen burly guards, the earl, his confessor, the steward, and several servants made their way across the darkened bailey to the chapel.

The blunted tower stood black against a starry sky. An ancient structure of crumbling stone and rusting iron, it was of a type built in ages past by returning crusaders and had virtually no windows.

A novice, who served at Mass and whose duty it was to recite prayers, bolted up from the altar rail at the sound of the chapel doors. Lost to his prayers and made deaf by the thickness of the walls, he rose, poised as if for flight, gaping open-mouthed at the host of men who entered unannounced. He was taken so by surprise that for an instant he forgot his obeisance, then, fumbling backwards, genuflected and withdrew to cower beneath the niche of a benevolent wooden saint.

Before the altar, a long black coffin lay between two rows of guttering candles. The sight of it halted John Croaker in midstride. He turned menacingly upon the old earl, a vicious slant to his pock-scarred jaw, demanding, "What trickery is this?"

"God's will, I am told," the old earl responded frostily.

John Croaker's broad mouth took on an ugly twist, and he shouted, "Where is your nephew?"

"He is there before God, just as I said."

"Surely," the sheriff snarled, "you do not expect me to believe your nephew is in that coffin, so conveniently dead?"

"My nephew fell at the battle of Hexham," Thurstan Hartley supplied grimly. "Though, truthfully," he added, mouthing the words as if they were something bitter, "it matters not to me what you believe." In truth, the old earl himself doubted the identity of the corpse which the Percy's servants had so dutifully returned to him, though that he wisely left unsaid.

It was all the sheriff could manage, to curb his temper, so intense was the urge to lay hands on the old earl, to strike and humble him. Instead, he commanded his guards to open the coffin. "Cast the lid aside. Quickly, you clumsy fools!"

Even with the lid in place, the odor of putrefying flesh hung heavily in the humid, still air of the ancient chapel. Once the cover was removed, the sickening stench drove the guards backwards and permeated every crevice of the chamber. John Croaker swallowed deeply and, drawing in as little breath as possible, drew nearer the black-stained box. The sick, putrid miasma of decay rising from the coffin caused his eyes to tear and seared the insides of his nostrils.

It was a hideously grotesque thing, ripe with maggots, yet he found it fascinating by the very nature of its revolting condition. The corpse, that of a young man, fully dressed, had been wedged into the coffin and was in such an advanced state of decomposition that the blackened flesh of the carefully placed hands had begun to fall away from the bones. Several massive wounds to the skull were yet visible, attesting to a death by violence—in battle, perhaps? Clearly it was no recent death, for the corpse was rather one that had lain too long exposed in the heat of June. Much too long, in fact—for what features of the face that had not been altered by decay had been mashed, distorted by the coffin's lid. Only the blue lion of the house of Percy was still recognizable on the blood-stiffened tunic.

Could another Percy knight be stricken from his list? John Croaker wondered. The body in the coffin might have been anyone—a traveler murdered by thieves, a nameless yeoman taken from the battle-field, a changeling — conjured up to spare a favored nephew . . . or to speed a message on its way? He was not a man to be easily duped; moreover, the old earl's trickery had rankled him. He had been played for a fool, led along like a silly, credulous girl. He was livid with anger. "Bring the boy here!" he shouted.

The boy, pushed to the fore by a guard, hesitated, horrified by the thought of what lay in the coffin. The sheriff gripped his scrawny shoulder, dragging his unwilling feet across the stones.

"Is that the man?"

He craned his neck, stammering, "No, sire," then quickly averted his eyes from the rotting thing.

"Look hard upon his face," the sheriff growled and, cursing the boy, snatched him by the scruff of the neck and thrust his face into the coffin.

The terrified boy arched his spine and braced his grubby hands against the coffin's rim. "No, sire," he whined, begging to be set free.

"You are certain?"

"The leg," he cried, bobbing his head like a cork and all but gagging on the words. "The leg was hacked!"

The boy had turned quite white around the eyes and the sheriff pushed him aside, though not quickly enough to prevent his boots from being splattered by the contents of the boy's stomach.

John Croaker uttered an oath and, stomping his fouled boots, gazed one last time at the corpse before stalking across the chapel to confront the old earl. "Pray your nephew lies there in the coffin," the sheriff advised him venomously. "For if I find him among the living, you will share his traitor's death!"

Only when the last of the horsemen had ridden from the bailey did Brother Osmond venture to speak. "Could it be that William still lives, milord?"

Thurstan Hartley gave a weary smile. "Anything is possible, Osmond. Do the Scriptures not attest to it?"

"Indeed they do, to the grace of God and to miracles. Even the prodigal returns home a wiser man."

"Perhaps we should not ask for too many miracles," he cautioned, though the smile was still on his lips.

Chapter Two

At nearby Lambsdale Mill, the ancient wheel creaked on and the mighty stones ground out the grain, uncaring for the fates of kings.

Above the miller's solar, the bedchamber was loud with laughter, bright and dazzling as the shafts of golden sunlight braced against the oaken floor. Mary made a moue and stuck out her tongue at her sisters—"Not the likes of you—or you." She laughed, quickly arming herself with a pillow.

Tess, the youngest of the three, gave a toss of her flaxen hair and pounced upon the bed, giggling wildly. She snatched up a goose-down pillow and, wearing an expression of mock indignation, wailed, "Did you hear? We are not invited to her wedding feast!"

Sybelle, the middle sister, laughed. Wielding her fat pillow like a weapon, she feinted right, then left, stalking her elder sister around the bed. "Methinks she is the queen, Queen of Goosie Down!" she declared with a gleeful squeal and boxed her ears. Mary retaliated, blow for blow. Back and forth the contest went with traded insults and feathers flying, peals of laughter, and cheers from Tess. Bouncing upon the bed, the girl recited, "We would not pick our noses, teeth, or nails—nor scratch our backsides, nor . . ." But before Tess could add another line, Mary turned on her and brought the pillow down soundly on her head. "I shall have the servants throw you in the midden," she threatened in a voice broken by giggles. Then Sybelle's pillow thumped her shoulders and sent her reeling forward with a resounding "Whoomph!"

All three romped across the mattress, slugging away amid gales of laughter. Tess clutched her pillow like a shield and, fending off the blows, sang out, "Oh Mary, Mary fair and sweet. She loves Ralph Baggyhose with the stinking feet!" Sybelle, teary-eyed from laughing, added, "Mary, Mary sweet as a rose. She lost her heart but held her nose!"

In the midst of their caterwauling, Bertrade's dark head appeared at the door. "For shame," she shouted in a scolding voice. "There is work to be done, and the morning be half gone. Mary, you are not yet Lord de Trafford's daughter by marriage. There is sewing to finish. Sybelle, you have not yet swept the solar, and you," she said, pointing her finger at Tess, "have eggs to gather." Bertrade could not disguise her mirthful tone, nor her amusement, and her idle threats of "switching the lot of you" elicited only another round of walloping pillows and riotous laughter.

Bertrade was the wife of their grandfather's steward, and it was she who had raised them after their parents' death. She was herself but a score of years older than Mary; and under her jolly permissiveness, the trio had grown up happily, if not properly, into high-spirited young women.

Only the stern voice of their grandfather brought them to heel. They had thought him gone to collect his rents until his gruff voice bellowed from the hall.

Their laughter choked off, and the trio jerked to attention. They sat pink-faced and breathless in the middle of the rumpled bed with their long fair hair swirled about their heads like demented haloes.

"Why are your chores not done?" he demanded in a voice unmistakably harsh and unyielding. He had little patience with his three granddaughters. At times he felt cursed to be saddled with three silly girls rather than sturdy, sensible grandsons. It was surely a punishment; still, he had fulfilled his duty. He had kept them and seen them grown and had arranged their marriages, good marriages all. Only Tess's betrothal had given him cause for concern. The marriage date had been twice set aside with no clear explanation.

He watched them, his eye severe, as they scampered down the stairs and wished him, "Good morning, sir," before dashing off to see to their neglected duties. They were comely girls, fair haired and well formed. Mary, the eldest, was very like her mother with her gentle ways and mild, pleasant face. Sybelle, the middle child, was stoutish with a broad cheerful face; she beamed with good health. Tess was

24

the youngest, and without a doubt she was the handsomest. She was as blond and fair as her sisters, but there the similarity ended, for she was a wild little creature, headstrong and determined as himself and with a quick shrewdness that was somehow unsettling to the male mind. She would, Adam Shaw decided with a wry smile, be a challenge for any man.

Later when Ivo, Adam Shaw's steward arrived astride his bay, leading the old man's mare, he mentioned having seen Tess walking through the meadow. "The geese have gone down the stream again," he reported with a note of concern. Tess, as he knew, could not swim; and Willowes Beck was swift and deep, save for the riffles downstream.

"Let her go," Adam Shaw remarked, settling into his saddle. "The geese are hers and hers to keep from harm." He had never been one to pamper his granddaughters, and he would not begin at this late date. His thoughts were on his rents. He was a wealthy man, as millers often were. His own grandfather had been a trusted villein of a powerful lord, and the mill and lands had come to him as payment for his brave and loyal service. Over the years, advantageous marriages had enlarged the holdings further, so that his granddaughters' dowries were desirable indeed and much sought after by the local barons. Not worthy of a first son, perhaps, but tempting to a second or third-born, one with no hope of an inheritance and whose sole worth was his noble name.

Chapter Three

Squinting into the bright afternoon, Tess scoured the stream's course. At Lambsdale Woods, the stream meandered from view. She could follow the water's edge, though there the banks were steep, or cut over the hill to the riffle. The route over the hill and through Tonbridge Woods was longer; but she was not in any hurry to return, reasoning that if she tarried long enough, the solar would be swept, the rugs beaten, and the peas hulled.

She pushed back a stray strand of flaxen hair and set off up the hill. In the warm June afternoon, sunlight danced upon the fluttering leaves, tossing bright shapes amid the shadows beneath the huge trees. Clumps of wood sorrel, fern, and lichen carpeted the dank ground, and the warm air was heavy with the breath of rotting leaves. At the crest of the low hill, the stream — bathed in sunlight — sparkled through the trees. The song of birds drifted on the mild breeze and another sound, faint, yet unmistakable to her, echoed up the hill. It was the deep musical call, "ha-lunk, ha-lunk," of her wandering geese.

A joyous feeling of relief surged through her breast. Her silly geese were not yet a fox's dinner, she thought with a smile, and hurried toward the sound.

She had not gone far when a loud crashing noise all but stopped her heart. Directly before her, the dense undergrowth shook violently and, with a brutish snort, the tossing head of a horse rose above a thickset clump of young oaks. Tess gave a startled gasp and stumbled backwards, calmly telling herself, "It is naught but a horse, just an ordinary horse." Though it was not at all ordinary. It was as white as a ghost where the speckled sunlight played upon its arched neck, and its finely chiseled head was that of a blooded animal. Even its harness was not ordinary but of black leather and brass, like that of a knight's horse. Perhaps it was the strangeness of finding it there or the dark gloominess beneath the trees that gave rise to memories of Bertrade's fireside tales of phantom knights who roamed the countryside seducing maidens and stealing their souls.

Graceful as a swan, the white horse turned its head and gazed at her with huge, dark, wide-set eyes. Tess held her breath; a shiver of fear raced up her spine.

It was not a conscious decision, rather an impulse, that moved her to turn and flee. She ran blindly, crashing through the underbrush, her heart pounding in her ears, her feet stumbling over the ground. She did not see the obstacle that checked her flight and sent her sprawling. It was as if the sky had turned over and the earth had come up and thrown

27

itself against her. Something struck her shoulder, and she cried out. Only then did she see the youthful face, darkened by the stubble of a half-grown beard, a dead man's face, not a breath away from hers.

The eyes blinked open, intensely dark, instantly alert. A shudder of horror pulsed through her, and she clawed at the earth in a desperate bid to gain her footing.

A hand seized her ankle with an iron-hard grip and slammed her down with such stunning swiftness and such force that it left her gasping for air. Above her she saw the flash of a blade. A brief startled yelp of terror escaped her lips; but before she could muster a full-blown scream, a filthy hand clamped over her mouth and she felt his crushing weight atop her.

Will Hartley stared down at the pale wisp of a girl in stupefied silence, like Lazarus wakened from the dead. His groggy brain was unable to control the hallucination of nerves, the frenzy that set his hands to trembling. In another instant he would have killed her, slit her throat, for there was the knife poised in his hand. She was hardly more than a girl, a blond, pale-skinned thing with a spattering of freckles across her nose and huge blue eyes. The thought of what he had nearly done left him suddenly giddy, weak, as if he had run a very long distance. A panting sound thundered in his ears, and only then did he realize it was his own breath whistling through his teeth.

"I meant you no harm," he said, his voice no more than a hoarse whisper. As if to give credence to his words, he slowly returned the dagger to the sheath at his side. He would have shifted his weight off her but feared she would scream. "I will not harm you. Swear to me you will not scream if I take my hand away?" the gravelly voice demanded.

Tess stared back at him with wild, terrified eyes. He was neither dead man nor phantom, but living flesh and blood. He smelled of horses and long-dried sweat, and his dark eyes were deep as wells. Deep enough to drown her. All at once she arched against him, thrashing her arms and legs and twisting like a dervish.

She had caught him by surprise, and now they tumbled in the wood sorrel and fern with grunts and gasps and grappling hands. Tess threw herself to one side, dodging his arms. In a heartbeat she was on her feet and running, a single thought exploding in her brain—escape!

He lurched up and bounded after her, skidding down the hill, favoring his injured leg as much as he was able as he dodged tree trunks and crashed through the brambles and close-set saplings.

Tess plunged through the thicket, a mindless terror gripping her heart. Brambles tore at her flesh and clothing, and the branches swept aside by her passage whipped back at her pursuer. With a fearful backward glance, she saw him closing ground. She could not run any faster; the calves of her legs ached, and her lungs burned as if they were afire. Free of the woods, she flung herself toward the willows and sedges at the stream's edge. But on open ground, her freedom lasted only as long as the reach of his arm.

He caught her by the shoulder and brought her down. They hit the ground and tumbled into the willows, coming to rest on the muddy creek bank in a tangle of arms and legs.

Tess opened her mouth to scream, but no sound came out. Before she could catch her breath, he pinned her face down in the mud with his one hand on the back of her neck and the other twisting her wrist behind her, jerking it to her shoulder blade. She heard him curse and threaten, "Be still!" Dropping his head, he pressed his lips to her ear, repeating, "Be still." He tightened his grip on her wrist and murmured, "I do not want to harm you, but you must not scream. Do you understand?"

Tess blinked. All before her eyes misted and flowed together. She nodded mutely. A millrace of desperate thoughts coursed through her mind. She heard his labored breathing, the distant honking of her geese, and voices—male voices—followed by the crash of brush.

Will Hartley also heard the voices. He swiveled his head toward the sound and, collaring the wriggling girl, clamped a hand over her mouth and dragged her deeper into the sprawling willows. In the struggle Tess had lost one of her leather clogs, and her bare foot scuffed across the pebbles as he dragged her backwards.

The harsh shouts and crash of brush grew steadily nearer. The geese, floating near the opposite bank, gabbled a warning and swam off downstream. Moments later, half a dozen Yorkist soldiers hacked their way through the tangle of brambles and dense willows and surveyed the stream. Their crossbows were slung over their shoulders, and one by one they returned their swords to the scabbards at their sides. To their left more shouts rang out, and another group of soldiers emerged from the undergrowth further downstream. They appeared like walking bushes, for leaves and branches ripped loose by their passage still clung to the crossbows that were slung across their backs. They splashed along the stream's edge and joined the first group.

"Do we go on, across the beck?" one from among the second contingent of soldiers asked with little enthusiasm.

"No, there is no purpose to it," the fat man who appeared to be their captain remarked. "No one brought a horse through there." His observation was seconded by several others.

"Not a hare could have crawled through them brambles!" a lanky, bearded youth said as he hawked and spit into the stream.

"He's gone to ground, that's what," a shorter youth asserted.

"Aye," yet another agreed. "There's many a Lancastrian sympathizer hereabouts. They're hiding him, an' John Croaker be damned. He'll get no respect till he's burned them out an' hanged a few what holds with the French queen and the Percys."

His words were met with hearty agreement. The

31

jolly conversation continued with several lewd references to Queen Margaret and King Henry followed by caws of loud laughter.

One crouched down and gathered up a handful of stones and sent them skipping one by one across the stream. A stone struck the shoreline directly before them. Will watched it bounce and roll and come to rest beside a girl's lost leather clog.

The small brown clog, lying on its side at the water's edge, loomed large as a house in Will's eyes. But the soldier, bragging loudly of his prowess at hurling stones across the stream, did not notice it. He continued to skip stones while others took the opportunity to relieve themselves.

Beneath the willows, Tess glowed with embarrassment. She feared her red face must surely be visible to all. The worst was yet to come, for the soldiers' activity soon deteriorated into a noisy and hotly debated competition, much on the order of a spitting contest, which caused Tess to blush to the roots of her hair.

Only after the uproarious laughter had died away was a discussion of how best to reach the Lambsdale road, and their horses. Shortly afterwards the two groups set off the way they had come.

In the humid closeness of the willows, Tess risked a glance at her captor. He was the one the soldiers were hunting; she knew it with a swift certainty. He had the same anxious dark eyes as the fox who had once blundered into the kitchen with de Trafford's dogs at his heels. Bold as brass, the fox had fled through the kitchen and into the hall, past the chair where her grandfather slept; and with a graceful bound, he had leapt onto the silver chest and out through the narrow slot of a window, leaving her thoroughly befuddled grandfather to be serenaded by the baying dogs.

Their eyes met and Tess whispered, "Let me go. I'll not betray you, I swear it. Please let me go." Tears brimmed her eyes, and her hushed words were choked with emotion.

For an instant it seemed he would relent; but, just as suddenly, his features hardened and he said, "No. They will search the farmsteads. They would question you."

"I would not tell." She spoke in a hushed voice, reasoning with him. "How could they know, if I did not tell?"

He ignored her, dragging her to her feet and down to the stream's edge. But she would not be silent. Finally, he said, also in a muted whisper, "You would not need to tell them with words. Look at you. There are grass stains on your back. You have blood on your skirt. Pick up your shoe," he commanded.

Her back she could not see, but there were no bloodstains on her skirt. Why should there be? Only then did her disbelieving eyes focus on the bright crimson stain of blood that marked her blue gown — and the cause of it: a bloody cloth bound about his thigh.

Tess stooped to retrieve her lost clog. It was wet and squished when she slid it onto her foot. With handfuls of water, she attempted to wash the telltale stain from her skirt. All the while, she had hardly taken her eyes from him. He was tall and slender, as young men were apt to be, though his shoulders were broad and, despite the coarse dark stubble on his jaw, his features were clear-cut and pleasant. Perhaps it was his eyes that frightened her most, for they were quick and intelligent.

"I will tell them I was searching for my geese," she suggested, hoping to convince him of her resourcefulness. From where she stood, she could not see the extent of his injury, but she saw him unbind the wound and dip the cloth in the stream. She watched the dark cloud of blood mix and mingle with the bright water.

"When I am asked," she went on in the same hushed tone, "I will tell them I lost my footing by the stream."

He looked up swiftly, his dark gaze boring into her. "You will tell them nothing. You are coming with me."

If the black look was meant to silence her, it served its purpose.

She pressed her lips into a pout and slowly, methodically, wrung the water from her skirt hem.

He bound his thigh with the cloth and was in the process of securely knotting it when Tess again pleaded, "Let me go. I'll not betray you, I swear upon all that is holy."

"In the next village," he told her. Then he took her by the arm and shoved her toward the wooded hillside they had so recklessly descended only a short time before. Perhaps it was then the idea occurred to Will Hartley or perhaps he had seen the possibilities from the very first. The Yorkists were searching for retreating Lancastrian knights, not common yeomen and camp followers. His decision, though quickly made, was not without guilt. Surely, he thought, it was a sin to risk another's life for a cause not of their choosing. But it seemed a greater sin to leave her, knowing what price she would pay if she were questioned.

There was no real danger. He argued the point silently with himself as he made his way painfully up the hill. At Bolton he would leave her at the abbey; no harm would come to her there and he would be safely away. How she might explain her disappearance to her kinsmen was another matter, one he had not the time to consider.

As they crested the hill, he took her arm and hurried her along. Tess balked with every step, her feet stumbling over twigs and tree roots. The clumsy clogs she wore were work shoes, better suited to barnyard mud than trekking through the woods.

He had not noticed; he had problems enough of his own. His injured leg ached with a fury, and he was no longer sure where he had left the horse. Sunlight winked through the trees. He halted for a moment, his gaze searching out a scrap of white hide among the myriad shades of green. Without the horse, he had no chance of evading the Yorkists.

It was white as a ghost, obvious as a drunkard's

nose; why could he not see it? He cursed softly, thinking he had been stupid to chase after the girl. Better to have let her go screaming home than to lose the horse. He pulled her along with him, his gaze searching the thicket. A thrill of panic tingled his spine. Finally, he spotted the animal, rather the flash of its white tail and silken rump.

At their approach, the white horse lifted its head and shifted sideways. It was a beautiful creature; and Tess, who was not ignorant where horses and country matters were concerned, saw it was a gelding. Her own palfrey that carried her to hear Mass on Sundays was a gelding, though it was a pony and, regardless of how much she groomed it, scruffy. A lovable pet that first Mary had outgrown, then Sybelle. Only Tess, who had not grown a whit taller since her twelfth birthday, had never outgrown the fat pony.

Tess raised her eyes to her captor's, intending to plead once again; but his features were set as those carved into stone, and her voice deserted her.

Without a word, he boosted her into the saddle, then, taking the reins, seated himself behind her. Tess's spine stiffened at his touch. She must do something, she thought. Save herself, though she did not know how. The utter hopelessness of her situation brought tears to sting her eyes.

Astride the tall white horse, she felt suddenly too far above the ground, displaced from reality. She was breathless, and gripped by the same uneasy sensation as when she had climbed too high in the apple tree one summer.

Beyond the stream, bright with the reflection of clouds and blue sky, were the green fields of Lambsdale, the distant bell tower of St. George's, and the humble rooftops of the village of Hovey. Moments passed, hardly bearable, as with each stride the white horse carried her away from all the years that had been, from all she had ever known.

The woods, which had at first been familiar were now strange, denser, marked with the dark, narrow trails of small animals and tangled with thickets of brambles and vines. For what seemed an eternity, they rode at a slow, steady pace. The only sounds were the muffled tread of hooves on the soft ground and the jangle of harness.

When Tess could no longer bear the silence, she whispered, "Why do they search for you? Are you a thief?" She expected no reply; and when he spoke, the sound of his whispered words startled her.

"No. Do I look like a thief?" he asked in a voice edged with what might have been either annoyance or amusement. It was impossible to gauge the emotion of the husky voice, the murmured words.

More a thief than anyone she had ever had the misfortune to meet, she thought. Yet, in spite of his filthy clothing and unshaven appearance, there was a look of honesty and decency about him that she could not explain. "Then what have you done?" she asked, half-turning in the saddle.

He smiled at her. The way young men do at comely girls. Because she was pretty as a summer's day and because he had been too long alone. He said, "The less you know of me the better." He had not meant to smile; it was as involuntary as the quickening of his pulse, the rush of blood, the gradual tightening in his loins. He was aware of everything about her—the sheen of moisture on her cheek, the pale dusting of freckles, the fine blue vein at the base of her throat, the scent of her skin.

"Why?" she posed, pushing aside a stray strand of flaxen hair and glancing back to him. "Are you one of King Henry's knights? My grandfather says the Yorkists hunt them down and hang them." In the sunlight his dark eyes sparkled with golden motes and his smile was so nice she could almost believe he meant her no harm.

"Is your grandfather a Yorkist?"

"No," she said too quickly. In truth, she had never given a thought to such matters. On reflection, it seemed far more likely that her grandfather gave not a care for either York or Lancaster as long as his business interests did not suffer.

Before them, the woods opened to dazzling blue sky and meadows dense with tiny yellow flowers. The mild breeze was almost intoxicating, filled with the sweetness of the blossoms; and the marshy ground beneath was meshed with little streams, rivulets of shining water that appeared for a short distance then vanished beneath the mat of grass and wildflowers.

"You speak of a grandfather. Have you a husband as well?" he quizzed, hoping, illogically, that she hadn't.

She frowned into the sunlight. "No," she said. "It is my grandfather who will search for me."

"Then he need search no farther than the abbey at Bolton."

"And what will I say to my grandfather? A soldier stole me away? He would not be pleased to hear that. There would be gossip, and my marriage contract would be set aside once and for all."

His smile broadened, dimpling his cheeks. "So you are betrothed. Would *he* not search for you?"

She shrugged her small shoulders. "I saw him only once when we were children. He makes excuses now, for he does not wish to marry me. My dowry is not grand enough for him."

"A fool, surely."

"He will have good reason now to set aside the contract."

"You could lie to him—or is he only a fool and not gullible as well?"

"What would I tell him? What will I say to my grandfather? That I wandered away like the village fool. Then I would be called weak-minded or a witch. I would rather they believed I ran off with a soldier. No matter what I say, truth or lie, no decent man will have me for a wife."

"Shall I come back and marry you?"

Her clear blue eyes flashed with annoyance. "To you it is a jest!"

"I did not mean it as such. I can think of no fonder place to spend cold eternity than in your warm and loving arms."

Her lips pursed spitefully, and she retorted, "Must I suffer your flattery as well as your company?" Perhaps it was the ring of snobbery she detected in his voice that vexed her so. He was no different from the de Traffords with all their airs and foppery.

" 'Twas not flattery, but fair truth, unbidden and from my heart." He was thoroughly enjoying himself.

"I doubt you have a heart. Have you murdered someone? Is that why they search for you?"

He chuckled. "In truth, it is I who have been fatally wounded by your many charms."

"Are those the words you say to all young girls?"

He gave a soft laugh. "You are a witch. Do you read all men so easily?"

"It is hardly magic. They have but a single thought in their minds!"

He laughed aloud, confessing it was the first time in days he had done so. "What is your name?" he asked, his breath warm on her ear and the smile still on his lips.

"Tess."

"Tess," he repeated. "It has a lively spirit to it. It suits you well."

The way he said her name sent a little tingle up her spine. In spite of her annoyance, she found herself liking the sound of his voice, as if she had been waiting all her life to hear him say her name. Her fears evaporated like mist in the sunshine. "Have *you* a name?" she pressed, glancing over her shoulder.

For an instant he was held captive by her eyes. They were blue as the sky, and somewhere in their depths was the promise of laughter and eagerness. "Will," he finally said.

"Will and no more?" she retorted.

She was much too pretty, he thought, and he was a fool to have brought her along. For no more than the shy, teasing tone of her voice sent his blood to singing and left him feeling clenched as a fist. He had no time for such pursuits. Shifting uncomfortably in the saddle, he replied, "Only Will, and you have asked enough questions." His smile faded and the loam-rich eyes gazed past her, lost to the distance.

Chapter Four

They rode out the afternoon in silence. He did not speak again except to point out a lake, shining in the distance, where they would stop to rest and water the horse.

All that day he guided the horse with a sure hand, not unlike a man riding over his own lands, and it seemed to Tess that he was not a stranger to the dale. At last they came to a broad meadow where the tall grass grew lush and thick. Stirred by the breeze, the grasses billowed like waves and their shadow, cast long and thin by the late afternoon sun, floated like a ship on an emerald sea.

At the lake, Tess slipped from her leather clogs and, wrapping her still-damp skirt about her legs in peasant fashion, waded ankle-deep beside the white horse as it dipped its head to drink. The lake's grassy banks extended into the warm shallow water, so at its shore it looked like a puddle left by a rain shower. Water beetles darted across its surface.

Tess patted the horse fondly. "What is his name?" she asked.

Will halted at the water's edge, crouched down, and, cupping his hands, drank several mouthfuls of the tepid water. "Navet," he said without thinking.

"A French name for an English horse." Her blue eyes smiled.

"He was not mine to name," Will said curtly.

She turned away, chastised, concealing her confusion behind a sweep of fair lashes.

Will sluiced a handful of water over his face. He had already said more than he'd intended. The days with little or no sleep and less food had taken their toll. He hardly recognized the haggard face reflected in the still water. His leg pained him enough that he knew it was still there, though the bleeding had stopped. A dark russet crust had formed on the cloth binding the wound. He drew his fingers tenderly across it, debating whether or not to unloose the cloth and rinse the blood away. Better not to disturb it, he decided.

He looked up to see the horse slosh from the lake, swishing its tail as it moved off to rip greedily at the luxuriant grass. His gaze settled once again on the girl silhouetted against the sun. With her long fair hair and simple grace

43

she might have been a heroine from one of Brother Osmond's Viking tales.

Beguiled by the gilded surface of the lake, Tess dipped her fingers into the warm waters. Ripples spread like molten gold. "It is beautiful here," she said in a wistful voice, meant perhaps for him, perhaps for the sun or for the shimmering waters.

"Yes," he agreed in much the same sense. These were his uncle's lands. His, if he lived to see the day and if the Yorkists did not seize Devrel in the name of the Crown. But it was best not to think of the future, just as it was best not to tarry.

He had been so close to food, a safe bed, and a fresh horse — for, despite their quarrel, he knew his uncle would not have denied him that. Perhaps it was best he had turned away; he had brought enough grief to Devrel Hall. He would die before he led the Yorkists there.

The war had taken an evil turn, and he did not understand this new ruthlessness on Edward's part. In the past he had been forgiving of his foes as long as they would pay fealty to him. Now, he sent his justiciar to hunt them down like vermin. "Kill the noble; spare the common man" had been the Yorkists' cry. Will had seen proof of it in Grassington and Hexley, where bloated corpses swung from trees and the rotting heads of Lancastrian knights adorned the town gates. He rose slowly and limped toward the horse.

Tess followed, pleading to his back. "Leave me here. You would be far and away before I reached my home. What could it matter to you?"

He turned the horse and led it back. "If ever you reached your home," he said, reminding her. "Have you forgotten the soldiers by the beck?"

"They were searching for you! Not for me," she finished lamely, knowing in her heart all he had implied was true.

"They would have hanged me and been done with it." A dark comma of hair fell onto his forehead. He brushed it aside with an impatient gesture, adding, "You would not have been so fortunate." He waited, watching as she unbound her skirts and shook the creases from the coarse material. Then, cupping his hands, he boosted her into the saddle.

Tess said no more. She could only imagine what would have been her fate had the soldiers found her alone by the stream. But, she wondered, was she any safer in his company? He, too, was a soldier — at least she guessed him to be, and the thought of the approaching night filled her with dread.

Toward evening, they came upon a rutted country lane. They halted there. Tess found privacy behind a bush, while Will made use of the roadside. After completing the ritual, he surveyed the countryside, determining the sun would be down in another hour and Bolton was yet a day's ride east. They would need a place to spend the night. From the appearance of the lane, it was heavily used. Will scanned the landscape for higher ground, a place where he might still view the path, but remain unseen.

A riot of pink daisies with centers as dark and velvety brown as an ox's eye spilled onto the lane. Tess paused to pluck one; but, as she reached out her hand, a peal of childish laughter turned her head. The playful note soon became a chorus.

Will quickly brought the horse round, hesitating, for the voices were clearly youthful and likely those of cotter's children from a nearby farmstead. They posed no danger, Will reasoned. Moreover, it was too late to hide. There was still time to gallop away, but it seemed unnecessary.

The gabble of chattering voices drew nearer. A ragged chase of children topped the rise. Only then did the others appear, heads and shoulders breaking above the rutted lane, half a dozen or so men and women—peasants all—tramping along on sturdy legs and dressed in whatever finery they possessed.

At the sight of the strangers, the children called and raced to greet them. In a twinkling, Will and Tess were surrounded by a mob of snotty-nosed moppets who jigged about, babbled endless questions, and clamored round the white horse, reaching out their small hands to stroke and pet the animal's moon white hide.

The children's elders, parents and kin, approached with equal good cheer. A middle-aged man, neither tall nor short, with a stocky build and a ruddy face, hailed them. "God's blessing," he said. The others came forward with similar greetings.

"Where are you going?" a younger man wanted to know. A round little woman with grey hair asked, "Have you come from Owlsey?" The children blabbed and jabbered until a young man with a thick overhanging brow shouted at them to be still and shooed them away.

Amid the commotion, Will answered good-naturedly but told them little. He was more concerned that his pretty blond captive would betray him. But when he looked for her, he found her crouched down talking to a little barefoot girl with thick dark braids.

The ruddy-faced man did most of the talking. Will learned they were on their way to the wedding feast of the man's brother.

"I see you are a soldier," the ruddy-faced man said.

It was a logical assumption. For in the weeks following the great battles in the North, hordes of returning soldiers trailed south, filling the roads and villages. Most were afoot, some astride horses they had come upon following the battles.

Like them, Will wore the rough garb of the peasant soldier of both York and Lancaster. All, like Will, carried either a sword or longbow. They wore hosen of leather or some other suitably thick material, a coarse woven baggy shirt, boots without spurs, and a leather *jaque* into which thin metal discs had been fixed between the layers of leather. The discs were small and not visible except for being outlined by wear.

Usually soldiers employed three discs, blessed and symbolizing the trinity. They were arranged with one larger disc between the shoulder blades and the remaining two on either side of the chest to shield the lungs and heart. At best they were paltry protection against the brutalities of battle. Unlike the proud knights and armed retainers of the lords, the peasant soldier wore no heraldic symbols and sported neither armor nor spurs.

"Yes," Will answered. "I fought at Hexham."

The ruddy-faced man inclined his head. "My brother who was married today has also just returned from the North," he remarked. "As have my youngest brother, Edwin, and our cousin, Beavis."

Will nodded amiably to the young men. They, too, were dressed roughly in leathers. The cousin was the taller of the two, not particularly friendly in appearance; his overhanging brow lent him a fierce, beetle-eyed countenance.

More introductions followed. There was the ruddy-faced man's wife, a stout woman with a wart on her cheek; the younger brother's wife, who was equally stout; and the men's mother, a barrel-shaped matron with grey hair.

"This is my father," the ruddy-faced man announced, clamping a hand on the shoulder of an elderly man. When the old man smiled, he hadn't a tooth in his head and his chin nearly met the end of his nose.

Beside the lane, a trio of little girls flitted along, laughing and plucking handfuls of bobbing pink daisies. The man's brother, Edwin, turned his attention to the white horse, particularly the saddle and the excellent metalwork on the harness.

"Where did you come by such a fine animal?" the brother asked in a loud voice. His implication was clear. A common yeoman would not possess such a horse unless he came by it dishonestly.

A little girl with wispy reddish hair offered Tess a bouquet of limp daisies. The cousin, the one known as Beavis, whose eyes were almost concealed by his thick overhanging brows, gazed fixedly at Will's blond companion.

"Don't ask such rude questions," the toothless old man grumbled. In his peasant philosophy, stealing was preferable to starving.

"I found him wandering on the battlefield," Will said convincingly enough, mentioning that he hoped to sell the horse for enough to buy a plot of land.

"'Twas booty, then." The ruddy-faced one laughed cheerfully.

"A Lancaster horse, I'll wager," the brother said, running a hand over the horse's hindquarters. "We beat the bloody Lancasters, cut them down and killed them all," he bragged.

Not all, Will thought, noticing from the corner of his eye that Beavis was staring at Tess as if he planned to make a meal of her. Will felt a sudden push of anger and an overwhelming desire to sink his fist into beetle-eye's jaw.

"Yes, be thankful to God you are not of Lancaster," the little round woman said. "The king's sheriff hanged four of them in Bolton only yesterday."

"Hanged them in the square before the church," said a skinny youth with reddish hair, who was not yet grown but was too old to run and play with the other children.

"If I were you," the brother advised, "I'd sell that horse before the sheriff's soldiers see it."

Tess, surrounded by chattering children, sat down in the cool grass and began twining daisies into a wreath, much to the delight of the little girls.

The beetle-eyed cousin drifted back to the circle of adults. "Who is the girl?" he asked with a toss of his large head.

"She is my wife," Will lied. A note of protective rage had crept into his voice, and his level gaze made clear his rights of possession.

"You must come with us to the wedding feast," the ruddy-faced man declared. "My brother would gladly welcome a fellow-soldier to his celebration and, of course, your wife as well."

At first Will declined, respectfully. "I could not impose upon your kinsman's hospitality."

But the ruddy-faced man refused to allow it. "There will be good food and ale and plenty of it."

"Yes, they are rich! Come along," the others echoed. "You must join us."

Will glanced at Tess, undecided, thinking she must be hungry. He was. He had not eaten for two days, or perhaps it was three. He finally agreed. Where better to hide than in the midst of your enemies? he told himself.

Tess was overjoyed at the invitation, relieved that she would not be forced to spend the night alone with her captor. She did not fear the peasants half as much as she did him. They were people much like her own, open and friendly, without pretense — not like the gentry with their foppish clothing and silly rules of conduct.

As the group made their way along the lane, the round little woman with the grey hair came to walk beside Tess and the gang of skipping, laughing little girls. The woman, whom the children called "Gramma," was energetic for her age, and her gossipy voice had a youthful lilt to it.

"It is my second son who has married," she said to Tess. "I am happy for him, of course, but I worry too. His new wife's family, well, they are wealthier than we." She lowered her voice. "They put on airs. Oh, you will see for yourself what I say is true. They believe no one is as good as they. But don't misunderstand me, I am pleased that my son did so well."

The inflection of the little woman's voice said infinitely more than mere words could convey. "The girl did have a handsome dowry," she granted. "But, speaking as a mother, you understand. . . . Well, she doesn't seem at all devoted to my son. Not at all like you. You were very brave to follow your husband to battle. I can imagine the hardships!"

Tess said not a word; she was too stunned. Husband! Was that what he had told them? She stared straight ahead and there and then resolved to escape somehow from his clutches before he had the opportunity to force his attentions on her. For why else would he have claimed her? It was all a jest to him, a game. Oh, it was plain enough to Tess, as was the fact that no one would raise a hand to stop him. A man's wife was his to do with as he chose.

The little round woman talked on and on, about many things, of raising pigs, and drying beans, and spinning wool, but Tess scarcely heard a word.

Several times, she looked ahead to where he walked, talking with the men and leading the white horse, who followed placidly at the end of the loosely held reins. Her phantom knight struck an easy stride, with only the hint of a limp, and the evening sun burnished his dark hair with copper highlights. It all seemed so unreal—he, his white horse, the soldiers, and the fact she might never see her home again.

For a brief moment in the morning sunshine, Tess had thought him different from other men, kindlier and more decent. But he was neither phantom nor chivalrous, only base and selfish like all men. Not different in the least. And recalling how she had smiled at him from the depths of her heart and soul made her cringe. Her face fairly burnt with embarrassment. She felt a fool, and that angered her most of all.

The thatched roofs of the prosperous farmstead stood out vividly against the dark green fields. The scene, wondrously tinted by the pastel blush of evening, reminded Tess of home, of the mill at Lambsdale. She felt a stab of sadness, wondering if she would ever see her home and family again.

Wedding guests milled about in the garth and before the houses. The homely colors of their clothing bobbed to and fro in the twilight, as the activity increased.

An ancient oak stood like a sentinel at one side of the garth, and there was ample evidence that another of equal size had once stood before the stone-and-half-timbered kitchen. All that remained of that immense tree, however, was a gnarled stump whose gigantic girth would have required the arms of half a dozen children to span it. The mounded dirt at its base was mute testimony to the farmer's futile efforts to remove it.

Upon their arrival, the peasant's children gleefully joined a horde of other children who romped over the mounds of dirt, sliding up and down, piling the dark earth into fortresses, throwing it at one another, and getting thoroughly filthy.

Will was invited to turn his horse in with several others feeding on hay in a wattled enclosure. Tess heard and saw it as an opportunity to lose herself among the crowd and slip away. But Will took her hand. "Come with me," he murmured, pulling her after him.

"Go alone," she hissed, attempting to twist her fingers from his grasp.

He responded with a smile as hard and unyielding as his grip. "Walk with me," he said.

She narrowed her eyes, whining, "You are hurting me!"

"I know," he agreed, still smiling, "and with all my heart I despise doing so."

"Liar." Her cheeks flamed with color, and her childishly thick eyebrows knotted into a severe line across her forehead. "Why did you tell them I was your wife? I will not have you!" she declared in a small but determined voice.

"What did you expect me to say, the truth?" Once they reached the enclosure, he released her hand so he could unsaddle the horse. "You are the cause of it," he told her. "You go around smiling at everyone you meet. Didn't you see him staring at you?"

She looked back at Will with a puzzled expression, angry yet pathetic. He almost felt sorry for her—she was so trusting. She'd soon learn the world wasn't as safe and beautiful as she thought. "The cousin with eyes like a beetle," he specified. "What was I supposed to tell him— that you were a camp follower—a slut I found in a tavern? Then he'd be looking for a tumble with you later." He slid the saddle from the horse's back, suddenly annoyed with himself for speaking so plainly. He swung the leather trappings onto the fence and turned to unbuckle the bridle.

"I hate you," she said with a quiet fury. "I hope the Yorkists hang you!"

"Why should the Yorkists want to hang me?"

"For the same reason you hid from the soldiers. Because you are one of King Henry's knights."

Damn her, he thought, she was a witch. He'd told her nothing, and yet she had guessed so easily. He sent her a sudden dark look, one of indefinable anger. "That was a foolish thing to say. I can only hope for both our sakes you will not repeat it. After all," he paused, giving her a quick, impulsive smile, "they might hang you as well."

Taking her by the arm, Will guided her up the path, through the garth, past the noisy children playing in the dirt, and into the house. No one seemed to notice that they were strangers, perhaps because they had arrived with the bridegroom's kinfolk.

There was much feasting and merriment, even musicians — humble local men who were a little tattered, but musicians nonetheless. Their happy melodies floated on the summer air.

The wattle-and-half-timbered barn which adjoined the house had also been pressed into service for the guests. The beasts had been chased out save for one broody hen. The manure had been forked, and fresh rushes strewn on the dirt floor.

The family was indeed rich, as country people went, for the father of the bride, Tess learned, was a steward to the earl de Lacy. Three long rough-planked tables groaned with food—roasted mutton, stuffed pigeons, and a soup of pork and green peas. There were breads, tarts dipped in honey, ale and cider.

The newly wedded couple began the feast by sharing a cup of ale and feeding each other a symbolic bit of bread. For a time, Tess, like the other guests who lined the tables, concentrated on filling her empty stomach. She had no way of knowing how far she had traveled that day, though she thought it could not have been too great a distance. As her hunger abated, she vowed to slip away at the first opportunity. If she could hide herself in the woods until morning, she was certain she could find her way home. She even considered shouting out that the man who claimed to be her husband was in fact a Lancastrian soldier who had forced her to accompany him. But glancing up and down the table, she decided it would not be wise.

Would they hustle her off to Bolton to be hanged with him, she wondered? Or would they simply think her drunk, like the fat woman seated beside her, and make a joke of it? She would wait, she decided, and in covert glances watched her captor eat. There seemed no end to his appetite.

Fireflies winked in the garth, and the children chased in and out of the buildings, playing games in the mild summer night. The humble country musicians again took up their lute, pipe, and drum, while at the tables most sat around nodding drowsily, or complaining of having eaten too heartily.

Will had no complaints. It was the first time in days he had eaten. But his eyelids felt as if they were fashioned of lead, a situation made worse by the bridegroom's long and much-glorified account of his exploits in the North.

After a time, the food was praised. Will roused a bit and lent his voice to the chorus of compliments. There were also good words for the ale, which was brewed by the bride's mother.

She modestly accepted the compliments and went on to tell that in the past she had sold her ale in the village on market days and all preferred hers to what was served in the taverns. "I would have sold this, too," she confessed, "but the ferryman demanded half the barrel for his fare and it wasn't worth my trouble."

"He is no better than a thief," the bridegroom's mother remarked, citing the unreasonable fare he had charged for her family's passage.

Farther down the table, a young man with a long neck and a raspy tenor voice said, "I have heard it whispered in Bolton that a wealthy merchant from Grassington took the ferry one evening and was never seen again."

Several others spoke up, attesting to the ferry-man's dishonesty, and a skinny woman with a long nose shouted at the children for fighting.

After the ferryman had been sufficiently con-demned, the bridegroom, who had seen a bit more of the world than his kinsmen and perhaps wanted to show off before his bride and new in-laws, took up the subject of fire powder and hand cannons for which he prophesied a great future.

"Fire powder," the bride's father muttered, in-specting a mutton bone for any scrap of meat he might have overlooked. "Of course I've heard of it. It blows stone walls to pebbles and does the same to men and beasts. It's an affront to God, that's what it is, a device of Satan!"

"Mother of heaven!" the bride's fat aunt ex-claimed. "We may all be committing a dangerous sin just by talking about such evil things."

A number of others muttered their agreement. But the groom, who was more enlightened, dis-agreed. "It is nothing of the sort," he told them. "It is naught but what a bat has shat out, only that and a bit of sulphur, and there's no magic to it at all! Why in London, I'm told, they shoot it into the night to light up the sky for celebra-tions."

"Well, that is proof enough," said the father of the bride, whose face was round and smooth as a pig's behind. "Everyone knows how evil Londoners are. And the court—" he gestured, raising his sparse eyebrows—"they are sinners of the worst kind!"

Tess hardly listened to the conversation. Her thoughts were devoted entirely to how she might escape. Neither had she noticed the smitten state of the beetle-eyed cousin seated directly across from her. He'd been openly staring throughout the meal.

Will had noticed, and it was beginning to thoroughly annoy him. However, at the moment it seemed less a threat to their night's lodging than the unpleasant turn the conversation had taken.

"I am entirely in accord with you, sire," said the bridegroom's ruddy-faced elder brother. He knew a good dowry when he saw one, even if his foolish brother didn't, and sent his younger sibling a warning glance before continuing. "Such forces are better left untouched, for who can say where it might lead?"

"The world is changing," the bridegroom announced, either missing the point entirely or persevering out of pure obstinacy. "People shouldn't remain ignorant of the facts. I, myself, am interested in all sorts of discoveries," he bragged, leaning toward his new wife. "Isn't that true, Bona dear?"

She looked up suddenly. She had been talking

to her sisters and had no notion what he had said. "Oh, yes, Jerem is very clever," she replied. "He's been away to many places and is always talking about strange things a normal person can't understand."

"Thanks be to our Holy Father," an elderly man from the bride's family said. "We have lived all our lives without having to understand such evil!"

"Yes," Bona's mother added emphatically. "We may be ignorant, but we have managed to live a good life and have married off our daughter with a fine dowry."

"That is God's truth," her husband concurred. "If we are so uninformed, why did you decide to marry into our family?"

An ominous silence followed. The bridegroom was speechless. Will took a swallow of ale and set his gaze on the opposite wall; anything he might say would only make matters worse. Tess, who had shown no interest in the conversation until then, was suddenly alert. She sat up uncomfortably straight, blinking into the hostile silence, and feeling as if she had blundered into someone else's quarrel.

The men's toothless old father was asleep with his head on the table and heard none of the exchange. But Jerem's ruddy-faced elder brother gave a flustered grimace and sent his sibling a harsh look. "My brother is honored to have mar-

61

ried into such a fine lineage," he countered quickly. "Isn't that right, Jerem?"

"Why, yes," the bridegroom stammered. "I have always respected your family. I did not mean to imply that you were unlearned. I only spoke of the fire powder because I understand it completely. Here," he said, jumping up from the table. He rooted through a pile of his belongings stacked nearby. After a moment, he drew a goodly sized sack from a worn leather satchel. "You see." He held it up for the inspection of all. "There is nothing evil about it. I will prove it to you." He returned to the table, sack in hand. "It can be used for the good of all," he explained placing the sack on the table beside a sputtering oil lamp.

In the instant it took Will to grab the lamp and distance it from of powder, he broke into a sweat. He, too, understood the new discovery and calculated that had the contents of the sack come into contact with the lamp flame the resulting explosion could have easily destroyed the room and everyone in it.

But the bridegroom was oblivious to all. He'd had more than his share of ale, and even the strained faces of his in-laws did not deter him from singing the praises of the miraculous powder.

His ruddy-faced, now quite red-faced, elder brother, however, had had enough and told him in a harsh whisper to be still about the damned powder. And in a louder voice, he said, "Jerem's head is full of air. If he weren't so drunk, he'd realize that this delicious ale brewed by his mother-in-law has the greatest future of all."

Tragedy, both social and actual, was averted. The bride's mother glowed with pride as further praise was heaped upon her brewing skills from all around the table.

The conversation turned to lighter matters and then gave way to singing. Jerem, having removed the powder from the table, set it on the bench between his legs. In a truculent voice, he called for more ale.

Tess noticed Bona's two younger sisters preparing to make a final journey to the latrine at the end of the garth. Seeing her chance, Tess rose quickly from the bench. "Might I go with you?" she asked, smiling hopefully at the girls. They were of a similar age and assented readily. They took Tess by the hands, and the trio left together, giggling through the darkness of the garth.

Tess would have been long away had it not been for the girls and their silly questions. Questions about falling in love, and all the nonsensical things young girls discuss, subjects Tess and her sisters had whispered and giggled over endlessly.

After the near disaster with Jerem's sack and

the lamp flame, Will had not taken his eyes off the drunken groom. He was caught off guard by Tess's sudden departure and dared not follow her for fear of what the bridegroom might do next.

But, presently, the bride's soulful glances found their mark and the bridegroom, recalling his duty, swayed to his feet. First, however, he retrieved his precious store of fire powder, tucking it under his arm. Then, with the bride's assistance, he staggered off amid encouraging shouts and well-meaning hoots of laughter.

One by one, Bona's parents doused the oil lamps and torches. Such luxuries were expensive even for the rich, and common folk normally lived only by the light of the sun, taking to their beds when darkness came.

In the barn, people milled about in semidarkness, selecting a spot to sleep on the rush-strewn floor. They stumbled over children who had long-since become bored and fallen asleep, trailing in and out as they embarked on final pilgrimages to the latrine or a convenient tree.

After a perfunctory search, Will determined Tess was not in the barn. Neither were the two girls, nor the beetle-eyed cousin. He stepped into the garth, surveying the area. A pair of stout women pushed past him, groping in the darkness. An old man peed leisurely against the garth wall, but there was no sign of Tess.

Will walked through the moonlight and halted

by a smaller wattled enclosure that smelled like pigs. As he relieved himself of the ale, he heard the purr of female voices and soft laughter. Looking towards the barn, he saw Tess's fair hair shining in the moonlight as she and the two girls entered the garth. He sensed an ominous movement behind him and whirled around. The hair on the back of his neck prickled in alarm.

"I'll give you four gold pieces for her." A man stepped out of the darkness. The beetle-eyed cousin.

Will cursed softly, and turned back, remarking, "No, I'll keep her."

"Five?"

"She's not for sale." Will adjusted his hose, adding, "I'm fond of her."

"Seven." The cousin offered hopefully. It was more than enough to purchase a small plot of cotter's land. Will could guess how he'd come by the gold — stolen it off the battlefield dead, the same way his kinsman had come by the fire powder.

"I told you, she's not for sale." There was no misreading the warning in Will's voice and the cousin, smiling nervously, took a step backwards.

"It is a great deal of gold," he reminded the soldier. "If you change your mind—"

"I won't," Will interrupted curtly and left him standing there beside the pig sty.

The girls lingered in the garth. Try as she

might, Tess could not slip away from her new-found friends. The girls were in awe of her, showering her with the same sort of adulation she had always displayed for her elder sisters. The girls hung on her every word, and she secretly enjoyed it.

To their adolescent eyes, Tess seemed so pretty and wise. Most important of all, she had a handsome young man, or at least they believed she did, and just talking to her gave them hope that they too would find a young man of their own and experience the wonders of love and life for themselves.

"Are his arms as strong as they look?" the plumper of the two girls asked with shining eyes. Tess gave a coy smile, assuring her they were.

"When did you first see him? And how did you know that you truly loved him?" the other girl quizzed excitedly.

Tess, not knowing what else to say, held them spellbound with her tale of how she met her young man. It was a story Bertrade had told her about the magical qualities of peas. Everyone knew that peas were the favorite food of dragons, and even jilted lovers could be consoled by the healing powers of pea vines. Bertrade, a consummate teller of tales, knew a thousand stories; but Tess said a strange old woman she met on the road had repeated it to her. It sounded more mysterious, somehow.

"I was shelling peas one day," Tess related, "just as the old woman had predicted. And soothly, in one pod I found nine peas! Now that is surely *odd*," she whispered, "And I, thinking the old woman must have been a witch, did just as she'd bade me do. I saved the ninth pea and, being careful that no one saw me, placed it on the window sill and waited for the first young man to cross our garth. Well, the very next day, a young man came to my family's house."

"Was it your soldier?" they demanded in unison.

"Oh, yes. No sooner did I look into his eyes than I knew he was my own true love," she swore, though not a word of her story was true.

"He is glorious tall," the plump one gushed. "And his hair is dark and thick!"

Their questions were endless, and Tess, trapped in her own fanciful make-believe, was not herself immune to such romantic notions.

Will found the trio huddled in the garth. He stood listening for a time to their hushed voices and lilting laughter. It was a pleasant sound, musical and as silvery as the moonlight. At his approach, they turned, bright-eyed and expectant. They had been talking about him. He had heard only a portion of Tess's story but knew its subject as if by a sixth sense. No less egotistical than any other male creature, he smiled at the girls and spoke to them, half-amused, half flirting.

They parted company at the doors, the girls with envious glances. Tess, continuing the charade, smiled cheerily; but in truth, she was terrified as she bumbled—in the darkness of the crowded barn. Eventually she was forced to take his hand and follow after him. When they found a vacant alcove near the rear of the structure, he whispered close to her ear, "What did you find to talk about for so long a time?"

He was smiling, for she saw the flash of his white teeth in the darkness. "I did not betray you," she retorted hotly. She was certain he knew as much, for she suspected he had overheard their chatter. And if he hadn't, she was certainly not going to repeat her words. He would laugh at her, and she would rather face death than humiliation at his hands.

Alone with him in the pitch blackness, she reluctantly lay down in the rushes beside him. She waited, listening for the sound of his even breathing. As soon as he drifted off to sleep, she intended to make her escape.

Chapter Five

The scents of the summer night wafted through the cracks in the wattle-and-daub walls and mingled with the fragrant smell of fresh rushes, meadowsweet, and clary. She heard every sound—the sonorous snores, the flatulence, the coughs, the rustles of bodies moving in their sleep, the scritching of the mice, and a dog barking at the moon.

It seemed an eternity before she heard his heavy, rhythmic breaths. He was asleep. She sneaked a glance to confirm her suspicions, then moved stealthily to her haunches, hardly daring to inhale.

Out of the swirling blackness, a hand caught her shoulder. His strong fingers closed over her lips before she could cry out. She was flung backwards into the rushes, seized securely as a moth in a spider's web—and not by a stranger's hands. Already she knew his scent as surely as she recognized his face. He smelled of horses and sweaty leather.

He had only pretended to be asleep; he had been playing with her. Now he laughed softly, as he mauled her. With all her strength, she tried to speak. She wanted to protest and to damn him, but his arms were tightly around her and his lips silenced hers with a kiss that was vehement and as hard as his body.

"Rogue," she breathed, battling against the on-slaught of his lips. "Liar. You swore you would not harm me!"

He eased his grip but still held her captive. In the darkness, his soft laughter tickled her ear. "What harm is there in a kiss?" he whispered. "Tell me how have I injured you? Shall I look? Have I broken something?" His fingers moved from her lips to caress her cheek and trace the line of her throat down into her loosely laced bodice. "Your lips, an ear—your heart, per-haps?" he suggested.

"No!" Tess squalled in a gusty whisper, wres-tling against his arms and prying his hand from the warmth of her bodice. She won no victory, though, for no sooner had she captured one large hand, than another took its place. "Stop it!" she scolded, her hushed voice growing shrill and her heart pounding furiously.

"What will you do?" he teased.

She felt his suppressed laughter in the dark-ness. "I will tell the truth," she threatened in a deadly tone, her face hot with anger. "I'll scream it out for all to hear!"

"You might at that," he conceded, relaxing his grip but not releasing her. "A man offered to buy you tonight."

Instantly she looked at him, her eyes huge and round.

"Your beetle-eyed admirer," he supplied, to satisfy her curiosity. "I turned him down, but I've no doubt he's somewhere near and likely not asleep."

She shoved at his hands, wriggling to free herself. "You are no better," she spat.

But he only chuckled and pulled her backwards into the curve of his body. "That is stingy payment," he told her—teasing—and called her "Greensleeves."

It was a reference, unflattering at best, to wandering musicians whose bawdy songs and tales enlivened taverns. Now she knew he had eavesdropped in the garth. She was mortified, and her blood boiled at his taunts. "I owe you nothing." She said the words through gritted teeth. "It is because of you—"

But his fingers touched her lips, and he murmured, "A truce, Greensleeves. A few hours rest is all I ask."

She lay butted against him, despising him and burning with fury. She was unable to sleep, tormented by the complexity of emotions that raged through her body. She no longer understood her own responses. The touch of his lips and his hands had bared her every nerve, her very soul.

Will's thirst woke him, and the taste in his mouth recalled the ale. The sun was up, for a whitish light filtered through the cracks in the wattle-and-daub walls. He looked down on the tousled blond head; she was sleeping soundly, her cheek pressed to him. His arm was asleep and felt as if it were fashioned of wood. He awkwardly pulled the tingling limb from beneath her head and rubbed the blood back into it.

She stirred in her sleep but did not wake. In truth Will had never known a woman who looked quite as lovely in the morning as she had the night before. Only his little Greensleeves, for she was as pretty as he had first imagined, even in the harsh light of morning.

In the hushed interior of the barn, a few children moved about and jabbered softly. Will sat up, yawned, and ran a hand through his sleep-rumpled hair. He heard a cock crow. An instant later, a resounding blast roared through the structure like a hot wind, shaking the earth beneath him and reducing the front wall to a pile of rubble. It was like nothing Will had ever heard; even the Yorkist cannon at Alnwick had no such voice.

Tess bolted up from the rushes. Instinctively, Will shoved her back down and threw himself over her, shielding her with his body. A thunderous hail of mud and clumps of thatch rained down. A fog of dust filled the air, dogs yapped; children wailed, and even the grown-ups screamed in terror.

Uncertain of what new disaster might follow, Will pulled Tess roughly to her feet, intending to shove her out the nearest door. But she clung to him like a burr, unwilling at first to release him and only vaguely aware of his shouted words of concern. When she realized what he was saying, she answered at the top of her lungs that she was not hurt. Her ears felt deafened, as if they were stuffed with wool, but that she did not try to mention, doubting his ears had fared any better.

People stampeded past as if the devil himself were in pursuit, the sobbing bride and her sisters, the horrified host and his wife, old men, young men, women, and children. Will and Tess made their way toward the rear cattle-door. As they did, Tess spied a little boy huddled in a corner, abandoned and crying. Will carried him outside, where a panic-stricken woman wrested him away without a word of thanks.

The dazed and shaken guests were reunited before the farmstead. Amazingly, all were accounted for and none had suffered any worse than scrapes and bruises. They gathered in little knots, some as dumb as cattle, others praising God and all the saints for their miraculous escape.

A skinny old man standing before Tess told his wife the world was surely coming to an end. A cloud of dust still hung in the air, and the bride's father and his closest kinsmen surveyed the damage with disbelieving looks and wagging heads.

Tess had never seen such a sight and only managed to tear her gaze from the destruction long enough to notice that Will had come to stand by her side. "I wager it rang the abbey's bells in Bolton," he said beneath his breath. His first thought had been that every Yorkist soldier in the dale would soon be searching for the source of the ungodly blast.

There would be no mistaking it, for the facade, common to both barn and living quarters, had suffered a death blow. Most of it lay on the ground in an untidy line of debris. As it was a bearing wall, much of the roof—timbers and thatch—had given way and come to rest inside the structure. More the wonder no one had been killed.

Will knew at once what had occurred. Scanning the crowd, he located the disconsolate bridegroom. He was muddied from head to foot and whatever he had said to his bride had sent her into another fit of sobbing.

The children lost no time in exploring the gaping hole left by the blast. The huge stump now rested squarely on a crumbled section of the garth wall, eight or ten strides from the crater . . . truly an amazing feat. The fire powder had certainly removed the stump—a fact the bridegroom was quick to point out to his father-in-law, though with less enthusiasm than he had originally intended. Owing, no doubt, to the dismal condition of the barn and living quarters, the bride's father, whose face had darkened to a shade very near to purple, ranted and raved, flailing the air with his fists. In his rage, he cursed Satan and the saints and threatened his new son-in-law with a dozen kinds of mayhem.

One among the bridegroom's kin spoke up in his defense, and soon the lines were drawn. Angry shouts and accusations flew back and forth with lightning swiftness.

Will dropped his head close to Tess's ear. "It's time we left," he murmured and slipped away to fetch the horse. Tess watched him go, half-amazed, half-angry. Was he so certain she would follow? He had not hesitated for an instant. How self possessed he was, conceited in his maleness, with his broad shoulders and narrow hips. She followed, what else was she to do? She did not want to go with him, but neither did she want to stay.

All morning, a pale metallic sun wandered through the haze and a cool, damp breeze pressed at their backs. Will broke the silence, drawing Tess's attention to the slow-moving clouds.

"Rain," he predicted.

Tess nodded in agreement. She felt the chill in the air and imagined how miserable they would soon be without a cloak to shed the rain.

"We will be in Bolton by evening," Will promised, stating again his vow to see her safely to the abbey.

As he spoke, Tess absently braided a lock of the horse's snowy mane, twining it, smoothing it, and twining it once more. She did not necessarily believe him; and by the measure of his kiss, she most certainly did not trust him.

Still, that was how their conversation began, for, in spite of everything, they were young and together and it was only natural they should discuss the startling events of the morning.

Tess voiced her concern for the sobbing Bona and the feckless Jerem. Will was less merciful, though his thoughts were put in such a way and in such words that Tess could not help being amused.

They fell silent. For a time Tess was content to watch the countryside unfold, from woods to meadow, with each new vista a delight. Blooming shrubs and wildflowers peeked from the greenwood and swayed in the tall grass, brighter, perhaps, for the somberness of the day.

When Tess had been small and still believed in

fairies, Bertrade told her how the tiny folk made their homes in flowers and that if one were caught sleeping, the unfortunate fairy would be forced to grant her a wish. She had searched relentlessly, wanting above all else to go to London and see the queen, for it was said that those who did were blessed with happiness and wealth for all their days. "I shall return dressed in silks and satins, with rings on my fingers," she had informed her sisters when they teased her for believing in fairies. Now, in all likelihood, she would return in disgrace. The thought spoiled her reminiscence, and the chill breeze raised a rash of gooseflesh on her arms.

Will reasoned the country paths to be safe enough. Nearer the river, he would be forced to take to the Bolton road, but by then he would have sufficiently distanced himself from the farmstead.

They came upon the cherry tree by chance, the chatter of the birds intriguing them. Out of curiosity, Will guided the white horse through a marshy hollow, tall with wild angelica whose nodding, tasseled heads bobbed and swayed in the cool breeze.

Beyond the hollow, they spied the ruins of a dark log hut and, before it, a cherry tree dense with shiny leaves and ablaze with fruit. Will halted, ostensibly to rest the horse. In truth, he could not resist the lure of the cherry tree and a pretty girl with whom to share its bounty. He had no need of a sword here; it would only hamper him. He was as eager as a boy and wasted no time in unbuckling his belt and hanging the sword and scabbard onto the saddle by looping the belt over the pommel. With a shove and trailing reins, he sent Navet off to graze.

Only at Will's approach did the greedy robins abandon their prize, flapping off with cries of protest to settle in the nearby trees. He lifted himself up through the sturdy limbs, mindful of his leg, though it seemed to pain him less to climb than to walk. Graceful as a cat, he settled with his spine butted against the scaly bark and offered Tess a hand to join him.

Perched in the tree, they ate their fill of tart, red cherries. Time slipped away and he cared not. Tess had eyes that could slay a heart, and the feel of her pale hair between his fingers gave rise to thoughts of more private places and deeper pleasures.

In lieu of rubies, he hung cherries on her ears and, coaxing her to laugh, told her all the foolish things young men say to pretty girls when all they truly want is to lay them down.

William Hartley was no amateur at such pursuits. Yet, he marveled over her. With her eyes blue as harebells and cherries dangling from her ears, she was an enchantment, a forest nymph with firm, full breasts that rose temptingly from her bodice.

He was so besotted with her that he did not immediately see the horsemen. Too late, the sound of drumming hooves alerted him. What he glimpsed sent a jolt of panic slicing through him like a knife. The horsemen were Yorkists, judging by their crested helmets, and riding full toward them.

His first thought was to escape, but where was the horse? "Navet." He cursed the arbitrary creature. The damned horse had wandered off again. He cursed himself for having known as much. Only then did he think of the sword. He reached for the limb above, lifting himself to view the horsemen once more. They had vanished from sight, but reappeared an instant later. It was then he realized he had glimpsed them through the fringe of trees. Could their view have also been clipped and brief?

He prayed it was so and, signing to Tess to be silent, whispered, "Soldiers. Hide yourself in the woods."

"The horse?" she asked, for she did not see the animal anywhere. She scrambled down, dangling from his arms to touch her toes in the cool grass.

"It is too late," he said. He stripped off his leather *jaque* and dropped it down to her. "Take this and go," he urged. "Quickly!" By doffing the *jaque,* perhaps he could convince them he was no more than a cotter. He did not wish to be questioned about his service in the North. The sooner he could get rid of them, the less chance they would have to discover the girl and the wandering horse.

"What of you?" Tess cried. A white chill of fear spread over her body like frost. Weren't they hunting him?

But he waved her away with a fierce gesture. So she stuffed the garment under her arm, snatched up her clogs and ran toward the brushy copse. Barefooted, she scrambled through the brambles and tangled tree roots. At last she crouched in the thicket, scratched and trembling. She clutched the short leather jacket to her breast and waited.

All at once, she heard a crashing sound behind her and turned with her heart in her throat. "You," she scolded softly.

The white horse, surprised as well, snorted and stared at her with huge dark eyes. She grasped the reins and held them fast, placing a hand on the horse's velvety muzzle to quiet him.

Beyond the blind of brush, she heard male voices, harsh and questioning, then laughter. She could not at first distinguish Will's voice from the broad, crude brogue of the soldiers. He was mimicking their way of speaking, just as he had the peasants'. A sudden smile touched her lips. He was as clever and as handsome as the running fox and—yes, she thought, as diligently pursued. The notion left her suddenly terrified, for if he was King Henry's knight, then he would pay the traitor's death.

She knew of such things. Several weeks before, she had overheard men talking in the mill. A Lancastrian noble had been hanged in Owsley, and it was said that while he yet lived, his body had been split with a sword and his entrails spilt out and burned before his dying eyes. It was too horrible to consider. Tess pressed her face to the horse's soft grey muzzle and murmured a prayer.

Surrounded by the soldiers, Will eased his spine against the tree's rough bark.

"Who is your master?" asked a broad-faced soldier with skin as tanned as a brick.

"The lord de Lacey," Will answered with what he hoped was an expression of genuine ignorance.

"What are you doing up there?" another shouted.

"Gathering firewood," Will replied, grinning.

"He's waiting for the tree to die," another laughed, amused by the peasant's lazy insolence. It was not unlike their own, and in that there was a sort of camaraderie. "I swear he must be your brother, Mull!"

"More likely yours!" the lank-jawed youth retorted.

"Throw down some cherries, lout!" the one

81

whose face was tanned as a brick commanded.

Will, eager to please, did so, and the fun began. The soldiers astride their horses hooted and shouted, diving after cherries. Grabbing and snatching like terriers after scraps of meat, they mingled and dodged as their horses trampled the fine grass beneath the trees. But soon they tired of the sport and, saluting the peasant, rode off through the hollow.

When he saw the last of their backs, Will lowered himself from the limb and dropped to the ground. "Tess," he called, his voice as weak as his knees. He had completely forgotten the nagging pain in his thigh until he had put his full weight on his leg.

A movement deep in the thicket betrayed Tess's position, and a moment later she and the white horse crashed from the copse. She led the gelding, her cheeks bright. "Thanks be to God," she sighed, holding the *jaque* out to him. "I was afraid."

"No more than I," Will confessed, flashing her a smile as he buckled on his sword. Settling the belt on his hips, he took the *jaque* from her hands and hiked into it, then boosted her upon the horse. It had begun to rain, a fine mist carried on the breeze.

As they rode, he noticed that a pair of cherries, having somehow survived the thicket, still dangled from her ear. He took them as skillfully as a thief lifts a rich man's purse and jiggled them before her eyes. Sudden merriment lit her face. She reached out to claim the shiny fruits and laughing merrily shared her prize. She fed one ruby red cherry to him, and with dainty fingers, kept the other for herself.

The taste of the cherry was tart upon his tongue. The touch of her fingers upon his lips sent a thrill of animal excitement coursing through his loins — a taut longing that was at once irritating, delicious, and exciting. He thought of her and nothing else. Seated as she was, before him, he feared she must surely be aware of his arousal, and he struggled to turn his mind to other thoughts.

He had no time for such longings, no more than he had the right to draw her deeper still into his affairs. The incident at the cherry tree was proof enough. Had he not been cavorting like a roe deer in rut, he'd not have found himself surrounded by Yorkists. He had come within a hairsbreadth of failure; and by his sworn word, he could not fail the task before him. He could not allow such wanton negligence to happen again.

His only consolation was that he'd soon be in Bolton. He'd leave her there and good riddance, else she would surely be the death of him.

They rode out the afternoon across a drenched and misty landscape. Occasionally they spoke, though it was only to comment on some curious sight—a hare that started up before the horse and bounded away or the jackdaw with ruffled feathers perched in an ancient cedar tree. Rain drifted in great grey clouds across lowland meadows cut by little streams. The closed-in skies hastened the dusk of the chill June day, and cattle stood knee-deep in ground fog.

From a hillock thick with gorse, Will at last sighted the Bolton road. With a nudge of his heels, he set Navet forward. It was late and on such a foul day, he reasoned, there would be few travelers afoot. Banks of milky vapor clung to the woods and as they travelled down the road ever nearer the river, the bitter-tasting fog thickened, enveloping them in a netherworld of mist.

The deep voice of the river greeted them. Will dismounted, and, lifting Tess down beside him, instructed her to hold the reins. He walked to the river's edge, cautiously, for all was lost in fog. Only then could he see the swift brown waters rushing past.

Tess wrapped her arms about herself to ward off the chill. The horse beside her shifted uneasily, his ears twitching at sounds, his nostrils flared. There was an eeriness about the swirling fog. Tess felt it, too—the strangeness of objects half-seen when every sound was muffled by the damp hush.

On the opposite bank, the glowing red eye of

a driftwood fire glittered and sparked through the wooly mist. Though Will could make out little more, it seemed reasonable to assume the ferry crossed just at the road. Whatever there had been of a levee was lost to the swollen river, swallowed by the rolling waters. He risked a few strides further along the rocky bank, and his hands encountered the ferry ropes lashed to a tree. The twisted cords laced through the murky fog.

Will shouted a loud, "Hallo!" Twice more he called before an answer resounded from the opposite bank. The garbled low male voices floated on the damp air as if several men were locked in a discussion. Finally, a woman's voice rose above the others, and presently there was an answering call. A coarse male voice asked, "How many fares?"

"Two and a horse," Will responded. The shouted exchange continued until they agreed upon a price, an outrageous sum. Nevertheless, in Will's estimation it was preferable to the long ride north to cross the bridge at Horse Pool, which was also a toll crossing.

Perhaps a quarter of an hour passed, punctuated by the curses and clanks that echoed from the far bank. Finally, the ropes slung through the trees began to jostle and groan. The ferry, which was box-shaped with side rails and ramps fore and aft for loading and unloading, emerged from the fog. It was large enough only for a single cart and team of horses. The swirling brown waters slapped against its low sides, sending up a spray and pitching it to and fro against the ropes.

Once tied off, the raft appeared more stable and the two men aboard made jokes about the roughness of the water. Will guessed they were father and son, for the elder man ordered the youth about with familial authority. He was of a right age, forty at least — a heavy man with a shapeless nose and unshaven jaw.

His son, though resembling him, was a brute of a fellow, as tall as Will and twice as wide. Useful, Will imagined, for towing the ferry back and forth across the river. The tops of his arms, even beneath the roughly woven tunic, were as large as hams.

Tess eyed the pair with alarm. Despite their apparent friendliness, something repellent about them, reminded her of beasts, of hulking creatures dredged from Bertrade's repertoire of trolls and grotesque water spirits. It was foolish, she told herself, but even so she could not dismiss the overwhelming sense of dread they inspired.

Perhaps it was the fog that drew them closer, so that they talked in one another's face. Like the peasants at the feast, they admired the horse and the fine saddle. The son drew attention to Will's sword, inquiring, "You're a soldier, aren't you?"

"A Yorkist, I hope," the old man chortled, "else we'll have to chuck you in the river."

"Aye," Will assured him, "a Yorkist unto death." He wondered uneasily if such a fate were just what the ferryman had in mind for him. He had been forced to part with a gold piece. Did they believe that a man so eager to cross the river might have a full purse? The thought disturbed Will.

Tess was completely unstrung by the ferryman's remark. She could not swim. She imagined frightful things, her premonition of disaster fueled by the sound of male voices from the opposite bank and the horse's initial refusal to be led onto the ferry. She felt she must say something to Will, to warn him, but she did not know how without alerting the ferryman and his monstrous son as well.

Where the horse was concerned, Will prevailed, and, balking and snorting, Navet finally clattered aboard. The ferry set out across the churning water. Will kept a quieting grip on the animal's fine leather bridle. But despite the attention, the horse rolled his eyes, showing white all around, and his hide twitched with a continual shudder.

Tess, who wished to avoid the odious ferryman and his son, came and stood beside Will. She was thankful for the arm he dropped round her shoulder as the raft pitched and swayed. Several times she tried to capture his attention with her eyes, to warn him. She dared not speak out.

It was impossible for Tess to judge the width of the river. Moments stretched out interminably, and the fog closed around them, at times rendering all objects beyond an arm's length away invisible.

Her horrible imaginings were groundless and the journey proved uneventful. At the opposite bank they were met by another burly youth who fetched and secured the ropes.

Will led the horse off the ferry, warning Tess to stand aside in case the animal should kick. The gelding, eager to be on solid earth, crab-stepped forward, tossing his head and fretting with the bit. "I'll be back for you," Will called.

Tess watched as he and the horse vanished into the dense fog. She had no intention of remaining on the bobbing, tossing ferry, and cautiously made her way forward. She thought herself alone on the raft until a voice just above her shoulder commanded, "You, come with me!"

At the sound of the voice, she jumped forward several strides, stumbling into one of the stanchions that supported the ferry's ramp, and whirled about. The old ferryman's gap-toothed grin leered through the mist, sending a shudder of fear through her every limb. "No," she said. It was all she could do to fight back the urge to break and run. "I'll wait," she stammered and, out of fear, added, "for my husband."

"He won't be coming back," the gap-toothed mouth replied.

Her mind had hardly grasped the words when she heard angry shouts echoing through the fog, followed by curses and the startled yaup of a horse. She shrank from the violent, punishing sound of blows and guttural snarls, not unlike the noises of a dogfight.

A hand grabbed at her. She ducked and scrambled away. A high, wild scream sliced through the thick mist; it seemed to come from every direction. Or perhaps it was her own voice she heard? The ferryman lunged at her again. She dodged sideways but lost her footing to the swell of the ferry, and he caught her by the hair, pulling her head backwards with a snap. She cried out in pain, shrieking for help. But the ferryman's hand struck her face, jarring her senses.

He grabbed her wrists, first one then the other. Tess lashed out at him with her feet and felt one of her clogs fly from her foot. The ferryman dragged her from the boat. She cried out again, a great gasping sob, and in desperation threw herself from side to side, fighting to free her arms. The roughhewn planks clawed at her flesh as she tried in vain to dig her heels into the gaps between the boards.

All at once the ferryman uttered a loud, uncouth, "Ouf!" and sagged forward with a grunt. His body toppled onto hers, nearly crushing the breath from her. Blind with terror, she strained against the limp form.

For an instant, she could not say who had booted the ferryman aside and sent him rolling down the ramp. But Will pulled her to her feet and shoved her behind him, warning, "Keep down!"

Shouts and commotion came from the shore. Tess saw the ghostly forms and screamed out, "They are here!" The silver glint of a sword cleaved the fog. The ferry shuddered, then jerked away, as Will hacked the mooring lines. Again she saw the flash of his blade. The boat yawed wildly and the current caught them, sweeping them away.

Shouts and curses echoed after them. Will staggered back to where she sat clinging to a side rail. He sank down beside her, still gripping his sword. "Are you hurt?" he asked.

"No, I do not think so. Are you?" For she saw him fumbling weakly to return the sword to its scabbard.

He did not answer but said instead, "They meant to rob and kill us."

She nodded in response, saying only, "I thought they would throw us into the river."

"Only our naked bodies," he assured her. "The horse is gone," he continued, afterwards thinking it an obvious, stupid thing to say.

But Tess took no notice. "Where are we going?" she asked in an alarmed voice, for they were blinded by the fog.

"Down the river," he replied, with little concern — as if he had wished someone a good afternoon. For some insane reason, one quite beyond explanation, the remark struck him as grotesquely funny, and he bit his lip to keep from laughing. It was as if he had no control over the muscles of his jaw. They had nearly died because of his stupidity. He had even been warned of the ferryman's dishonesty. How gullible he had been!

The ferry lunged and pitched with the rolling current. They could not control it. They had no rudder; even the pole that had secured the ramp was gone. A torrent of water surged up the ramp and sluiced over the ferry, soaking them to their skins. Will's every attempt to raise the ramp was beaten back, defeated by the pitching motion of the boat and the roaring waters.

The ferry lurched and bucked, changing ends. It was hopeless, and he crawled back to where Tess clung to the side rail and crouched beside her. He secured an arm round her and, in a soothing voice, said, "Eventually the current will carry us to shore." But he did not believe it would be before they were forced to swim.

They were sinking, dipping with the swells and taking on water at a perilous rate. His only thought was to hold on to her somehow, for he knew if he lost his grip, the raging river would snatch her away and he would never find her.

The bow reared upwards; the floor fell away, and a great dark deluge of water thundered over them. Tess cried out and clung to him. Closing her eyes, she held on tightly as the water rushed over her head, filling her mouth and ears and pulling at her, trying to drag her away.

Chapter Six

They were bound together by Will's strong right arm as the water dragged them on, tumbling them over and over until it seemed their lungs would burst. With all his strength, Will fought against the crushing weight of the cold, dark water. And with one final effort, he exploded onto the surface, sucking in great gasps of precious air.

The water hammered against their bodies, rushing onwards, plummeting them swiftly down its course. From the fog, dark shapes loomed before them, black as the river, huge and distorted.

Tess clung to him, conscious only of her fear and the desperate need for air. Buoyed up by the churning tide, she drew in a ragged breath and, in that instant, glimpsed the rock-bound shore. Wicked entanglements of roots and driftwood snatched at them, deadly traps that could rip and tear and seize — and hold them down and drown them. Tess tried to cry out, but no sound came from her throat. Water crashed against her, filling her mouth and choking her.

Will flung out an arm, groping, grasping for a handhold, catching a slippery limb only to have it break with their weight and the force of the rolling water. He caught another, a tree root, more solid.

Something in the water, drift perhaps, struck his side with a sickening impact, momentarily stunning him. Balls of light burst before his eyes, and he felt his hand slipping. He clawed at the roots, catching still another and, with great effort, he slowly, painfully pulled himself and the limp girl from the torrent.

Will half-carried, half-tugged her into the limbo of fog, willows, and driftwood. She was as cold as death. But she was alive and—like him—strangled and coughing.

When they were able, they climbed higher on the shore, finding refuge in a clump of close-set pines. Beneath the trees, the earth was carpeted with a thick mat of needles, and they lay down together, shivering.

There was no hope of lighting a fire. Will's flint striker was in the satchel tied behind Navet's saddle; but even if he had still possessed it, everything about them was sodden, reeking of the dampness. Above all, he had no notion where they were or to which bank they had been swept. He knew only that they had survived. For the moment, that was enough.

Toward dawn, Tess awoke, sobbing, clawing her way from the bottom of a watery nightmare. She lurched up, terrified, with the feel of the black waves weighing her down, suffocating her. "We will die," she wailed. "We will. We will!"

"No, no, no," he mumbled in a voice thick with sleep. He pulled her near, stroking her hair. "We are alive." Gathering his scattered wits, he lightly mentioned the cold and the misery they shared as proof to her.

Somewhat consoled, she laid her head against the damp warmth of his chest. "I want to go home," she sobbed.

"I know," he whispered, holding her in his arms and pressing his lips to her hair. "I will take you to Bolton," he promised. "They will be kind to you at the abbey. In a few days, your kinsmen will come for you." He said the words in the same smooth tone of voice the young ladies at court had always found irresistible. For above all he was kind, disarmingly so, and, despite his more obvious male failings, at times as sincere as a small boy.

She raised her face to his suddenly and pushed against him. "You would not lie to me?"

"No, upon my word," he murmured. "Nor could any man with a heart."

She examined the words, like pretty stones, turning them over in her mind, unable to decide whether she believed him or not. She was too exhausted to care and, after a moment, lay back in his arms and fell asleep once more.

The sun lit up the eastern sky with a pastel blush of pink and yellow. Layer upon layer of soft mellow colors melted upon the mild blue arch of morning. As the sun rose higher, the couple ventured from beneath the towering pines into the yellow warmth. Below their refuge, the river rumbled past, swift and brown with silt.

"How ever will we cross it?" Tess asked. It seemed as impossible a feat as removing the tangles from her long hair. She looked at him with a hopeless expression—directed as much toward the task of grooming the knots from her hair with her fingers as it was to their predicament.

"Mayhap we have," Will murmured, surveying his surroundings. In the fog he had lost all sense of direction. Now he mentally retraced his route from Alnwick and the moor. He had traveled south and west, to Devrel lands, knowing he must eventually turn east, toward Bolton and the route south. Two days before, he had ridden toward the river with the setting sun at his back; but on this day, as he faced the river, the rising sun rose over his shoulder. It could be naught but the east bank, he concluded. A smile etched itself upon his lips, and he remarked, "It is so. It must be."

"Are we on Bolton's shore?" she questioned,

wincing with pain as she tugged a stubborn snarl from her long fair hair.

"Yes." His tone was confident and, turning to gaze at her, he added, "Though I would not give a tinker's promise to cross that way again."

Since they had no other choice, they set out on foot. Tess had lost her clogs to the river, and Will walked before her through the heavy brush, tramping down a path. Crushing the tall weeds, he filled the air with a sweet green infusion. Their soggy clothing soon dried in the warm sunshine, except Will's multi-layered leather *jaque*. Next to his skin it was still damp.

By a tumbledown wall, they found a wealth of wild strawberries. Gathering the tiny red fruits by handfuls, they sat on the stones and ate, savoring even the grit.

Later, they crossed a meadow where sheep grazed in the distance. The cropped grass made the walking easier for Tess, though she was more concerned for Will than for herself. He favored his injured leg more and more; and where an islet of oak trees divided the meadows, they found him a stout stick to use as a cane.

It was still early when they came upon the road. Its course was broad and even, though deeply rutted and no less muddy than the country paths. They were alone until a blond boy with a switch, herding four pigs before him, overtook them.

As the barelegged boy and the pigs galloped past, Will shouted, "Be this the road to Bolton?"

"Aye," his voice carried back amid the squeals. " 'Tis market day, and I'm fair late!"

The boy and the pigs disappeared from sight. Will and Tess trudged on, keeping to the roadside, avoiding the deeper ruts. Where a country lane joined the road, they met a prosperous peddler and his wife seated on a handsome cart drawn by heavy horses.

Will bought a wooden comb for Tess's hair and a seat for both of them on the rear of the jouncing cart. The peddler knew the countryside, the people, and the gossip. His wife was dressed in cloth of mousy brown. She had a wart upon her cheek and seldom said a word, but the peddler hardly paused to catch his breath.

"Look," Tess said to Will, and pointed to the distance. "There's something hanging in a tree."

"Ah, 'tis but another pair that's croaked. You see them hanging everywhere," the peddler said.

"Croaked?" Will repeated, puzzling over the vernacular. It was a term he had never had occasion to hear.

The peddler chortled. "Those who've been hanged by John Croaker!"

"He is the king's high sheriff," the mousy brown wife exclaimed, devoutly making the sign of the cross upon her breast as they passed the tree. "He is as cruel as Satan, he is!"

Tess glimpsed the bloated corpses swaying from the limb. She turned her head away and closed her eyes in horror.

They had been Lancastrians; Will plainly saw the Percy badge upon their tunics. "He was but a captain," Will remarked. He felt enraged, angered by the recollection of the Yorkist's battle cry, "Kill the noble; spare the common man." But Will said only, "I heard they hunted down the nobles, not the commoners?"

"John Croaker hangs them one and all," the peddler chuckled, and with a wry look, added, "He lets Saint Peter sort them out!"

Before they'd gone another league, they came upon a virtual caravan of peasants bound for Bolton's market. They drove their cows and sheep before them or bounced along in carts, some drawn by oxen, all stacked high with country produce, willow cages with honking geese, and clucking chickens, barrels of cider, or mounds of vegetables.

The peddler knew a multitude of tales. In time, it seemed to Will and Tess, they heard each one twice over. Then, mercifully, a group of peasant boys shouted back, "Horsemen, horsemen up ahead!"

A moment later half-a-dozen riders came into view, looming larger with every stride — Yorkists, by their tunics, and as public as a pack of dogs. Why not? Will thought with a grimace of disgust. The victory was theirs. What remained of King Henry's forces dangled from the trees, a forest of dead men.

Closing ground, they waved the peasants aside, shouting, "Clear the roadway! Clear the way for His Majesty, King Edward!" With prancing horses and the flats of their swords, they chased the peasants from the road. "Hah, hah ya! Damn ye sluggards, off the road!"

Above the grumbling voices of peasants, donkeys brayed, oxen balked, and horses shied. Drovers and carters trundled from the muddy roadway, slipping and sliding as they took to the swampy roadside. Will leapt down from the cart and used his weight to steady it as it teetered on the berm, then slid among the cattails in the ditch.

A company of armored knights and mounted troops with banners fluttering led the long procession. The sun glinted from their gleaming armor and mail, and the jangling of their swords and harnesses filled the air. After them paraded the barons, arrayed in velvets, and then their squires in silks of the same colors.

Edward of York, King of England, rode in their midst. He did not lack for grandeur, even returning from war. Behind him stretched a long train of richly garbed officers of his household, judges, councillors, courtiers in ruffled hats, and exquisitely gowned ladies. They were laughing gaily, secure in their privileged world. On and on they passed — knights, villeins, yeomen, archers, and goods wagons.

The peasants squatting on their haunches in the mud merely stared. They did not cheer, and it seemed to Will, if you looked closely, you could see the hatred in their wrinkled eyes and smell it on their sweaty shirts. It was a different view than he was accustomed to.

John Croaker, accompanied by a small troop of soldiers, rode out from Bolton with due haste. He had returned to the abbey only to be informed that King Edward had passed through the village some hours before. As they rode, Damon Swift drew his horse abreast of his lord sheriff's. In halting phrases, he shouted, "King Edward made a gift of gold to the altar and received the abbot's blessings! All went well, though Norfolk made merry of your absence." Swift, shouting into the wind, gave a full account.

"Before God, one day he will choke on those words," John Croaker vowed, thoroughly annoyed by Norfolk's glib remarks. His mood was further fouled by his own self-recriminations, his failure to be present to greet the king.

John Croaker knew full well that Norfolk's retainers searched night and day for Henry Lancaster. If Norfolk succeeded in running to ground the former king, where *he* had thus far failed, there would be no further glory for John Croaker, the lord sheriff of St. Albans. That he could not bear, for his ambitions knew no bounds. No! He would not be denied. He had come too far to be thrust aside by a fat and pompous boy. Damn Norfolk! What had he accomplished in all his twenty-one pampered years, aside from bedding whores?

John Croaker had chosen the abbey at Bolton as his center of operations and would have certainly been there to greet Edward had it not been for a mysterious incident which occurred shortly before dawn of the previous day. A strange and unexplained tremor caused the abbey's bells to sound. He wondered now if Norfolk had not orchestrated the entire affair in order to draw him away on a fruitless search of the countryside.

Edward's handsome young head was turned to several of the noble ladies and their companions who rode nearest him. He was laughing as he told an amusing anecdote. He was aware of his sheriff's approach, having been advised by one of his squires, but continued his story.

John Croaker wove his well-lathered mount through the assembly. Horses bumped and snorted, jostling their riders. Edward ignored him a moment longer, concluding his tale. The ladies tittered and the gentlemen laughed. John Croaker seethed.

"Ah, but here is my justiciar," Edward announced with a droll smile. "Have you brought me Henry Lancaster or merely the messenger?"

"Neither, sire," John Croaker was forced to admit. "But my lieutenant, Damon Swift, has returned only recently from the North, and I have good reason to believe Henry Lancaster has not slipped across the border. He is yet in the shires, hidden by sympathizers. I am certain he will soon be in my grasp."

Edward's condescending smirk remained firmly in place. "And the messenger? Has he fled to Scotland in place of his master?" Edward taunted. Edward was unequaled in his vainglorious arrogance. He smiled and, casting a glance to catch the eyes of the surrounding nobles, suggested, "Or perhaps he has flown to the moon!"

John Croaker paled with restrained fury. Norfolk, who rode beside the king, laughed, a loud guffaw that caused his large bay stallion to throw up its head and jangle the bit.

"Sire," John Croaker intoned, "I am certain the messenger exists."

Norfolk could not resist a retort and, reining in his sidling horse, quipped, "Only in the minds of a clever boy and a dullard sheriff!"

The sheriff sent him a murderous, lancelike glance. He hated Norfolk, whose ears, he observed, stuck out beneath his ruffled, green-velvet hat like jug handles. One day, John Croaker

103

thought, he would take great pleasure in nailing them to a tree. "Sire," the sheriff addressed his sovereign, "where the messenger is concerned, there is a promise of success."

"A promise," Edward scoffed. "The king of France sends me promises. I expected more of you, my faithful servant."

"Sire," the sheriff protested.

"Enough!" Edward said. "You have darkened my day with your feeble excuses," and smiling roguishly at his young friends, he confessed, "I have quite forgotten my other story."

Two young noblewomen riding near mirthfully attempted to retrieve the threads of the conversation. With the sound of their foolish laughter ringing in his ears, John Croaker turned his horse and cantered back toward the small troop that had ridden out from Bolton with him. As he rode, he passed a group of peasants. His gaze roved over them, unseeing. He saw them as a single face, lined with dirt and disgruntlement.

He had seen a thousand such faces in recent days, and today was to be no different. On his return to the village, he would be obliged to sit in at the abbot's court. It was at best a boring chore, one John Croaker did not relish. He was sick to death of hearing peasants squabbling over wandering sows and stolen hens. Time was being wasted, for he was certain the messenger was close at hand. He himself had spoken to a cotter near Grassington who had seen a young man astride a white horse. The peasant had watched him lead the horse to water. He described a young man who walked with a limp, just as the horseboy had said.

The peddler nudged Will with his elbow, and said, "That's him; that's John Croaker." Will watched him ride past, noting the pock-scarred face.

Tess, who was braiding her blond hair, looked up to see. He was an ugly man, she thought, with his pitted skin and a mouth too broad for his face. But, no, there was something more, something almost evil about him. She shrugged away the feeling, as one might a sudden chill, and went back to her plaiting, and watching the passing parade of archers, yeomen, and goods wagons.

In the wake of Edward's cortege, the peasants again took to the road. On they traveled through the mire and ruts, down the muddy track to Bolton. It was but a country village with a maze of cottages and shops. There was a church near the market grounds and a guildhall. Farther on, the grey stone tower of the abbey rose above the cluttered rooftops.

With the sun warm on their shoulders, Will and Tess bade the peddler and his wife adieu and wandered through the village. It was market day and they sauntered past the stalls, glancing at the mounds of beets, fine green cabbages, and heaps of pungent onions. Plump rabbits and fowl hung from staves, and silvery fish were heaped in willow baskets lined with reeds. Ironware, crockery, woven cloth, and leather goods were displayed like a pannier of gifts.

The enticing aroma of food the permeated air. At one stall Will bought a pair of pork pies, chunks of pork wrapped in a delicious crust of pastry. He and Tess ate them as they walked. They looked at everything and everyone. Peasant women, with faces wrinkled and tanned as old gloves, sold peas and greens while their menfolk sat together beneath the shade trees and talked behind their beards.

An old woman with eyes as bright and as black as beads offered ropes of dried mushrooms for sale—and fresh ones, too, with the gritty black earth and pine needles still clinging to their smooth white skins. Nearby, a man with shoulder-length, flowing auburn hair hawked crockery bowls, shouting, "Three for a penny!" Village wives and serving girls bustled past with overburdened arms and baskets. Soberly dressed matrons haggled with fishermen, sharply questioning them over the age of their fish, and snotty-nosed children raced down the aisles with dogs barking noisily at their heels.

Will led Tess by a stall were knives were displayed on a red woolen blanket, then on to a cobbler's booth. He had been fortunate not to lose his coins to the river. The coins, like the message, had been secreted inside his *jaque,* and both had survived the drenching. He had sworn to buy Tess a pair of shoes and so he would. On the road she had agreed, but now she balked, embarrassed by her muddied feet. Will thought her feet as pretty as the rest of her. They were neither large nor small, but of a middle size, with here and there a pale brown freckle on the tops.

"A fortunate size," the cobbler said with a ready, eager smile. "A moment," he begged, raising a hand and going to root through his stock of shoes. "These," he said, displaying a pair of red slippers. "They are lovely, are they not? The dye won't fade, I promise you. No," he swore, "as God knows my name, it won't. And they've right stout soles as well."

Tess smiled shyly. They were as handsome as he claimed, and when he knelt to slip the scarlet slippers onto her dirt-etched feet, the strict newness of the leather did not even pinch her toes.

"Five silver coins," the cobbler said. "You'll not find a finer pair of shoes 'twixt here and Tadcaster."

Will offered him four and he agreed so readily that Will was certain he could have had them for three. It annoyed him, but there were soldiers drifting through the marketplace, and it seemed wiser not to bargain too loudly.

As they walked, Tess watched her feet, step by step, in the new red shoes.

"You should have a shawl," Will told her, spying some at a distant stall.

Tess glanced up, smiling. "The sun is warm today."

"All the same," Will told her. "The other women are wearing shawls, and you should have one too. You must look like a decent sort when you go before the abbot."

"What of you?" Tess asked. "You look like a beggar, and your beard grows bigger every day."

"It is all to my advantage," he joked. "More so the beard, for it hides my face."

"Your leg is no advantage," she reminded him. "It pains you, doesn't it?"

"A bit."

"No, more than you say. You should save your coins to buy a horse," she said, sweetly practical.

"I've coin enough to buy a horse. Now, about a shawl," he insisted, placing a hand on her shoulder and turning her toward a dazzling patchwork of brightly colored cloth strung out on ropes and gently undulating in the breeze. There were shawls and lengths of cloth of every color, save for purple, for it was a noble color and not allowed for common folk, even those who could afford the price.

"Red to match your shoes?" Will suggested, ducking amid the forest of cloth.

"No," she said, laughing as she fumbled from beneath a length of saffron velvet. "The abbot would certainly˙ think me indecent! A softer shade, I think, grey or brown."

"A little brown hen," he teased, reciting a silly verse and making her laugh, as he trailed after her through the many narrow aisles of billowing cloth.

When it came time to settle on a price, Tess touched his hand, and softly said, "Let me bargain with her."

In the end Tess got the shawl for a single coin. Will was amazed. "I should let you bargain for the horse," he chuckled.

Tess looked up through her fair lashes, beaming, pleased by his praise. "Oh, I would be glad to bargain for you. My grandfather often left me to bargain with his tenants over grain."

"Then you must not let them know you are at the abbey," he teased, "or they may pay the abbot to keep you here."

Side by side they strolled leisurely through the crowded streets. Before the guildhall, where the metal craftsmen kept their shops, the staccato chorusing of hammers filled the air, and shoppers mingled with guildsmen and soldiers.

From a narrow, shaded street they entered the abbey garden. The bells were tolling nones; and pigeons, routed by the dull iron sound, swirled lazily into the sun. Before them, roses bloomed in riotous splendor, spilling over the half-walls of grey stone, blazing from the hedges and trellises so that the warm air was sweetly steeped with their scent. A sundial stood amid a bed of thyme, and sulphur yellow butterflies fluttered through a haze of blooming chamomile.

A feeling of sadness descended over Tess, bittersweet and intense as the overpowering scent of roses. "I am glad we met," she said, stumbling over her words a bit, "though, I do not even know your name, 'Only Will and no more.' "

"Will is enough, and even that is best forgotten." He took her hand as they walked the flagstone path. "When you are questioned, you must say you fell and struck your head. Tell them a passing peddler and his wife found you lying still as death. Say you passed the days in a fever and, since the peddler and his wife were bound for Bolton, they left you at the abbey."

"You have thought much on my dilemma, haven't you?" Tess smiled, thinking perhaps he was after all as good and decent as she had first imagined. "I, too, thought of something similar," she confided. "Though it is sinful to lie, is it not?"

"Not if the reason is virtuous," he countered, his dark eyes thoughtful and reflective. "If there is any sin, then it is mine. You are as good and right as sunshine, and I could never again be easy in my heart if I thought harm had come to you."

Color rushed to Tess's cheeks in a flush of searing premonition. It was as if all she'd ever wished for had been captured in that instant, in the unexpected scent of roses and their sun-warmed flesh. And it would be lost, beyond her reach forever, if she spoke or turned away.

"Do not let them catch you, 'Will and no more,' my soldier." She tiptoed up to kiss him suddenly amid the scratchy beard. "And see to your leg," she admonished.

As quick as that, she slid her hands from his and turned to go. She must leave, she thought, or her trembling heart would surely stop. She hurried down the path. She did not look back or even blink away the stinging tears.

Soon, she thought with a touch of regret, she would return to the mill; and, once again, her life would take up its dreary routine. One by one, her sisters would marry and raise families. Only she would be left to live out her days at the mill, day in, day out, until she was old and no longer filled with dreams and longings. Her beautiful red shoes were but a blur before her eyes.

Near the abbey stables, the traitorous horseboy

who had first brought word of Henry's messenger to the sheriff, crouched on his haunches gouging a stick into the mud, aimlessly striking lines. A fly, blue and iridescent, zinged past his nose. The horseboy cocked his head toward the droning sound. He a reached out and grasped the fly in midair. He held it to his ear and heard the telltale buzzing. He was about to send it hurtling into the sun-washed stable wall, when he noticed a tall, dark-headed young man go limping past the abbey garden gate.

"It's he," the horseboy muttered, his voice barely audible. "It's he!" he said aloud, releasing the fly and sprinting toward the stable. "It's he!" he yelled still louder. "It's old King Henry's knight!" he shouted at the quartet of guards who lounged near the well swapping tales and barracks jokes. "Don't you hear?" the horseboy screamed as he dashed past them. "It's King Henry's knight. He's here in Bolton!"

The guards lurched to their feet, uncertain what course of action they should take. In the end they ran after the horseboy, knowing that if they lost him, the sheriff would have their hides.

Near the kitchens, Tess met a lay brother who directed her toward the chapter house. She stepped into the ivy-shaded alcove and lifted the heavy brass door-knocker. It made a dreadful noise. She waited half in fear that someone would come and scold her for making such a racket. It was oddly cool in the shaded arch, and her eyes played upon the intricate design of the brass knocker. It coiled and turned and wove into itself and seemed for all the world to be a lion swallowing a serpent, or perhaps it was the other way round. It was gruesome, she decided.

She waited for what seemed a very long time before a fair-haired brother appeared.

"What is it, my child?" he inquired. His eyes, at first cool and condescending, softened at the sight of the fresh faced young girl.

"I seek an audience with the abbot," Tess replied in a small, careful voice. She detected a wrinkle of skepticism on his smooth pink brow and she quickly added, "It is a matter of great importance, a matter of a gift to the Virgin's altar." She had no doubt that her grandfather would give a gift for her return.

The curate made an odd grimace, which Tess supposed he meant as a smile, and told her the abbot was at present unavailable.

"It is the day of the abbot's court," he announced. "Though you may wait, if you choose to." Stepping aside to admit her, he directed her across the hallway to a small, crowded chamber where a host of petitioners sat in silent contemplation.

As she entered the room, Tess was aware of their scrutinizing stares. Men and women lined long benches set against the walls. Peasants, all

113

of them, and of every conceivable variety—tall and short, fat and thin—smelling of sweat, earth, and manure. Tess squeezed in beside an enormously fat woman who reeked of sour milk and whose too-big clogs were stuffed with straw. Flies circled and roamed across the yellowed plaster walls; and above the door arch, a wooden Christ hung in a pose of eternal suffering. How appropriate, Tess thought, and reconciled herself to a very long wait. No one moved or spoke a word, and after a few moments of the unnatural silence it seemed to Tess that she could hear the taking and exhaling of each and every breath.

A noisy disturbance in the hall shattered the silence and captured the attention of those waiting. Several farmers leapt to their feet. An old woman, her shawl wrapped tightly about her, hurried after them, and a moment later three plump girls squeezed in beside them at the door arch. All locked in a great huddle, peering cheek by jowl to see what was the matter.

The fat woman beside Tess craned her neck to see, though she made no move to lift her immense bottom from the bench. "What is it? What's going on?" the fat woman asked.

"I don't know," the broadest of the plump girls answered, as she wiggled in beside the others to get a better view.

Tess, no less curious than the rest, rose from

her seat and perched on her toes to catch a glimpse.

A brother with a tonsured head strode past, mumbling to himself, followed by two soldiers scuffling with a young man, who shouted at the top of his lungs. "It is against the law! They will not cheat me of what is rightfully mine!"

Tess was still staring after him when the bride's father burst through the door, ranting, "He is a madman. He has destroyed my home, and I will have my payment!" In the clutch of women who trailed after him, Tess recognized the sobbing bride, her sisters, and her quarrelsome mother.

Horror of horrors, Tess thought, and slipped quietly back to the bench. She prayed they would soon be gone, for if they saw her, they would have another story to tell the abbot.

"Well, what is happening?" the fat woman asked Tess.

"No one knows," Tess mumbled, shrinking back against the wall.

The broadest plump girl was determined to learn the facts and, leaning out into the hall, motioned to a young soldier who guarded the door. "Psst," she whispered. "What is it all about?"

"Yes, tell us," the others chorused with hushed and baited breaths.

The soldier paused and, looking round, sauntered over to them. In a low voice, he began, "Some fool of a soldier—" but whatever else he intended to say was lost to a sudden disturbance at the entry door, the trample of boots, and loud voices. The door burst inward. A teenaged boy ran past with four or five soldiers at his heels.

"Open the doors!" the boy yelled, skidding to a halt before the abbot's chamber and battering against the stout panels with his folded fists. "I must see the sheriff! I have seen the lame knight! He was here! Here at the abbey!"

His words brought Tess to her feet. She edged to the door arch of the room and saw someone within the abbot's chambers crack the doors enough to angrily demand, "Silence! No one enters!"

Thwarted, the boy, as if gone mad, began to shout. "It is King Henry's knight! I have seen him! He was here in the abbey garden!" Surely all within the chamber heard him. As had Tess, who hovered at the door arch, hollow with dread, her hands trembling at her sides.

The doors to the abbot's chamber opened wide, and a surge of men met at the doors, with shuffling feet and loud inquisitive voices. One face stood out among the group of men, the pock-scarred face Tess had seen ride past on the road. As she looked on, mesmerized, he raised his head from questioning the boy. His gaze swept past her and, in his glance, Tess saw such a look of hatred and baleful ugliness, that she bolted for the entry door. In an instant she was in the sunshine, running, the red slippers skimming swiftly past the privet hedges, down the garden paths, and through the postern gate. An uproar of voices wildfired through the abbey, soldiers ran, and hastily saddled horses stamped and shied.

Before the guildhall, Tess slowed her pace with halting steps and mingled with the crowds. Where? Where would he go, she wondered and, recalling his promise to buy a horse, hurried breathlessly toward the square. In the distance she saw the gaily draped stalls of the market and the milling throngs of people.

Chapter Seven

Will Hartley proceeded toward the market at a moderate pace, favoring his injured leg. He was in no particular hurry. The village streets were crowded with people; moreover, there was nothing to distinguish him from the groups of tattered and footsore soldiers who loitered about the village. Among so many others he would not be singled out, stopped, or questioned. In his present circumstances there was no danger of his being mistaken for a Lancastrian noble. At the moment, the only threat to his success was the fever in his leg. Throughout the day the pain had grown progressively worse, and the heat of the sun had set the wound to throbbing. He felt dizzy, suddenly too hot.

Halfway through the square, he paused at a plaster-and-lath shopfront and leaned his shoulder against the rough surface, resting his leg for moment. People passed by, coming, going. A whitish skim had formed on the mire of the muddy square. A few carts creaked past, and a horse dealer with a string of several animals made his way toward the market grounds.

Directly across the square, the doors of a tavern stood open to the afternoon. Voices and laughter floated on the warm air. An assortment of prostitutes, soldiers, village swains, shepherds, and cotters drawn in from the countryside loitered before the doors, drifting in and out by twos and threes.

An alleyway ran beside the tavern and, directly behind it, half-hidden by a row of empty ale barrels, was a small courtyard where horses were tethered beneath the shade of a large chestnut tree. He glimpsed hindquarters and several twitching tails. The alleyway ran only a short distance before it joined yet another and ended in a clutter of half-timbered dwellings and wooden courtyards.

Will was considering that the alleyway ran east toward the river, and other aimless thoughts, when he saw a large man riding a rangy sorrel turn the corner of the alleyway. At first he was uncertain, but as the image grew sharper there was no mistaking the rider. It was the ferryman's burly son, and he was leading a white horse by a rope looped round its neck. Navet. Will at once recognized the floating gait, the sculpted head, the graceful neck.

Had the burly son been sent to sell the horse? It seemed logical to Will. As did the son's next move, which was to tether the horses with the others behind the tavern. Will watched closely as he emerged from the shaded alleyway. The fact that he could walk at all astounded Will; he could have sworn he'd crushed his skull. He'd certainly done his best. But the hulking lout had only a blackened eye and a nasty bruise on the side of his jaw where the blood had suffused beneath the skin. Will watched with something near to awe as he shoved several country lads aside and entered the tavern.

After a few moments, Will crossed the square at an unhurried gait. The lout would have his ale by now, he thought. He was equally certain that a single pot of ale would only serve to whet his thirst for more.

Will slid between the horses, touched the satiny white flank, and felt the quiver of response. "Hello, old friend," he murmured. At once, Navet's head went up. His ears swiveled round, and the great dark eyes turned to him. Will found his saddle, the woven saddle rug, and bridle on the sorrel—a situation he soon rectified. He was about to lead Navet into the alleyway and mount up when three small boys armed with sticks came whooping up the passage, parrying back and forth.

The empty barrels were too great a temptation for boys with sticks. The trio attacked the barrels with savage glee, whacking away with murderous blows. At the sound of the noisy barrage, Will towed at the reins, pulling the white gelding back into the line of horses.

Just as he did, a paunchy man wearing a soiled apron charged from a side door shouting curses and making a show of chasing after the boys. They fled, but not before shouting taunts at the fat tavern keeper and sticking out their tongues.

Will flattened himself against the chestnut tree and waited. He heard the door slam shut. He took the reins and steered Navet into the open, determined to make away before anything else could go amiss. But no sooner had he taken the reins and laid a hand on the saddle, than he heard the quick breathing of someone running behind him.

He spun round, his hand on his sword, his every muscle tensed, only to see Tess come sprinting toward him, breathless and gripping her skirts with one hand to keep from tripping.

"Where are you going?" he asked, dumbfounded by her sudden appearance.

The words burst from her lips in a gusty torrent, "They know you are here! Hurry!"

He did not believe her.

"Yes!" she panted, her full lips gulping air. "A boy saw you at the abbey! He ran to tell the sheriff!" She lifted her hands in a small, significant gesture of helplessness. Could he not understand? "I overheard!" she wailed, her voice gaining momentum. "Go, please. They are coming!"

He vaulted into the saddle, but once astride the restless, stamping horse, he hesitated. "Did anyone see you leave the abbey?" he asked.

She shook her head. She did not know. "Hurry," she cried, frantic now.

How could they overlook the golden hair? No, he could not leave her there, knowing what her fate would be. And, yet, to take her might mean failure.

Voices, shouts, and the trample of hooves filtered into the space between the buildings. He had to choose — now.

"Come," he urged, offering his hand.

Her lips parted as if to speak. She cast a startled bright-blue glance toward the square, then took his hand, clambering up to sit before him in the saddle.

Figures darkened the top of the alleyway and dashed forward, blurred with motion. A single shout, of, "Here! He's here!" in a heartbeat echoed up and down the square.

Men burst from the tavern's side door. "There!", a cry went up in unison. One among them shouted, "Stop, thief! Stop!" In full flight, the two groups converged grappling and swearing oaths. A large figure dodged the jostling mob and plunged ahead. With a superhuman bound, he sprang at the white horse and grabbed for the bridle rein.

Tess screamed, just as Will drove a heel into the gelding's flank. The white horse lunged forward, knocking the large figure aside as it shot down the alleyway. At the foot of the lane, Will reined the gelding to the left. He saw a group of riders thundering toward him and abruptly wheeled the gelding round and galloped north.

This route led unavoidably toward the market grounds and certain capture, for boxed and hemmed in by the wooden stalls and narrow aisles, they would be an easy target.

At the top of the square, John Croaker heard the hue and cry go up—a man on a white horse had been sighted. His blood beat faster. Here was his chance to prove Norfolk a fool, and more, much more. From atop his fretting horse, the sheriff sent crossbowmen and horsemen scurrying to close off the village and the market grounds. He turned in his saddle, shouting, snapping orders, beckoning. Through the square he cantered, with Damon Swift, his closest stalwarts, and the horseboy who'd first told the tale of the messenger, at his side.

Villagers scrambled to clear the way. Women screamed, dragging their children to safety. Crowds gathered before the village taverns, and merchants gawked from doors and window openings.

John Croaker caught but a fleeting glimpse of the galloping white horse and its tall, supple rider. He saw the fair-haired girl as well, and recognized her from the abbey—the golden hair at least. He turned to the horseboy, an expression of rage upon his face and demanded angrily, "What girl is this? Why did you not mention her to me?"

He knew nothing of a girl, he swore. Damon Swift, tempted to believe him, said, "Perhaps she is a villager? I, too, saw her run from the abbey. She must have gone to warn him."

"A villager?" the justiciar said, with the voice of an inquisitor, and swore before God, if her family was within his reach, he would hang the lot of them. Damon Swift had no such information, but asserted, "They'll not go far, double on a horse. All will be revealed to us milord sheriff." John Croaker was certain of that. No detail would escape his torturers.

With the market grounds before him, Will led his pursuers on a drunkard's course. People sprang for cover as horsemen thundered through the narrow aisles. Booths were flattened, knocked askew, produce scattered and trampled under hoof. Baskets of fish went sailing, cabbages rolled and bounced. A tangle of boards and a sea of broken crockery was all that remained of the bowl-maker's booth.

From the corner of his eye, Will saw the crossbowmen cut through the swarm, halt and cock their bows. He heard them call, "Bring down the horse."

A blaze of color filled Will's eyes as he hurtled toward the aisles of billowing cloth. A gaudy patchwork, half-seen moving with the breeze was their only hope. He chose a middle course, hung three aisles deep with cloth. He bent low over Tess and gave the horse its head. Down through the aisle they dashed, whipping past the display of colors. The thrum and thud of crossbow darts shot against the lengths of blowing cloth, marked their passage. Those launched higher hissed above their heads.

A length of bright red cassimere, strung perpendicular, closed the aisle. He saw it, but too late. The color red filled his eyes. He pressed Tess to the horse's neck and felt the rope skim his shoulders as they tore past. They plunged onward, lost in blackness. Blind and helpless beneath the smothering weight of the cassimere, Will fought the cloth, one-handed, like a foe.

A crowd of dashing men and charging horses descended after them. Men swore, colliding into one another, and horses blundered, shoulder and flank. Crossbowmen halted to cock their bows, and cursing, they fired again, but their range was lost.

John Croaker, his voice coarse from shouting, glimpsed the streaking white horse and the billowing crimson cloth for an instant only, before it disappeared behind a row of stalls and then a cotter's hut. "After them!" he rallied, with a violent forward motion of his arm. "After them!"

With a mighty heave, Will flung aside the cloth and sent it sailing in their wake. Before them, a meadow deep with grass rolled and rose toward a dense woods. Where the meadow dipped, then crested, Will saw the tumbled wall overgrown with vines. Behind them, the horsemen blackened the meadow, closing ground. There was no other course.

Will judged the wall to be knee-high to a man and he prayed it was not too high for a double-weighted horse. The jarring ground rushed past. The air pressed against their faces, heavy with the scent of earth and trampled grass.

The wall jolted up to meet them. Tess felt the horse's muscles bunch as, with a lunge, he took flight. She closed her eyes and held on dearly. Down they came, as if into perdition, skidding, sliding sideways. The gelding faltered, dragging himself forward, then gamely found his legs and, with a bound of powerful hindquarters, lunged into the greenwood. A stampede of riders swarmed across the meadow in hot pursuit, John Croaker at their head.

The woods closed around them, impossibly thick and close. Entanglements of trailing vine and bramble made the going treacherous. Windfalls, branches,and briars thrashed and clawed at their passage. At their backs, the violent crash of breaking brush grew fainter until only silence followed them.

In time, Will and Tess dismounted and walked the lathered horse. They talked rapidly in hushed tones, until Tess, unable to suppress it, gave a mirthful little laugh as Will related how he'd found Navet and reclaimed him from the ferryman's son. They followed an animal trail to a glistening forest stream, shallow and bright with stepping stones. Away from the ribbon of water, here and there a pine tree appeared and soon the forest was overtaken by them.

They were tall and stately pines, whose bright green tops stood out against the white clouds. Perhaps the breeze that pushed the frothy clouds along touched their tops, but in the dark and gloomy shade beneath them, not a whisper of a breeze stirred. The warm air was hushed and silent so they spoke softly, as one might in church. Here, the pines were in bloom and, wherever they brushed against the branches, a dense yellow cloud rose up, dusting them and the white horse with a golden powder that settled slowly and spiced the still air with the scent of resin.

They spoke of it like children, discovering something new. How good and simple nature was, so unlike the world of men. Will knew without a doubt that he had been betrayed. . . . But by whom? For all his effort, he could not recall a boy amid the chaos on the moor that night.

As they walked along, he questioned Tess. "You say the boy recognized me? What did he look like, this boy?"

Her thick brows arched into a quizzical expression. "Oh, he was half grown—not a child, near fifteen years perhaps. His hair was brown, and as best as I could judge, he was little taller than myself."

Her thick brows, Will noticed, were several shades darker than her flaxen hair; combined with the blue of her eyes, the contrast was striking.

"He said you were King Henry's knight," she added. "He shouted it out when they would not admit him. And, he knew your leg was lame."

There was the answer, Will thought, for his leg had been hacked as their small group fought a desperate retreat to save the king. Confused and contradictory, the images returned, and all at once it struck him with the sickening numbness of a blow. Yes, the horseboy had been sent to fetch a mount for him. "This boy," he asked, "had he a delicate look . . . a soft face, like a girl's?"

"I did not pay as much attention to his face as to the words he spoke," she replied, wishing that she had. Ducking to avoid a pine bough, she asked, "Do you recall him now?"

Will nodded. "Yes," he said. But what troubled him more was the question of what else the boy might have seen or overheard. For if he'd seen the king seal the note, and Will stow the missive in his leather *jaque*, there'd be no greenwood deep enough, no place in all of England where he might hide.

"Who is he?" Tess inquired.

"A traitor," Will said simply, fending off further questions. He chose his words with care. He was of an age to recognize the wiles of women, having been their victim more than once. Like all her sex, she was astonishingly clever at ferreting out the truth, and he was determined to tell her nothing of the missive. She knew too much already.

Each stride was an agony of pain for Will. A searing ache began in his left thigh and radiated upwards into the muscles of his back. He knew he could not walk much farther; and the exhausted horse could not carry them any longer. Hopefully, he thought, the darkness would soon put a halt to the sheriff's search.

As the evening sun silhouetted the black-stained woods, they found a secret little hollow where the open ground beneath the trees was deep with fern. Tess spied a large stone and slumped down on it. "You have walked far enough," she announced. "If you do not rest your leg, you will be useless."

Her remark, the bitter truth of it, made him laugh, a short hoarse little laugh, though the effort left him shaky and weak. He sagged to the ground, still clutching the reins, and sat waist-deep in fern.

"To have but one leg is not at all amusing," she reminded him and, spying another stone set on end like the first, walked over to investigate.

The tone of her voice took him back to the time when he was a small boy and at the mercy of his aunt. He felt afire with fever, and the scorching heat seemed to infect his thoughts. As he watched, Tess crossed the hollow, stalking yet another stone. She stooped and pushed aside the ferns. He was dying, he thought, and all for an insignificant cut on his leg. The irony of it tempted him to laugh again. Instead, he asked what she was doing.

"They are curious," she answered, pointing out the pale grey stones to him. "Look, they are set in a row." Her exploration led to a final stone, half-hidden by vines and weeds. Pressing her way into the wall of vegetation, she exclaimed, "Look! Oh, look! It is something built of stones—perhaps an altar."

Intrigued, Will dragged himself from the ferns, and hobbled after her. Beyond the fringe of cling-ing vines and brushy young trees, he saw a tiny meadow, as round as a fairy circle. At its center, peeping from the tall rye grass, was a tumble of pale grey stones, which bore little resemblance to anything . . . other than a pile of rocks.

They settled there for the night. The tiny meadow contained an abundance of grass for the horse, and even Will had to agree that the humble, wholesome rye had a more familiar feel, if not a pleasanter scent, than the dark, mysterious fern.

The reedy call of an owl heralded the night. They lay together, listening to the horse crop grass, alert to every sound. Will slept fitfully, awakened several times by the sound of his own voice mum-bling back at him from dreams.

Tess woke as the first rays of morning sunlight dappled the treetops. She glanced up at Will. He was sleeping soundly, though his face was flushed and it seemed she could feel the fever burning in his body. She lay beside him a moment longer, aware of the curiously strange feeling that they were not alone.

Looking around, she saw no one . . . nothing. But the sensation would not go away, and she drew her gaze back across the darkened fringe of woods. It was then she fancied she saw a huge, dusky, shapeless thing lurking in the darkness beneath the trees.

A cold shiver of fear ran through her. It was naught but her imagination, she told herself. Even so, she looked nervously over her shoulder for Navet. In the early morning gloom, she saw his satiny white hindquarters, the rhythmic swishing of his tail. All was well.

She heard the crack and crunch of twigs. Hazarding another glance, she saw the huge, shapeless thing was still there. A mellow shaft of sunlight crept toward it through the trees. Soon the golden light would touch the very spot.

It is silliness, Tess thought, a bug a boo of branches, nothing more. Unendurable moments passed. The lagging sunlight was nearly touching it. She looked away—then, with a desperate determination, she forced herself to look again.

Before her stunned and staring eyes stood a bear, as broad as a rowan trunk and near as tall. Sunlight spilled over its brutish form, and murder glinted from its eyes. A sinking feeling seized her heart. She gasped for breath, unable to utter a sound or even move.

With a savage roar, the beast charged forward, a length of rope bouncing after it. Tess shrieked, and the panicked horse shied and bucked. Will jolted up, his hand groping for the sword beside him in the grass.

Tess heard the scabbard rattle as he shoved her behind him and rose to meet the onslaught. Staggering with sleep and fever, Will brought the sword up before him and cleaved the air.

The beast halted in its tracks, then stumbled backwards, reeled, tripped, and fell upon its nose. Will rushed forward to strike a blow, but what he saw stayed his blade. The gigantic bear began to quiver as if taken by a fit of ague; and, unbelievably, a dwarf, an ugly little man, dressed half in black and half in white and striped from end to end, red-faced and bald on top, crawled from under it.

Still the hide quivered and another, a half-grown boy, slithered from beneath. A cheeky, rat-faced youth with a dagger clutched in his hand. Like a cornered rat, he rolled upon his back, shouting, "Eh! Eh! We only meant to scare you off! 'Tis the horse we want. Ain't that right, Luigi?"

The little man, ugly as a wart, nodded and darted to the safety of the trees.

" 'Tis the horse, you see. An' we'll take it from you all the same," the cheeky boy said.

Will was about to give him the flat of his sword,

when from the far edge of his vision, he saw the boy's reasoning, as two more youths armed with staves moved menacingly into the sunlight. "Yes," Will agreed, looking round. "But one of you will die."

Tess's frantic gaze darted from Will to the circling boys and back again. Suddenly a voice called out, "Here! What are you lads about?" A thin faced man, skinny as a reed, appeared among the sunlit trees. The boy lying on his back saw his chance and scurried off on his elbows and knees.

"We got him, Tom," he addressed the skinny man as he scrambled to his feet.

"Aye, we've found a horse!" One shouted past Will's back.

"He's mine," a greasy blond haired boy piped. "I saw him first!"

"Call them off!" Will threatened, swaying a bit. He felt as if he might burst into flame—the fever was consuming him.

The skinny man took note of his unsteadiness, but decided there was still enough fight left in him to be dangerous. "Off with you, lads!" He raised an arm and gestured, "Git on!"

Grumbling, the boys lowered their staves and trailed across the clearing to come to heel beside the skinny man. "I ought to knock your empty heads together, you bunch of bungling asses!" he directed at the boys in an undertone.

"Aw, Tom, we had him, till you come!" the rat-faced boy countered.

"You had sheat," he snarled. "An' git that hide back to the cart!" He raised his hand as if to strike. The boy cowered back, and stooped to grapple with the bearskin. Two other boys dove to help with the unwieldy hide.

The skinny man then turned to Will and, with an oily smile, said, "They forget their manners on occasion. No harm done."

Will opened his mouth to speak, but all his senses had deserted him. His eyes grew dim, there was a roaring in his ears, and all at once the noisy blackness snuffed him out as if he were a candle-flame. He hit the ground and did not move.

Tess ran to him, kneeling by his side, cradling his head. The boys exchanged hopeful glances. The horse might yet be theirs.

At the sound of a feminine voice, Tess looked up, distractedly, her face wet with tears, to see a fat woman charge into the clearing, followed by a barrel-chested barefooted man dressed only in his hosen. The woman's hair was flaming red. Her face was painted like a plaster saint's, and even after she had halted, she seemed to still be moving. The illusion was heightened by her girth and garish parti-colored clothing.

"Soldat!" she panted, pointing a fat dimpled arm. Breaking into English, she screeched, "Soldiers! Soldiers!"

The half-naked man behind her stubbed his foot

and cursed out loud, unmistakably in English, and ranted at the skinny man. "Now you've done it," he swore. "Killed him, have you? You and your witless little whillylillies!"

"He fainted, or some damn thing!" the skinny man shouted back defensively.

This theory was seconded by the lanky boys. "Aye, he flopped over on his own, we never laid a stick on him!" the blond-haired boy called. "We never cudgeled him! We never got the chance!" the others chorused, gathering up the bearskin.

Tess's blood ran cold as ice. She again saw the corpses swaying from the tree. Her soldier would be hanged, and likely she as well. Wild with fear, Tess raised her face and screamed above their bickering voices. "He's a Lancaster! He stole the horse, and now you'll all hang with him."

Every face blanched white. Except, of course, the fat Frenchwoman's, though she sagged as if she'd been deflated and her painted lips pursed in a knot.

"There, there," the half-naked man cajoled, attempting to calm Tess. "We'll just not let the Yorkists find him or the horse. Now won't that be the best for all of us?"

Tess stared back in petrified silence. What did they mean to do? The bare-chested jongleur mistook her momentary hesitation for assent, and he and his skinny friend flew into a flurry of activity, barking orders and gesticulating wildly.

"Noam," the skinny man shouted to the greasy, blond-headed boy, "Hide the horse."

"Here!" the bare-chested man called out. "Luigi, Cedric, Elgar, fetch the hide and stuff our pilgrim in it, an' be quick, damn you!"

Confused and terrified, at first, Tess misunderstood. She grabbed up a stone from the pile of rocks and held them all at bay, threatening, "No! Stay away! Don't you touch him!"

"Mon dieu, chérie, be reasonable," the fat woman pleaded. "It is but a bit of trickery for our common good. If they see before them a stupid bear, they'll not hang him, or us!"

Slowly, Tess released the rock and lent a helping hand. Never had a man vanished so swiftly, though it took seven pairs of hands to stuff Will's limp body into the cleverly fashioned hide.

The skin itself was altogether genuine, with glinting eyes of glass. A hideous creature and chillingly authentic, it was so real it made one shiver, for it was all but impossible to see the closures in the front unless one drew near enough to press the thick fur aside.

At the sound of cracking brush, the fat woman who had called Tess, *chérie,* took another look at her, as a mother might look at a tardy child. "You're much too pretty," she said with a tsk-tsk of her tongue and, whipping a scarf from around her waist, bound up Tess's golden hair. Still, she was not satisfied. Stooping down, she rubbed her hand

136

in the dirt, spit on it, and smudged it over Tess's nose and cheeks.

The youngest boy, whom someone had called Cedric, pointed with a look of horror at the sword and scabbard lying in the grass.

"Pitch it away!" the skinny man snapped. Quick and wiry, the boy jumped as if on strings, snatched up the sword, then the scabbard, and sent both cartwheeling into the woods.

All told, ten Yorkist soldiers rode into the clearing, disappointed to find nothing but a motley group of jongleurs poking at a bear. Confronted, the jongleurs stood still. One leaned against his stave. The square-jawed youth who led the soldiers urged his horse nearer to view the curious sight.

"Is it dead?" he asked the bare-chested jongleur, with one red leg and one of blue.

"Nah," he said, and gave it a poke with the stick as if for proof. A muffled groan came from the bear. Tess held her breath.

"Is it dying then?" The Yorkist captain stretched his neck to see.

Tess looked up to see a horse beside her, a fat youth in the saddle. He winked at her.

"Looks near dead to me," the captain observed.

"Nah. Not our Growl. Stupid beast got away an' ate a sheep is all. Ate it whole, it did. You see," he imparted with a confidential air, "it's the wool bears can't abide." He then went on to relate how he'd raised the bear and that was why it didn't

137

know what was good to eat and what was not. "But never you fear," he assured the youthful captain, "He'll bring the wool back up, just like a cat, an' he'll be right as rain."

At the prospect of such a sight, the soldiers quickly lost interest, and moved on with jokes and laughter.

"Come an' see him dance in the grand city of York, lads!" the bare-chested man called after them. "It's Botte Bleu's troupe, an' we'll be in the square! Bring your silver coins!"

When the voices faded, a boy ran and fetched a length of cloth from their props and the "bear" was hauled away. Though it was not an easy chore. They dared not remove the soldier from the hide for fear of other passing soldiers, and so they hauled and dragged the "bear" the distance to their carts.

The blond boy, known as Noam, huddled in the greenwood with the horse, and did not dare return till dark.

Tess helped to stretch Will out in the back of the narrow, crowded cart, and the struggle to remove him from the hide began. Inside the cramped cart, they heaved and twisted, pulled and tugged. When at last it was accomplished, all were perspiring mightily.

They stripped him of his *jaque,* boots, and hosen. Tess heard the coins jingle, but what was she do? In desperation, she reached to grab a leather sleeve, protesting, "He risked his life for those."

But the bare-chested jongleur gripped the *jaque* and in a waggish tone, remarked, "Did we not do likewise?" He held her captive with his eyes, suggesting, "Surely his life is worth as much as this?"

Tess watched him scoop the coins into his hand and go, stooping as he made his way from the cloth-covered cart. She tugged the leather *jaque* to her chest and said no more. Her soldier lay before her like an effigy upon a tomb, still and ghastly white, naked to the world, save for the coarse woven jupe that covered only what a shirt affords. And though her eyes sought to avoid it, she could not help but see his maleness, fat and lazy, nestled in its foreskin amid the crisply curly hair. It shocked her. She had never glimpsed a man shorn of his clothing.

Perhaps Tess blushed, for the fat woman pressed close to her, and said, "I am called Fleur." She patted Tess's hand. "We'll mend your soldier's leg," she promised. "Make him *bon sain* for you again. Vinaigre Tom knows how, don't you Tom?"

"Well enough, I do," he grumbled, inspecting the leg and calling to the big-nosed boy, Elgar, to fetch a candle and light it from the fire. The boy returned quickly with the candle, holding it for the strange, skinny man, as he heated a dagger's blade in the flame, turning it with care.

Tess shifted miserably, her pale face tense with worry. She moved closer to Will and took his hand in hers, fearing she had done wrong to trust them. But what else was she to do? she wondered wretchedly. He was raging hot with fever, and she did not know how to help him.

Distorted by the candlelight, Tom's long thin face and fleshy mobile lips took on a fiendish look. "You will not harm him?" Tess asked, suddenly, pathetically.

He smiled at her. "No," he murmured. His voice was almost kindly. "I'll not harm him."

Cedric leapt to his defense. "Tom pulled my arm straight when I broke it," the boy chirped, holding out a healthy brown-skinned arm as proof.

"Do not fear, *chérie*." Fleur comforted her with a broad rouged smile. "Tom is finer than a barber. Is it not so, Botte?"

"So he claims," the bare-chested man attested with a chuckle. He stood at the end of the cart. He had fetched a jupe with bellowed sleeves and was in the process of pulling it across his shoulders. "See you do it right, Tom," he said, peering into the cart's dim interior. "We don't want his one leg shorter than the other."

Tess helped them to gag and hold Will down. Mercifully, he was little aware. She thought herself a villain to be a part of it; but when the wound was opened and she saw the purulence ooze out, she felt somewhat redeemed. It was an ugly wound and deeply infected.

Tom theorized that it was a broadsword slash

and that a bit of cloth carried in by the blade had set the wound to festering. "A bit of cloth you cannot even see, but 'tis enough to kill a man, no matter what his size."

For three days, Will lay in the suffocating heat of the cart, drifting in and out of consciousness. Tess's first act was to find a light cloth amid the untidy mounds of material stacked in the cart and cover the lower part of his body. The cloth served to keep the ever-present flies from the wounded leg, as well as to ease her aching modesty.

Every night she said her prayers. "Matthieu, Mark, Luke, and John, bless the bed that I lie on, and bless all those who I hold dear. May the saints protect and hold them near." She prayed for salvation and mercy for the lost and for her soldier — for a miracle, that he might walk again.

She seldom left his side as the cart jounced and jolted southward. At times Will would toss restlessly, cry out, or mumble incoherently for hours. The days became an endless round of daubing him with water and shooing away the persistent biting flies.

Fleur, and once the dwarf Luigi, brought food to Tess and her ailing soldier, though the small amount of liquid she coaxed down his throat did not seem enough to keep him alive.

The others did what little they could. Noam contributed a big red rooster that soon became a pot of soup. No one asked where he had found it.

141

For the most part Tess was alone with her soldier, save for Cedric who drove the cart and fetched the water for her. When they made camp, he slept with the other boys beside the turf fire.

Their voices and laughter drifted on the air. Tess pushed aside a corner of the dowlas cover to see them walking through the sweet-smelling smoke as they settled for the night. But on the second evening the rain returned, and Cedric, dripping wet and still smarting from the older boys' hazing, was forced inside the cart.

Day by day, Tess came to know them more. It seemed a society where no one had a proper name and questions were not asked. Fleur, who was the freest with her words, seemed near to forty . . . quite old to Tess's youthful mind. She was a large woman, hard-featured; and in her parti-colored frock, she appeared truly like a huge, overblown flower. Even so there was a certain charm about her, a sensuality beyond the faded prettiness, the painted face, and the russet hair.

Near evening on the third day, Will's fever broke and he was bathed in perspiration. His first thought was for the leather *jaque*. Tess shushed him with her fingers pressed to his lips and, signing with her eyes, she directed her glance toward the voices beyond the cart. In an undertone she whispered, "The coins are gone. They took them from me," she finished lamely, feeling somehow to blame. She fetched the jacket from amid the jumble of the cart and brought it to him, for he would not be satisfied until he'd seen and handled it.

"Where are we?" he finally asked, dizzy with relief, realizing the missive was still there between the layers of leather, undisturbed.

"Do you not recall the bear? The jongleurs?"

He closed his eyes, uncertain. Fantastic images came to mind, a sense of unreality, as if he were still wandering, lost in a dream. "Some of it," he said, unwilling to admit his total lapse of reason. But when Tess told the tale, he was astounded. As he listened to her words, his admiration grew. She was a little wit, and very determined. She was pretty, too, even with a dirty face.

"I could have done no better," he assured her, and asked about the horse.

"He is pied," she said, smiling.

Had she said, he died? No. He was pied. Will was lying helpless on his back and she was suddenly talking riddles. He asked again, perplexed. But she could only laugh into her hands. At last, she said, "They painted him with spots." Drawing nearer, she softly murmured, "I think they are a pack of thieves."

Will's legs were shaky as a newborn foal's, but wrapped in the cloth from the makeshift pallet and with Tess to steady him, he ventured out. He took a deep breath, looking with pleasure at the world around him, the grass, the trees, to be alive and standing on his own two legs. He would live, he thought, and with one hand braced against the cart, the other grasping reality, he relieved himself against the wheel.

His little excursion into the world left him exhausted. Even so, he was determined to clothe himself. It was no easy matter. His leg was sore, and wrestling the leather hosen onto his sweaty body in the cramped interior of the cart was near to impossible.

"I can help you," Tess offered, rushing toward him eagerly, tugging here, and tugging there on the stubborn trousers.

The struggle became a contest of endurance. Will laughed weakly in defeat and Tess pulled with all her might, her budding breasts jiggling as she giggled. Much to Will's surprise, his cock bobbed up impudently between them. She was intent upon the hosen, pulling, tugging, and she did not see. He grinned with embarrassment and turned his back to her.

"Did I hurt you?" she asked with genuine concern, fearing she had injured his wound. He had turned away so abruptly—she was frantic.

"No," he assured her. His face felt hot. He gave a soft laugh, thinking there was more life in him than he had expected. "I'll manage now," he told her and asked her to wait outside for him.

At the foot of the cart, she glanced back. Suddenly she was overwhelmed by the thought of him, as if she had only that instant become aware of the dark, heavy-lashed eyes, the straight perfect nose, and the sheen of perspiration that glistened on his lean, muscular body.

Fragrant smoke and bits and scraps of conversation greeted them as they joined the others by the fire. Will's feelings toward the troupe were mixed at best. In truth they had saved Tess and him from the Yorkists. And he had no doubt that Tom's barber skills had saved his leg—perhaps his life—for the wound, unopened, would have slowly festered, poisoning him. Indeed, he would have considered the gold well spent, but there was still the matter of the horse . . . without a horse, he had not a prayer.

Unfortunately, it seemed the jongleurs also needed the horse. For three days, Navet, now sporting handsome bay spots, had pulled the cart in which Will lay. Botte explained their cart horse had recently gone lame and been traded to a farmer for a sack of oats. Without Will's horse, they had but an old mare and a mule, and would be forced to abandon one of their carts.

"We'd be left to hitch up Fleur." Tom chuckled, holding out his bowl.

Botte laughed, slapping his knee, while Tom and the boys exchanged snickers. Fleur was not amused. She raised her eyes from the bubbling stewpot and silenced them with a look. Beside her, the dwarf, a wiser man, awkwardly dipped stew with a wooden ladle. His lips tightened in a grin, but he made not a sound.

Botte, passing round his empty bowl, cast an appraising eye at the young man and said, "I don't know where you're going, young soldier. I don't even know your name. But you've a share in our troupe now, and it might be to your best advantage to travel on with us."

More than a share, Will thought, considering he'd had five gold coins and six silver ones in his *jaque*. But he was not keen to go on with them, and by way of refusal, said, "I've a long way to go."

Tom sopped a stale chunk of bread in his steaming bowl of stew. "If you're headed south, you've a better chance with us. We're bound for London. There's fatter purses there." He winked.

"London." Fleur sniffed, passing a bowl of stew to Botte. *"Eh bien,* for myself, I'll not be happy till I see the Seine again."

"I'd only be a danger to you." Will spoke up honestly with leveled eyes, "There're those among Yorkists who know my face."

"The Yorkists are no friends of ours," Botte said, tipping a bowl of stew to his lips. He was a loud-voiced man and stout, but with a good-humored bonhomie about him, a benevolent fatherliness that inspired a person to trust him in spite of one's instincts.

Fleur tucked an errant auburn curl behind her ear and settled beside the waggish Botte, remarking, "It's because of the stinking Yorkists we have no bear."

"You mean the poor beast whose hide is in the cart?" Tess asked. "How cruel!" she shivered.

Cedric raised his eyes from his bowl and blurted out, "Nah, 'twas Milo they hanged."

"The bear died on its own," Noam informed her.

Elgar, who was the oldest of the youths, agreed, adding, " 'Twas years ago, before we joined. There was a lad named Bob who wore the skin, but he drowned in the Swale two years ago. Then there was Milo."

Fleur nodded sadly. *"Alors,* poor Milo. He and a soldier got into a fight. The soldier was killed, and they hanged our Milo." She paused, to blow the steam from her stew, remarking, "And such a shame it was. He was a big, strong boy. A little stupid, but tall ones are not so easy to find."

Botte sucked at his stew, then wiped his hand across his mouth. "This bunch of twigs," he said, motioning toward the boys, "they'll never be his size. It takes two of them to fill the hide, one on the other's shoulders, and that's no good. It makes them clumsy as a drunken whore, the head saying, 'Go here,' and the feet saying, 'Go there.' It's no good at all."

Tess brought two bowls of stew and handed one to Will. She settled down beside him on the ground, pressing her hip to his.

"What about him?" Will asked, inclining his

head toward Tom. "He's tall enough."

Botte's lips twisted in a smile. "Only got one arm, haven't you Tom?"

Tess had noticed something odd about him from the first, though she could not say exactly what it was. The way he stood, perhaps. And then she recalled how he had ministered to Will's leg single-handedly. But she could plainly see he had two arms, or did he? Although the sleeve was filled, it was tucked into his tunic, as if from habit. But when he opened his shirt to reveal the mutilated half an arm, he convinced her. The sight of the withered stump made her wince.

"There was the finest juggler in all the world," Botte assured them with a flourish of his hand.

Tom gave an artful smile and bowed his head. "Alas, one-armed jugglers are of little use. Still, I search for those to teach. The boys here have some talent for it, they're fair enough, and I've taught them to be acrobats; they've no match at that."

"Mon dieu, for the old days," Fleur mused wistfully. "We were famous—*Le Magicien* Botte Bleu and his troupe. In France, the nobles knew our names. We performed at St. Po before the king and in the Hotel de Nesle, but that was long ago, *dans le passé."* She shrugged.

"I've no talent for sleight of hand," Will told them. He wanted only to be on his way.

"You needn't any to be a bear," Botte said. He ripped off another chunk of bread. "You need only be big and dumb. Well, what say you, young soldier?"

Will did not answer him at once. How close, he wondered, were his pursuers? He needed time to think and to regain his strength. At the moment, it seemed he had little choice but to agree. He could not go far afoot, and what of his golden-haired Greensleeves? The opportunity to send her away was gone. In the eyes of the king's sheriff, she was no less a traitor than Will. In a sidelong glance he glimpsed her profile; and settling his gaze on Botte's round face, he said, "I'll take a turn at it. Though, I'll not promise anything."

In the days that followed, the troupe fell back into their accustomed routine, which was no routine at all. Rather, it was a vagabond existence in which all lived cheek by jowl and there was no such thing as privacy; one lived not as an individual, but as a member of the troupe.

In dry weather they would break camp early. For the most part, there was no morning meal other than a bit of flat oatbread left over from the night before and a sip of cider. However, the keg lashed to Botte's colorful blue cart was nearly empty.

If an unlucky rabbit wandered into one of the snares set the night before, there would be meat for supper. If not, perhaps a stream might yield a gudgeon or a trout; otherwise the boys would shinny up the trees in search of bird eggs.

All day, they would jolt along at an unhurried

pace, the only speed at which the heavy carts could negotiate the rutted roads and country paths. Come evening, they would choose a campsite. The mule and horses would be cared for and firewood would be gathered. The preparation of the food was most often left to Fleur and the dwarf, Luigi, with the boys often pressed, somewhat glumly, into service. Tess was glad to share the cooking chores, and Fleur much preferred her company to that of the rowdy boys.

A little tributary of the river Nidd provided fish for the troupe's supper as well as a much-needed bath. Fleur and Tess took their turn in the beck first, sharing a bar of Fleur's precious lavender-scented soap. It had come from Paris, and Fleur never tired of singing the praises of all things French. She told Tess tales of long ago, of the French court, of extravagance and delicious indiscretions.

When the women returned, the men headed to the stream. Their voices and laughter carried on the lazy summer air as Tess and Fleur, crouched in the cool shade of the towering beeches, prepared the glassy-eyed fish for roasting on the fire.

The men returned smelling of homemade soap, a peculiar scent, a musky mingling of lard and wood ash, but in any case a definite improvement. They had shaved as well, and all appeared somehow odd-looking, as if they had put on new faces.

On returning, Botte, with characteristic bonhomie, sidled up to Fleur and announced in a theatrical tone that he was as clean as a newly baptized babe.

Tess giggled at their banter, but when she looked at Will, she laughed at him. Without the beard, he looked silly, no older than Elgar. Every time their eyes met, Tess had to look away, or smile or giggle.

Botte had trimmed his red-gold beard in the French style with two dramatic points, giving him a devilish look. Fleur teased him, tugging at the points and tweaking his cheek coquettishly.

Tom's face, shorn of the whiskers, appeared twice as long. And Elgar, still preening, showed off the modest beginnings of a mustache to everyone. Noam, too, proudly sported a yellow haze above his lip, while Cedric moped about dejectedly because he had no beard to shave.

Little Luigi, who was not a bit prettier without his growth of beard, pummeled Cedric's thin shoulders. "Look here," he remarked, polishing his bald pate, "I wish my hair was on my head and not my face. Now there's a magic trick for you, Botte!"

"Aye." Botte laughed. "If I could conjure that, we'd all be rich as kings!"

Each night, Tess slept chastely in her chemise with naught but a thickness of linen between herself and her soldier. She lived beside him, slept beside him. She truly liked him, without knowing why, without knowing who he was or even where he was going. She was certain he was fond of her,

151

and she did not lack proof. There was the look in his dark eyes, and a certain smile, both meant for her alone. Yet there was nothing more between them than the cool white linen cloth.

At first she thought him courtly and gallant, but then she wondered, did he find her unattractive? Because he was a knight, was she not fine enough for him? Or worst of all, had he a ladylove somewhere? A thousand questions crowded upon her tongue, but her pride kept her from speaking. She lay beside him, tortured.

Sounds drifted on the warm night air with wafts of wood smoke from the fire. For a long while she listened to the drone of boyish voices beyond the cart, then to the crickets chirping. She heard a night bird call, then drifted off to sleep.

Will's every sense longed for sleep, but it was slow in coming. When at last it came, he had but short, heavy snatches of rest tormented by violent dreams of pursuit and combat.

The horrors of the battle were still fresh in his mind, mayhap they would always be—the drilling rain, the bottomless mire. He saw again the corpses and the mayhem, the humped and blackened forms of men and horses littered across Hedgeley Moor.

He awoke from the nightmare with a jolt, shuddering, and with a pounding heart. In his dream he saw again the multitude of broken bodies, and the abbey where they had retreated with the king. Compelled, he moved amid the throng of men, brushing shoulders with the priests, the squires, and knights. Dead men, all, whose bloated bodies and distorted features passed before his eyes, crying out to him. The wounded and the dying lined the walls, and the flagstones ran with blood.

And in their midst, frail King Henry in his ragged robe danced about with shouts of glee, skipping through the pools of blood like a senseless child through a water puddle.

Margaret, his ambitious queen, came forward carrying a severed head. "Take this to my enemies in London!" she commanded, thrusting the grisly thing at Will and screaming in his face, so that all eyes stared at him and a host of bloody hands reached out to seize his cloak. And then he saw that the head was his.

After a tormented moment, he pushed the dream from his mind and fell into a deep exhausted sleep. But it was no less troubled, and time and again he shifted restlessly. His tossing body woke Tess, and afterwards she lay awake for a long while, watching the flap at the rear of the cart sway with the breeze, and wondering what it was that haunted him so.

Chapter Eight

A string of small villages marked the route to the walled city of York. The troupe made their camp in a meadow near the first of the villages. Since they intended to remain there for several days, perhaps as long as a week, they set up a trio of small gaily colored pavilions in which they could store and repair their props and costumes. Will noted that the rounded tents were not unlike the sort used by knights at tournaments. His and Tess's pavilion was of a wine color and marked with garish white diagonal stripes. The carts, unloaded of their burdens, seemed almost spacious.

Will found the dreaded bearskin to be every bit as smelly and as hot as he had imagined. It fit well enough, though a bear's legs were not fashioned quite like a man's and, in order to walk on all fours or even upright, Will was forced to hunch forward and plod along in a lumbering gait.

The head presented yet another problem. Will quickly discovered that the world when viewed through the glass eyes took on a distorted tilt. It took a bit of practice just to keep from falling on his nose. There was, however, no mastering the summer heat, and Will emerged from every practice session red-faced and dripping wet with sweat.

One morning as Tess sat alone plaiting her hair, she thought of her family and the mill at Lambsdale. Surely by now her sister had married, and she wondered hopefully if Mary were happy as a wife. It seemed an age since Tess had awakened in the large bed she shared with her sisters—a memory so distant, it might have belonged to another's life. In counting back the days, she was astounded to find only a fortnight had passed. She could hardly believe it.

It was not that she had been unhappy at the mill, nor had her grandfather been cruel. No, it was the everlasting dullness. Her life had been as monotonous as the turning of the millstones—day after weary day passed as if the mighty stones were grinding every moment slowly down to dust. It was a giddy feeling to break free, and she recalled how as a child she had watched the acrobatic displays of the swallows in the spring. Now she knew what they must feel—the wild, delicious, ever-veering delirium of soaring free. She reveled in it.

At times, though, she wondered, guiltily, if her family believed she had drowned in the beck. Or perhaps they thought that the marauding soldiers had murdered her. She wished there were a means to tell them not to worry, to tell them that she loved them, and she wondered if they would understand, even if she had the chance.

Fleur, who had earlier shown Tess the finer points of painting her face for an audience, was in the process of helping her sew a colorful costume. She could not help smiling at the young girl's bubbling enthusiasm and, with a touch of sadness, thought that she, too, had been that young once. A peasant girl, she had fled the despair of her ruined village with a pair of English mercenaries.

Tess posed before the scrap of mirror. She was unsure about the costume. She thought the neckline immodest, particularly when she learned she could not wear a chemise beneath the clinging silk. She would die of shame, she thought. But when she broached the subject, Fleur's painted eyebrows nearly leapt off her face.

"A chemise!" Fleur exclaimed. "Non, non, *chérie*. You want the silk to move with you. You want the men to drool, to tease the coins from their palms."

Tess was scandalized. "But I must wear more than—"

"Wear your lovely skin. *Mon dieu!* I wish I still had such a skin; I'm wise enough to wear it now. *Eh bien,* God only knows what I would have done, the sins I would have sinned."

Every day the sun blazed down from a cloudless sky. Tess and Will worked together in the summer heat to perfect their act. He was lumbering and clumsy in the bearskin, while Tess towed on the braided rope and ordered him about with a long brightly colored stick. Both suffered from the heat and the rough edge of Botte's tongue, for he was a hard tutor.

Nearby, Elgar and Noam stomped past on ten-foot stilts, and Luigi strolled by upside down, walking on his hands. Later, Cedric, Noam, and Elgar practiced their tumbling tricks, cartwheeling recklessly along, back-flipping, and leaping into human tableaus.

Botte and Fleur were accomplished at making almost anything seem to appear or disappear, including themselves. Tess, and even Will was fascinated. It was all arch-trickery, of course, and worked by means so incredibly simple and so sly that once it was explained, both would gape with amazement and mutter, "How is it I did not see this until now?"

One of Botte's more amazing stunts was to make coins, preferably gold ones, appear and vanish in mid-air. But in Tess's mind it was Fleur who was truly the conjurer, for with some scraps of silk and ribbon, she had fashioned Tess a costume. Tess had gratefully helped her to sew the seams and set the gaily colored ribbons. Completed, it was beautiful. Upon her skin, the silk was as soft as sin, and the bright fluttering ribbons cascaded over her bare arms like rainbows. Even the wreath that graced her fair braids was fashioned of blooms made of silk and ribbons.

Fleur was inordinately proud of her creation and, viewing the pale, lissome young creature, turned her about and about, declaring, *"Ma belle dame sans merci,* men would die for an hour with you!"

Her praise was seconded by Botte who exclaimed, "By God and all the saints, she'll need a bear beside her to keep the men away!"

Approving glances came from all around. Elgar nudged Noam with his elbow, and Cedric, clearly awed, said, "I didn't know she looked like that."

Will turned, taken by surprise by Tess's flustered smile, pink-flushed cheeks, and breathless lips. He hesitated awkwardly; all eyes were on him. He cleared his throat, but still his voice rasped. "You look beautiful," he finally said.

That evening, with the wagons packed, they made their plans for the following day. Botte, whittling a stick into a toothpick, spoke slowly. "Tomorrow we work Lutsby's square. We'll keep it simple till I've had a word with the tavern-keeper. Mayhap I'll get us a night's work. If not, we move on. Tom, you know what to do."

"York's the place we ought to be," Tom said. "I hear there's twenty taverns in York."

"There's coins to be made everywhere. We'll be in York soon enough."

The evening meal was more spartan than usual, a few bird eggs and some gathered greens. The cleaning chores were left to Fleur and Tess. They loaded up the pot and trenchers and trudged off toward the beck.

It was already dark beneath the trees. Tess fumbled with the bowls. She dropped one into the water and swore an oath. Blue and French, it was one she had heard from Fleur's lips, Tess had no notion what it meant. The bowl, fashioned of wood, made a plopping sound as it fell into the black water and, caught by the current, bobbed just beyond her reach. A fallen tree lay in the beck. Tess stepped out quickly, balancing precariously on its mossy bark, slipped and, with a yelp, fell into the stream. The dark water drew her down. She thrashed her arms and legs, terrified and gulping water.

Fleur ran back and forth like a frantic hen. She was unable to reach Tess and could not swim herself. She screamed as only she could scream, which brought the men racing through the meadow.

Will waded in waist deep and pulled her out. He was laughing. Everyone was laughing. Safe on the shore, Tess spluttered and pushed her straggling hair from her eyes. It was then she realized, to her profound embarrassment, the water was but waist deep on Will. In the dark and with the slippery mud beneath her feet, she had panicked. She could have stood up if only she had tried.

All the way back across the meadow, through the hazy twilight, they laughed, teasing her unmercifully. Luigi put a bowl on his bald head and danced before them through the tasseling grasses.

Tess was soaked to her skin, as were her lovely scarlet slippers. Will set them by the fire to dry. Perhaps from guilt, he asked, "Would you like me to hang your kirtle there in the tree? It will dry more quickly than in the cart."

At the foot of the cart she paused and glared at him. "You have helped me enough tonight." With that she flounced into the cart and jerked down the ragged rug that served as a flap.

Will came and stood by the foot of the cart. He heard her moving about inside, heard the sound of her wet clothing dropping to the floor. "At least you were not hurt," he said, still smiling at the thought of her thrashing in the waist deep water, and Fleur screaming like a Viking warrior.

Tess's voice came to him from within the darkened cart. "You did not ask me if I was hurt—until now. You were laughing too loudly."

He was about to deny it when she pushed aside the worn rug and then stepped back, running a comb through her wet hair. She had donned a monstrously large chemise, one of Fleur's. It was too large, and it hung from her slight form in folds.

Will lifted himself into the gloomy interior of the cart and began to shed his wet clothing. Even his shirt was soaked. "You do not look too badly hurt. You seem to be as I recall," he teased, taking stock of her. "Two arms, two legs," and catching a glimpse of pale breast exposed by the enormous neckline, added, "two of every part."

"The hurt was not a part you see."

He sat back on the bed of rags and pulled off his boots. "Shall I look for it?" he offered.

She gave him a sour face and turned away, pulling the comb through her hair.

He stood up, barefooted, and stripped the shirt from his back. "I swear, I did not know the water was so shallow."

"You made me look a fool."

"I pulled you from the beck."

"At my expense."

He wadded his shirt into a ball and thrust it into her hand. "Here, take my heart and step on it."

"I do not want your heart!" she exclaimed, though she could not keep from smiling. She put down her comb, shook out the shirt and draped it over a huge willow basket. There was hardly space to move, amid the confused mass of costumes and props.

In the semidarkness, Will watched her supple body stretch and bend. Random thoughts of a

161

forbidden nature flashed through his mind. He turned his back to her and concentrated on the ties of his hosen, peeling the leather from his body. The mere thought of her left him feeling tense. He was not at all surprised to find his arousal was complete and slapped against his stomach when he crouched to rifle through a pile of rumpled clothing. Earlier he had seen a pair of Milo's hosen lying atop a pile of filthy silken tunics. He could not find them. He slid down on the bed and covered himself. It was no use. He made a tent beneath the linen cloth. He rolled over on his side.

Moments passed. At last Tess put away her comb and lay down with her back to him. She was still angry, he thought, and, shifting full length beneath the covering, he propped himself on one elbow. He smoothed her hair aside with gentle fingers and caressed her shoulder. "I thought I'd lost you to the beck," he murmured, proceeding carefully. "I'd sooner die than live without you." It was the truth, for at that moment, spurred on by the sharp pangs of desire, he wanted her above all else, more than even life itself.

As much as she wanted to, Tess did not believe his pretty words. Such words came too easily to him, and the soft, husky purr of his voice, the gentle touch of his marauding fingers, sent a delicious chill racing through her limbs, tingling her flesh and heightening her every sense. She fought against it. "It is all a game to you," she accused, though she did not push his hands away.

Will hesitated, but only for an instant, responding, "What is a game? Because I care for you?" The smooth subtleness of his tone seemed to invade Tess's body, to strike a chord deep inside her. She half turned to him, shivering, and when her eyes met his, they were as dark and soft as velvet. She felt suddenly weak, helpless to resist his nearness, the warm scent of his skin, the broad shoulders, and the strong arms that so skillfully drew her to him.

He lowered his head to bring their lips together. Like a thief, his tongue slid along her parted lips, touching her teeth and slipping between them to claim her tongue and steal away her breath. As he continued to kiss her, his hands began to roam, to caress and stroke the smooth, sweet curves of her body. With a single practiced movement, he slid the shift from her shoulders and pressed a trail of damp kisses down her throat.

Tess's body was warm and pliant, melting in his arms. Her hands slid over his shoulders in acceptance, uncaring, heedless of the consequences. In her excitement she could no longer breathe properly; and when his lips fastened onto a nipple, to mouth and lick and suck, she felt a jolt of passion surging through her lower abdomen.

He moved forward, locking his mouth on hers,

and covered her body with his. What had begun as a hollow ache was now a pulsing heat between Tess's legs and even when she felt the urgent bump of his hardened shaft against her thigh, she did not struggle against him. She was so eager for him, so willing to spread her legs, she was ashamed.

She panicked, pushing against his chest. "No," she cried. She could hardly speak, her heart was beating so against her ribs. "You only care for me because I am here within your reach." She quickly turned away from him, drawing the shift over her naked breasts. Her dignity was not so easily regained, and she burned with embarrassment, angry at him and at herself. "You are a knight, the boy at the abbey said as much. What could you care for me?" she asked, her voice thick with reproach. "I am naught but a miller's granddaughter. I have no noble name or fine estates."

Miller? Had she said *miller?* Nothing could have doused his ardor so completely. He knew of only one mill near his uncle's lands, and that was Lambsdale Mill. "It was not your fine estates that I admired," he mumbled. He could think of nothing else to say.

No. In his mind he denied it. It was unthinkable that the desirable creature beside him was Theresa of the betrothal contract—the miller's brat he'd seen but once, years before, when he

164

had been a boy of barely fourteen and she a child of six or seven — a fair-headed girl, fat and so shy she had to be dragged from behind her nursemaid's skirts. No, he had seen no mill, though he reflected, he had not seen what lay beyond the wooded bend of the beck. Holy Christ and Mother Mary, was this the girl he had refused to wed? How was it possible she had grown to be such a beauty? What a clever cock I am, he thought. I deserve to be thrashed. He shifted away, miserable, and said no more.

Even later he kept quiet when she murmured, half-heartedly, "It was good of you to save me from the stream."

He merely grunted his acceptance and lay there staring into the empty blackness of the cart, his thoughts in ruins.

Chapter Nine

Their first performance was in a little village that was no more than a straight-through rutted road with a few houses and shops between. At one end was a deserted marketplace, at the other an abbey, and beside it a graveyard. From birth to death, the villagers' lives had not far to go. The village had but a single tavern, and it was owned by the brethren of the abbey, so jongleurs and their ilk were unwelcome. The brothers viewed them collectively as a blight, a scourge upon the souls of the faithful.

Botte returned with downcast features to tell the troupe there would be no work that night. "An abbot owns the tavern," he related, with a sneer. "They've sanctified rogues and repentant whores hereabouts. They don't want the likes of us corrupting them."

The coins had been few and far between, but all agreed to play the square a bit longer. They left the village in the summer dusk and camped at dark. By the fire, the coins were counted. A full day's work in the blistering sun had netted them little reward. But with all eyes on the entertainers in the square, Tom and the boys had taken the opportunity to loot the wool merchant's shed. Grinning like border raiders, they showed their booty.

Fleur inspected the half-dozen sacks of wool, declared it of good quality, and suggested, "We should sell it in the next village, we're in need of food."

"We'll get a better price in York," Botte said, calculating its worth while Elgar and Noam lounged against the cart.

"Our little flower of France is worried she will starve," Tom snickered.

Fleur hissed at him and walked away. Tess followed after her. Will heard them speaking in rapid whispers as they passed.

He, too, felt uneasy about the stolen goods. "There is a penalty for stealing wool," he mentioned. He did not like the idea of an irate wool merchant following them to the next village, for it would not require too much intelligence to guess where the wool had gone . . . and with whom.

Botte smiled and, slicking back his red-blond hair, said, "There is a penalty for everything young man, even life."

With Lutsby behind them, it was a village a day—a hectic pace. They would play the square for several hours; Tom and the boys would do their work, and before dusk they would move on to a campsite well beyond the village and the victims.

Then, with the small villages behind them, the jongleurs took a much-needed rest. Costumes ware repaired and readied and new tricks were perfected. One new trick was discovered quite by accident as the troupe prepared to pack. Cedric was disassembling the *table,* which consisted of a section of heavy clay pipe and a board of several feet in length.

Acting the fool, Cedric put the pipe on its side and attempted to balance himself on it, while rolling about. Will, who was brushing down the horses and the mule, laughed. "Now try it on one foot," he joked.

"Come on," Cedric called back. "You try it."

Will laid down the brush and walked over. "Let's make it a bit more difficult," he suggested, taking the short length of board that had served as the tabletop and laying it across the pipe to make a sort of rolling teeter-totter.

Cedric christened it a roly oly, because the minute he stepped onto the board, it began to roll and his next words were, " 'oly Christ!" as the board rolled away from beneath his feet and dumped him on his back.

Will soon discovered that the roly oly was more difficult than it looked. He, too, hit the ground with bruising regularity until he finally got the hang of it. He learned that if he first stepped on the lower end of the board, then placed his other foot on the upper end, he could shove off safely. Then, as he put his weight on the upper end, the board would roll away from that foot, and in order to keep his balance, he had to shift his weight rhythmically from foot to foot as the board made a seesaw movement. The knack, he found, was to keep his upper body still and only move from the waist down.

Before long, all work had stopped. Fleur and Tess ·abandoned folding costumes to watch, and each boy had a try at the roly oly. It was great fun until Tom and Botte decided it would make a clever trick for Growl the bear. The first time Will tried it dressed in the bearskin, he nearly broke his neck.

The sun was still high and hot on their necks when they sighted the great city of York. "Tomorrow," Botte called, striding back to his cart, "we'll pay York a call, and she'll pay us!"

That evening by the fire, Tom had the boys set up a wooden framework from which he dangled a merchant's purse. He placed a coin in the purse and strung the purse and frame with little hawking bells. Amid much laughter and heckling, each boy took a turn. The coin was the prize; the object was to seize it without ringing the bells.

Elgar, with his pointed nose and bobbing Adam's apple, was the victor. He grinned from ear to ear and, holding up the coin, challenged Will. "Come on, Growl, it's yours if you can nick it!"

Tom laughed at the prospect. "Yes, let's see what we can make of you."

Will, seated beside Tess, rose good-naturedly and took a turn at it. He was not as subtle as the boys, and Botte, red-faced and laughing, suggested he should use a sword. When the laughter and the hazing had died out, a few sticks were added to the fire and plans were made for York.

Cedric listened, poking at the embers with a stick until Noam knuckled his head, and warned, "Quit playing in the fire, you donkey. You'll piss yourself again tonight!"

Alone in their cart, Will stripped off his shirt and stretched out, exhausted, on the pallet of rags that served them as a bed. A moment later, Tess slid in beside him and laid a cool hand on his shoulder.

"That is why Tom has no arm," she said in a breathless whisper.

For a moment, Will was at a loss. She had the most disconcerting habit of beginning her conversations with a single mysterious phrase. At times he found it maddening. It was almost as if it were a game she played, and he was meant to guess the rest. "For thievery?"

"Sh, yes. He has killed men, too."

He shifted position and made a place for her inside his arm. She was as soft as he imagined and the faint female scent rising from her bodice sent his blood racing to his loins. He blinked in the darkness; coherent thought escaped him, but at last he managed to mumble, "How do you know these things?"

"Fleur told me." Lowering her voice still further, she whispered, "It is all my fault. I told them you were an outlaw and that you stole the horse." She did not pause for breath and went on rapidly. "You must think me very sinful. I am not, I swear by Matthieu, Mark, Luke and John. I would not have told a lie, but I — well, don't you see? They think you are a thief!"

Of all his muddled emotions, desire, confusion, and amusement, Will felt the pang of guilt most strongly. It was because of him that she was there and most certainly in danger. For even if Tom's thievery did not get them hanged, there was still the message, and clearly men would kill to have it. He dropped his head close to hers and breathed, "Listen, my little *sainte*. It is only because of your clever lie that we are still alive. If there has been a sin, it is mine. I should not have brought you into this. You were safe at Lambsdale Mill. I had no right to take you from your family."

That he had called the mill by name did not at first occur to Tess. His fingers roving up her spine and his lean efficient body close to hers, sent her thoughts to racing and filled her with a burning ache to draw him near. "You promised you would take me home again." She had no notion why she said it. Perhaps, to save herself from the velvet voice, the tender smile.

His hand faltered. She was like a fever in his blood, one for which there was no remedy. "I have not forgotten," he told her, his voiced hushed. As much as he desired her, he could not confess, for surely she would hate him. Nor could he in good

171

conscience seduce his own betrothed, the very woman he had rejected. Of all the fair damsels with pink-nippled teats and silken thighs, why should she have been the one to fall into his arms? 'Twas no more than he deserved, he thought. He took his arm away and shifted onto his side, reminding her, "Do not forget your prayers."

Tess had never seen such a sight as York, which, in the pastel mist of morning, rose from the plain like a fairy city—with bastioned walls, gleaming rooftops, and towering spires that nearly touched the clouds.

She stared at the spectacle, looking first one way and then the other, afraid she would miss something. Each view was new and grand; but at the Micklegate, a more familiar sight met her eyes. Yorkist soldiers manned the walls, halting all who entered.

The caravan of three ancient carts drawn by a mule, a ginger mare, and a faded piebald joined the queue of tumbrels, carts, and pack animals awaiting entry through the city's walls. A gate tax was demanded. All who entered were forced to pay—merchants, farmers, even jongleurs.

In the misty morning light, the soldiers moved lethargically from cart to tumbrel. Occasionally they would poke their heads into a cart, then continue on, striding down the line of weary pack horses.

With a dreadful sense of anticipation, Tess watched their every movement. Cedric, seated beside her, gripped the reins, his knuckles showing white. One look inside the carts would seal their fates, for they were laden with stolen goods—from sacks of wool to knives and little silver bowls.

Will, sweating in the bearskin, peered through a rent in the dowlas covering. He waited tensely. At last the guard sauntered past. He paused, then turned about. Tess's heart skipped a beat. But he only smiled at her, then waved them past.

York, they soon discovered, was an immense and crowded web of narrow streets and close dark alleyways. Carts and pedestrians choked the winding thoroughfares, and at the bustling docks, a multitude of tongues was spoken. The river Ouse brought Hansa ships from the Baltic and beyond, and ships from France and Spain to trade for English wool.

The market was no less crowded. Every available space was occupied. In frustration, the jongleurs set up beside the Church of St. Mary. The morning, which had dawned with overcast skies, now threatened rain.

They had not earned a dozen pennies before the dreary day gave way to large, intermittent drops of rain that splashed their faces and drubbed against the dusty ground. Faster and faster it came, streaming down and driving them to cover in the tent they had raised for changing costumes. All across the market grounds, people darted for shelter; shoppers abandoned their search for goods, and merchants crawled beneath their carts and stalls.

Inside the tent, the air was stifling. Fleur swore in French and peered from the tent flap. "It will rain all day," she glumly predicted.

"Not in this season," Botte said, idly flipping a gold coin. "It's only a shower. It will be dry in an hour."

Fleur shot him a peeved glance and said abruptly, *"Mon dieu!* Look at the sky. Even an old fool like you can see it's as black as if a horse had kicked it."

"If you're going to argue," Tom said, scratching his jaw, "why not wait till you're alone?"

Fleur glared at him.

"She blames me for the weather, too," Botte chuckled, snatching the coin from midair. "Don't you, my shapely little dove?"

She swore at him again in French, and Elgar, who had been lounging on the dusty floor beside Will, stood up and stretched. Noam scooted to one side for him, then went back to rolling dice with Cedric and the dwarf. The humid heat was intolerable.

Will pulled his head and arms free of the skin and ran a hand through his dark hair. His face ran with perspiration, and his hair was pasted to his head. Tess crouched down beside him, her back aching from standing.

"Eh! That's cheating," Cedric accused, taking a swipe at Noam, who ducked away, laughing, a layer of greasy blond hair falling across his face.

174

Tom kicked at them. "Shut up," he said.

A gusty draft of rain blew in the tent flap. Fleur shook the wetness from her arms and turned on Botte, her black eyes blazing. "What are you going to do, stand here all day? Get out and find us a tavern for tonight. We haven't had a decent meal in days. And don't brag to me about the stinking wool; we can't eat that."

"I'm going, too," Tom said, motioning for Elgar to come along. Botte snapped his fingers; the coin vanished, and leading the way, he pushed from the tent. Fleur stood victorious with her pudgy hands on her hips and watched them go darting through the mud, past the untidy rows of stalls.

Inside the tent, the dice game continued. Tess leaned her head against Will's shoulder, and together they watched the rain teem down.

The church bells sounded sext, and afterwards, the rain ended as suddenly as it had begun. Townspeople ventured out from taverns, homes, and shops, eager to get on with the day, their chores, and shopping.

The jongleurs reappeared with the sun, hoping to cadge a few coins from the passing crowds. Fleur draped her dimpled arms with necklaces of glass beads and finely braided silk on which she'd sown amulets—little silken bags filled with couch grass and meadowsweet, a few pine needles, and a pebble to give weight and substance. The "magic" necklaces of rose-colored beads and bright silk made tempting baubles.

"Messieurs, mademoiselles, capture love everlasting!" Fleur called to passerbys. *"Amour, amour,* only three pennies for your heart's desire! A powerful charm to bring your love to you," she promised as she smiled and dangled her silken pouches before the townsfolk who gathered round to watch the jugglers and the girl with a dancing bear.

Noam began the juggling, sending three brightly colored balls into the air. Cedric, by his side, snatched one with his right hand. Noam continued while Cedric—with a comic face—stole another with his left, and, pitching the first ball into the air, captured number three. Now Noam was left to juggle only air . . . until he stole them back. But as he stole one ball from his right, then another from his left, Cedric astounded everyone by continuing to juggle three balls. It was a clever trick in which Cedric held two balls out of sight with his smaller fingers, then simply brought them into play.

"Eh bien, are they not amazing for ones so young," Fleur praised in a honeyed tone, smiling a lot as she moved through the knot of onlookers, collecting coins on the troupe's behalf.

The baking sun was transforming the puddled marketplace into an oven. Will moved slowly, miserable inside the bearskin; perspiration ran from every pore. Tess led him about as a gang of children squealed with pleasure. Luigi, dressed as a fool with bells on his long, pointed shoes, followed along playing a flute. At Tess's command, Will rose up slowly on his hind legs, pacing heavily to the tune.

Young and old gathered round to see the huge, muzzled creature dance. Will glimpsed their faces through the glassy eyes, wondering what savage need it fulfilled in humankind to see a creature brought to this. Little wonder, he thought, that the bear had died with a leer upon its face.

Tess prodded him once more with a brightly colored whip, commanding him to dance. He was sorely tempted to knock the whip from her hand, but he clambered up once more, dizzy in the heat, and paced around and around, stomping out the simple tune.

Afterwards, Tess, fearing he was too hot, led him into the tent. The violet-hued shade of the interior kept out the sun, but there was no escaping the steamy heat.

Will's body chilled with gooseflesh as he pushed his way from the fierce head-piece. Half in, half out of the wretched hide, he flopped down on his rump, his furry legs stretched out before him. He was drenched in sweat. His hair was wetted flat against his head, and perspiration streamed down his spine.

Tess plunged a cloth into a jug of water and rushed to offer it to him. "Did you see the coins fall?" she gushed. "And the faces of the children? Oh, you are such a good bear." She giggled, hanging onto his neck and hugging him.

He dragged the cloth across his face, and only

then did he see the imprint of his perspiration on her silken bodice. It had become transparent, and the nipples of her breasts budded out and thrust against the cloth with her every breath. A stab of desire forked through him as if he'd been pricked with a spur.

"What is the matter?" Tess asked, made anxious by his staring eyes. She cocked her head and looked at him, frightened by his silence. "Are you sick?" she cried.

"Yes." It was no lie, for at that very moment he was dying of desire, monstrously uncomfortable where he strained against the bearskin.

A traitorous smile gave him away. And when Tess glanced down, self-consciously, her cheeks flamed with color.

The marketplace was all but deserted when the trio returned from their rounds of the taverns. Their high good humor was partly due to ale and partly due to their success at arranging a night's work in the Black Duck Tavern. Tom had plans as well, the sacking of a merchant's house in Goodramsgate.

When their gear was packed, they made a procession through the streets. Tom had hired half-a-dozen urchins to run ahead, calling out for all to hear: "Come tonight! Come tonight! See magic done at the Black Duck! A dancing bear, jugglers, and ale by the cup!"

True to the tavern's name, above the door, hung a wooden duck whose peeling paint was more grey than black and, like the tavern, worn by time. In the quick mud of the tavern's back lot, the carts were unhitched, the mule and horses led into the tavern's stable.

It had been a long day for all, particularly for Will. He had not been completely free of the bearskin since early morning, and even an action as simple as taking a drink was all but impossible without Tess's assistance. Only if she opened the hide a bit at the throat could Will duck his head enough for Tess to tip a cup to his lips. Relieving himself was a bit more complicated, but in the melting heat of the hide, he seldom felt the need.

The tavern supplied them with a meal of meat pies and ale. When the cook offered Tess a bloody bone and gristle for the bear, Tess rolled her eyes heavenward and exclaimed, "Oh, I wouldn't dare to feed him that. He might decide to eat me next. I feed him the same food I eat." The cook, a broad woman, not too bright but kindly, saw the wisdom of Tess's simple logic and heaped three more meat pies on the tray.

Without the weight of the bearskin, Will felt as light as a feather. He joined the rest of the troupe to eat. It seemed unlikely an extra head would be noticed, and he wisely did not stray far from the cart or the bearskin.

As the troupe wolfed down the pork pies, plans were laid. The tavern's ceilings were too low for stilts, so it was determined that they would do a juggling routine and some tumbling. There was work for later as well, but that required fast moves of a different sort.

The dim light cast by the tavern's oil lamps was perfect for sleight of hand and all illusions. Botte proposed the chains and the basket, remarking, "We can't go wrong with it."

"Oui," Fleur agreed, her mouth filled with food. "Of all our little *tricheries,* it is my favorite."

A shoulder-to-shoulder crowd packed the Black Duck Tavern. Tradesmen and merchants milled about with soldiers, farmers, and sailors fresh from the docks on the River Ouse. The sights Tess saw set her blue eyes shining. There were Hansa merchants, dressed as finely as princes, side by side with common yeomen, cartmen and drovers, and richly garbed members of the knightly class. There were scruffy, coarse-looking men, cutpurses, and girls no older than herself who plied their trade with come-hither smiles and wagging hips.

In such an atmosphere, it was inevitable that Tess would be pawed and pinched and grabbed. Even the rowdier crowds of the marketplaces had not prepared her for such a gauntlet of crude advances. She very quickly learned to dodge, push, and shout out loud.

But one bold sort, a Yorkist soldier full of ale, came after Tess, determined to steer her towards the back rooms for a tumble. Tess felt his fetid breath on her face, his iron grip on her arm. She shouted, "No!"

He countered by grabbing her shoulder with his

other hand and jerking her about. "You little whore," he cursed. "I'll give you something to make you yell!" He'd no sooner got out the words, when Growl the bear, a leer upon his face, swung round his furry rump and knocked the fellow lengthwise. Howls of laughter filled the tavern as the man's drunken friends, who were laughing just as loudly, hauled him from the floor and dragged him off to swill more ale.

Preceded by a fanfare of lute, fife, and tambor drum, Botte, garbed in his azure blue tunic and namesake blue boots, stepped before the crowd. In his booming, accomplished voice, he introduced himself and his troupe. All came forward and took a bow. Botte then gave the crowd his usual spiel, and said, "But let us have a little music first, something to set you fine gentlemen to drinking hearty!"

This was the cue for Fleur to come forward, carrying her lute, followed by little Luigi with a fife, and Cedric, disguised as a girl, with a tambor drum. They struck up a merry tune, then Luigi skipped to the fore and sang:

> Bring us in good ale, lads.
> Bring us in good ale.
> Don't bring us in no mutton,
> For that is often lean.
> Don't bring us in no tripes,
> For they be seldom clean.

Just bring us in good ale, lads.
Just bring us in good ale."

Dressed in a garish outfit and wearing a fool's cap adorned with bells, Luigi jigged about and sang another chorus:

"Don't bring us in no fair maids
As soft as downy beds.
Don't bring us in no lassies
With big teats on which to lay our heads.
No, just bring us in good ale, lads.
Just bring us in good ale!"

Coaxed on by the crowd, Luigi let one bawdy song lead to another, until presently he crooned:

"Beneath a weeping willow in foul and stormy
    weather,
A rogue and a whore took shelter together.
But oh, that randy rogue,
He screwed her on the spot,
Stuck it in and got it caught.
Now even He who made the thunder
Can't pull that rogue and whore asunder!"

As the musicians trooped off to applause and shouts, Noam and Elgar cartwheeled into the circle of lamplight. Botte, on the sidelines but in view of the audience, rapidly produced six brightly colored balls from thin air—or rather from the depths of his ragged sleeves, though the trick was completely undetectable—even to Tess, who knew how it was done, and she was standing only a short distance away.

The two boys made quite a show in their gaudy silken tunics of red and white as they combined their skills at juggling and acrobatics. They sent the colorful balls cascading through the air. They passed the balls back and forth, sending them in fancy directions, under their legs, behind their backs, and sliding off their heads. At the end of their routine, they sent the balls back to Botte, who made them vanish with an effortlessness that was truly amazing.

After the boys had taken their bows, Botte stepped forward and announced to the audience, "My friends, my friends, I hope you have enjoyed our entertainment so far." Applause and cheers rose from the crowd. "There is more, do not fear. Let me first introduce you to a very brave and daring young daughter of France who has subdued and, yes, trained one of the world's most vicious beasts. I give you Mademoiselle Tessa and Growl, the dancing bear!"

Tess, whose face was painted like a doll's, walked confidently into the mellow ring of light, leading the lumbering bear. Accompanied by lute, fife, and drum, Growl went through his paces. Tess, remembering to smile, bowed and accepted the crowd's applause. As the tune ended, Noam ran out carrying the length of pipe and board. Both pieces of the roly-oly had been painted suitably bright colors and gleamed in the lamplight.

As planned, Will, alias Growl the bear, at first balked at the trick. Tess prodded the obstinate bear with her whip, then pretended to whisper in his ear. Growl, protesting with a grumble, rose up slowly on his hind legs. Then, to a drum roll on the tambor, he cautiously risked one foot, then the other, balancing himself on the teetering board as he rolled about in a circle.

A cheer went up from the audience. Growl exited the board in a bearlike fashion, more of a bounding roll. In Will's opinion the exit had been the hardest part to learn. Tess patted and praised him and, pretending to take a treat from her silken skirts, she stuffed it into his mouth. He was very credible as a bear, so much so, that at times the fierce glinting eyes and the sincerity of his lumbering gait sent a shudder through her. Noam trotted out to collect the pipe and board. As he did, the haunting notes of Luigi's flute filled the tavern, and Tess commanded the bear to rise on his hind legs again. With another word from Tess, Growl clasped her loosely in his fierce paws. Like dancers in a dream, they swayed to the melody, turning slowly around and around to the wild approval of the audience.

After bows and much ado, Tess led her bear back across the room, returning to a small bench by the wall. Will flopped down beside her on the floor, leaning his back against the bench. Something solid to lean against made it easier to maintain a bearlike posture; otherwise, the strain of holding his body in such a pose was killing to his spine.

Botte again held up his hands, calling, "My friends, I know you are enjoying yourselves, but we must interrupt our show for a matter of grave importance." Jeers and hoots came from the audience. "Please, my friends. Listen. We have among our troupe two men who have fallen in love with the same lovely maid."

At that, Cedric, still dressed as a girl, minced onto the stage—to much laughter—and curtsied. "As I said," Botte continued, "neither will relinquish their claim to the fair lady. Alas, they must settle it in battle. I give you, Squire Green and Squire White. May the victor have the maid!"

All at once two hilariously small men burst from behind the jongleur's screen, already locked in a furious struggle. Tess could not help laughing. Seen in the dim light of the tavern they looked quite real, though they were only half the size of Luigi.

Squinting through the smoke of the oil lamps, Tess saw that although Squire Green was the larger, Squire White was quicker on his feet. Their arms were clasped so tightly about each other's shoulders that only the backs of their heads were visible as they pummeled one another, twisted, and grunted. Over and over they rolled, fighting ferociously and inflicting terrible blows.

Just when it seemed Squire Green would be victorious, plucky little Squire White would leap onto Green's chest and throw him to the ground. The pair fought without once releasing their grip, as the crowd urged them on with shouts of encouragement.

Finally, the two impetuous little fighters fell exhausted to the floor, still gripping one another tightly and calling for Botte to declare one of them the victor.

Botte viewed them from one angle and then another, scratching his head in indecision. At last he turned to the audience and said, "Who do you choose?"

"Squire White! Squire White!" they chanted.

Botte acquiesced, and gallantly led the fair maid, Cedric, forward on his arm. At that, Squire Green stretched out his legs and then, before disbelieving eyes, Squire White slowly rose into the air, as if he were doing a handstand above Squire Green. Suddenly Squire White's peasant boots fell off to reveal hands. Hands which reached down and grabbed Squire Green by the tunic and peeled off Squire White like a piece of clothing, to reveal Luigi's exhausted red face and bald head. A rousing round of laughter and applause filled the tavern as Luigi took a bow and exited with Cedric on one arm and the crumpled Squire White hanging from the other.

Botte stepped fully into the light and once again engaged the audience. Fleur was introduced. After much comic bantering back and forth, Botte, with characteristic braggadocio, began pulling one brightly hued scarf after another from the air. With a flourish, he presented each to Fleur, who would smile with amazement and then remark, "It is very nice, but I would like . . ."—and whatever color he conjured up, she, of course, wanted a different color. Finally, having run out of colors, he whipped a black scarf from the air. Fleur pretended to be furious. "I want a white scarf!" she scolded.

Botte, smiling at the audience, began waving the black scarf slowly to and fro between his hands. As he did, the black scarf magically changed into a white one.

"Non, non, non!" Fleur shouted, having changed her mind again. She planted her plump hands on her hips, and in a carping voice, she began to lecture him. "You are as stupid as a goose! You do everything wrong. I don't know how I put up with you!"

While Fleur continued to berate him, Botte took a step closer to the audience and, in a conspiratorial tone, said, "You see how she treats me?" The audience, comprised mostly of men, was quick to take his part and to respond sympathetically.

"Then you won't blame me for what I'm about to do?" Botte asked.

The crowd responded with shouts of, "No! No! Stuff her in a sack!"

One drunken cotter yelled, "Skin her out and make a tent of her, brother! She's fat enough!"

"I'll keep that in mind, my friend," Botte said, stepping back to Fleur and adopting a contrite countenance. "Will you ever forgive me, my dove?" he begged, taking her hands as if to kiss them. But no sooner than he did, he whipped a scarf from nowhere and bound her wrists.

"You little pricklouse!" Fleur cursed at him, shouting threats at the top of her voice.

Botte made a show of holding his hands over his ears. From one ear, he pulled another scarf, which he used to gag her. The audience cheered with hoots of laughter. They were even more generous with their applause when Botte pulled a sack from the air and stuffed her inside.

Fleur wriggled and struggled, protesting with grunts, as Botte rolled her across the floor and into a huge wicker box. He then proceeded to lock the box, by inserting a stout metal bar through the hasp. From the sidelines, he gathered up lengths of rope and a chain.

He carefully tied up each end of the jumping and shaking box and, as a final safeguard, wrapped it with chains. Turning to the audience, he dramatically dusted off his hands and took a bow. Accompanied by their thunderous cheers, he pushed the box behind the large screen.

An instant after he and the box had disappeared behind the screen, a figure emerged from the other end, casually folding up the screen. It was Fleur, not Botte! And she was wearing a victorious smile. But as the screen was folded away, the audience noticed that the box was still jumping about and muffled cries came from inside it.

Fleur, looking genuinely confused, turned to the crowd and shrugged her shoulders. The audience responded with shouts of, "The basket! Open the basket!" When they became sufficiently loud, Fleur obliged them by unbarring the hasp and slowly untying the ropes and chain. Finally, when she opened the lid, the sack rolled out and, to everyone's amusement, Botte emerged, gagged and tied.

Tess laughed, too, even though she knew the basket had a large panel in the back which provided an exit for Fleur and an entry for Botte. The critical moment was when the basket was pushed behind the screen and the pair quickly exchanged places. The lock, ropes, and chain were necessary to give each of them time to get in or out of the scarves and sack. But in the dim light of the tavern, it appeared truly magical.

Even seated off to one side in the gloom, Tess was propositioned numerous times. One fellow, a fat sailor from the docks who was stinking drunk on ale, offered her two gold pieces for her affections.

"I have a husband with whom I am content!" Tess shouted back at him.

The bleary-eyed sailor looked both ways and answered with a grin, "You ain't got no husband."

"An' you don't have two gold pieces. Go away, before I feed you to my bear!"

It seemed he would persist, but several villeins pushed him roughly aside to get a better view of the entertainment. "Move on, you fat piss. You've seen enough. Make room for your betters." If they were spoiling for a fight, the sailor gave them no satisfaction. He merely shrugged off their insults, and weaved away into the crowd.

The villeins quaffed their ale and watched the youthful jugglers. Though Will's view was hampered by the bear's glass eyes, it was apparent from the villeins' blocky forms that they were wearing mail beneath their fine silk tunics. All three were middle-aged and had the look of hardened fighters, most likely armed retainers of a local lord. Will could not make out which noble's badge they wore.

Presently, two younger men joined them. They were nobles, judging from their rich attire and the size of their heavy silver spurs. Both carried a knight's sword at their side and clearly wore the Beauchamp coat of arms. Will's tenure at court had served him well, for he knew the Beauchamps to be kinsmen of the earl of Warwick, the most powerful lord in all of England.

It was Warwick who had placed Edward on the throne. Henry's queen, Margaret, hated and feared him. Before the battle of Towton, she had offered a thousand gold crowns to the man who brought her Warwick's head. But Warwick, not Margaret, had been victorious; and now, Will thought, the glove was on the other hand.

Will watched the young nobles freely. It was the single advantage to being a beast. One could stare holes through people without arousing their suspicions, much less their hostilities. Will tilted his head slightly in order to view Tess. If she had seen the men, she took no interest in them. Her eyes were on the jugglers and the brightly colored balls rising swiftly through the smoky air.

A sudden movement by one of the nobles drew Will's attention back to them. The taller of the two had halted a tavern girl and pressed a coin into her hand. A short time later, she returned, threading her way through the crowd, with Botte close behind her. Will could not hear their voices above the babble of conversation, laughter, and shuffling feet, but to judge from their actions they seemed to be haggling over money.

Chapter Ten

John Croaker paused before a window of the bishop's guest quarters. Beyond the lancet opening, great misty clouds of rain swept across the city of York. The persistent rain had made him edgy. He clasped his hands behind his back, his thoughts running with the low, ragged clouds. Time, too, was running past, racing like the rain that fell in sheets across the tiles and spouted from the gaping mouths of gargoyles on the tower.

For all his efforts, he had little to show. In the weeks since the battle, John Croaker had ridden out half-a-dozen times prepared to capture the fugitive king only to find that Henry's Lancastrian supporters had whisked him away to yet another hiding place.

His search for Henry's messenger had been equally frustrating. Day in, day out, his men at arms had scoured the countryside. They had zealously dragged an assortment of lame peasants, wandering yeomen, carters, and drovers before him. Some possessed a white horse, some not;

none was the young man for whom he searched.

The horseboy was key; John Croaker felt sure of it. He often sent for the boy and had him relate the events following the battle. One phrase provided Croaker with a glimmer of hope, and he had the boy repeat the words uncountable times. "I heard the old king say *London* and *Christ-tide*."

Had it merely been a prayer muttered by the pious Henry, or had it some deeper meaning? John Croaker well knew the barons were to convene in London at Christ-tide; it seemed a certainty that the message was in some way connected. But when and where and for whom was it intended? Or was the message meant to shame Edward, to be read before the assembly? The barons would decide if Edward's crown were secure. Without their support, he could not rule England. Or was the message meant perhaps for but one among the barons? Or for Edward's rapacious younger brother, the duke of Clarence? A plot to regain the throne? No, Croaker decided, Henry had not the subtlety for such a game. More likely he would appeal to Edward — make a plea for peace, for amnesty that Henry might be left to his prayers and books. Such a thing Edward would never permit, for so long as Henry lived, Edward's crown was in contention.

Only one thing was certain — the messenger must be found and stopped. Why was there no trace of him? Where had he gone? Had he shaved his beard? Abandoned the white horse? And what of the girl? Had he abandoned her as well? His injured leg would not be so easily altered. Though in time even that would heal and his lameness become but an imperceptible limp. Still, even if all of it was true, somewhere there must be a tavern owner, an alewife, a cotter, or a shepherd who had seen a young stranger riding south.

A sharp rapping sound swiveled John Croaker's attention to the chamber door. "Enter," he muttered thickly, still lost — deep in his own thoughts.

Damon Swift strode into the room. He was a large youth, in his mid-twenties with a tendency toward fleshiness. He was fond of food, and the full face beneath the square-cut, lank brown hair would have lent him the appearance of a foolish child were it not for his eyes, which were small, piercing, and as yellow as those of a bird of prey. He was followed by an anemic-looking monk who carried an unwieldy bundle, wrapped in coarse woven sacking.

"Milord Sheriff, Brother Raymond has been sent by the abbot at Bolton," Swift said, stepping to one side and turning to the monk.

The brother bowed his tonsured head. "Abbot Whitby sends his greetings and God's blessings to you, sire. It was the abbot's wish that I should deliver this sword and scabbard into your hands."

John Croaker took the bundle from the monk's extended arms and placed it on a table before the window. He quickly unwrapped it.

Damon Swift moved closer. Upon seeing the finely wrought hilt, he remarked, "It is a knight's sword."

"Yes," Croaker agreed, separating the sword from the scabbard, noting the rust upon the blade and the armorer's mark. If he were not mistaken, it was the mark of a London artisan. "Brother, who found this sword?" he questioned. "Where, and when exactly was it discovered?"

"Wednesday last, milord," the monk replied. "A woodcutter employed by the abbot discovered it on the edge of a small clearing as he was gathering dead wood for use in the abbey's kitchens. I myself returned with him to the very spot. By the cotter's road the clearing is scarcely three leagues from the abbey."

"The sword was lying in plain sight?" the sheriff asked, incredulous.

"No, milord. It was lying deep in a briar thicket on the fringe of the clearing. The woodcutter would not have noticed it but for the sun glinting from the metal."

"He found nothing else?"

"Our woodcutter is a simple man, milord. I, however, did notice that a horse had been kept in the clearing at some time in the past. There were droppings, not recent, to be seen."

"Nothing else?"

"No, sire, but there was a campsite a short distance away near the road. Perhaps by calling it a road I mislead you. It is little more than a right of way, and used mostly by country folk, drovers, peddlers, and the like. Consequently, there are many campsites along its course. This particular campsite was the nearest to the clearing, and I found remnants of campfires, also a number of partially burned rags amid the ashes." He paused to rummage through his robes, withdrew a folded cloth, and offered it to the sheriff. "I found these as well. They were scattered on the ground."

John Croaker held the cloth in his open palm and cautiously turned back a corner. "Beads?"

Swift, standing beside his lord, had little difficulty glancing over his shoulder. "Every peddler sells this sort of thing," he remarked.

Brother Raymond quickly corrected him. "The beads are made of glass," he pointed out. "Notice the rose color, milord. They are French and the sort used in rosaries. You will find none like them in England."

"That is interesting, Brother," the sheriff intoned, thinking he would soon have the opportunity to test the brother's theory.

The pale brother's adamant expression faded, and he seemed suddenly ill at ease. "In any case, milord Sheriff," he stammered, "I hope I have been of some assistance."

"Yes, of course, Brother. I am grateful to you and to Abbot Whitby as well. Will you be staying here as the bishop's guest?"

"Alas, only until tomorrow."

"I see. Then I shall have one of my clerks call upon you later in the day with a gift for the abbey's altar, some token of my appreciation."

"God bless and keep you, milord."

After he had seen the brother from the chamber, Swift returned. "Do you believe him?" he asked.

"We'll soon know. I have an appointment to keep." Croaker gathered up his gloves and cloak. "Have a servant bring two horses to the chapter-house door." He glanced at the window. "I do believe the rain has ended."

In a shop just off the Lendal road, John Croaker pinged the glass with his fingernail. It rang like a bell. The shade of blue was most remarkable, reminding him of the sky on a fair February day. "This color is more to my liking," he said. The price, however, was not. Twelve pence a foot for the design, added to the cost of the additional glass and the framing of the window, amounted to considerably more than he had intended to spend. "Something not quite so large," he suggested, adding, "It will be for my private chapel." Sheriff John Croaker went on to describe a lovely structure, one that had formerly belonged to the Catesby family. As they were Lancastrians, their estates had been seized by the Crown. Such estates were awarded by those in power to favorites.

John Croaker had longed his whole life for such a fief and for the title which accompanied it, that of earl. And he would have it — no matter that the cost be treachery and murder; he was adept at both.

The glazier listened attentively to his description, advising, "Perhaps a rounded window would be more suitable, milord. I recently completed one for Lord Beauchamp to be set above the altar in his family chapel."

John Croaker smiled inwardly. The thought bolstered his ego, fed it as a draft feeds a flame. He, John Croaker, would have a window as fine as Lord Beauchamp's. "Yes?" he replied, inquiring, "What was the subject?"

"The Virgin crowned as Queen of Heaven," the glazier eagerly replied. "I have my original *vidimus* here — if you would care to view it, milord?"

"Yes," the sheriff nodded. "I would very much like to see it."

The glazier returned with the sketches, carrying them as one might a precious object. Every glazier drew his own sketches or *vidimuses,* literally, 'We have seen,' and when he died, these valuable drawings, patterns for making the great colored-glass windows, would be passed down to his heirs along with his property.

All around the shop, men labored over lime-washed boards where the designs had been reproduced and the colors of the stained glass indicated by letters. At the very rear of the shop before the open doors, pieces of clear glass were being rough cut with irons whose red-hot points were pressed into the sheet of glass, allowing it to be cut in any direction. Damon Swift watched, intrigued.

Other workers trimmed the rough glass with flatish, notched tools. Several shaped pieces were being laid out on a design board as Swift strolled past. To his left, a completed design, that of St. John, was being painted. Damon Swift was curious about the foul-smelling tint, and questioned the greyheaded man who was painstakingly applying the color with a fur-tipped brush.

" 'Tis enamel, sire," the man said. He paused at his labors, explaining, "It be no more than a mixture of powdered glass and treated metals."

"Nothing more?" Swift inquired. "What causes it to be liquid?"

"Ah," the old man sighed, grasping his meaning. "Most often we use wine. It depends on the color we want. This here is urine. Here, see this shade of green, compared to that?"

Swift nodded, intrigued by the process.

"Now for darker shadings," the old man revealed, "I do it with the brush. Like this. A heavier stroke is all." When he had completed the movement, he looked up with twinkling eyes. " 'Course the firing makes a difference," he advised, inclining his head toward the kilns, clearly visible beyond the open rear doors. Small mountains of ash were piled about the yard, and the bare ground surrounding the kilns was white with lime.

"After the glass is fired," the old man continued, "we lead it in and set it in a framework. There's one what's finished."

Swift walked over to inspect the window. "What is the weight of a window this size?"

The old man grinned, scratching his grizzled head. "That, sire, I could not say. I only know four strapping lads set it there and they was glad to put it down."

Across the lengthy shop, John Croaker was completing his transaction with the master glazier. Still another charge was added for preparing the finished window for transport. It rankled Croaker, but he made no complaint. He was considering the cost, when he recalled the beads. "Before I take my leave," he said, producing the cloth-wrapped packet from his tunic, "I would like your opinion on a certain matter."

"Certainly, milord." The glazier was always willing to please a customer and watched attentively as the sheriff unrolled the cloth.

"I was told these glass beads are not made in England. Can that be true?"

"Glass beads are made in a shop two doors away," the glazier assured him. However, upon examining the beads, he amended his remark. "These are French," he said positively. "The rose color is an invention of the French and they guard the process with their lives. Such color must be fired *into* the glass, not painted on it." He held a rose-hued bead between his thumb and forefinger, displaying it in a ray of sunlight from the window. "It is a lovely shade, is it not?"

John Croaker felt a deep sense of accomplishment as he took his leave.

Swift held the shop door. The sheriff strode past him into the puddled street, where a servant waited with their horses. John Croaker had not gone ten steps when he was accosted by a loud, familiar voice. He turned to see Oliver Neville bearing down on him and prepared himself to be battered about the shoulders. Oliver was a member of the exceedingly wealthy and prolific Neville family, and a cousin to the powerful earl of Warwick.

"Croaker! You little swine!" Oliver exclaimed, thumping the sheriff heartily on the back. "I had no idea you were in York. I imagined you'd be in the North, chasing geese. Haven't found Henry Lancaster and that damned Frenchwoman yet, have you?"

Croaker winced. It annoyed him beyond endurance to be bantered with in such a fashion. It was all he could do to force a sour smile. "Not yet," he said, the irritation in his voice barely under control.

"You make it sound as though you might." Oliver laughed. His laugh was as huge as he was—somewhat of a braying sound.

"I have no doubt of it," Croaker maintained.

"Not Margaret and the prince, you won't. They're safe in France I hear." Oliver Neville had an almost feminine love of jewelry, and his many rings and necklaces glittered in the sunlight.

"Where did you hear that?" Croaker asked.

Oliver Neville threw back his large head and gave a roaring guffaw. "Ah," he gasped, "the consummate mouser. Cousin Simon Beauchamp told me, of course, and you know where he heard it."

Croaker pulled his broad lips into a straight line, thinking he could have heard it from no one but Warwick; but he did not give voice to his conclusion. The sheriff was well-acquainted with Simon Beauchamp, who was another of Oliver's cousins. Even so, the sheriff had had no idea that Simon was privy to Warwick's confidential affairs. Frankly, John Croaker found the fact more than a bit unnerving. He wondered how many others knew of his most recent correspondence with the earl of Warwick.

"I wouldn't have thought it possible for my words to have traveled to London and back again so quickly," Croaker remarked testily.

"No?" Oliver laughed. "Well, Cousin Simon had good reason to ride swiftly. His daughter is being married this weekend. Heloise, the eldest. . . . She's over twenty and ugly as sin. Have you ever seen her?"

"I don't believe so," Croaker replied, "though I

imagine poverty has forced many a young man to marry for more than beauty's sake."

" 'Tis no landless knight. 'Tis Salisbury's son."

"Salisbury's!" Croaker was taken completely unaware. "To what purpose?"

Neville's long face cramped in a grin. "Why, love, of course." He winked. "That and Edward's best interests. He'll need the Beauchamps behind him when the barons convene. Edward will be there; there's talk of it at least. Won't you come back to Sandal with me?" he said, suddenly. "Simon would be dashed pleased to see you. Say you will. I'm staying in a house near the guildhall. I leave in the morning. Do ride back with me."

"Perhaps I shall, yes. Why are you in York?"

"Buying a damned present, of course. Simon's sons are here as well, looking to hire entertainers or some such thing. Till the morning then."

John Croaker prepared himself for another pummeling, but Neville, glittering with gold and jewels, strode off, his servants trailing after him. Mounting his palfrey, the sheriff could hardly believe what he'd just heard. Salisbury's son marrying Simon's daughter, and King Edward present for the ceremony. Croaker had not intended to leave York until his chapel window was completed, but this was too tempting to miss. He would definitely be present, he decided.

On his return to his lodgings at the bishop's residence, the sheriff concluded his affairs in York. To

Damon Swift, he said, "I want the horseboy brought along as well, and twenty men at arms. After the festivities at Sandal we'll head south to Tadcaster. And Damon, call in Lewis and Stanton. See that each has a bead. Instruct them to question the peddlers they meet, the hawkers at village markets and the like. Advise them we will be in Tadcaster by the new moon. Oh yes, tell Stanton he's to transport the window. Caution him that if it arrives in pieces, I shall have his hide as payment."

Chapter Eleven

It was late when the troupe trailed out through the kitchen of the Black Duck Tavern. Botte, loud with ale, raised his voice to a faltering falsetto and recited a lewd ditty as he led the way through the smoky kitchen. Once in the yard outside, he jigged about, herding his troupe together in the manner of a jolly shepherd, and announced, "We're off to Sandal Castle on the morrow! Tra-lee, tra-la. Thirty-five crowns! Tra-lee, tra-la!" Fleur stared at him with a hardened face and told him to shut up, then snatched at him, attempting to catch him. Back and forth she darted, shouting curses in French and gesticulating wildly.

The commotion brought Tom from his cart. Botte grabbed him about the neck and whirled him round, babbling about his great success. Tom wrenched away and, grinning, called for Elgar. The two of them steered the drunken Botte to his cart, where Fleur was waiting, her pudgy hands planted on her broad hips.

Will looked both ways, and, seeing no one about, stood up and climbed into the cart. Tess followed but remained at the rear of the cart, watching nervously up and down the alleyway. From where she stood she could see the back of the tavern, and the yard, which was lit by the sickly wash of light from the kitchen.

Voices and laughter still drifted from the tavern. Tess heard Fleur's shrill voice, and in the darkness of the alleyway, she heard someone retching. She was about to turn away when a figure came from the tavern with a pail in each hand and emptied them noisily into the ditch beside the latrine. Tess watched the figure trudge back to the kitchen before she pulled the rug across the rear of the cart and hooked it on a nail.

"It was only the cook," she reported, surprised to find Will standing beside her, a knife in his hand. He remained a moment, half expecting to see a troop of Yorkist soldiers rush across the yard.

"Do you think he will betray us?" Tess whispered, while watching Will as he moved through the darkened cart. She, too, had seen Botte bargaining with the nobles.

Will put the knife aside and returned to carefully arrange the bearskin so that the air could have a chance to dry the linen lining and thick padding. In the beginning he had worn his leather hosen inside the skin, but the heat was so intense that he'd taken to wearing the ill-fated Milo's linen hosen. They were thinner, cooler, than the leather, yet protected the more tender parts of his anatomy from the constant chaffing caused by contorting his body in order to amble on all fours.

He sat down on the bed. "Perhaps," he answered, stretching out with an arm under his head, and adding, "when he no longer needs a bear and a pretty face to draw the men."

The thought terrified Tess. She could think of nothing else as she fumbled in the blackness, undressing from beneath the enormous shift. "What shall we do?" She unloosed the plaits from her hair. It fell over her shoulders, crimped and ashen in the darkness.

"Nothing," he replied in a quiet voice. "If he had betrayed us, the Yorkist soldiers would have come by now."

Tess could not help thinking there was a more desperate reason the Yorkists searched for Will, one beyond his Lancaster oath. It was not fair that he should keep the truth from her, and she was determined to learn his secret. She crawled beside him, searching for the end of the cover, when the rug at the end of the cart was flung wide and Cedric bounded into the cart.

He stood there, stock still—then in a flustered voice, said, "Tom run me out. He said there wasn't no place for me with them."

Will lay back down, sliding the knife between the bed of rags and the side of the cart. "You scared me near to death," he muttered in a low voice.

"I didn't mean to," Cedric slurred the words, and quickly began stripping off his costume. He was slight and thin, white as a trout's belly in the darkness of the cart. "Tom says we'll be able to use the stilts at the castle. I never been in a castle. Tom says they're full of gold and treasures, and—" He went on and on. Finally Will told him to be quiet and go to sleep.

Before dawn, the jongleurs made their way through the narrow streets to the appointed rendezvous, the pageant grounds, where the wagons of the nobles and the musicians awaited their escort. Teams of horses were being harnessed, and here and there small groups of carters stood about talking. The sound of lutes floated on the misty air, and a girl with long black hair sang a mournful lai.

An escort of a dozen armed retainers of the earl led the wagons through the turreted Micklegate. Those in the wagons caught only a glimpse of the nobles, who rode swiftly ahead on horseback, surrounded by their company of guards. The roads were often perilous. Years of civil strife and roaming bands of unemployed soldiers had bred a dangerous situation for travelers. A degree of lawlessness existed, particularly in the more remote areas, where armed bands roamed freely.

On the third day, near to sext, the towers of Sandal Castle were sighted above the dark emerald-green of the treetops. In the castle's bailey, garlands of flowers were draped about the courtyard. Masses of servants scurried in all directions, making welcome the arriving lords and their parties. The vibrant hues of their clothing and their servants' matching livery gave the jostling crowd the appearance of a living tapestry.

Fleur and Tess followed a group of servants from the kitchens who gathered by the walls to watch the noble lords and ladies. It was quite an education for Tess. She was dazzled by the veiled hennin headdresses, jewels, and low décolletages of the younger ladies. And when she commented on some of the ladies' total lack of eyebrows, she was told by a serving girl, "Oh, 'tis the height of fashion. They pluck them out, an' some even pluck the hair on their heads, halfway back to here"—she gestured—"to make their foreheads all the higher!"

Tess thought it a stupid thing to do, and wondered how they must look without their tall headdresses, although, she did not voice her opinion.

The jongleurs and musicians, too, had been relegated to the rear garths. Some were offered space in the armory, but Botte had viewed the accommodations there, returned with tales of overcrowding and vermin. He had made the acquaintance of the musicians and found them a friendly lot. While they unpacked their lutes, harps, flutes, and drums, Botte came to terms with the leader of the group, and they discussed the sequence of the evening's entertainment, the tunes and routines.

Will, who for the most part stayed out of sight, eased his boredom with the paper, ink, and pens he had found among the loot from York, in a wooden chest stolen from a guildmaster's house. As in his days at court, he amused himself by drawing pictures of his surroundings. Sandal Castle provided a new and fascinating challenge.

When Tess returned, she found him sitting cross-legged in the cart making dark lines upon the paper. Gothic arches, crenellated towers, and gates surmounted by guardian figures all flowed from his pen with perfect symmetry. Tess forgot for a moment her chatter and watched him with a sense of wonder.

Completing a line, he looked at her and smiled. "Where have you been?" he asked.

"To see the nobles. How did you learn to make the lines?" She was amazed. After a moment she peeped from the dowlas cover to see his view. "How do you do it? How do you make it look just the way it is?"

"Here." He dipped the pen into the ink pot and offered it to her.

"No, I would only spoil it."

"No, here." He made a place for her inside his

arm. "Hold the pen like this." He placed it in her hand. "Now draw a window for me, a little one."

"Where shall I put it? Here?"

"Yes, just there."

She did so, laughing. "It's a bit crooked, isn't it?"

"Just a bit. Now make another here."

Tess giggled. "I do not think they would have windows placed as near as that."

"Yes. See for yourself."

She leaned forward and peered out. It was so: The windows were set one beside the other.

"It is the garderobe," he advised.

"How do you know?" She laughed.

"See how the stones corbel outward? And see the streaks down the wall? That is where the waste has blackened the stone, and there," he directed, "is the ditch."

Tess's gaze followed the sloping banks. "But it runs into the stream below the kitchen!"

"Yes," he smiled. "Remember that, when you go for water. Did you see the fine and gracious nobles?"

"Yes, the ladies have no eyebrows, and their breasts are hanging out."

"In that case, I'm sorry to have missed it." He laid out another scrap of paper. "Here, draw a picture for me."

"I can't." She blushed. "There were too many of them."

"Draw one, one lady, for me."

"No." She smiled, "I do not know how."

"There is no mystery to it. Think of one lady you saw. Do you remember her? Now, what shape was her face?"

Tess looked up, her eyes dancing with amusement. "Round."

"Draw it then."

Tess did her best. She looked at it, and laughed, declaring, "She looked less a pig, I think."

"Ah," he chuckled. "But you can make it right again by placing a hat and veil on her." He lent a hand.

"It's only worse, and besides, she has no body."

"Make another larger circle," he instructed, happy with her in his arms, her golden braids brushing his cheek.

"Oh, now she looks like a keg of ale!"

They were laughing like two children when Cedric's head appeared at the foot of the cart. "It's me," he announced with a lopsided grin, and clattered inside. "I need the stilts," he said excitedly and began to root beneath the jumble of the cart. "We're going to do the giants tonight. Botte says the hall is tall enough!"

Will placed the cork stopper on the inkpot and helped him extricate the stilts from the tangle of props and costumes. At the last moment, Tess leapt up to save her necklaces and comb. Cedric staggered backwards under the burden of heavy props. "There's no soldiers about," he said to Will. "Can you catch for me?"

"Why can't Tom or Botte?" Tess scowled, her arms laden with belongings.

Cedric looked at her as if she were stupid. "Tom's only got one arm, an' there's three of us on stilts!"

"I'll catch for you," Will said, reaching for the bag cap he often wore. He glanced at Tess reassuringly. "No one will notice me. They're far too busy."

She smiled at the sight of him in the silly hat, though she could not as easily dismiss the fear she felt. She had seen soldiers loitering about the armory. However, they were dressed in livery of green and gold, unlike the soldiers of the sheriff, who wore no livery. Clad in the leather and mail of armed retainers, their only distinction was the white shield upon their leather *jaques* and the badge of York with its belled falcon.

Tess laid her belongings aside and folded the drawings. She placed the pens, ink, and paper in the little wooden chest. For a time she watched Elgar, Noam, and Cedric stomp about on their stilts. Luigi tumbled, dashing through their legs. Occasionally a boy fell, for the ground was uneven and the tall grass of the meadows behind the castle had not been scythed.

When they fell, it seemed they would surely kill themselves; but they would twist and turn as they

213

toppled, so as to land on their hands and knees. Then they would raise themselves to a kneeling position so that Will and Botte could lift them by their knees and upper stilts. It was a simple matter to be raised if they supported themselves by holding onto the men's shoulders. In only an instant, they would be upright again.

Tess squinted into the sun, following their progress as they stomped across the meadow, ten feet tall, improbable giants, with the narrow stilts lashed to their legs. Crickets leapt before them in the grass, and their voices blended with the noisy gabble of the servants in the garth.

Excitement was running high as evening fell. The troupe gathered in the garth amid their carts to eat a supper of cheese, bread, and ale. The cook in charge of the kitchen was a truculent sort, puffed up with rich foods and his own importance.

"No meat and pastries," he told the jongleurs and musicians. "These dishes are for the feast, not for the likes of free-and-easies and servants!" But when he'd turned away, a little brown-haired serving girl with a gap-toothed smile pulled Cedric aside and said, "They'll be plenty o' leavings. I'll save you some if you come back tonight."

The meal was eaten off the rear gate of Tom's cart with everyone standing round or sitting on the ground. Fleur, with much gesturing and shrugging of her shoulders, condemned the rich. "You see

214

why they are so rich. They give nothing away! The cheese is rank, the ale is weak as water!" she harped. *"Mon dieu!* We ate better at the Black Duck!"

Chapter Twelve

John Croaker thoroughly enjoyed such affairs. The very atmosphere of so much wealth and opulence excited him, and he longed for the day when he, too, would be counted among the nobles of the realm.

A servant bearing a large silver tray offered him refreshments. He chose a cup of wine, and moved off to mingle with the crowd. He was particularly interested in the two long tables laden with gifts for the bride and groom. He lingered over each item, calculating its worth. There were illuminated books whose finely worked covers were gilded and set with jewels, gold and silver statues of saints, silver plates, gold vessels and spoons, and jeweled crosses. One entire table was devoted to tapestries and colorful oriental rugs. Many of the tapestries were of floral design, but a few were of a religious nature.

He was quite impressed by one large work, whose subject was the lamentation of the Virgin with St. John. The colors were strikingly vibrant, and it occurred to the sheriff that he must have one exactly like it for his hall. He was memorizing the design, as much as he was able, when he noticed his lieutenant, Damon Swift, step from the crowd.

"Edward is here," Swift said in a hushed aside.

Sensing a movement in the throng of people, John Croaker raised his eyes. He smiled, and both he and Swift bowed their heads slightly as their hostess, Alyse Beauchamp, passed regally by on her son's arm. She was a rather tall, gaunt-looking woman who glittered with jewels and was attired in a gown of darkest green velvet, topped by an over gown and long train of gold cloth on which her family coat of arms had been embroidered. Her headdress was of starched gold cloth and fashioned in the shape of a huge rounded heart, which only served to accentuate the hard angles of her face.

"You have seen King Edward?" Croaker calmly asked, sipping from the cup of wine he held.

"Yes. The lords Herbert and Hastings are with him, only they and a few knights and servants. I hear he rode out from Coinsborough. The Woodville woman is with him," he said. He paused to gauge the sheriff's reaction, before suggesting, "Perhaps there is some substance to the rumors?" Damon Swift had first reported accounts of a secret marriage — between Edward and the young widow — to the sheriff in early June. Croaker had dismissed them as foolish gossip. But Damon Swift was not so apt to discount their accuracy. "It would be to Edward's advantage to keep the wedding a close-guarded secret."

Croaker scoffed at the suggestion. "Whatever failings Edward may have, stupidity is not among them. He may well be a whoremonger, but he would not endanger his crown by marrying such a lowborn woman. Her father is not even an earl. No, he will marry Bona of Savoy this autumn just as Warwick has arranged."

A hush descended over the throng of guests, and heads turned. A herald stepped forward and announced the king. A cheer rose up and the guests heartily greeted their sovereign. By his side, arrayed in a magnificent gown of scarlet and gold, was Elizabeth Woodville.

Edward, making a grand gesture, placed Elizabeth Woodville's hand on his and led the assembled guests, surely two hundred or more, to the garlanded tables where he gave his hearty congratulations to the bridal couple.

After the obligatory speeches and toasts, a grand parade of liveried servants appeared, carrying trays laden with a profusion of exquisitely prepared dishes. The great hall was redolent with the aroma of stuffed suckling pigs, roasted ducks and capons, swans and bitterns whose feathers had been reassembled after baking so the birds looked as if they might suddenly take flight from the serving trays. There were also meat and fish aspics, rissoles of beef marrow, black puddings, intricately sculpted pastries of venison, and vegetable dishes adorned with flowers.

Musicians played tirelessly throughout the meal. Later, minstrels dedicated romantic lais to the bride and groom as servants plied the guests with trays of honeyed fruit, peeled nuts, comfits, and sugared cakes.

Oliver Neville leaned forward with his elbows on the table. "What do you think of all this, Croaker?" He was well aware of Croaker's ambitions. Frankly, they amused him.

The sheriff looked up, noticing Neville had slopped gravy down the front of his splendid azure-and-purple silk tunic. "The food is excellent," he said. He did not mention the gravy. "It seems Simon has outdone himself once again."

"Yes," Oliver chuckled. "He shall have to raise his peasants' taxes twice to pay for it. Did you see the Woodville woman? Very comely, isn't she?"

Croaker chose a comfit from a tray. When the servant had stepped away, he replied, "Edward's path is strewn with comely women." Too late he discovered the sugary bit of fondant was flavored with licorice. He hated licorice but, not knowing what else to do, he swallowed it.

Oliver laughed. "If you think that tastes bad, wait till you hear what Norfolk's been up to." Oliver delighted in baiting Croaker. It was plain to see from his dumbfounded expression that he hadn't heard the news.

John Croaker took a swallow of spiced wine to rid his mouth of the taste of licorice, cleared his throat, and asked, "What are you talking about?"

"I hear Norfolk's men came very near to capturing Henry. He's ridden north to join the search. That's why he's not here. Hadn't you noticed?"

The fact that he hadn't noticed Norfolk's absence annoyed John Croaker even more than Oliver Neville's patronizing tone of voice. "When did you hear that?" Croaker pressed.

"A few hours ago, Edward's cohorts were discussing it. I heard them. They made no secret of it. I imagine everyone overheard them." He laughed. "Except for you, of course!"

Damon Swift sat silently beside the sheriff, listening, wondering. Did King Edward no longer trust his former allies? Did he fear that they would place Henry on the throne once more and rule England in his name? Clearly nothing less than Henry's death could assure Edward's crown.

Across the immense hall, Botte Bleu's troupe had gathered in a passageway, nervously awaiting their cue. Through the wide archway, the jongleurs could see the festively bedecked tables and noble guests. A multitude of candles burned, and servants holding torches lined the walls like human candlesticks.

The sound of drums was their introduction, and

the troupe made a grand entrance. Act by act, they entertained the nobles, drawing much applause and a generous quantity of coins.

Elizabeth Woodville was particularly taken with the brave young girl who danced with the bear and sent a page to deliver a gold piece to her. Upon receiving it, Tess smiled radiantly at the noble lady in the scarlet gown and made a low curtsy.

As Tess raised her head, her eyes fell upon a squat, ugly man seated near the king. His gaze was set, not on her, but on the lady in scarlet. With a tremor of horror, Tess realized it was the same evil, pock-scarred face that had branded itself upon her memory at the abbey.

For a long moment she gazed in terror. Why was he here? Had he somehow learned of their whereabouts? Had they been betrayed? Numb with fear, she led the bear away, following the troupe from the hall. She dared not ask Will if he had seen the sheriff. Not there, in the crowded passageway with servants pressing past. There were many ears to hear.

Following the troupe's performance, a harpist flanked by flautists and lute players filed into the hall. Many of the younger nobles deserted the tables to form a dance line. Amid the torchlight, the colorfully dressed guests glided across the hall, and the tall starched headdresses of the noble ladies stirred like sails.

In the confusion, Tess and Growl became separated from the jongleurs and the musicians who had accompanied their performance, and wandered through the maze of dim, torch-lit passageways. They met fewer and fewer people, until at last they were alone.

Will halted, grumbled, and pulled himself erect. His spine felt broken. "We should have turned right at the last passageway," he told Tess.

She was about to disagree with his reasoning, when she heard voices and approaching footsteps. "Someone's coming!" she advised in a rapid whisper.

Will went down on all fours. A moment later, two grandly attired young couples appeared in the shadowy passageway. The young men poked the bear and laughed. One barked like a dog. The young women giggled.

Without warning, Will gave a ferocious growl, whirled about and lunged, slicing the air before them with a huge, deadly paw. The young women screamed, and all four took off at a run.

As they disappeared around the corner, Tess began to laugh. "Did you see their faces?" Will did not answer her. But she could hear his hushed laughter coming from inside the hide, and the sound of it tickled her all the more.

After a bit of backtracking, they found their way from the castle, emerging into a small unfamiliar courtyard where crickets chorused. They followed a flagstone path through an archway overgrown with rambling roses. Beyond the walls, they saw the garth, the carts, and the armory. No guards were about.

The moon was full and there were stars above, but in the distance lightning flickered and the still warm air seemed charged with a latent fury. Before them, the rolling lawn stretched out broad and silvery to meet the darkness beneath the spreading trees.

Meanwhile, away from the grandeur and the dancing nobles, a poorer version of the splendid celebration in the hall was underway in the castle's armory. There, those of the lower classes gathered—the soldiers of the lords, and the servants, and the hired entertainers. Wine and ale flowed freely, and servants from the household scurried back and forth between the castle's kitchen and the armory, delivering the picked-over remains of the nobles' feast.

The musicians who had accompanied the jongleurs' performance began to play for the rough crowd in the armory. Bawdy lyrics rang out above the oily smoke. Loud laughter; the lively notes of lute, pipe, and drum; and the constant shouts of the dice players resounded from the armory's dismal stones.

Beneath a brace of slotted windows, a girl with long black hair sang a soprano duet with a pretty boy in a red-silk jupe. The boy's jupe hung open to his waist, and his smooth-skinned chest was as hairless as the girl's.

Several butts of ale fueled the rowdy festivities, and there was not a sober soul in sight. For a time, the traitorous horseboy sipped his ale and watched his guards gamble at dice. It was only when he wandered off and fell into conversation with several serving boys that he began to drink in earnest. During the course of the boys' lewd and randy discourse, they downed innumerable cups of ale and wine and even took a turn at juggling when two young jongleurs joined their group.

Just as Will and Tess found their way from the castle's hall, the bleary-eyed horseboy staggered out onto the armory's ramparts to clear his spinning head.

The area around the armory was as busy as a village street. Men urinated in the dark. Soldiers and servants roamed in and out the armory doors. Shouts and laughter echoed in the blackness and from somewhere out of sight, the horseboy heard a man and woman arguing.

At the wall, the horseboy took a deep drought of air. It seemed to set his head to spinning. The warm, oppressive night collided with his rolling stomach. He gagged and, staggering forward, leaned out from the embrasure and brought up a sour-smelling stream of ale and wine.

The horseboy gripped the wall with both hands, his legs as weak as a newborn foal's. Then he saw two shadowy forms emerge from a blackened courtyard near the hall. Once the figures ventured beyond the low stone courtyard wall and moved across the lawn toward him, he saw it was the performing bear and the girl who camped with the jongleurs.

He'd seen the girl that afternoon in the garth and had been unable to take his eyes from her. She looked no older than himself, and he thought her very comely. She was slender, fair, and blue-eyed, and when she gracefully walked, she seemed to be dancing. He watched closely as she and the lumbering bear melded with the shadows beneath the trees. He did not think it strange to see her there, for logically, bears, like other creatures, must relieve themselves. And ones so large, in quantity, he considered with a chuckle.

Ah, but what a comely girl, the horseboy thought. He would have staggered back to the armory had he not hoped to catch another glimpse of her. He scowled into the darkness. It was then he decided to follow after her, and in a swaying stride made his way down the armory's worn stone steps.

Will ambled on all fours. Tess trotted along, hurrying to keep abreast. Under the trees, she tugged at the lead to halt him. "It is safe here," she said, glancing over her shoulder at the bleak outline of the castle. Voices carried from the direction of the garth and the armory, she reasoned they could not be seen beneath the canopy of leaves.

But Will pulled her forward, towing her along through the copse. The uneven ground fell away quickly, and Will—going on all fours—rapidly gained momentum. Tess ran after him.

The air of the little wood was close and moist, heavy with the breath of summer. Through the trees, she saw the stream, silver in the moonlight, and heard the deep harmony of the frogs.

Will plunged down the rise, faster and faster until it seemed he would tumble forward and roll into the stream. Directly before him, the moon floated on the black water. He could not stop. At the last moment, he threw out a paw and awkwardly snagged a tree trunk to halt himself. The startled frogs splashed away. Will sank to the ground, crouching on his haunches, and fixed his gaze on Tess.

At times the bear's leering face frightened her. Just then, its glassy eyes sparkled in the moonlight, raising a rash of gooseflesh on her sweaty skin.

Nearby, the horseboy staggered along through the wood, stumbling as he descended the hillock. Midway, he halted and looked about. But he saw only empty blackness, the ghostly moonlight glancing from the leaves, and the queer shifting shadows of the trees. Where had she and the bear gone? The horseboy's head reeled from drink and exertion. He swayed forward, grasping at trees for support. His searching gaze swept to the stream, and there, where the trees thinned at the water's edge, he saw the girl and the bear. He watched as the bear lumbered up on its haunches and stood full force, its thick fur gleaming in the silvered light.

Unaware of the watcher in the wood, Tess turned back to the hulking bear. "I did not think to ask if you were thirsty," she confessed, breathless and apologetic. She recalled the stifling heat of the hall, and guiltily admitted that she had not given a thought to Will, trapped inside the skin.

She quickly unloosed the hooks so he might free his head and afterwards his arms and shoulders. "I was afraid to offer you a sip from my cup in the hall, afraid someone would see." It was the truth, though she still felt heartless to have neglected him. The sight of the sheriff seated at the banquet table had driven every other thought from her mind.

She said suddenly, "John Croaker was at the banquet table. I saw him. He was seated by the king."

Will did not answer, but continued to free his upper body from the hide, emerging like a moth from its cocoon. He took a deep breath of air and coughed. His throat was as dry as dust.

Above them on the hillock, the horseboy, who had paused to catch his breath, heard the murmur

227

of voices. The girl's, and a deeper voice. Was it the bear's? Voices, surely, though he could not make out the words. He craned his neck to see better. As he watched, the girl appeared to make a sign before the beast and, unbelievably, the bear's fierce head became that of a man. The horseboy stared — dumbfounded — as, through the gently tossing leaves, he witnessed the bear alter, grow arms and glistening shoulders, become half-man, half-bear.

The horseboy shook his head in denial. "I am tetched," he blubbered, burying his face in his hands and sinking slowly to the ground. He lay there cringing among the tree roots, recalling the many cups of ale and wine he had consumed. The more he thought of it, the worse his head spun. He shut tight his eyes to keep from being sick and soundlessly recited the only prayer he knew. Without any sense of passing time, he mouthed the words over and over again.

Below, by the stream, Tess stepped to the water's edge, and, crouching down, cupped her hands and carried water back to Will. Most of it ran through her fingers, but the precious little that touched his tongue revived him. "I did not see the sheriff," he said finally. His view from the bear's glass eyes was distorted, myopic at best. "Are you certain?" he asked, rising to his feet, half-in, half-out of the accursed hide. He swore an oath. "I would not wish this damnable hide on an enemy," he muttered, fumbling in the darkness with the wire hooks and positioning himself before a tree.

Tess squatted behind a thorny bush. The trailing ribbons of her flower circlet dangled before her eyes as she carefully raised her skirt. "I am not mistaken. I will never forget his face. He was the one we saw on the road to Bolton, the one the horseboy spoke to at the abbot's door." No answer came back. Did he not believe her? "I saw him!" she insisted, rising and shaking the folds from her skirt.

"I don't doubt you." Will adjusted the linen hosen. "The king was there, was he not?" He had seen the king, or thought he had, but not the sheriff.

"Yes," Tess responded, coming from behind the bush. "It was his lady who sent the page to me with a gold coin. Why was John Croaker there? Do you think Botte has betrayed us?"

"If he had, we would be dead by now or captured." He came and stood before her, taking her small shoulders in his hands and smiling at her. "Perhaps it means nothing. Only that he is Edward's justiciar, and he has come to lick his master's hand."

A gust of breeze rippled the surface of the stream and faraway lightning flickered. A cool draft touched Tess's face and sent a chill through her. "I am so afraid," she sobbed, and sagged against Will's chest.

"I know," he soothed, folding her inside his arms. "It is all because of me. I am to blame. I should not have drawn you into this."

"Tell me why they hunt you. Tell me what you have done."

He hesitated, a moment only—what was the use of lying? "No more than to defend my king and country."

"But Edward is king now. Is that why he searches for old King Henry?"

"To murder him, yes—and, failing that, all of England if he must . . . to keep the crown he stole."

"But what have you to do with all of that? Do they believe you know his hiding place? Or is it because of the missive in your leather *jaque?*" Her eyes grew wide in confession, and she added hastily, "I did not open it. I would not have found it. But when Botte took the coins, I searched the *jaque* hoping he had overlooked some."

"I have no knowledge of the king's whereabouts. The letter is naught but a plea for peace, for reason. King Henry asks nothing for himself. Only that the barons force Edward to put an end to the slaughter." It was the truth or nearly so. The rest he could not tell her.

"But that is good and just."

"Yes, all that Edward is not—though perhaps my view is tainted by my father's and my brothers' blood."

"I am sorry for your loss," she said with sympathy in her voice and eyes. From somewhere across the shimmering waters a night bird called, and Tess, because she felt that she must know, naively asked, "Once you have delivered the missive, where will you go? Have you a lady who waits for you?"

Her question was unexpected and brought a smile to Will's lips. "I have no lady," he said, circling her waist with his arms and dropping his head close to hers. "None but you, Greensleeves. Shall I return and marry you?"

Tess felt the color rush to her cheeks. "You would not lie to me?"

Only a breath separated their lips. "No," he murmured, "that, I could never do." Of all the promises Will had ever made, none was truer. She was all he wanted. Perhaps it was the heat, the tantalizing female scent of her, or no more than the sound of the restless leaves that first spurred his blood to racing, singing with desire. He felt an overpowering need to hold her near, to love her, to wear her like a glove. He wanted to fill her full of him, to grasp eternity if only for an instant and lose himself in it.

A breeze rustled the leaves overhead and in the distance, lightning continued to spark the darkness. Tess sighed, and touched her lips to his. From the very first, she, with her childlike sensuality, had affected him as no other ever had. Will claimed her mouth in a deep lingering kiss, a confirmation of all he felt—the hunger, the passion, and the terrible disorder of being male and lost in love.

Tess clung to him, warm and willing, running her hands over his broad shoulders and his sides. She had wanted him long before that moment. Long before his hands caressed her breasts, his lips wetted them with kisses, and the feel of him pressed hard against her raised a pulsing heat between her thighs. So intense was her need for him that she was hardly conscious of shedding her clothing, of his hands and hers, or of the rumpled silk lying at her feet.

Will marveled over her soft, silken body. "You are beautiful," he whispered as his hands petted and stroked her slender, lissome curves. His eyes devoured her delicate fairness. Even the tight curls of her mons shone pale and silvery in the moonlight. He had never known a woman so fair.

Will was trembling like a stud horse, and the realization that Tess wanted him just as desperately intensified his ardor. He knew that to have her there was dangerous, foolish, but the fierce animal urgings of his glans blinded him to rational thought.

His suckling lips drew out her hardened nipples. Tess sighed, making little mewing sounds as her hands, faltering with innocence, moved over him. With a single deft maneuver, Will undid the ties of his clammy linen hosen. The fact that his lower body was still imprisoned in the bear's skin did not at first occur to him.

Tess saw his cock curve sweetly up, tumescent, blooming from its foreskin, and thought that if love were poison she would surely die . . . and did not care—she longed for a death so sweet.

Only then did Will realize his legs were trapped. He could not free himself, not easily. He was throbbing with desire. He had no time. His lips brushed her, and he breathed into her mouth. "You will have to come to me."

"Yes," she agreed, her voice a dulcet murmur. She would have willingly walked through fire to reach him, to satisfy the greedy ache inside her.

Will sat flat out with his imprisoned legs stretched before him. There was no other way. He drew Tess to him, his hands positioned on her slender waist. She steadied herself with her hands on his shoulders and straddled his seated form, that half of him imprisoned in the fierce and brutish bearskin.

Instinctively, she reached to grasp his hardened shaft and guided it to fill the moist, aching emptiness between her thighs. The intrusive first touch sent cramps of pleasure pulsing through her belly. Tess moaned and twitched, splaying her knees as wide as she was able. She clasped again the swelling muscles of his shoulders and impaled herself on him. A searing, stabbing pain forked through her like a flame.

233

Tess thought that she would tear in half. A wordless cry choked her throat. But she was also wild with excitement. The sudden, tearing pain, mingled with the pulsating, throbbing feel of him inside her, urged her on to flex her legs and thrust her hips, driving him still deeper into her.

She moaned, and Will, fearing she would cry out, locked his mouth on hers. For one ecstatic moment, Tess felt that he might swallow her. Her blood pounded in her ears. He seemed to pierce her every orifice. And when she thought that she would surely die of love, she was seized by a joyous, shuddering convulsion and a burst of cold inside, while a tingling sensation washed over her.

Will had no control. She was like a wild animal, riding him. He could not move, nor could he hold back his surging climax. His seed spurted from him, again and again, and he could only sob softly as he emptied himself in her.

The horseboy, who had shaken off his drunken stupor and risen to his feet only a few moments before, turned and ran. Fear sent him scrambling up the hillock as if the fiends of hell were snapping at his heels.

For a moment in the woods, with his head still buried in his hands, the horseboy had nearly convinced himself that it was all a dream, a nightmare born of wine and ale. But the sound of hushed voices had pricked the hairs on his neck, and he had looked again, almost against his will.

234

He had seen quite plainly the girl's naked body, pale as alabaster in the moonlight, her youthful upturned breasts, and her smooth white buttocks. The horseboy had watched, gripped by a strange mingling of fear and sexual arousal, as she heaved herself upon the beast's upright cock, swaying and writhing in pleasure.

She is a witch! he thought. Images of hell and damnation flashed through his brain as he ran toward the armory. He did not stop until he stood atop the ramparts. He waited, watching, panting with exertion, his mind besieged by a maelstrom of unnamed fears.

The moon sailed above a cloud, and thunder rolled in the distance. Suddenly, the girl appeared from the shadows that verged onto the lawn, with the bear lumbering beside her.

The horseboy gasped aloud. A scuffling movement behind him in the dark caused him to whirl about. A drunken guard lurched into him, careened away, and cursed. The horseboy gave a startled cry, as if he'd been burnt, and fled inside the armory. He was terrified and resolved to say nothing of what he'd seen, lest he be thought addle-brained or, worse, a heretic.

As Tess and Will entered the garth, they noticed that a fight had broken out before the armory. A handful of drunken servants, who had been drinking by the kitchen door, dashed past them, hooting and shouting as they ran to join the cheering crowd of onlookers. The garth was now deserted, except for a couple copulating against the kitchen wall.

In the cart, Tess's soft laughter rippled in the humid blackness. Will, free of the bearskin, could not keep his hands from her. They spoke in whispered voices, both of them perfectly naked in the dark. He loosed her flaxen hair from the braids and played with it, from her back, his breath warm on her neck.

"Why?" Will asked, unhurried, squeezing her waist, drawing her smooth pink rump to rub against his erection. "Why be afraid? No one will come," he promised, touching his lips to her shoulder, and coaxing. "Touch me. Kiss me."

Tess hesitated, tortured by his nearness and her own desire. Her body throbbed in response to his every touch, his every kiss. "It is not because of that," she sighed, though truthfully it was. "I do not even know your name," she accused him. "Will and no more, Will o' the Wisp, will I turn one day and find you've gone?"

His laughter made a hushed sound. "I will not disappear, though you may wish me to one day."

"No," she breathed, allowing him to draw her closer and run his hand between her legs.

He kissed the hollow of her throat and felt her blood purr beneath his lips. "Do you know that I have loved you since my eyes first saw you. Do you know?"

But she could only smile, turn, and offer him her lips. It was a kiss without words, for none were necessary.

Negotiating the jumble of the cart, they rolled upon the bed. Tess moved beneath him, spreading her legs in anticipation. She tried to pull him to her. But he told her, "No, not yet," and kissed and stroked and petted her. He licked her straining breasts; mouthed and teased out her nipples; and, taking each by turn, suckled them. A heat of such intense need built deep within her that she arched her hips to him, pleading.

"No," he breathed, ignoring her, kissing, stroking her until she ached for want of him. She tried to clasp him and launch him into her to put an end to her torment. But her groping hand could not reach him, and the agony continued. And when his lips touched the soft, damp curls of her mons and his tongue invaded it, she gasped and bit her lip.

How queer it looked to see his head between her legs, lapping her like a dog laps water. She wanted to protest, to tell him, no, thinking it was surely sinful. But the raw pleasure of his touch was so intense that she spread her trembling legs still further. When she could no longer endure the rough caress of his unshaven jaw and probing tongue, she begged him to come to her, arched against him, and moaned, "Please."

He took her by the ankles, raised her legs to rest upon his shoulders and, with a hand to guide himself, thrust into her with a groan. His body trembled with each rhythmic stroke. For Tess, each probing impact exploded into escalating bursts of pleasure, then into white-hot nothingness. She cried out and, with a final forceful thrust, Will took his release. It came as violently as his pounding heartbeats, precise, with its own fiercely spurting rhythm.

Cedric hung at the foot of the cart. Shouts came from the direction of the kitchen. He looked about nervously, but still he held back. He had been waiting for them to finish, for the grunts and panting sounds to end. But the trample of approaching footsteps galvanized him to action. He leaped over the cart gate and flew past their nude bodies, diving into his bed of rags and pulling a cover over himself.

Will bolted up, groping for the knife. Tess gave a startled gasp and lunged away from Will so quickly that her bare foot hit his shoulder and nearly knocked him off the bed. Burning with embarrassment, Tess buried herself in the assortment of rags. She could have died of shame.

Seeing that it was only Cedric, Will swore at him and settled back on the bed. His heart was in his throat.

"Don't let 'em find me," Cedric pleaded in a

shrill whisper. "I didn't mean to spoil your fun, but I couldn't wait no longer. Her brother and his friends is after me!"

Will was softly laughing. "Whose brother?"

"A kitchen girl's. He had me. I thought I was good as dead. He said he was gonna cut off my terse. I got away, but him and his friends is hunting for me."

Tess made a groaning sound and buried herself deeper in the covers. Will's large, warm hand closed over her shoulder, gently kneading it. He was still chuckling when he asked, "What did you do to her?"

"I didn't do her no harm," he protested. "I didn't even get it in." The voices were outside the cart, as was the sound of shuttling feet. "Hear that?" Cedric breathed, his whisper rising to a soprano pitch. "That's her brother. Can you see 'em?"

Will leaned over Tess and peered through the rent in the dowlas cover. "They're leaving, headed toward the armory." When he turned back, Cedric was peeping out from under the rags. "Are you hurt?" Will asked.

"My nose is sore, an' I think my teeth are loose."

"You're lucky," Will remarked. He was still laughing to himself when he lay down and pulled Tess into the curve of his body.

She refused to say a word. Even later, when he

239

pushed her hair aside and planted a kiss at the nape of her neck, she was still too ashamed to speak. She lay there like a stone, unmoving, even though her thighs and the bed beneath her were wet from their lovemaking.

The morning sun had not yet reached the garth, but already it was hot. The storm that had passed by without a drop of rain the night before brought no relief from the late summer heat. No sooner had they abandoned the bed, than Tess rolled up the cloth they had lain upon. She did so quickly, not wanting anyone to see the telltale smears of blood-flecked semen. She had suffered enough embarrassment as it was. When she thought of her innocence in such matters, she blushed. She felt angry as well, angry at Bertrade for concealing such things from her.

As she quickly braided her hair and knotted a scarf at the back of her head, she thought of her sister Mary, and of a conversation she had overheard between Bertrade and her sister. It had been after the banns of Mary's marriage had been announced. Bertrade had said to her, "Now that you are going to your marriage bed, there are certain matters . . ." That was when Mary had giggled and confessed to Bertrade that she had discovered all that on her own long before. Even then, Tess had not guessed.

When Tess announced she was going to the stream for water, Will turned from where he was carefully stretching the bearskin over the wicker basket, a chore he had neglected the night before, and offered to go with her and carry the water.

Tess was horrified that he would even consider doing such a thing. His arguments that no one would be about so early, were quickly pushed aside by Tess. "No," she said, louder, and in a more determined voice than she had intended.

Finally Cedric, lounging on the jumble of props and rags which served as a second bed, dropped the coin with which he had been practicing sleight of hand into his pocket and offered to carry the water.

Will shrugged and went back to the bearskin. The musty smell of the hide seemed to permeate the cart and everything in it.

Cedric waited, gawking out the rear of the cart, looking anxiously up and down the garth, until Tess poked him in the back and, with a look of impatience, shoved a pail into each of his hands. She then gathered the cloth into a bundle and pushed past him. He skulked out of the cart behind Tess, glancing all around.

"Hurry on," Tess said, shortly. She was in no mood for his foolishness.

"What if her brother sees me?"

"You said you were innocent."

"I am."

"He was probably drunk, like all the others."

"But he said . . ."

241

"I know what he said," she snapped, not wishing to hear it a second time. She hadn't realized how hungry she was until she caught the scent of food drifting from the kitchens. "He has no right to accuse you; and if he confronts us, I will tell him so."

It hardly seemed likely, for there was no one about. Nor was there any movement at Tom's cart. Cedric, swinging the pails to the ground, lifted himself on the cart's gate and looked inside. "They're all asleep," he reported, taking up the pails again and following after Tess.

At Botte's cart, it was the same. But Tess tapped on the side of the cart and called to Fleur. After a lapse of several moments, clunking noises came from within the cart and Fleur poked her head out the front. She was red-eyed and complained of a headache.

"Do you want to go to the stream with us?" Tess asked.

"Uh, *non, chérie*. This moment?" She yawned, rubbing her neck. "Very well. All right, but you must wait for me."

In the stark, unforgiving sunlight, Fleur's disheveled red hair matched her eyes and she walked as though her head were made of glass. The dew was still on the grass, and Fleur, fearing she might slip, took Tess's arm to steady herself. As they walked, she described the celebration in the armory in glowing detail. Her narrative, emphasized by much gesturing and shrugs of her shoulders, had progressed to the moment when two drunken soldiers galloped round the hall on chairs in a comical joust.

Tess paused, as Fleur, with dramatic pantomime, delivered the *coup de grâce*. Tess laughed, glancing back to Cedric. As she did, she noticed a troop of mounted horsemen gathering before the armory. One in particular spurred his horse from a patch of shadow into the sunlight. It was John Croaker, and riding beside him was the horseboy who had betrayed Will's presence at the abbey in Bolton. Tess said nothing, but as they continued toward the stream, she glanced back, watching until she saw them ride out through the castle's gates.

It was pleasant at the stream. A slight, warm breeze ruffled the leaves overhead, and the shadows of the trees floated on the water. Everything looked vastly different in the sunlight, and glancing round she saw no sign of her and Will's presence there the night before, or of what had transpired between them. In fact, if it had not been for the tenderness she felt below, well, she could almost have doubted that it had ever happened.

While Fleur soaked her swollen feet in the stream and nursed her aching head, Tess washed the bed cloths. Cedric stalked through the shallows hunting crayfish. He had an ugly bruise on his jaw, and blood had dried beneath his swollen nose. Occasionally he'd dip and, splashing in the stream, capture a wriggling crayfish, break off its head, and suck the meat from its tail. It nearly made Tess gag to watch him.

As Tess wrung out the last of the cloths, she noticed Cedric standing beside her. He said, "Look at my teeth."

Tess set the last cloth aside. It embarrassed her even to look at his face, but she felt sorry for him, and he had always been kind and helpful when Will was sick. She flung the water from her hands and stood up. She was as tall as he.

"See," he said, opening his jaws, pointing, then pushing, at his upper teeth. Blood seeped from the gums above the loosened teeth.

Tess pulled his filthy fingers from his mouth. "Don't push on them," she scolded, frowning at him in the manner of an older sister. "And keep your dirty fingers out of your mouth!"

"Men are crude beasts, aren't they?" Fleur exclaimed, wriggling her toes in the warm water. "*Eh bien,* it's a wonder to me they live as long as they do."

"If you leave them be," Tess admonished Cedric, "they might heal. And don't chew with them."

"Do you think they'll all fall out?" he asked, horrified by the thought.

The look on his face brought a smile to Tess's lips. She released his smooth jaw and, giving him a shove, said, "No." She kindly added, "Go and wash your face, there's blood on it."

When they returned to the garth, the men were harnessing the horses and the mule. Will, wearing the silly bag cap on his head, caught her about the waist and whispered something she could not hear above Tom's grumbling voice, as Tom, one-handed, buckled the mule's harness and cursed the young noble who had hired them, for he had come and told them to get out. "Like we was garbage!" he spat.

Botte had managed to prevail upon the cook, with gold or otherwise, and promised there would be fresh bread and jam for later.

Within the hour, they left Sandal Castle behind them for the London road. They had not made two leagues when they were overtaken and forced to give way as King Edward and his retinue galloped past.

In the rear of their cart, Will and Tess were bathing, sharing the pail of water between them. They were tossed and jounced by the motion of the cart and only just managed to save enough water to rinse the soap from their bodies. Cedric, driving the pied horse, heard their laughter and, jiggling the reins, bobbed his head to a whistled melody of his own composing.

Chapter Thirteen

Thurstan Hartley and his steward Hamo watched from horseback as the cotter's boys scampered through the horse-high weeds and spreading willows. The quartet of blond heads bobbed along through the dense greenery toward a huge entanglement of brush—a dam of limbs and debris swept down from the upper reaches of the beck.

One boy clambered atop the tangle of limbs. The others waded crotch-deep into the beck, peering into the depths of the mountain of debris. Their youthful voices rose and fell, brush was pulled and flung aside. After a time, one called back, "There's nothing!" Another seconded, "Tree roots an' branches is all!"

The old earl raised a hand to signify he had heard. To his steward, he said, "I did not think we would find her here." He, and Hamo, and a dozen men—more, at times—had searched for two long months for some sign of Adam Shaw's missing granddaughter. The de Traffords, too, had searched, but with no more success.

" 'Tis my opinion, she was carried off," Hamo declared. "Shaw's own cotters said there was Yorkist soldiers about the day she went missing. Mayhap, the same lot that rousted the hall."

Thurstan Hartley nodded sadly. He had thought it likely from the very first, though he had not had the heart to say it before Adam Shaw. Thurstan Hartley knew too well the pain of loss. His only brother and his two nephews lay moldering beneath the chapel. Who was left to defend the Hartley lands? An old man and an infant.

He refused to accept it, just as he had steadfastly refused to believe that the corpse in the coffin was his youngest nephew, William. Despite his sister's pleas, he would not permit the body to be placed in the crypt below the altar.

But the weeks passed and William did not return. There had been no word of him, and now it seemed that his betrothed was dead as well . . . or ravished, and too ashamed to come forward.

Hamo called to the boys, motioning them back with a wave of his arm. The sun was hot and the boys would have preferred to shed their clothing and swim, but they reluctantly made their way through the weeds and climbed the embankment. They reached the top just as half a dozen of the earl's villeins emerged on horseback from the woods. They had found nothing—a few snares set by poachers, nothing more.

At Lambsdale Mill, Sybelle sat motionless before her loom. The yarn was placed upon the spools, all was in readiness, yet she could not bring herself to begin. That morning there had been a fog, the scent of autumn in the air, and it had broken her heart.

The half-finished pattern on the loom blurred before her eyes, melting into nothingness. The date of Sybelle's own marriage was quickly approaching. The banns had been announced. Caught up in the bustle of activity, she had not thought of Tess. But today, she could not stop the tears.

She had been very brave at Mary's wedding feast and even in the days which followed, always hopeful that her younger sister would be returned, safe and unharmed. And if that was not God's will, found at least, so she might be mourned by those who loved her. But the hurtful days and weeks and months had dragged past without a trace of her.

At the sound of footsteps, Sybelle quickly brushed the tears from her face. She turned and, seeing it was Bertrade, buried her face in her hands and bawled.

Bertrade crossed the room with rapid steps and put a comforting arm round her. "Sh," she soothed. "You must not let your grandfather see you crying."

"Oh, Bertrade," she sobbed, "why must life be so cruel?"

Bertrade could think of no reply. She, too, grieved for her littlest babe. She'd had no children of her own, and the three little orphaned girls had filled her life with happiness, given it a purpose. Tess most of all, for she had been the youngest, naught but a babe in her cradle when first Bertrade had come to the mill to live.

* * *

Somewhere among the villages of summer, of Kirkby and its kindred kind, where the shadows of the oaks played lightly on the dusty roads and village squares, the jongleurs amazed the townsfolk with their art and brought the children skirmishing round with squeals of glee to stare with rounded eyes and mouths at the dancing bear and hulking giants ten feet tall.

Will had learned to juggle. Tom had tried to teach Tess as well, but she was happier to sit with Fleur and repair costumes or design new ones. At times she would look up to see Will sending a trio of bright balls into the air.

His hands would move—throw, throw, catch, catch—and Tom would shake his head and say, "Your second throw is going late." Will would smile and try again—throw, throw, catch—and Tom would make a face. "You're lifting your hands. Keep them level!" Again and again Will would try—throw, catch, drop, drop—and then he would swear and Tom would laugh or shout, "Too far! Too short! Now close your eyes and try it!"

In time Will mastered it. He could keep the balls in the air, pass a ball over his hand before grabbing it from above, roll one over his knuckles, or bounce it off his forearm before catching it in midair and sending it up with the others.

Botte, most often bare-chested in the heat, spent his time devising new and even more astounding sleights of hand. He and Fleur would curse and swear at each other until a trick was perfected, then they would laugh and praise each other's cleverness.

They were an odd lot, Botte and Fleur and Tom. Tess could never quite decide what sort of agreement existed between them, though over the months it had provided her with many moments of fanciful speculation.

In the warm summer evenings Elgar, Noam, and Cedric were never still. They practiced new routines. They would hurl themselves over backwards and land upon their feet, walk through the campsite on their hands, or challenge one another with the purse and hawking bells.

The notes of Luigi's flute made a haunting sound in the rosy sunset. He could play a lute as well, but Fleur was truly the mistress of the lute and when she sang, her voice was quite enchanting.

Fleur taught Tess enough to play a simple tune — a little lullaby, whose words in French made a sweet and soothing sound.

"It goes like this," Fleur said, and began to sing. *"Bénis la nuit. La nuit où de deux chairs il a créé ta vie,"* she crooned. Suddenly, she paused, then said, "I had a baby once, a poor little fellow who did not live out the night."

"Oh, how sad for you," Tess said compassionately, for she was fond of Fleur.

"Eh bien, it was years ago. It was my own fault. It was I who killed my child, only me. They warned me not to cross the stream alone. The stones were slick and mossy. I fell, and, well, you see the child was harmed. I was foolish, but very young, and afraid

when my belly got so swollen. I did not understand how I had got that way!" She laughed, and then went on to tell how the war had raged in France, all the peasants starved. She, Nicolette, the rye thrasher's daughter, was left an orphan.

Her black eyes sparkled as she spoke, and there was a smile upon her lips. "I was not yet of an age to get a flux when a group of English soldiers came through our village. They gave me food. They gave me an education, too," she tittered, nudging Tess. "But you know what I mean. Two of them, Botte and Tom, deserted from the others and, when they did, they took me with them.

"We joined a troupe of jongleurs, and the three of us lived a merry life together until the day one put a child in me. To their credit, they did not leave me. Both cared for me, but afterwards only Botte took me to his bed. It was an understanding between them, I suppose. Life is strange, is it not, *chérie?*"

For a moment Tess was speechless, and before she could recover, Fleur said, "That great stupid bear you sleep with, does he mean to care for you?"

"Yes," Tess stammered. "Well, I . . . yes," she sputtered, now uncertain, her thoughts completely scattered.

"Believe me, *chérie,* they all want the fun, but not always what comes after it. How long have you been with him?"

Tess was so startled by the bluntness of her question that she told the truth. "Two months, or three."

"Ah," she said wisely. "But it has been hot, and in

the bearskin, well . . . the heat down there . . . of course, that is why." She concluded with a shrug.

Tess was mystified.

It must have shown, for Fleur tweaked her cheek and hugged her with a pudgy arm and laughed. "You are so innocent, *chérie*," she said. "You see, at the court in Paris, the young men who sold their services to fine ladies would soak their sacs in hot water, so that when they went to pleasure a noble lady, they would not get her with child. Oh, yes, there were others, too, who sold their services to men exclusively, such is the world." She shrugged and, chuckling, added, "Of course they did not have the same concerns." A swift smile crinkled the corners of Fleur's sharp black eyes.

"Ah," she laughed, "Have I shocked you, by telling you that some men are no more particular in what they do for gold than some women? Here, it is too fine an evening to carry the cares of the world. La! La," she began, strumming the strings of the lute, "Sing a song with me."

For days Tess could think of nothing else. Sex, she discovered, was everywhere. She even saw a pair of grasshoppers so engaged. Not that she had never seen grasshoppers before, just not in the same light. It seemed the entire world pivoted on that one raw principle. Why, she wondered, had she never been aware of it? Was she simply to accept it, and not try to understand? Was that what others did?

Several times she had nearly shared her burden with Will. Was it, as she feared, that everyone in the world

252

was aware of this truth with the exclusion of herself? She did not quite know how to put her concerns into words, and always at the last moment, she would lose her courage.

Moreover, Fleur's heart-wrenching tale of her early life had left Tess to draw parallels to her own life. What would become of Will and her? What did the future hold? Indeed, was there a future for an outlaw knight, one beyond a hangman's rope? How could she ever return to her family after what she had done? She was already a sinner beyond redemption, and if she came home with child, so much the worse for her poor baby.

He said he loved her. He said he would not leave her. But did he love her? Would he leave her? And if he did, to whom could she turn? She tried to push such thoughts from her mind. She could not believe Will would abandon her.

He was good to her, gentle and kind. He could make her laugh, and he was teaching her to read and write, to make the beautiful black curved letters on the paper.

It was true he could not keep his hands off her. He seemed to feel no shame in that—a squeeze or a kiss. And whenever they were alone in the cart, Tess would find herself seduced. There was no other word for it, though she was just as often to blame. She wanted him, despite all her forebodings, and it would end, as always, with heaves and grunts and sighs and a damp spot on the bed.

Will seldom spoke about the future; and whenever

Tess would broach the subject, he would artfully steer the conversation to more immediate matters, to foolishness or kisses. What could he say to her? Certainly not the truth. That he was the very man who had refused to wed her because she was naught but a miller's granddaughter and he had had more ambitious plans — a Percy heiress with a dowry of three fiefs. How foolish he had been, and the cruelty of it was that he'd discovered it too late. In all, he felt an overpowering guilt.

The troupe traveled on through the golden harvest, village by village, moving ever southward. If the cotters and the village folk were generous with their coins, the troupe would stage a dazzling nighttime performance, in which jugglers sent blazing torches end over end through the dark and a bear on a rolling teeter-totter wheeled through a ring of fire. There were magic tricks to awe the onlookers. A fat lady vanished before their eyes, and hen's eggs were pulled from a dwarf's ear.

As summer languished on to dusty death, the troupe approached Northampton. With only half-a-dozen villages between, the jongleurs took a respite from their labors.

Will and Tess lay late abed or found a shady spot beneath the trees to make love. Tess was pregnant by him, at least she suspected that she was. She had not thought it could happen so quickly and at first denied the truth of it . . . even to herself.

But her flux had not come again and, lately of a morning, her stomach felt unsettled. It was a certain sign, Fleur had told her, as was the rosy fullness of her breasts and the darkening of the midline down her abdomen.

Fleur was thrilled. Tess was uncertain, more afraid than anything, afraid that Will would leave, and she made Fleur promise not to tell another living soul. Though she was certain Fleur told Botte, for he slyly teased her—one day when Will was not there to hear—not openly, but in such a way that Tess knew.

Before they journeyed on, there was much to do, and in the final days, they repaired costumes, practiced, and rehearsed. The carts were also in need of repair, and in a nearby village, the horses and the mule were reshod.

Navet's spots had grown fainter with each successive shower. The dye, similar to ink, made of oak gall and iron salts, could only withstand so many drenchings. What's more, there was not enough remaining dye to repaint the pattern.

Fleur suggested alkanet root. It was henna, the very substance she used to color her hair. She was well-supplied and she generously offered to help color the horse. "Oh, it will not harm the beast," she insisted. "After all, look at me."

Tom, who seldom missed an opportunity to strike a blow, grinned and set aside the tinkling hawking bells. "That's right," he said, "An' once it grows to twice the size, you can make two horses of it." The boys, lounging by the carts, snickered. Fleur's pudgy hands flew to her hips, and she sent Tom a murderous look.

For all her bluster, Fleur seemed to take no deep offense; her hide in such matters was as tough as the dowlas covers of the carts. Before long, she had retrieved the sack of henna and the trio set out for the stream. Will lifted Tess upon the horse. He offered to boost Fleur onto its back as well, but Fleur only laughed at him and began walking.

The stream was bathed in sunlight. Half-grown birches grew from the soft green grass, and the swift little stream hurried past, stealing the rippling reflection of the trees. Their voices sounded above the call of birds and splashing water. When they had finished, Navet's hide was as bright as the copper dome of York cathedral save for his four white feet where he'd stood in the stream.

To Tess it was a summer's day filled with sights and sounds that brought back memories of her childhood—a gust of warm breeze, the color of Will's shirt, a certain way he held his head.

"I had a horse this color once," Will confided, stepping back to admire the horse in the sunlight. Even then, Tess did not recall. But later when they returned through the damp meadow grown thick with horseheal weed, she for an instant sensed something exceptional about his voice, the red-brown horse, and the nodding yellow flowers.

For weeks the summer memories of long ago seemed to haunt Tess. Sudden images of the past returned unbidden—as bittersweet as the death of summer—images of burnished leaves and fallen apples rotting on the ground. Bit by bit, her memories took form. The yellow flowers of the garth, Bertrade tug-

ging at her hand, and the boy on the red-brown palfrey who sulked and refused to talk to her. The memories, as much as her condition, troubled her; and in
spite of her present happiness, at times she longed to
see her family, and to see the mill once more.

Their arrival in the grand city of Northampton was
heralded by the autumn rains. The city was much the
same as York, with its proud churches, broad
squares, guild houses, and multitude of shops.

Day after weary day, the rain fell. Will and Tess,
made restless by their imprisonment in the cart,
garbed themselves in hooded cloaks and wandered
through the squares, where they were jostled and
bumped along with the crowds of shoppers. It was a
freedom Will had not known for many months and he
enjoyed every moment of it, walking with an arm
loosely around Tess, mingling with the throng of
townsfolk, drinking in the sights, and inhaling the
scents of onions and apples. At a bake shop they
bought two sugar-dusted buns and ate them as they
walked along.

Near the open market they were forced to cross
through the flesh shambles, where the stone walks ran
with the blood of slaughtered beasts, and the sweet,
nauseating, rusty smell seemed to hang in the damp
air. There were tanneries there as well, and many taverns filled with soldiers, who spilled onto the streets
in noisy brawls.

That evening round the soggy cookfire, the boys
braised some strips of meat. Standing in the mud and
draped in cloaks, they looked like demented friars.

The fire smoked, leaping, flaring orange and yellow in the evening mist. When the meat was cooked, they carried it back to the carts. Fleur had come to take her meal with Tess and Will, for she and Botte were embroiled in another of their quarrels. Cedric brought their share, climbing into the cart with it, bringing the mud of the market on his boots. Fleur, who tasted it first, swore it was horsemeat, not beef, despite Cedric's cries of outrage. Fleur cautioned him sharply. "You ought to be more careful what you steal!"

Cedric spent the rainy evening with them. He had come by a deck of cards, which he produced from the clutter of the cart. Will taught them a gambling game that had been popular among the soldiers. Cedric could not hear enough of knights and armor, and Fleur laughed at Will's amusing anecdotes. With his dark good looks and easy smile, Will could be very charming. Once he playfully chastised Tess for neglecting to draw a card. His expression—the dark, quick glance—and his teasing mention of the mill, stirred her memories of long ago. She lay awake half the night, unable to put her thoughts to rest.

Outside the cart day had dawned. A grey light lit the disorder of the cart. Props jutted from clutter and stacks of neatly folded clothing adorned the disorder.

Tess awoke by degrees. Beside her, Will was sleeping soundly, quite unaware. A glance across the narrow cart, literally an arm's length away, confirmed that Cedric was beneath the huddle of rags. He stirred in his sleep, an elbow sticking out from beneath the covers.

The musty smell of rain hung in the air. Tess rose up on her hip and leaned over Will's sleeping form to peep from the dowlas cover. She was not surprised to see the rain, more of a mist, a predictable drizzle that, judging from the dingy grey skies, promised to last out the day.

Looking around, Tess saw the market was all but deserted. They would earn no coins. Amid the empty stalls and carts, tethered horses stood with drooping heads, their hides slick with rain. Before a nearby cart several men in hooded cloaks poked at a fire, trying to revive the sodden embers. A drenched dog tied to a peddler's cart began to bark, and Tess saw an old woman, with a basket on her arm, trudging through the puddled mud.

Will stretched full-length beneath the covers and, reaching out, slid an arm round Tess's waist. "What do you see?" he asked softly, before he yawned.

"It is raining."

"Good," he said, pulling her down and folding her in his arms.

Tess rolled her eyes and pushed against his chest with the flat of her hands. She whispered, "Cedric is there."

Will pulled himself up on one arm and looked. He smiled at Tess and, stretching out a hand, brushed the elbow hanging over the edge of the makeshift bed.

Cedric stirred and rolled over, his face smashed against the wadded tunic that served as his pillow.

"He's asleep," Will concluded, turning his attention once more to Tess.

"Then we can talk," Tess smiled, parrying with his hands.

"Yes," he agreed, though it was not what he had in mind. He lay back on the bed.

Tess moved beside him. "How did you know?" she asked.

"About the rain, or about Cedric?" His smile broadened. He hadn't any notion of what she meant.

"No. About the mill. How did you know about the mill?"

At first he did not recall. His gaze shifted to Cedric, then back again. "I must have seen it."

Cedric opened his eyes to slits, raised his head, and yawned.

"No," she told Will. "You could not have, not from the woods, nor from the beck. You called the mill by name. How did you know?"

"Perhaps you only thought I did." He saw Cedric lay his head down and close his eyes.

"No," Tess replied in a hushed voice. "You said it. I remember."

"Did I?"

"Yes." Her voice strengthened, taking on a firm tone. Will's lips were still smiling, but his eyes were set straight ahead without showing the slightest emotion.

It was, Tess decided, the cunning expression all men wear when they are lying. It was the same expression her grandfather had worn when he told her that her wedding date had been delayed.

She heard the truth from her sister Mary, who had heard it from the wool merchant's daughter, who had heard it from the cook, who had heard it from her sister by marriage, who was a kitchen servant at Devrel Hall. And the truth was that the old earl's nephew, William Hartley, had refused to marry a miller's dowdy granddaughter. Her eyes narrowed, and her lips twisted. "You are William Hartley!" she accused, in an exultant whisper. "Will and no more! It was all a game to you! You have known all along, haven't you?"

"No." He denied it and, glancing at Cedric, saw his eyes were closed so tightly he was squinting.

"Oh, you are such a liar!" She thrashed out at him, pounding her hands against his chest. "Damn you! I was not good enough for you to marry!"

"That is not true. Tess!"

"Oh, yes, it is. Do you deny it? Do you? Don't you think I heard the gossip?"

He reached for her. "Tess, I swear I did not know you, not at first. How could I? It was years ago! I did not —"

"Not when you refused to wed me. I was good enough to romance under a bush. But not good enough to marry." She slapped at his hands, cursing him and shouting, "No, don't you touch me!" She leapt up from the bed and grabbed her clothes. He followed her from the bed, naked, wearing only a helpless expression, trying to explain away the truth. She would not listen. She turned her back to him, crying as she struggled into her clothes. When he tried to reason with her, to take hold of her arm, she kicked him soundly in the shin.

She was like a furious little beast, and anything he said only served to fuel her anger. In a storm of tears, she threw on her kirtle and snatched up her shoes. Great heaving sobs escaped her lips. She was crying so hard that she could no longer shout at him. He caught her by the shoulders, pleading with her, but she would have none of it. When he tried to stop her from leaving, she slapped him alongside the head with her cloak and ran out into the rain.

He called after her, but she did not even hesitate. She lifted her skirt and cloak and ran on through the mire toward the straggly line of trees that marked the boundary of the market grounds.

Will turned to grab his clothes and collided with Cedric.

"Why is she angry?" Cedric asked, bewildered. He, too, was stark naked. "Where is she going?"

Will grumbled something unintelligible and hiked into his leather hosen. He reached for his shirt and hastily dragged it across his shoulders. He could not find his boots at once and cursed loudly.

Cedric flung on his clothing. "I'll go with you," he shouted as Will hopped from the cart, one arm in the leather *jaque*.

Chapter Fourteen

John Croaker could not be everywhere, and time was growing short. That was why he had come to Northampton in hopes of locating the source of the rose-colored beads. He had precious little else to go on; he had learned nothing from the sword. The armorer who wrought it could not be found, and the inscription, "I hold none above you, my Lord," engraved in English — which in itself was unusual, French or Latin being far more common — gave no clue as to who had wielded it in battle.

The beads, unlikely as they might seem, were his only hope, and with winter coming on, many peddlers headed south. Northampton lay along their route.

On this day the market was a virtual swamp. Few people moved about through the patchwork of mud and wooden stalls. From his vantage point before the tavern, Croaker was debating whether to continue on, or return to St. Sepulcher's until the rain abated.

The sheriff's sergeant at arms, Hugh Stanton, was certain to arrive later in the day. The fact that he was already several days overdue did not overly concern the sheriff, who reckoned — and logically so — that Stanton had slowed his pace due to the fragile nature of the glass window he was transporting. John Croaker was itching to see his prize. The thought of it gracing his private chapel thrilled him beyond measure.

There was, however, still the vexing problem of Henry Lancaster and his damnable messenger. In truth, John Croaker had no intention of turning the luckless Henry over to Edward, who would most certainly murder him in the Tower. No, Henry would serve a higher purpose. He would be the means by which John Croaker would attain his fondest dreams, the Catesby estates and the title of earl. He lived for the day when he could stand before Oliver Neville as his equal.

Warwick had placed Edward on the throne so he might rule through him. Now that Edward had made it clear that he and he alone would rule England, Warwick planned to replace him with Henry. Mild and pious, Henry would be clay in Warwick's hands, particularly since the imperious Margaret had taken the young prince and fled to the safety of her native Anjou.

Damon Swift came from inside the tavern. At the open door, he stepped aside as a lethargic old woman pushing a broom drove the filth of the tavern into the muddy street. He waited for her to clear the door, then took up a position beside the sheriff and asked, "Shall I have the men bring the horses round?" Rain dripped from the overhanging upper story of the tavern, drilling a trough in the mud.

"Yes," Croaker replied, peering out through the drizzle. "It's a pig sty today. I've had enough of it." The scent of fall was in the air, the tarry odor of woodsmoke and the musk of leaves.

Swift stepped back into the tavern, dodging the old woman once again, and called to the men. They drained their cups of ale, cutting conversations short, and shuffled about adjusting their belts and swords.

John Croaker slid his hand into his glove. As he did, a girl came bursting from an alleyway beside the tavern and dashed past him. He glimpsed her face momentarily, long enough to see that she was very fair and that her full lips were set firmly in a pucker, as if she were attempting to hold back the flood of tears which glistened on her cheeks.

Perhaps it was the sheer emotion of her expression, the drama of her tears, that piqued his curiosity. He turned, his gaze following her as she hurried away. In her haste, the hood of her cloak had fallen back to reveal a wealth of golden curls that bounced enticingly with every stride.

All at once it came to him. The fair face, the skimming gait, the bouncing golden curls. Bolton Abbey, yes, he was almost certain. It was she, the girl who had fled from the abbey to warn the messenger. It was there he'd seen that glorious golden hair.

With a quick motion of his gloved hand, he alerted Damon Swift. He said to him, "It is the girl from the abbey. I'm going after her. Follow with the men and horses. Mind you, keep a proper distance — I do not want this bird flushed." Swift nodded and sent the men at a run to fetch the horses.

The street was only just beginning to come to life. A few housewives and servant girls with baskets on their arms passed by, heading toward the market. John Croaker kept his distance from the girl. He made no attempt to overtake her, believing she would lead him to the messenger. How droll, he thought, after all the searching, to have the mystery end so simply.

He followed the girl at a leisurely pace, down a short alleyway and onto a street given over to leather workers and harness makers. At one point, a group of tanners on their way to work whistled and cawed at the girl, but none made a move to approach her. Farther along, near the wool merchant's guild, she slowed her pace, drew a cloth from her cloak, and dabbed at her dripping nose.

She seemed to be wandering aimlessly, without any particular destination in mind. Croaker's instincts sharpened; he feared she had noticed him. But his suspicions proved groundless, for she neither turned to look nor made any effort to elude him.

After an hour or more of wandering in circles, Croaker was becoming bored with following her. Traffic moved along the streets, heavier than before.

Townspeople went about their daily chores, mindless of the drizzle and the dismal chill of the day. Carts appeared, adding to the crush of traffic as he neared the city's main thoroughfare.

Better to have the bird in hand, he thought. He had the means to get the truth from her. She would tell him all; they always did.

But he had not reckoned on the unexpected. By chance alone, Cedric trotted from an alleyway onto St. Giles'. Only a moment before, Will had sent him in that direction, while he dashed off toward St. Mary's Priory in hopes that Tess had sought shelter with the sisters.

Clear of the alley, Cedric glanced both ways. In the distance he saw Tess's golden hair glinting in the grey afternoon. He would have called out to her had he not noticed the man garbed in a fine fur cloak who followed her with measured strides.

He was squat in appearance and, for some reason quite beyond Cedric's understanding, the man seemed to be evil embodied. As Cedric stared after them, the man glanced over his shoulder. Cedric recognized the pock-scarred face as that of the man at the wedding feast, whom a servant had pointed out as the king's high sheriff. If any further proof were needed, there were the horsemen lagging behind. They wore the badges of York, and held their mounts to a walk, halting, then moving forward, slowing the flow of traffic on the street, purposely keeping pace with the two figures striding ahead.

The fact that they were Yorkist was enough to put Cedric on his guard. He imagined Tess had been recognized, but how? And why? Unlike now, when she was painted with Fleur's cosmetics, her face was artificial, not unlike a painted *sainte's,* and her hair, braided tightly and wound about her head, was all but obscured by a circlet of silken flowers.

As to why, well, she had freely confessed her lover was a horse thief. And for all Cedric knew, there had been murder and robbery involved as well. Of one thing he was very sure: If she led the Yorkist sheriff back to the troupe, they would all hang, for the carts were once again filled with pilfered goods.

He must warn her, he thought. But how was he to accomplish it, without revealing himself? Moments passed. A sound from the street reached his ears. He turned, and there jammed into a butcher's cart was the answer to his dilemma. The piercing squeals of half-a-dozen pigs echoed from the rear of a cart driven by a fat man with short-cropped bristling hair.

The cart creaked past. Cedric slackened his pace, waiting; then, moving with the swiftness of a cutpurse, he dropped behind the cart, tripped the latch of the cart's gate, and was gone, to blend with the shadows of a walkway sheltered by two shops.

The pigs stampeded from the cart, darting off through the mud in all directions. The cartman towed on the reins, shouting obscenities. Traffic halted; women screamed, and the horses of the men at arms reared and danced as pigs darted twixt their legs.

The plan had far exceeded Cedric's wildest expectations. Errant pigs dodged away, defying capture, and the noisy commotion caused everyone on the street to turn and look, including Tess. She had seen the man, too, because she hurried forward and abruptly ducked into an alleyway.

The man following her on foot broke into a run and disappeared after her. The horsemen reined in their mounts, kicked them to a fast trot, and followed after him, scattering pigs and pedestrians as they went.

Cedric edged from the shelter of the buildings, wondering desperately what to do next. A pig galloped past him, and he heard the cartman cursing. Sprinting from amongst a group of onlookers, Cedric crossed over to the other side of the street and ran toward the alleyway. He had no plan; he only knew he must not lose sight of Tess.

Halfway down the narrow twisting course, he saw the horsemen grouped at the foot of the alleyway. He slipped unnoticed behind the wattle fence of a poultry yard. Shouts and cries echoed up the soggy lane. Peering cautiously around the corner of the fence, Cedric watched helplessly as Tess was hustled away. Her cries ended suddenly, as if she had been gagged. He saw them boost her onto a horse, her hands bound, and one of the men pulled the hood of her cloak forward to conceal her face.

Cedric followed along as closely as he dared. The route led through a shabby section of the city, where idle workers loitered before the taverns, mobs of filthy children roved the streets, and unkempt women stared from the doorways.

A great church dominated the rabble of leaning housetops and tunnel-like passageways. Veiled in mist and rain, the dark, brooding structure, with its pointed towers and guardian figures, appeared like a gigantic black beast, with its brood of young clambering round its feet. A stout curtain wall surrounded the holy building, and in places the walls of the close-set houses abutted it.

The horsemen entered through an imposing stone arch, riding two abreast. Proceeding slowly, they halted in the forecourt until the guards raised a large iron portcullis which slammed shut after them with the force of a thunderclap.

Desperate to see where they were taking her, Cedric ran up and along the wall. A shed roof provided an unhindered view of the compound. From his perch he spied the horsemen passing the church's chapter house and cutting through a graveyard filled with statuary and grey stone crosses. They seemed to be taking a shortcut, avoiding the front of the church as they made their way toward three long low buildings which were set discretely back from the huge rotunda and pointed towers. The trio of buildings possessed none of the grandeur of the church and were set in a crescent shape, forming a sort of courtyard.

The horsemen dismounted before the center building and Tess, held between two burly guards, was rushed inside. The squat, broad man and another taller, younger man with square-cut hair followed. The others moved off, leading the horses to the stable, which was nearest Cedric's lookout. He could see only the rear of the building, and the piles of dung which, stacked to one side, steamed in the rain.

The building opposite appeared to be a barracks and kitchen, for smoke curled from its chimney, and it was there, after leaving their horses with the grooms, that the soldiers entered.

Cedric, brushing the rain from his face, dropped from the shed's roof and dashed off to search for Will. By luck—and with a silent prayer—he found him in St. Mary's Square and told him in rapid, breathless words, "We've got to hurry. The Yorkists got Tess. They took her to a church. I know the way." Cedric told him the story as they walked at a steady, rapid pace.

Will said little; he forced himself to listen. He was sick with worry, but knew he must not give in to his emotions. He must not panic. Recklessness would only defeat him. He must make his plans carefully, forget that Tess was his. Otherwise, what he felt so deeply in his heart would only work against him.

Cedric led him back the way he'd come, through the confusing maze of houses, sheds, and wattled fences. "What are you going to do?" Cedric asked, his peaked face tense with concern.

"Wait till it gets dark, and take her out of there."

"I'll help you."

The look of determination on Cedric's young face took Will by surprise. He smiled and ruffled his unruly brown hair. "Good man. Stay here and watch for me. When we reach the wall, you can help get her over."

"No, I want to go with you. 'Twas the likes of them what hung Milo. He was my friend." Cedric did not say that they had beaten Milo's face to a purple jell and broken both his arms and legs before they put a rope about his neck and hauled him up to strangle slowly. He did not even want to think of it, and he hoped they would not be too late for Tess.

There was nothing they could do, however, other than to wait out the soggy afternoon and explore the boundaries of the wall. They found several other places where it was possible to breach the wall, where trees had grown up against the stones; but none were as accessible as the shed's slanted roof, and it was there they returned to keep their vigil. A cold drizzle fell, and now and again the wind sent a shower of burnished leaves drifting past, heavy and slick with rain.

Will gazed at the leaden skies and tried not to think of Tess. For all he knew she was already beyond help — or dead. Of one thing he was certain, she had not betrayed him, for no troops had left the compound.

Will had no weapon and, truthfully, not much of a plan. During their earlier reconnaissance of the wall, he had discovered a door at the rear of the guest quarters by which they might gain entry, though he had no way of knowing in which room she was being held. He only knew that somehow he must find her. At that moment he realized she was all that really mattered to him. The message, his sworn word, even his honor, were nothing compared to the possible loss of her.

Just as dusk was falling, a large group of horsemen and several goods wagons entered the compound. It was a final blow. His plan was all but hopeless now; how could they succeed against such odds?

The walls of the dimly lit chamber were lost to shadows. Tess was aware only of the smoking brazier before her; her lungs were choked with the stench, of it and the glowing coals seemed to pierce her eyelids with a dull red burning.

The rapid, persuasive voice went on. "Make no mistake. You will tell me, I promise you. What you have suffered so far is nothing, nothing at all."

Tess was barely conscious of the voice that had risen to a savage pitch. Images blurred before her eyes, and she no longer bothered to listen to the snarling words.

"You will regret your stupidity. I will find your accomplice, just as I found you. And your foolish refusal to spare yourself will have been in vain." There was a pause, and John Croaker spoke again. "Well? Will you say nothing?" His fist struck the table before him. "You stupid little cow! Don't you see? I must find him! I *will* find him! Even if I must break your every bone! Damon! Start with her fingers."

A loud rapping sound swiveled the two men's attention to the door. "See to it," Croaker commanded.

Damon Swift moved to the door. He opened it a crack. "What is it?" he demanded.

The guard delivered the message and waited as it was relayed to the sheriff. The guard was at once aware of the heavy, acrid stench of burnt hair. From where he stood, he could see but a slice of the dimly lit library, enough to glimpse the fair-haired girl whom they had brought to the guest quarters earlier in the day. She was lashed to a chair with ropes; her head had fallen forward on her breast, and what remained of her beautiful golden hair lay on the floor beneath her chair.

"Have the men at the gate admit him," Swift directed, slamming the door.

"Norfolk!" John Croaker spat. "What an insufferable nerve the bastard has! And, moreover, how has he located me here?"

"Shall I remain?" Swift inquired, signing with his eyes toward the girl. Unchecked, he was certain he could wrest the truth from her in a matter of moments.

"No, she is not going to run away. Accompany me."

"Perhaps we should put a gag on her," Swift suggested. The sheriff nodded, and Swift did so roughly. Jerking her head backwards before he left, he whispered lewdly into her ear, then jolted her head forward as if to add emphasis to his words.

At the door, Croaker instructed the guard, "No one is to enter." Damon Swift glanced back into the room. He would have preferred to stay. He hung at the door a moment, closed it, and with long strides drew even with the sheriff.

The wet darkness of the courtyard was filled with the sound and smell of horses. Iron-shod hooves clattered on the stones amid shouts, the jangle of harness and mail, and the creaking wheels of goods wagons. From the direction of the kitchen, several servants came running splashing through the puddles, with lanterns swinging before them.

"Where is Norfolk?" Croaker swore beneath his breath. "Does he expect me to walk out into the rain to greet him?"

Swift's gaze roved the darkness, settling quite unexpectedly on a carelessly wrapped bundle which had been secured by ropes to the back of a horse.

"Ho!" A shout came from the midst of the milling horses, and an arm rose above the mob of riders. Pressing forward through the crowd, Norfolk moved his mount to the fore. His sergeant at arms leant over and caught his horse's reins, holding them so he might dismount.

The ridiculous green velvet hat with the scalloped lappets hid Norfolk's protruding ears, but there was no disguising the childishly chubby face beneath it. "Come out," he called to Croaker. "Otherwise, I shall have my men carry the thing in and lay it at your feet." He turned in his saddle and barked an order at the soldier leading the burdened horse.

"What foolishness is this?" Croaker ground out, irritably stepping into the misting rain.

"See for yourself," Norfolk answered, gesturing to the soldier, who had dismounted — and shouting for a lantern bearer.

When the dripping canvas was thrown back and the harsh light of the lantern revealed the dead man's features, it was Swift who said, "My God, it is Stanton."

"What of my goods wagon? What has become of it?" Croaker inquired urgently, his shock giving way to panic.

"It is there," Norfolk advised, indicating it was among his goods wagons. He added with a chuckle, "Whatever was in it apparently wasn't worth stealing. They did steal the horses. You're indebted to me for a pair."

"How could this have happened?" Croaker mumbled. He regretted the loss of Stanton, though he was relieved to the point of tears that his window had been spared. "The others, are they . . . ?"

"In the goods wagon, the ones I found."

Croaker stalked to the wagon. A boy with a lantern jogged after him. His concern was not the bodies, but the window. Once he saw it was still encased in its crate, he climbed from the wagon. "Thieves would not be so bold as to attack my forces," he insisted, suspecting something far more sinister.

Norfolk, who had dismounted, shrugged. "Either that or retreating Lancastrians. I hear they've been stirring up a rebellion of sorts north of the city. Don't you hear these things?"

Croaker was far too upset to take offense. His thoughts were reeling. Even the rules of simple etiquette had escaped him.

"Well?" Norfolk blustered. "Must I stand here in the rain and die of thirst?"

"No, of course not," Croaker said, forcing his broad mouth into a smile. Norfolk's companionship was the very last thing he wanted at the moment. After giving a series of brief, clipped instructions to the servants concerning the bodies, he graciously escorted Norfolk and his closest aides into the small hall of the guest quarters.

Servants scurried before them, lighting the wall sconces and setting a fire in the hearth. Norfolk was removing his riding gloves, when Damon Swift appeared in the passageway and waved in two youths carrying trays of wine for the guests.

The thought of having Norfolk under foot until the following day was intolerable to John Croaker.

He said, "I trust you have arrangements here in Northampton?"

Norfolk looked at him and laughed. "I shan't force you from your bed, if that's your concern. I intend to make Farthingay Castle yet tonight. In truth, I would not have troubled myself with the tiresome chore of collecting your dead had I not been passing through the city." He took a long draught of wine, for he did nothing by halves. "Tell me, Croaker," he said, adopting a casual air, "have you found your mysterious messenger?"

"As I recall, when last we met, you questioned his very existence." The sheriff's lower lip protruded, and his expression was contemptuous.

Norfolk smiled into his wine. "I don't deny I made light of the story. But if it were truly so, if he could truly lead us to Henry . . . well then, it might be worthwhile for you and me to join forces. After all, we do seek the same goal, to keep our beloved Edward on the throne of England."

It was a sweet sound, to know that Norfolk was no closer to capturing Henry than he was. Though at the moment Croaker was a good deal closer than he wished anyone to know. And had he not been so anxious to return to his questioning of the girl, he would have taken immense pleasure in listening to Norfolk's left-handed efforts at mending the rift between them.

The rain had stopped and the wind risen, driving light waves of mist along the ground. Will shimmied from the shed roof onto the wall and soundlessly dropped to the ground. Cedric followed.

They crossed the open space at a run. It was not as dangerous here, with the stable to block the view. Will covered the distance quickly. At the rear of the stable, he brushed past the cockleburs and weeds, flattening himself against the wall. A moment later Cedric ducked to the wall beside him, his eyes fixed in an unnatural stare. The damp air vibrated with voices and the sounds of milling horses in the courtyard.

As calmly as he was able, Will sighted their objective, mentally measuring the distance to the rear of the guest quarters. For a short span they would be clearly visible from the courtyard, but it was the only way; they had no other course.

Will waited, drawing in long draughts of damp air. His nerves were keyed to a fever pitch, heightening the sharpness of his senses. The noise from the courtyard seemed deafening. He sprinted toward the blackness beneath the eaves of the guest quarters, Cedric's pounding footfalls chasing after him.

They leaned against the wall, their hearts beating violently. No cry of alarm went up; the dint and babble of conversation from the courtyard went on undisturbed.

The door was barred. Will tried it again to be certain. He swore softly, though he'd half-expected it would be locked. Desperate moments passed. He glanced up, noting that the few windows were set impossibly high. In any case, they appeared to be too narrow for even Cedric to slip through.

"Yes, I can. I can do it," Cedric insisted in a breathy whisper. "I can slip through a mouse hole. Just give me a hand up."

A combination of Will's height and Cedric's nimbleness quickly put the window within reach. Will took a step backwards, his face stiff with tension as he watched Cedric thread himself through the outrageously slim opening. All the while, images of the boy trapped half-in, half-out of the slitlike window exploded in his brain. After what seemed an eternity, the awkward elbows and knees vanished into the building.

Voices and footsteps sounded from the darkened passage below the window. Cedric paled, his face expressionless as he molded himself to the window embrasure, his knees jammed against his chin. Lantern light bounced along the passage as two young servants passed directly beneath him, locked in a conversation.

After a moment, Cedric lowered himself. Feeling with a foot, he discovered a sconce, steadied himself, then dropped with a muffled thud. Quick as a flea, he darted to the door and, groping for the latch, slid back the bar.

Will eased inside, pushing the door to. Cedric's smile gleamed in the darkness. They had managed thus far, but now, the task of finding Tess loomed before them. They had no idea in which part of the building she was being held.

Tess strained frantically against the ropes which cut painfully into her breasts and wrists. If she could but free her hands. . . . she did not think of her bruises, her bloodied lip, her beautiful hair, shorn by handfuls and dropped onto the floor or fed into the smoking brazier to writhe and blacken before her eyes. She would not allow herself to think of it, of the hopelessness of her situation. Hers was the instinct of all creatures, to survive, and she struggled against the ropes with a renewed recklessness.

In the hall, Norfolk said, "The French are our true enemies. Burgundy is no better than Louis; both of them are only waiting to see which way to jump, and Margaret will do anything in her power to advance their cause." Norfolk, completing his thoughts, glanced round for agreement. By now it was clear to Norfolk that the sheriff was not about to collaborate with his efforts.

A sudden crash sounded from the passageway, followed by weaker, scuffling sounds. All eyes turned.

John Croaker, noting the look of surprise on the faces of Norfolk and his men, smiled. Swift rose suddenly from the bench where he had been sitting. He was not smiling.

"The servants," Croaker mentioned, with feigned casualness. He smiled once more. "They are a clumsy lot—intolerable, really. I wonder what damage they have done?" At a furtive glance and a nod in the direction of the passage, Swift sprang from the room.

"Of course, there is nothing we can do about Margaret," Croaker philosophized. "And as for Henry, even he has proven to be more elusive than any of us imagined. But I must not keep you from your journey. Farthingay is half-a-dozen leagues away. You'll be fortunate to reach it before lauds."

"Yes," Norfolk agreed. It seemed the good sheriff was anxious to be rid of him. Rising from the heavy wooden chair, he listened for further sounds, wondering what could have made such a resounding crash. It was almost as if someone had deliberately turned over a piece of furniture.

The sheriff walked from the hall with Norfolk. Beyond the doors the rain had stopped and there was a chill breeze blowing.

In the passageway, Damon Swift shoved the guard aside, cursing angrily. The guard stammered excuses about not leaving his post and was still blabbering when Swift slammed the library door in his face.

Concealed in the shadows, where the darkened passages intersected, both Will and Cedric had seen the man with the square-cut hair stride quickly past. They noted the doorway he entered and heard the slamming of the door.

Will had his answer. He knew where to find Tess. He only hoped he was not too late. "Now," he breathed, glancing to Cedric, who gave a nod of his head and watched Will turn the corner and walk toward the guard with a confident gait.

A single wall sconce fueled by oil, fish oil from the smell of it, cast a wash of light over the doorway where the guard stood sentry. The guard turned at the sound of footfalls but assumed the man coming toward him was another of the sheriff's armed retainers.

As Will stepped into the halo of light, the guard, not recognizing him, moved to challenge his presence.

Will was ready for him. The guard never had the chance to speak. Will's hardened fist made a hollow sound as it met solid flesh. The guard doubled over with a low groan. A second rapid blow felled him. Will caught him before he hit the floor and eased him down. He quickly drew the guard's sword and, for good measure, cracked the hilt against his skull.

As quickly as if he had wings, Cedric was there. With practiced ease, he relieved the guard of his dagger.

Neither of them had been aware of voices within the room until that moment. One weak and protesting, the other savage and coldly calculating. As Will took the latch in his hand, a scream—a high, wild shriek of pain—sliced through him to the bone. It was Tess's voice. He knew it even though he could not see her.

Will shoved the door violently open, Cedric right behind him. In the flickering candlelight of the chamber, they saw Swift leaning menacingly over Tess.

His surprise was complete. Had he not been so startled, he might have thought to hold them at bay by threatening to kill the girl. But the long figure armed with a sword hurtled toward him and sent him backward in a frenzy of panic, fumbling to draw his weapon.

He was Will's equal in size but not in hard experience—of Towton and the battles on the moors. He had not known the fury of such combat. That was how Will came at him, in a furious, deadly onslaught, his dark eyes bright, as black as lacquer, and a small, rigid smile upon his lips.

Tess tried to turn her face from the red-hot glow of the brazier. Shadows leapt past her, and the deafening clang of steel against steel rang in her ears.

Suddenly the ropes were no longer cutting into her flesh. She heard Cedric's voice. An arm went round her, preventing her from falling.

"It's us, Tess. It's me and Will," the familiar voice said.

Tess clutched at him desperately, crying, "Will! Where is Will?"

"He's here. Come on now. Can you stand?"

It took every bit of Tess's strength to sway to her feet. She forced her eyes half open. She had to find Will. She could see Cedric's face, blurred and uncertain, a pale disc. But where was Will?

Swift hacked out frantically, edging forward, only

to be sent backwards in retreat by Will's withering assault. Will was the master. It was no contest. He broke through Swift's defenses easily. But the blow that should have landed between Swift's neck and shoulder glanced away as Swift grasped an iron candle standard and toppled it before them. Even so, Will's sword did not go entirely amiss, for the downward stroke of the blade caught Swift's side and sent him to his knees, his eyes wide with amazement, to sprawl amid the splattered candle wax.

A faint odor of burning hung in the air, and Cedric, glancing round, saw a sparking in the shadows. A candle flickered where it had rolled against a stack of scrolls.

"Hoy!" Cedric shouted with alarm. "There's a fire going from the candles!"

"Yes. Careless of him, wasn't it?" Will agreed, overturning the brazier with the point of his sword as he passed it by. The iron stand and base clattered to the floor; glowing coals bounced away, sending up a bitter smoke. Across the chamber, the scrolls burst into flame with a sudden whoosh, flaring in the darkness.

Will came toward Tess. She looked very small, crumpled and hurt. He put his hand to her face. She raised her arms to him. She tried to talk, but she could only cry and cling to his arm. She was aware of moving, of being swept along down the darkened passage, and of Will's voice, deep and smooth, urging her onward.

As they cleared the door, shouts carried from the building, then from the courtyard. They ran, Cedric sprinting on ahead. Will grasped Tess, pulling her along, carrying her forward.

She was conscious of her heart pounding, her legs moving beneath her. She felt the burning ache of exhaustion in her lungs and in her legs, the same desperate effort which she had felt at times in dreams, the terrifying feeling of going nowhere, of her feet dragging, sticking to the ground. She stumbled, felt herself falling, but Will's strong arm pulled her up, and on toward the wall.

Cedric was there, perched above them, his hands outstretched. Will cast the sword aside and, gripping Tess by the waist, propelled her upwards to Cedric's waiting hands.

Atop the wall, Will cast a backward glance. Smoke rolled from the rear windows of the building, and shouts of "Fire" rang out above the frantic activity of the courtyard.

They fled through a nightmarish labyrinth of blackened streets and alleyways, splashing through puddles and ditches, running down earthen paths and dank, eroded stone steps.

At the straggling line of trees above the market, they slumped down in the wet weeds and waited, watching. Below, all was still. Only a few cookfires, long gone to embers, glowed orange in the wet blackness. They ventured from the shelter of the trees. A peddler's dog slunk from beneath its master's wagon to bark at them, and in the distance church bells tolled.

The swampy mud of the market grounds sucked at their feet. Will swung Tess into his arms and carried her through the worst of it, lifting her into the cart.

Cedric slumped down by the tattered rug at the end of the cart, straining his eyes in the darkness. Will helped Tess to the bed; there was no other spot to sit, in the cluttered cart, aside from the niche where Cedric slept.

Will sat beside her, a protective arm round her. "Are you hurt?" he asked. He could not see in the blackness of the cart. Again, he asked, his hand gently exploring the features of her face. Bitter tears rose in her throat. She could only softly cry and shake her head, knowing that if she dared to speak, it would unleash a torrent of emotions.

"They did not . . ."

"No," she whimpered, lifting a hand helplessly to her shorn head. "Oh, my hair, my hair!" Then she could not speak for sobbing.

Will held her, felt each bruised cry and heaving recovery. He planted a kiss on her forehead and, running his hand through the uneven short-cropped stubble, pressed her face against his chest. "It will grow back, in time," he promised. "It will be just as lovely."

He did not know what else to say to her. It was enough for him to have her back, to have her safe inside his arms. He did not care about her hair, though now did not seem the right time to say it. His hand moved to caress her neck tenderly. He felt the ragged, swollen laceration, the sticky blood thick as jam that glued his fingers together. "What did they do to you?" he asked, his hushed voice filled with pain and outrage.

Between her gasps and choking sobs, she wailed, "He bit me."

"Who? Which one?" Recalling her scream, he prompted, "The one I fought?"

She nodded, fighting back the sobs, coughing.

The muscle in Will's jaw tightened, and he swore, adding, "I hope I killed the bastard." He gently turned her head and ran his fingers over the wound once more. It was too dark inside the cart to see. He got up quickly, fumbling for a candle.

Cedric found one, a pathetic little stub, and hopped out of the cart to light it from the embers of the cookfire.

In the uncertain light of the candle, Will saw the ugly, jagged marks, the purple swelling. He thought of the jug of water in the front of the cart and made a move to rise, but Tess clung to him. "No, do not leave me, please."

He passed the candle to her. Her hands were as cold as marble. "Just to get water and a cloth. I will come back."

She agreed, dumbly, and sat there shielding the little flame, trembling, sucking at her lower lip, and trying not to cry. Her nose was dripping, and she raised a hand to dab at it.

Cedric turned to see Will clunking forward in the cart. "I don't see no one," he said. "It all looks clear."

"Good," Will muttered, cursing the darkness and searching for the cloth they used for washing. He found it, dipped it in the water, and lurched back to her. In the darkness, the candle made the dowlas-covered cart a beacon. He knew that he must hurry.

Will checked her over quickly. What he saw in the feeble light brought a wave of searing anger to heat his face. Her hair was shorn near to the scalp in places. Her face was marked with welts; her lip was bloodied, and her arms and legs were etched with dark-blue bruises from the ropes. He did not know a way to touch her that would not hurt.

Tess sat stiff and shaking as he tried to clean the blood away. Once she found her voice, the words poured out of her in an endless stream. "We have to go," she pleaded. "He will find us here. He knows of London; he has your sword, and . . . and yes, the beads. He found them. I think that's what he said; he said so many things." She paused, then began again. "Oh, Will, he found the beads where he found the sword and. . . . we must go or he will find us!"

"No, we're safe here. The lord sheriff will expect us to run."

"But he is looking for a peddler selling beads, Fleur's beads. There was something different about them, but I cannot remember what he said. If he comes here searching, someone is bound to remember where they bought—"

"Before, the beads were all he had," Will said. "Now, he has a quarry. He'll search the roads south for a time . . . until the scent is cold."

A sound outside the cart sent Cedric bounding to his feet so suddenly that he cracked his shoulder against a wooden prop. The youth's sudden movement, the suppressed yelp of pain, caused Will to whirl round, his heart hammering against his ribs.

Botte's voice came from the dark beyond the cart gate. "Where've you been all day, an' half the night?"

"We had a go-round with some Yorkists," Cedric said, grimacing and rubbing his shoulder.

"They after you?"

"Not yet," Will responded, reaching out to snuff the candle with his thumb and forefinger. "They're putting out a fire. Did you see us cross the market grounds?"

"No. 'Twas Fleur, damn her. She swore she heard a woman crying, and shook me out of dead sleep." Botte pushed back the cart covering, and his eyes surveyed the darkness. His gaze settled on Tess's small pathetic form. "Is she hurt?" he asked.

"A little, yes."

Botte glanced quickly at Will, beginning to understand. "If you need to go, take the horse. It's yours, and you'll not have a prayer without it."

"We'd do better to stay. They'll search the roads first, not here." After a moment, Will added, "I'd sooner stay . . . if it's all right with you."

Botte gave a nod of his head. "It's right enough with me," he said.

"We've got nothing to hide," a second voice affirmed. It was Tom, standing in the dark at Botte's elbow. He gave a bland smile and added, "We sold it out today."

Chapter Fifteen

The following morning found Elgar making his way down a brushy embankment to the river. The air was chill and there was no mist to blur the bleakness of the landscape. Elgar took notice of such things — the myriad shades of brown, the grey light, and the shadows playing on the water. All of it pleased his eyes, and he hummed to himself as he forged on through the tangle of weeds and stark branches.

A dry north wind cut at his cheek and tugged at his cloak. Above him the stone bridge that spanned the river Nene stood out vividly against the dull white sky. Sure-footed as a goat, Elgar made his way nimbly down the steep hillside. Stuffed inside his tunic was a sack containing the remainder of Fleur's beads. She was none too pleased to part with them, particularly after she had only just fashioned the last lot into necklaces — lovely little baubles. She could have sold them for a handsome profit.

Fleur, who was in her heart still a Breton peasant, could not help calculating the cost of everything in pennies. She had instructed him specifically, "Sink them deep." The thought that her loss might be another's gain galled her Gallic soul.

On the bank, Elgar found a suitably large stone, trussed it in the sack and cast the burden as far as his youthful arm could fling it. It struck with a loud *kersplash* and was gone. Satisfied, he crouched down to poke through some pebbles whose colors had caught his eye, when he heard sounds of traffic upon the bridge. He watched with interest as a large company of soldiers departed the city. They appeared to be in two groups. The first moved swiftly; the second, with goods wagons and a troop of guards, lagged behind.

Fleur toiled over Tess's hair for hours — surprisingly, for so little of it had survived the brutal shearing. Fleur combed and snipped, snipped and combed, looked at it from every angle, from far and near, and clucking to herself repeated the entire process once more.

In the end, when Tess held up a little shard of mirror, the sight of her hair no longer made her gasp. It was ungodly short, not unlike St. Joan's before they burned her, but not as hideous as before, no longer like a dog with mange.

For lack of her golden braids, more flowers were added to the circlet which adorned her head. A flower here, a few ribbons there; Fleur was in her element. She even taught Will the knack of making silken flowers. He was, for the most part, a prisoner to the cart, and, out of boredom, willing. It was a simple process, once he learned the moves. Even so, he found his thumbs were often in the way.

One day for foolishness, or boredom, or simply

because he had a fondness for entertaining ladies, Will tucked a large silk flower behind his ear and, taking up Fleur's lute, strummed and sang a repertoire of silly tunes for them. His lack of talent on the lute was more than made up for by his comic pantomime. Fleur laughed as if she would burst and even Tess was forced to giggle.

Tess's scrapes and bruises were easily disguised with cosmetics; even the vicious marks on her neck faded from view. Nothing, though, could dispel her apprehension about the future, the nagging sense of uneasiness that seemed to grow with every passing day.

Tess was slow in healing. Not her flesh, for that healed soon enough, since she was young and healthy. It was her emotions that rejected mending. At times, and for no apparent reason, she would retreat into silence or burst suddenly into tears.

Will did not understand. He had told her that he loved her, sworn before God that if he did not end his days hanging from a rope, or cast into a ditch with his head beside him, he would gladly wed her. It was a fact. He had said it with a true heart and therefore considered the matter settled.

But still she moped and nothing seemed to comfort her. Will did not understand. She had become a mystery to him; yet he sensed, innately perhaps, that somehow he was the cause of her unhappiness.

They played the market through the week until the sky cleared and the roads became less of a quagmire. There was a chill wind blowing the day they packed and traveled on with none the wiser. At the city gates they drew only a passing interest from the guards — no more than entertainers with their gaudy carts and clothing were due.

As they traveled south they passed through villages no different from a hundred others. They performed in the square or market grounds, camping where they could and eating what they found — a snared rabbit, some fish, or partridges trapped beneath Elgar's net and quickly dispatched with a twist of his wrist.

At midday in a village north of Latham, Fleur, who held the troupe's purse strings with an unrelenting grip, announced they had earned enough coins for the day — a boon, since they now had the afternoon for play. She was so pleased that she proposed to buy meat pies and ale for everyone from the local tavern.

They all ate heartily, including Tess. Unfortunately the food did not stay with her. An hour later she brought it up again and blamed it on the ale.

When they camped later for the night, Will led the horses and the mule to drink at a little stream. Tess walked along, through the crunching leaves, breathing in the chill, spicy scent of autumn.

They watched the horses and the mule wade into the shining water and dip their heads to drink. Will clasped Tess by the waist and smiled at her. In the speckled light beneath the beech trees' amber leaves, the dusting of freckles on the bridge of her nose shone golden in the sunlight, as if they had been touched with gilt. He squeezed her waist and, pressing his lips to the coolness of her cheek, asked, "Do you feel better now?"

Her blue eyes shaded darker. "I am fine," she assured him, vaguely annoyed that he should ask. She was not; she felt oddly ill and, after the walk down the hill, woozy-headed. Even so, she could not bring herself to tell him of her condition. She wondered desperately how much longer she could keep her secret and if he would still love her and desire her if he knew.

Her greatest fear was that he would send her home, unwed. Her grandfather, who was very proud, would be unable to comprehend such a misfortune. He would be furious with her because of all the talk it would cause, and because of his position as a landholder. He would die of shame, she thought, though probably not before he beat her for her lack of decency. He would shout at her and demand to know where she had got it, and she would rather die than confess to being a foolish slut.

For after all, why should William Hartley marry her? If what he said was true, his brothers both were dead, and he would one day be the earl—unless he remained an outlaw. In either case, her modest dowry would mean nothing to him. Nor would her maidenhead, for he'd already taken that.

When they returned leading the horses and the mule, Tess's cheeks were as pink as blossoms from the effort. Fleur saw them top the hill and leaned from the blue-painted cart. She called to Tess, "I have your kirtle for you, *chérie.*"

Will busied himself tethering the mule and the horses for the night. Navet, for all his draft work, was still fit. Will stooped to inspect the horse's legs carefully, then rose to scratch his tawny forehead fondly, noting that the gelding's henna color was beginning to fade.

Cedric wandered over, offering to lend a hand, though he did little more than watch. After exhausting several topics of conversation, he suggested, "I can sleep by the fire tonight — if you ken my meaning?"

"Do I look so sorely in need?" Will chuckled.

" 'Tis what I'd be doing, if I had me a girl."

"Did you never have one?"

"Haven't found one I fancy."

"Before long," Will said with a grin, "you'll fancy every one you meet."

Fleur peered from the fore of the blue-painted cart. *"Non, chérie."* From where she stood she could plainly see Botte and Tom sitting by the fire. "No one will come. Try it on, to be sure it fits." She saw the boys and Luigi there as well, tossing dice.

"They may come to get something from the cart," Tess suggested nervously.

"Non, they are sitting by the fire talking of important matters and farting." Fleur heard a peal of laughter. Her black eyes turned to Tess, who wriggled from beneath the shift.

"How do you know they are farting? Can you hear them?" she asked, in a voice filled with mischief.

"Men are always farting. *Eh bien,* let me help you. There it fits very nice, you see?"

Tess again donned her shift and ducked from the cart, carrying the kirtle over her arm. She crossed beneath the trees, crunching through the leaves, and saw Will beside their cart, bare-chested, scraping the stubble from his face. He had propped a scrap of mirror on the cart's side and was straining his eyes to see in the fading light.

He had not seen her, and she stood there watching, struck by the beauty of his body: the lean efficiency of his broad shoulders and well-muscled arms, his broad chest with its crisply curling hair, and the long, sturdy legs. Her greedy stare must have put a cat's paw on his neck, because he turned suddenly and smiled at her. His smile alone conjured up a plethora of unexpressed emotions that made Tess blush. She returned his smile, walking on with a sway of her hips, mindful of the achy feeling between her legs and of her nipples, already sensitized by her condition, rubbing painfully against her shift.

She was not at all surprised when he came to her later, smelling of honest soap, and planted kisses on her bared shoulders. He laughed softly and put words in her ears. The words tickled the nape of her neck and made her laugh and blush again, though not with innocence, for her hand had already slid down his body to fondle him and clasp what she sought.

The touch of his lips and hands seemed to set her body throbbing, and in her mind she could picture his cock rising from the thatch of pubic hair, red-capped and straining from its foreskin.

She was beyond rational thought; she wanted only the simple, brute impact of his body moving against hers, the pressure and the probing feel of him inside her.

He was eager to give her all of that and more, to pump her full of him until she ached and throbbed with pleasure, until their peaking passions climaxed with thrusts and groans and left them breathless, lying spent in a tangle of arms and legs.

Afterwards, he nuzzled her with kisses and told her that he would always love her. He stroked her, absently, as he spoke, then gently squeezed her breasts and dropped his head to kiss each one in turn. Truly everything about her pleased him, too well, it seemed. And knowing he must ask, he laid a large warm hand on her abdomen. How pale it was, white as milk, and sprinkled with freckles. It was full, lusher, like her breasts, and in a quiet voice he said, "You've got a child, haven't you?"

For a moment she could say nothing. She felt about to cry. "I think so, yes. I have not bled since—"

"From the first," he interrupted, calculating back. "I had not given it a thought before today. Why did you not tell me?"

"I did not believe it . . . I thought. . . . I did not know," she whimpered. "I did not think it could happen so quickly."

His smile was gone, and his face had taken on a thoughtful expression. "Once is often enough, I'm told." He did not quite understand it himself. He'd had his share of young ladies at court, but none had ever graced him with a child; at least none had been able say with any certainty that he had been the father.

In all, he blamed himself. He had lusted after her from the first moment he had seen her, like a stallion who scents a mare. He had wanted her and she had not said no to him. It was as simple as that.

Tears spilled from her eyes. She made no effort to brush them away. "I cannot go back to the mill," she said in a teary voice, like that of a whipped child.

Only then, looking into her very large, very blue eyes, did the full implication of his act descend upon him with the force of a felled tree. He was so amazed by his own stupidity that for a moment he could think of nothing to say. At last, he managed to stammer, "As soon as I am able, I will send you to my uncle with a letter." Will had no idea how he would carry out such a plan, but the fact that he had said it seemed to ease his conscience.

"No." Tess was horrified. She buried her face in her hands and began to weep.

"You can return north with my uncle and remain at Devrel Hall. He will see that you do not lack for care." Will's words dropped off abruptly. "Tess," he murmured, touching her shoulder gently. "I love you with all my heart. Believe that I would have no other for my wife."

His words seemed to console her somewhat, and Tess let herself be taken into his arms. She listened patiently as he explained that they would be separated for only a short time. He had every intention of making good the marriage contract . . . however it might look, particularly to her grandfather. Will went on rapidly to assure her that he was not without property. And unless he had the misfortune to be hanged or named publicly as an outlaw to the crown, he would inherit the Devrel lands.

"Perhaps," he said, thinking it might yet be only half-bad, "my uncle may still be able to arrange things with your grandfather." Certainly Will did not wish to make an enemy of him, and since the old miller was known throughout the dale for his thrift — more truthfully his greed — Will suggested, "My uncle could agree to grant grazing rights for your grandfather's sheep or return a portion of the dowry."

In the end, Tess tearfully agreed. She felt humiliated, like one who has been easily deceived, to learn that love, like all else in life, came eventually to payments, contracts, and agreements.

Village by village, life went on for Tess. At times, garbed in her costume with her white-painted face and fluttering silken ribbons, she could almost imagine nothing had changed. Then she would notice the children.

She seemed to notice them more and more, watching their merry faces as they gaped and stared at the bear. Girls and boys of every imaginable description — chubby, scrawny, carrot-haired, rosy-cheeked, and all of them with runny noses. Some days she would choose one, the prettiest or the handsomest, from among the swarms of children and think, yes, that is what my baby will look like.

Will desired her as eagerly as before, reasoning the damage was done, and she no longer suffered from the bouts of sickness. Their time alone, though, had become more and more infrequent as the weather grew colder and Cedric was forced to sleep in the cart with them.

Whenever they were alone, Will would talk about the baby. He seemed more fascinated by it than pleased and, as her belly began to swell, at every opportunity he would press an ear to her abdomen to listen for a heartbeat.

Pitchley was a larger village than they had seen in quite some time. It boasted squares, several churches, markets, and guilds, as well as an inordinate number of taverns. The Three Angels, so named for its proximity to the Church of St. Michael, was one of the larger establishments.

At the Three Angels, Botte met with the owner, a small, glum-looking man with a drooping moustache, and arranged several days' work for the troupe. Everyone was overjoyed, for the weather was miserable, cold, and wet.

The day of their last performance, Noam, Elgar, and Cedric spent the morning cruising the markets. Normally they returned with a wealth of small goods under their cloaks, but on that day they reported having seen a number of soldiers in the markets and they were a bit more cautious than usual.

The moment Cedric saw Will alone, he sidled up to him and said, "They was asking questions, talking to peddlers. I saw some of them talking to the bald-headed man we was camped next to, but I couldn't get close enough to hear what it was they were saying."

"Did you recognize any of the soldiers?" Will asked, but not before he had glanced round the muddy lot to be certain Tess was out of earshot. She was still standing by the end of the cart with Fleur. The kerchief had slipped back on her head and her pale blond hair looked all the fairer for the greyness of the day.

"No," Cedric admitted. "But I didn't hang round either."

"Don't say anything to Tess."

"I won't. I'm glad we're leaving tomorrow. It gave me a feeling."

The feeling proved to be a premonition, for shortly after Fleur, Cedric, and Luigi struck up a medley of bawdy songs, soldiers began to drift into the tavern. They were rowdier than the usual lot of customers—the guildsmen, traders, and assorted types—and before an hour had passed, they'd packed the tavern.

The glum little proprietor of the Three Angels seemed pleased enough; he actually smiled. The ale and wine flowed in a steady stream, and the buxom girls were sure to be black and blue before the night was over.

One group of drunken soldiers paid extra to see

the *demoiselle* dance with the bear again. There were the usual lewd remarks, cheers, and shouts. When they had finished their act for a second time, Tess led the bear to the sidelines and stood there leaning against the rough, lime-washed wall. There was no place to sit, so she stood. Will, who had become even more protective of her lately, sat down before her on his haunches, effectively shielding her from any unwanted advances.

A ruffle of drums brought out Cedric and Luigi dressed as a comic pair, to prance about the stage and sing, Luigi as an ardent swain and Cedric disguised as a blushing maid. "Oh when he got her in the bed, she let him have her maidenhead!" The crowd roared with laughter at the verses and the comic antics of the pair.

Tess was watching, smiling and thinking her own thoughts, when she noticed a movement in the crowd. A group of soldiers shifted back from the doors, giving way to a man dressed in dark velvets. She could not say which shade, brown perhaps or black, for the lighting was poor. With his fur hat and cloak, he might have been thought a wealthy guildsman, but for the men accompanying him. They were armed and wore retainer's badges.

The crowd closed about the man in velvet as he made his way forward. He was short in stature and among so many taller men Tess could see only his fur hat. He and his company halted, watching the performance. As Cedric and Luigi made their bows, he turned to a man beside him, to speak and laugh out

304

loud. With a start of horror Tess gazed into the ugly, pock-scarred face.

She must have made a gasping sound, for she felt a brush of fur, and when she looked, the bear's glassy eyes were set upon her. She raised her head, signing with her eyes. She was too terrified to speak and too afraid someone might hear. The fierce head lifted as if to sniff the air, and with glinting eyes turned back to her. She was certain Will had seen, for when Botte strode before the crowd to announce the jugglers, the bear rose up restlessly on all fours.

Tess understood. 'Twas unlikely she'd be recognized beneath the painted face, but if she were, they'd be trapped inside the crowded tavern. The side door through which they had entered lay directly before them. To reach it, they must make their way across the room. The crooked doorway seemed a league away; a sea of heads and shoulders blocked their path.

Inside a ring of torches, Noam, Elgar, and Cedric, who was still attired as a girl, astounded all with their juggling feats and acrobatic prowess. Tess and Growl wove a path through the close-packed patrons. All gave way freely to the huge lumbering beast. In covert glances, Tess watched the sheriff. He did not turn to look; his eyes were on the showering balls.

People reached out grubby hands to briefly touch the fierce, ponderous-looking creature, so they might brag of having laid hands on a bear. Just as often Tess was their target and half-a-dozen times she

305

slapped away their lustful grasps.

In the eerie darkness just beyond the door, Tom stepped unexpectedly from the tilting passageway. Tess gave a startled little cry and nearly swallowed her heart, which was already in her throat. Will, equally taken aback, lurched upright in a most unbearlike stance. Seeing it was only Tom, he uttered a single furious obscenity and lowered his fists.

"We're moving out tonight," Tom advised. "You can help me harness up."

Will focused the glass eyes on him. "Why?" he asked, his voice deeply muffled by the hide. He glanced round and, reasoning that no one could see in the pitch blackness of the passage, continued on upright.

"There was some trouble tonight," Tom muttered. "Some fat, squealing merchant. Be best if we weren't around on the morrow."

Inside the skin, Will was sweating. "Dead?"

Tom glanced back. The passage was narrow and they were forced to walk single file. "That's right," he tossed back over his shoulder.

"The high sheriff's in the tavern," Tess breathed, steadying herself as she walked with a hand against the tavern's wall, her body all gooseflesh.

"Is he for a fact?" Tom chuckled. "I hope he likes the show."

Chapter Sixteen

A porter, only half dressed, opened the door. He had been roused from his bed by the clanging entry bell and was not yet completely awake. Even so, he at once recognized the distraught face of Edmund Lutter, his master's business associate and neighbor.

"Quickly, man," Lutter cried. "Fetch your master. Thieves have passed among us!"

The porter dashed away. In the steam-filled kitchen, several women plucking partridges heard the commotion at the door and halted their labors to peer across the hall.

From the floor above, doors closed and there was the sound of hurried footsteps. In only a few moments, Owen Kempston shuffled down the stairs in his slippers, clutching his velvet robe about his girth. "God's greetings to you, Edmund. What is this my servant tells me? Have you been robbed?"

"God's blessings to you as well, Owen. No, not I, but our good friend Stallo. He is lying near to death, attacked by thieves during the night!"

The middle-aged pair, Owen Kempston and Edmund Lutter, were Pitchley's wealthiest citizens. They and the banker-financier Giovanni Stallo had grown immensely rich on wool. Their status and wealth were mirrored in their stately mansions, which dominated St. Michael Square. It was here, in the home of Owen Kempston, that Sheriff John Croaker had passed several pleasant days on his journey south. He and Kempston had met at King Edward's court, and over the course of several years, the sheriff had often been a welcome guest.

Lutter's anguished baritone sounded to the very rafters. "They made off with gold, how much, I cannot say. You must rouse the sheriff!" he insisted. He was beside himself. "Perhaps, if he acts swiftly, these murderers can be brought to justice."

Kempston, knowing well his associate's love of exaggeration, tried to comprehend. "You say our friend Stallo is dead?"

Shaken with emotion, Lutter blabbered. "Not when I left him, but his condition is most grave. Owen, in the name of Our Saviour, alert your guest!"

"I have already done so," said the tall young man with square-cut hair who strode across the hall toward them.

Kempston gave a brief nod of acknowledgment. "Ah, here is Damon Swift, our good sheriff's trusted lieutenant."

Lutter could not help noticing the large scar that marked the left side of the young man's face. It appeared to be the result of a burn, a recent one, from the look of it. "Greetings to you, sir." Lutter said. "Did you chance to hear our—"

"Yes," Swift replied, cutting across his words. "The sheriff will be with us shortly. Tell me what you know of the incident."

At the Stallo mansion, the men were met by the eldest

of the banker's two sons and taken directly to the wounded man's suite. They found the banker lying in his velvet and gold-embroidered draped bed. A physician was leaning over him. His weeping wife stood nearby wringing her hands, and a constant stream of servants came and went.

No sooner had the son announced the visitors, than Stallo pushed the physician aside and leapt up from the bed, pulling the swatch of bloody bandages from his head. But for a slight unsteadiness of gait, he seemed little harmed by his adventure.

"Look!" he demanded, pointing to his injured head. "Do you see? They tried to murder me! Me, Giovanni Stallo!" He was swarthy and thick-set, and his voice heavily accented.

John Croaker noted the abrasion; it was clearly visible through the man's thinning hair, as was a lump the size of a hen's egg. The injury did not appear to be life-threatening, despite the copious amounts of blood.

On the contrary, for with yet another audience before him, the impetuous Stallo flew into a ludicrous reenactment of his battle with the thieves. A vein stood out menacingly on his forehead, and John Croaker thought it far more likely that he would be carried off by apoplexy than by his wounds.

"Here," he ranted, "They were here in my accounting room when I came upon them!" He went on to tell, most graphically, how he had struggled with Herculean strength to single-handedly battle three vile murderers. "Fortunately for them, I am no longer in my prime, otherwise I should have their dead bodies to display to you."

He cried out suddenly, as if in pain, giving everyone

in the room a start. His wife gasped, the physician paled.

"Here, but here, I have nearly forgotten," he exclaimed, lurching across the chamber to a long, low, carved chest, and retrieving an object from atop it. He whirled round, displaying his prize. "I tore this arm from one of the murderers!"

Amazement marked every face as Stallo displayed what for all the world appeared to be a man's arm, complete with gloved hand. John Croaker would have thought it a very bad joke had it not been for the remnants of the cloth harness that had been used to hold the arm in place. It was not unknown for thieves who had lost a limb to punishment to disguise their past in such a way. He had never before been presented with, and accompanied by such a melodramatic flourish.

The sheriff promised to give the matter his immediate attention. He further agreed, "It is unconscionable that citizens must live in fear of being attacked in their homes." And, to add perfume to the salve, he stated "I applaud your courage, sir. If there were more citizens like yourself, there would be fewer crimes."

Swift suggested that the arm might prove helpful in identifying the thief, but Stallo steadfastly refused to part with his souvenir.

On their return to the Kempston mansion, Swift did not enter the hall, but continued on toward the servants' quarters and stables. A small company of the sheriff's retainers were lodged within. Swift walked on through the chill morning with rapid steps. He had been instructed by the sheriff to send a rider to the city's armory, alerting the troops there to the crime.

A majority of the men had staggered in drunk the

night before and were still asleep. Only the horseboy and the two guards charged with watching him had been ordered to remain behind. Swift soon kicked the others from their cots, with curses and the toe of his boot. He was in the process of berating them for their drunkenness when two horsemen rode into the courtyard.

One was Lewis, the sergeant at arms, the very man for whom the sheriff's message was intended. The yeoman accompanying him was unknown to Swift, as was their mission.

Swift wondered what had brought them from the armory with such haste. Afire with curiosity, he dismissed his bleary-eyed men and went to gather answers. The armory was located on the other side of Pitchley, where the remainder of the sheriff's goods wagons and troops were billeted.

"Hoy," Swift shouted, striding quickly across the leaf-strewn cobblestones. "What brings you from the armory?"

Lewis gave a nod of greeting, remarking, "This goat turd here, that's what."

The young yeoman to whom Lewis referred was no more than a boy and wore a downcast face.

"Why? What has he been about?"

A servant came to take their horses. Dismounting, Lewis drew a necklace from beneath his cloak and held it up, displaying the rose-red beads. "He had this all along, afraid we'd confiscate it."

"By Christ," Swift exclaimed. "It's the beads, an' fashioned in a necklace! Quick, you must come and show it to the sheriff."

"Aye, I thought he might be keen to see it."

The two struck out with rapid strides. The yeoman followed meekly.

They rang at the door to the mansion. A dismal bell sounded somewhere within, and the porter admitted them. The yeoman was herded into the library, where a fire had been laid to ward off the chill of the day. Owen Kempston and the sheriff were seated in the warm glow of the hearth, sampling Kempston's imported French wine.

The sight of the necklace brought the sheriff from the embrace of the chair. "Where did you get this?" John Croaker inquired in an exacting tone.

The young yeoman stared at his boot tops and said, "Northampton, milord."

"Where in Northampton?"

"The market, milord."

Croaker fired one question after another. "Who sold it to you?" he demanded.

"A fat woman, milord."

"What did she look like?"

"To tell the truth, milord, I don't quite remember. Only that she was fat."

John Croaker rolled his eyes to the ceiling in an expression of impatience. The boy was as thick as pudding. "There must be something else you remember."

When the young yeoman did not speak up at once, Lewis boxed his ear. "Answer straight away, you hear!"

"Mayhap she had red hair," the yeoman squeaked, his voice rising to a prepubescent whine. "Aye, it was red, red as that." He pointed a finger at Owen Kempston's extravagantly long-toed boots. "And she was a Frenchy. I could tell 'cause of the way she talked."

"And?"

"I can't think of nothing else, milord. It was the necklace I was buying."

Lewis sent him a murderous look, and the young yeoman flinched as if he expected to be struck.

John Croaker went on doggedly. "This woman, was she a peddler?"

The young yeoman quickly licked his lips, casting sidelong glances about the room as if he were looking for an avenue of escape. After a moment, he said, "Yes, milord."

Croaker was determined to learn more. "What made you believe she was a peddler?"

"Well, milord, she was in the market, wasn't she? I mean she wouldn't a been there if —"

"Shut up!" Lewis growled, clenching a fist.

"Leave him be," Croaker cautioned. "Go on."

The young yeoman grimaced and lifted his shoulders, remarking, "She was standing by a cart, what looked like a peddler's cart."

"What else did you see? Think, man."

"There was some boys juggling balls. I stopped an' watched 'em for a time, but I don't know if they was with her."

The interview continued for another hour before John Croaker was satisfied that the young yeoman knew nothing more.

Later, amid much laughter and many goblets of wine, Kempston, the sheriff, and Damon Swift rehashed the events of the morning. They were laughing heartily when a servant came to the chamber door, calling Kempston away on some matter of business. After he and the servant had gone, the sheriff said to Swift, "It seems wherever Henry's messenger has been, so have

313

the beads. I am certain if we can find this peddler woman, we will find the messenger as well."

Swift's thoughts had wandered in other directions. "Do you think the theft last night could be in some way connected?" he asked, draining his goblet and rising to his feet.

Croaker turned his gaze from the fire. "What? No, of course not," he replied, thinking it a foolish remark. "Go and make preparations. We shall leave on the morrow. We go in search of peddlers. And by God, on this occasion I shall find pious Henry's messenger."

Swift was more interested in finding the messenger's blond-headed accomplice. There was much unfinished between them. She would not slip from his grasp a second time. He had thought of little else since her escape. And, as illogical as it was, the theft of the banker's gold seemed in some way connected to all the rest, the messenger, the girl, though he could not say how.

The jongleurs abandoned the roads, fearing harsh reprisals, since wealthy merchants were sometimes known to keep armed retainers in their pay. They would have chosen to travel farther from the road's course, had not the sodden ground bogged down their heavily laden carts.

Botte alternately cursed and prayed for a heavy frost to set the ground, but the damp weather remained only cold enough to make life miserable for man and beast alike.

Fleur, normally the first to complain, was as happy as a hedgehog. The gold she counted avidly would buy their way to France, and finance a tavern of their own in

314

Paris. She talked of nothing else, except Tess's baby. And while she waited for the hue and cry to die away, she spent her time sewing a christening gown from scraps of batiste, silk, and lace.

"You and your great stupid bear should come with us to France. Paris is like heaven. You would be free in France, and I would have the little one to hug and kiss."

The words tugged at Tess's heartstrings, and she wished that it were possible. "Oh, Fleur, I will miss you," she cried, hugging her pudgy neck. She could not keep from weeping.

"*Non, non, chérie.* You must not cry. It is not good for the little one. Your tears will cause it to have the colic later. *Eh bien,* look at this lace. What do you think of it? Is it not exquisite?" Fleur smiled, wiping the wetness from her cheek. "Tell me *oui,* and we shall use it — lavishly."

Will and Tess passed their days in hiding with the troupe. It was a forest world, carpeted with leaves and draped with mist, where the blackened tree trunks stood out like sentinels. The chill of November came, so that away from the warmth of the cookfire, their nostrils were moist from the cold. Even the bedclothes were icy, but for the cozy hollow they had warmed with their bodies. Cedric slept in their cart, but during the day he left them to themselves. His leave-takings often embarrassed Tess, for she suspected that he and Will had arranged a signal between them. Even so, she was glad to have time alone with Will, to lie in his arms and talk.

"Am I getting large?" Tess whispered, her small hand resting atop his as he stroked her abdomen. It was swollen only slightly, a little soft hump.

"It is only four months since. Do you expect to look

like Fleur? It is only a little belly," he assured her, smoothing his large warm hand over her.

His voice tickled her ear, and she turned her head to smile at him. "Are you certain?"

"Yes."

"Then tell me, what day is today?" she posed, clearly skeptical.

"It is Saint Catherine's Day, the fourteenth day of November."

She laughed softly. "No, you cannot know that."

"Yes I can."

"Then explain to me, how is it you know?"

He was more than willing to oblige her, and, drawing her into his arms, he explained. It was hilariously complicated, of course, a subtle trap, and ended as most of their conversations did — although the encounter lacked the vehemence of their earlier couplings, for of late he was mindful of his ardor and careful not to put his weight on her.

She worried about the strangest things. One day after Cedric had gone, she asked, "What will your uncle think of me? I will be large by then, won't I?"

"Yes," he replied, unthinking, his hands cupping her little belly and his voice soft against her ear. His thoughts were centered entirely on his erection, the pulsating feel of her, the scent of her freckled skin.

Positioned as she was with her back to him, couched upon her knees, spraddle-legged, and securely snugged into the curve of his body, the future suddenly seemed very distant to Tess. She felt no shame, only the warm tingling excitement, the solid measure of him gently thrusting into her. "He will know what we have done," she sighed.

316

"Yes," he agreed, his hands lingering over her breasts, to pet, and squeeze, and stroke, then dropping to caress her pale-skinned hips as he pumped into her.

A soft smothered sob of pleasure escaped her lips. "He will think me sinful." She moaned again, softly, and, bracing with her knees, bore down on him.

He had wanted to say no, to reassure her that his uncle, would understand, but her sudden movement drove every thought, save one, from his mind.

He could not have enough of her. He thought her silly, wise, and wonderful; and it tormented him to think he would have to leave her, but the days were passing. It would soon be December. Unless the troupe moved on to London, he would be forced to leave. There was no question of Tess's coming with him. She could not sit a horse all the way to London, not at the pace he would be forced to keep.

He had sworn a vow before God to defend his king, and now he must keep it—keep it or know for all his days that the lives of his father and brothers had been wasted, spent for nothing.

He tried to convince himself that she would be safe with the troupe. Cedric, whom he trusted most among the jongleurs, had promised solemnly to see Tess to his uncle. There was no other way if he were to have both— to have Tess and his honor. Still, it made him feel like a coward to leave her so.

The rains had washed Navet nearly white again, and Will reasoned that it would take but a glimpse of him riding south on the white horse to lead the sheriff's troops away. Neither the merchant's death, nor the gold, would interest the sheriff nearly as much as the prospect of capturing Henry's messenger. Will had all but made up his mind to go, when fate intervened.

Nearly every day the boys would trek the distance to the road and watch from a concealed spot. On several occasions they observed companies of soldiers moving south. As the days passed with no further sightings, it seemed safe to assume the searchers were leagues away, perhaps as far south as London. And in London, amid the massive city's squalor and overcrowded conditions, they could search for all eternity.

That night by the cookfire, the troupe discussed their plans for the future.

Tom dumped the leavings on his plate into the fire. It spat and sputtered as he spoke. "I say we move on. I, for one am damn bored with sitting round here on my bum."

The boys were in hearty agreement. Luigi, who had gone back to dip himself a second bowl of stew, added his voice.

"If only you hadn't killed that damn merchant. They won't be forgetting that anytime soon. But you're right about London, we can lose ourselves there, and they never will find us." Botte had whittled himself a toothpick and was prying a bit of rabbit from between his molars.

Fleur lifted her shoulders and pulled her rouged lips into a pout, announcing, "I am not staying in London."

Tom glanced at her, his eyes expressing nothing, other than perhaps a slight impatience. "Well now, you bloody well have to go there if you want to hire a boat to France."

"I am not staying in this miserable country!"

Botte patted her on the shoulder. "Calm down, my lovely little dove. You'll get to France, but first we must get to London." Fleur made a disgusted grimace, but said no more.

Cedric sat listlessly poking at the coals with a stick. "I ain't too keen on leaving," he mumbled, "An' I don't much like boats."

"Well you'll not get there on foot," Botte said with a snort of exasperation, and turning to Will, he asked, "What say you, young man? Do you go with us?"

"No, my home is here," Will replied. "But I'll stay for London."

"What about you, *demoiselle?*" Botte asked. He knew the answer. She had been holding her soldier's hand all during the discussion.

"I want to stay with Will," she said softly. In the past two weeks her condition had become more noticeable. Even Cedric had perceived that something was not quite right.

Chapter Seventeen

Several days later, they played their first village in nearly a month. Fleur had designed a new costume for Tess, one that effectively hid her thickening waist. It was of heavy red velvet with a short, low-cut bodice. The material gathered under her breasts and fell to the ground in deep rich folds.

The village was called Watham. It was small and the population, admittedly sparse, was also thrifty, for coins were few and far between. Even before the day began, it was marked by ill-fortune. The morning pot of oats, left unattended for a short time, scorched. Fleur muttered and cursed all the while, as she scoured the iron pot. Later, Noam and Elgar had words over a knife both claimed, and one blacked the other's eye before Tom could separate them.

The weather, however, was relatively mild, though it soon turned blustery. In the village square, the boys had trouble keeping the brightly colored balls on course. Luigi missed a back flip, wrenching his shoulder, and a bit of dirt blew into

Tess's eye.

By midafternoon they'd had enough of Watham's windy square, which by now was silent, but for the rustle of dead leaves carried along and worried by the wind. Away from Watham, where the road turned south, a gust of wind caught the carts' dowlas covers and set them to flapping like sails.

The rain, which was inevitable, came in great shimmering sheets that swept across the road and lashed at the carts. The troupe huddled in their cloaks, soaked to the skin. Will had given his cloak to Tess, while he busied himself inside the cart attempting to spare what he could from the drenching rain. He needn't have bothered.

The horsemen first appeared as a blur, a watery mirage hovering where the road and sky merged in a vaporous grey mist. The word quickly passed back through the three-cart caravan. "Yorkists."

The word alone was enough to terrify Tess. She climbed from the cart seat and stumbled back through the jumbled interior to help Will into the bearskin. She had just closed the last of the hooks when she heard shouts.

There were fifteen of them by count, led by a paunchy, disagreeable-looking sergeant with a grizzled beard. He ordered the carts to the roadside. Soldiers milled about the string of carts like hounds circling a downed beast.

"What be your goods?" the sergeant bellowed.

"We are performers, sir, not peddlers," Botte informed him with a grand gesture and, leaning from the cart, affected to draw a coin from the ear of the sergeant's horse. "You are indeed smiled on by fortune, my friend," he said, offering the coin to the sergeant. "To own such a talented horse."

The sergeant accepted the coin; he even looked mildly amused. But no sooner than he'd tucked the coin into his leather and plate-mail *jaque,* he commanded, "Down from the carts, the lot of you. I'll see for myself what goods you're hauling south."

The rain beat down relentlessly. All were herded from the carts to stand in the rain and the mud, to watch helplessly as their possessions and props, those the soldiers did not choose to steal, were tossed from the carts into the mire. They made a sorry picture—a drenched bear and a troupe of jongleurs with painted faces. The hoods of their cloaks provided some protection, but the driving rain caused their painted faces to melt, lending them an even more bizarre appearance.

Soldiers splashed through the mud, hooting with laughter. The knife that Elgar and Noam had argued over disappeared into the *jaque* of a chunky youth. Tess's comb was claimed by another. When the sergeant's men had finished with the cart, he turned on the jongleurs. "I've been told to look for a fat woman," he said, dismounting into the mud. "Do you know how many fat women I seen? You." He pointed at Fleur. "You're fat enough.

Let's have a look at you."

Botte laughed. As if by cue, the others began to snicker. Except for Tess, who did not understand, and was too frightened in any case.

"Our brother here may be fat, my friend. But he is certainly no she!" Botte's delivery was so casual, so confident that the sergeant halted. A short distance away an ugly little dwarf broke into a shuffling jig, reciting, "Oh, he is no she and she is no he. They were made for each other, you see!"

The sergeant turned angrily on him. "Shut up!" he growled. "Ya miserable little piss." He then drew his eyes back to Fleur's garishly painted face. Perhaps it wasn't a woman. He looked closely, still he was unable to decide. He felt foolish.

All at once Fleur's thick rouged lips skewered into a lascivious smile and one kohl-blackened eye slowly closed in a vulgar wink. The sergeant's forehead jerked smooth, and he jumped back as if he'd been bitten. Laughter sounded, and a string of obscenities sputtered from his lips.

The sergeant whirled about, glowering at his laughing troops. His hand shot to his sword hilt, and he lunged at Botte. "You," he bellowed, threatening him loudly. "I ought to put my sword to you and your lot of freaks!"

A few of the soldiers were still chuckling, but another menacing glance from their commander straightened their grinning faces.

The jongleurs stood by in silence. One bowlegged soldier elbowed another, suggesting, "We could have us some bear meat."

Will tensed inside the bearskin, his heart pumping painfully. Cedric moved in close to Tess, signing to her with his eyes. Tess acknowledged him with a glance. She, too, had noticed the chunky young soldier circling them.

"Bear tastes worse 'n sheat," said a soldier, climbing from Tom's cart with an armload of boots.

"Aye, there's the reason why his breath stinks," the bowlegged soldier rejoined with a loud guffaw.

Suddenly the chunky soldier, who had been circling Tess and Cedric, lunged. "This here's a girl," he shouted triumphantly, seizing Cedric by the shoulder. "I know it is! I saw 'em in York, in a tavern." He dragged Cedric forward. With their faces painted and draped in the voluminous cloaks, he and Tess looked much the same.

Cedric protested most convincingly, but when the cloak was stripped off and the tunic torn away, the bare chest of a boy was revealed. The soldiers howled with laughter. The sergeant joined in as well. The chunky soldier's face turned scarlet, and he retaliated by shoving Cedric down in the mud and kicking him soundly.

"Makes me skin crawl," the chunky soldier swore. One of the other soldiers, wheezing with laughter advised, "You need a few ales in you, Arn. Things look better then."

"I saw some like them in York, too," said an-

324

other soldier, as he struggled from the cart with Will's saddle. "Might have been them. They had a bear." The soldier had Navet's bridle draped over his shoulder. As he hefted the saddle up, he said, "They sure fooled me. I thought for sure that young one was a girl. Wouldn't that be a fine hello when you reached under her skirt?"

The sergeant was no longer interested. He mounted his horse and ordered his men to do likewise. In a matter of moments, though it seemed much longer to the jongleurs, the soldiers had mounted their booty-laden horses and cantered away in the pouring rain. Tom watched after them until they were lost to the curve of the road. "They're gone," he called back.

The jongleurs' props and all their clothing lay in the mired road. Rain drilled into the silken costumes and bedding material. No one spoke. They simply set to work, furiously gathering up what little was worth saving. The first thing Fleur did was to fly into the blue cart and see if her gold was still safe in the cart's false bottom. She returned with a smile on her face.

Will shed the bearskin, and set to work helping. In an amazingly short time they were again on their way, for in the back of their minds was the fear that the Yorkists might return.

They pressed on until near dark. By then the rain had ended, and the wind was as cold as a whip. In the blue twilight they spotted a peddler's cart a little distance from the road. The two men, two brothers, drying themselves before the fire, had suffered the same fate earlier in the day. They were glad for company, feeling there was safety in numbers.

As it turned out, it was a fortunate encounter for the jongleurs. The two brothers were familiar with the routes to London and, having had enough of the sheriff's justice, had decided to take the drovers' road.

"Aye," the stoutest brother said, " 'Tis the drovers' path, but with the cold coming, the ground'll be set. Me and Tad's taking it while we still got some goods left."

"It runs on to London, you say?" Botte questioned.

"Aye, an' it's free. There be no toll. Mind you, the ruts is deep, an' there's no villages to speak of along its course; but it's better 'an being at the mercy o' John Croaker's men."

"Amen to that," Botte agreed.

The jongleurs spent a miserable night. More brush wood was gathered and several more fires lit. Like all the others of the party, Will and Tess huddled before the fire and wrapped themselves in whatever cloth they could find that was not completely sodden.

Wrapped snug as a louse in a length of rough woolen cloth, Will and Tess were no longer shivering. Little by little, the shared warmth of their bodies eased away the tenseness from their muscles. After a time, Tess was able to think beyond her physical discomfort. "They know, don't they? That's why the sergeant was looking for a fat woman. Someone remembered Fleur selling beads in the market. Oh, Will," she whispered, her voice choked with emotion, "what will we do?"

Will soothed her with a kiss. "We haven't much choice but to go on to London." His warm breath tickled her ear, and the sound, sensible tone of his voice reassured her. "As soon as I am able, I will find a way send you to my uncle." Even as he spoke, he knew all was uncertainty. His uncle, he believed, would surely be present for the meeting of the barons. He had no idea, though, when he would arrive, two weeks before the meeting or a single day. Just as he had no way of knowing exactly where in the vastness of Westminster his uncle would be lodged. In truth, he was no longer sure that Tess would be any safer at Westminster than she was at his side. For John Croaker knew her by sight, and he was King Edward's justiciar.

Lured by the moist heat of their melded bodies, Tess nestled deeper in his arms. "I want to stay with you."

"No, it will soon be too dangerous," he said, thinking if the worst came he would send her away with Cedric, to his uncle, or to wait for him at an appointed rendezvous.

"Because of the child?" Her eyes flashed in the firelight and a sudden wave of resentment welled up in her breast threatening to suffocate her. It had affected her so for weeks. At times she was deliriously happy, awed by the thought of the child growing within her. But there were other times, such as then, when she felt angry and frustrated — no longer in control of her own body.

"Because I love you," he said, nuzzling her throat.

"No," she whined. "Because I am swollen and awkward." Tess could not stop the tears. She was frightened and confused, at the mercy of her emotions.

He folded her in his arms and spoke to her in a soothing voice. "Tess, will you listen to me? It is not because of what I have put into you. It is because I love you, and I would not care to live without you. Tess, do you know how much I love you? Do you?"

When she at last lay calm and quiet in his arms, he told her of Devrel Hall, of his family, and of the life they would share. What had once not been grand enough for him — the ancient hall, the quiet dale, and the miller's granddaughter — was now all that he desired.

In the bitter cold before dawn, Thurstan Hartley reined in his horse, bringing it round. He could hear nothing above the group of riders at his back — the jostle of harness and of stomping hooves on the frozen ground. A thin line of fog clung to the edge of the woods. There were stars above, and the continuous line of hills was yet lost to the deep purple haze of night.

Hamo, his steward, moved his horse forward, and, in a low rasping voice, asked, "Do we wait any longer?"

"For a time," Hartley replied. He had ridden too far to leave now, without some sort of satisfaction. In fact, if the boy, who arrived at the hall limping and stiff-legged from long hours in the saddle had not insisted that he had been sent by Roger Percy, Hartley would have never considered riding out in the middle of the night to keep a mysterious rendezvous.

A shrill whistle sounded. Heads turned and the horses' ears pricked. The high-pitched warble seemed to come from across the clearing, and six pairs of eyes strained into the predawn darkness. The sound of horses moving through the thicket reached their ears long before they saw a single horseman break from the mist and enter the meadow at a trot.

As the rider reached the halfway point, Thurstan Hartley recognized the large slouching figure astride the horse. He gathered up his reins and dug in his heels, loping into the meadow to meet his old friend.

"Devrel, thank God," Roger Percy exclaimed. "I was unsure. I thought you would come alone."

"Alone. You are fortunate I came at all—to a meeting on my enemy's lands."

Roger laughed softly. "You have not changed. You were always one for scenting a trap at every urn."

"And I am still alive. Is the king with you?"

Roger Percy nodded, "Yes. Can they be trusted?"

"They are my men, certainly."

Roger Percy turned in his saddle and raised his arm as a signal. Moments later a small group of riders appeared from the mist.

Thurstan Hartley hardly recognized the king. He looked thin and frail, and it seemed a great effort for him to speak. As they rode toward Devrel Hall, Hartley, who had fallen back to ride with Roger Percy, said, "He does not look well."

"He is not well, and it is more than weariness."

"His mind?" For it seemed to Hartley that the king hardly knew what was about.

"Yes, at times he is like a child."

"He is welcome in my hall for as long as he wishes to stay."

"I am in your debt," Roger said, turning his head to his friend. "But there is something more."

"You have only to ask."

"No," he sighed. "There is more to it than that. My servants returned the body of your nephew, did they not?"

"Yes, after Hexham. Later you must tell me about it."

"It was not William."

Thurstan Hartley leaned forward from his saddle. "What? What did you say?"

"It was not William. I could think of no other way. I thought if they believed he was dead, they

330

would not search for him. I know, it was inhuman of me, and I would not blame you for—"

"Why in God's name . . ."

"He is carrying a message south for the king. I would not confess it to you now, only I need your help."

Hartley's mind reeled. He did not know what to say. "Edward's sheriff arrived at the hall shortly afterwards, demanding William's surrender. He called him out by name. Later, I heard he searched for all your knights."

Roger inclined his large head. "To hang them, yes. Was he satisfied the corpse was William's?"

"Yes, perhaps. Where is he? Where is William?"

"I do not know. Still among the living, I pray."

"You say a message, what sort of message?"

Roger shifted in his saddle, straightening his back. "A plea for peace."

"To Edward?" Hartley snorted, "That is a wasted effort."

"To Warwick."

Thurstan Hartley nearly choked. "Warwick! You cannot mean that."

Roger looked away, ducking a low limb. "It was Henry's wish."

"You mean Margaret's."

"The words are Henry's. He wants only peace, an end to the slaughter."

They were fine words, but Thurstan Hartley had heard them before, too many times. "And what does Margaret want?"

"Time. She is in France trying to raise an army."

"Warwick will not be lured into parleying with Henry, least of all with Margaret. The idea of it is insane. William agreed to this?"

"He does not lack courage."

"No. It is sound judgment he lacks, but he is yet young. You spoke of something more, what?"

"Will you journey south this Christ-tide to meet with the barons?" Roger asked.

"I have little choice, if I wish to keep my lands."

"Then let us ride together to Banbury, for King Henry's sake."

"I will have no hand in combat," Hartley said plainly. "I am determined to save my lands."

"So be it. Well, what do you say?"

"A pox on you Roger."

"Will you be our escort?"

"Yes, but only that. Surely you do not trust Warwick?"

"Like you, I have no choice."

For several days the jongleurs' and peddlers' little caravan plodded south along the drovers' path. Its rutted course twisted and turned, snaking through woods and weed-snagged meadows. The day they drew near to London, snowflakes drifted from a mottled sky.

The peddler had set them right, for they entered the city where the cattle markets and slaughterhouses stood. There were no guards to question travelers, and no road taxes to pay.

Beneath a brittle blue sky, Tess first glimpsed London. She could scarcely believe her eyes. It was every bit as wonderful as she had imagined as a child.

A thousand towers and spires seemed to stand against the sapphire sky—with fluttering pennants and windows gilded by the sunlight. There were abbeys, and churches, and guildhouses, and a broad river flowing through their midst. There was a bridge as well, the likes of which Tess had never seen nor could even have dreamed of, for there were great houses built upon the span and endless traffic passed through them.

But down among the city's narrow, crowded thoroughfares, the sights were neither grand nor beautiful. For with London's massive size came squalor, and it stared barefaced at them from every turn: hordes of filthy ill-clothed children, and garbage-littered streets. The city's sights and smells and sounds were overwhelming.

In a city of such size it was inevitable that there were many taverns. The jongleurs found work almost at once in such an establishment near the markets and within the sound of St. Mary's bells.

The proprietor of the tavern was a small, shifty-eyed fellow with more angles than an eel. He also owned a carting business and hauled goods from the city's markets for wealthy merchants.

On the lot behind the tavern were his stables

and a number of shacks which he rented out to workers by the week. He let one of these hovels to the jongleurs. The rent was ten times what an honest man would have charged; but because of the bitter cold, the jongleurs agreed to meet the price. It was preferable to shivering in their carts.

There was a hearth, such as it was, constructed of mud bricks, but the cost of fuel—like everything in London—was above the reach of all but the wealthy or dishonest. Tess and Fleur strung cloths to lend a modicum of privacy, but in the cramped closeness of the dirt-floored hut, every whisper could be overheard.

Their carts had been backed behind the shack and everything of value unloaded and piled inside, so that the interior of the ramshackle structure was as crowded as their carts had been.

The empty carts, however cold, were the only place where Will and Tess might go to talk in private and make love—but in December it was uncomfortable to do either for very long.

Tess glanced past the rug at the cart's end. Snowflakes drifted past. "But how will you get into the palace?" she asked, her voice making a frosty comma in the air.

"On a wagon hauling meat into the kitchens." Will considered it a stroke of luck to have met the carter, though it was not by accident. In order to board the two horses and the mule in the tavern owner's stables, Will had agreed to fork manure. Working in the stables he had occasion to talk with the carters. Once he learned that they delivered meat and poultry to Westminster Palace, he let it be known he was looking for work by the day. He desperately needed a way into the palace. He hadn't long to wait. Only that morning, he had been mucking out the stalls when a tall, round-shouldered man called to him and offered him a day's work.

Tess looked at him with obvious concern. "What if someone recognizes you?"

"It is not likely, not riding on a butcher's cart." Four years had passed since Will had set foot in Westminster Palace. But nothing would have changed, save that Edward was now king. "I must know if my uncle is there among the barons."

"What of the message? Will you deliver it tomorrow?"

Tess did not know the exact wording of the message, nor for whom it was intended, but Will had told her all the rest. "If I am able," he promised faithfully. "I would be done with it, if I could, and be free to take you myself to Devrel Hall."

Fleur's shrill voice sounded through the lot. Tess raised her head to glance again past the rug. "She is looking for us. It is time to put on our costumes. We should go."

Will captured her face between his hands. "Do not frown." He smiled, smoothing his thumb across her forehead. "I will return." He kissed her quickly, promising, "I will redeem myself with you."

Long before daybreak, the stable yard was a beehive of activity. Near to a dozen carts were being readied for the day's work. At the appointed hour, Will was waiting at the stable. He and the cartman harnessed the horses and set off toward the slaughterhouses. It was still dark when the caravan of carts jolted from the stable yard.

The order was for three beeves, cut in quarters, five hogs, also in quarters, and four suckling pigs, dressed out for roasting whole. Inside the wooden-beamed storeroom, a forest of beasts hung from hooks. Watery blood drained from the carcasses and puddled on the plank floor.

The carter himself did none of the loading, but stood passing the time of day with several idle butchers. After Will had loaded the cart, the cartman unrolled a dowlas tarpaulin and with Will's help lashed it down over the meat.

During the journey through the dismal streets, Will learned that the carters were kept busy when the king was in residence.

"Our King Ed knows how to live. Good food and ale and comely wenches!" the cartman bragged. Like most Londoners, he held Edward in high esteem. They had always favored strong, flamboyant kings. Edward did not disappoint them. He was a fair Plantagenet; he was a womanizer, and he was brutal—all that mild Henry had not been. Saintly Henry was too interested in books and prayers; and, of course, they had hated Margaret, referring to her as "the bloody Frenchwoman."

Listening to the cartman's words, Will felt the sting of defeat more sharply than he had at Hexham. He felt shamed as well, to recall his argument with his uncle—their bitter, angry words. His uncle had been right. It was over, ended, even then.

The cartman was in no hurry and, as they jounced along, he talked incessantly. He told Will that before he had bought his own cart, he had worked hauling fish and the like.

"Mind you, fish is filthy, an' eels is worse. The stink soaks into the boards of your cart and follows you around for the rest of your life. You'd never catch me eating a stinking fish, nor an eel. Gawd, them slimy snakes. You eat fish?" he asked, squinting his eyes at Will.

Will had been deep in his own thoughts, but managed to reply, "I like sausage, myself." Apparently he had passed the test, for a broad grin split the cartman's windburnt face.

"Ah, now that's proper food, sausage is," the cartmen agreed, jiggling the reins and bringing the lagging horses up to gait.

From Cockspur Hill the winter-dead landscape spread out in shades of brown and amber. The broad course of the road skirted the river, rising, and dipping into hollows as it wound toward the West Abbey and the massive palace that rose up from the river's edge like a behemoth of grey stone, whose battlements gleamed in sharp relief against a cold, curdled December sky.

At the east gate the iron-grilled portcullis stood open, and the guards were so involved in conversation that they waved along the string of carts without bothering to turn their heads.

In the broad yard before the kitchens, as many as thirty other carts, only recently arrived, were being unloaded. Above the shouts and confusion of voices, kitchen workers dashed about directing the cartmen and their helpers.

As Will stripped the dowlas tarpaulin from the cart, his gaze searched the standards of the barons which hung before the great hall. Fashioned of silk and as long as a man is tall, the colorful coats of arms hung lank in the still morning air. His uncle's standard was not among them; he had not yet arrived. Neither did he see the red standard of Richard Neville, the Earl of Warwick, Margaret's hated enemy, the very man to whom Henry addressed his plea for peace.

Will worked steadily, hefting quarters of beef and pork, following the line of cartmen who streamed like insects into the kitchens and down a long flight of worn stone steps into a huge storeroom where the moist, heavy air was filled with the stench of mold and spoiled meat.

Will was up and down the stairs a dozen times. The calves of his legs were beginning to ache, and he was glad to see that only two hindquarters remained on the cart. He climbed into the back of the cart, his eyes vacant, only to have the tall figure of a man imprinted upon his retina. At a glance he saw the man striding back and forth, directing the unloading of a goods wagon. But it was the square cut of the man's hair that caught his eye, and now he saw it was the sheriff's lieutenant—the man who had beaten Tess, the very one he had fought and meant to kill. He was far from dead, though when he turned to shout an order at one of the servants, Will saw that his face was marked by a large scar—a burn perhaps?

"You waiting for it to spoil!" the cartman shouted. Will jolted to action, swinging the quarters from the cartbed. As he walked, he glanced back several times to see the sheriff's lieutenant directing half-a-dozen servants who struggled to remove a huge wooden crate from the goods wagon. When he returned from the cellar, they were gone.

The return journey was uneventful, but for the cartman's endless tales and ruminations. In the winter dusk, the stable yard was filled with snorting, stamping horses. Men moved about unharnessing their teams, swinging their carts into a line and leading the horses off to their stalls.

Will made his way from the stable, with its smell of horses and of subtly mingling scents of hay and manure, and walked toward the rear yard.

Tess was standing by the door, wrapped in her shawl, watching for him. When she saw him turn the corner of the yard, she ran to greet him.

She had been terrified all day, afraid he would not return, though she did not say so. She merely flung her arms around his neck and kissed his stubbled jaw.

He was glad of the feel of her in his arms. He squeezed her waist, smoothing his hands along the sides of her belly. "You should not run," he cautioned, returning the chaste kiss.

She was tired of being treated as if she might break. "Do you think it will drop out of me?" Her eyes looked very blue and they were filled with mischief.

"No," he conceded with a short laugh. "I expect it will cause you more effort than that."

Tess took his hand in hers and tugged. "Come into the cart with me," she said.

"Now?"

"Yes."

"Tess?"

"Shh!" she told him.

When they were inside, she whispered, "Is anyone in the yard?"

Will angled his head so he might see past the edge of the ragged rug. "No." He chuckled, reaching out for her. "Could you not wait?"

She caught his hands and looked up at him impatiently. "Well, did you deliver the message?"

He had already decided to say nothing to her of the sheriff's lieutenant. "No, the man I seek was not there. Neither was my uncle."

"Is anyone nearby?" she asked again.

"No, there is no one. What is it?"

"I have so much to tell you," she began in a

rapid whisper. "I do not want to forget any of it. This morning, after you had gone, a guildsman came to hire the troupe to represent his guild in a pageant two days hence. He said he was the master of the woad-dyers guild. Is that not a blue dye?"

Will nodded, though he was not certain.

"I thought it must be," Tess said, "because the man from the guild mentioned he had been drawn into the tavern by the name Botte Bleu."

Will had not given the pageant a thought. The yearly madness began before the guildhouses, and wended its way to Westminster Hall, where the representatives of the various guilds presented gifts to the king and his councillors. Surely the man he sought would be present, for he sat at the head of King Edward's council. But what of Tess? Though after what he'd seen at Westminster that day, he wondered if she would not be safer at his side — and with a painted face.

"Do you hear what I am saying?" Her voice drew him from his thoughts. "Botte has arranged passage to France," she repeated and, hardly pausing for breath, went on. "Do you know when they are leaving?"

"No." He nearly laughed, thinking that he loved her.

"The night of the pageant. But that is not the worst of it. They intend to cut the nobles' purses before they go. I heard Tom and Botte discussing it."

He made no response. Nothing was going as he had planned. He needed time to think. His mind felt as if it were going to explode. He smiled at her and hugged her to him. "It will be all right," he said, thinking that he must not panic, he must not loose his nerve—not now, when so very much depended on it.

"Was the palace as you remembered it?"

He looked down at her. Everything about her was simple and good. How easy it was to forget the world when he held her in his arms. "It was not nearly as beautiful as you, not even as lovely as just one of your freckles."

She giggled at his silliness. "They are hardly marks of beauty."

"They are to me. Do you know that I have counted them?"

She laughed, allowing herself to be cinched in his arms. "You are such a liar," she admonished, "and we will be cold without our clothes."

He kissed her, murmuring against her lips, "Then we shall leave them on."

Cedric heard their soft words and laughter, and caught a glimpse of them as he walked past the cart—the broad shoulders, a slice of pink leg. He sat down on the stoop of the ramshackle cottage and waited. Presently Tess appeared, with flushed cheeks, and Will behind her, adjusting his hosen. He hopped down from the cart and lifted Tess to the ground.

Cedric stood up and walked toward them, explaining, "I came looking for you before, but you was—" he paused, abandoning the words, and began again. "You're not going to like what Botte had me do to the horse."

"My horse? What are you talking about?"

It was nearly dark, but Tess noticed Cedric's hands were dye-stained. She was going to ask him about it, but before she could, he and Will began walking toward the smaller of the two stables.

Chapter Eighteen

The dreary December day cast a cold rectangle of ashen light across the chamber floor. A fire blazed in the hearth and the tap-hammering of workers echoed throughout the suite of rooms at Westminster Palace. In the midst of it all, John Croaker stood with his hands on his hips, observing with a critical eye as his magnificent stained-glass window was painstakingly removed from its crate.

Of late he had little to be pleased about. The old king remained free, hidden by his sympathizers, and his messenger had vanished once again. The possibility of failure, utter and complete, hung over John Croaker like the sword of Damocles. His sole consolation was that Norfolk had fared no better than himself.

Failure, however, did not appeal to John Croaker. With every fiber of his being, he lusted after the Catesby estates, and the title of earl; and he was determined he would have them both. He had made his plans; now he must wait. Evil ends make evil means. Well, so be it, he thought, stepping into the pale rectangle of light.

The window was just what he needed to give him the necessary incentive. As the workmen labored, he carefully inspected the rectangular wooden framing. "There is no danger of this toppling?" he demanded of the master carpenter.

"None, milord. 'Tis more likely the moon would fall out of the sky."

Croaker rubbed his hands together in anticipation. He could hardly wait to have it positioned before the long lancet window of his solar so that he might see, at least in part, how the light played upon the vibrant shades of blue, violet, green, and white.

In an alcove set off from the sheriff's solar, Damon Swift leaned with one shoulder against the wall and looked on as the horseboy described King Henry's messenger. The elderly monk seated beside him listened attentively, making one sketch after another.

Swift felt certain that the messenger and the man he had fought in Northampton were one and the same. In Bolton, Swift had caught only a glimpse of a dark-haired young man on horseback. But in Northampton, he had crossed swords with him; he had seen him eye to eye, and he would never forget his face.

The brother was accomplished at his craft and,

before long, a face emerged. The very face Damon Swift had expected. "Yes, that is the man," he said. "That is the man I fought in Northampton."

The tap-tapping of the workers continued, interspersed with sharp reprimands from the sheriff for any imagined carelessness on their part. Meanwhile, in the alcove, the mild-spoken brother curved his fingers about the stylus, reproducing the lines of the messenger's face with a startling accuracy, the dashing good looks, the bold dark eyes.

Swift did not necessarily share the sheriff's confidence concerning Christ-tide and the meeting of the barons; but if he was correct and the messenger did indeed try to deliver the missive to one of the barons, then they had only to wait for him to walk into Westminster. They would know his face.

The sheriff's duplicity in the matter of the messenger and the fugitive Henry was unlikely to be discovered by King Edward, who was in any case too busy with Elizabeth Woodville.

And of course it was to their advantage that Norfolk did not know the messenger by sight. Norfolk had even done them the service of diminishing the messenger's importance in the king's eyes. Still, it concerned Swift. For if it were discovered that the sheriff plotted with another to place Henry on the throne as a puppet king. . . . well, many had been executed by Edward—and with far less provocation.

* * *

Navet was blue! Woad blue, the very color the ancient Britons smeared upon their bodies when they went to battle. On a horse it appeared tawdry, less than noble, almost an affront to nature.

For fully a minute, Will said nothing. He ran his hands over his still-damp horse as if he expected to find some integral part missing. He was furious. He grabbed a filthy cloth from the side of the stall and shook the dust from it, rubbing over the horse's withers, along its back, and down its legs where it was still wet and the blue dye the darkest.

"I didn't want to. Botte made me do it," Cedric babbled, glancing from one to the other. Will's deadly silence and the black angry look on his face only deepened Cedric's anguish. He wished he could think of something to say to lessen the damage, and he blurted out, "It washes off with water . . . mostly. Will, I'll wash it off him tomorrow night. I swear . . . unless it rains an' I won't have to . . . rain'll wash it away."

Tess hadn't said a word. She was still posed before the stall, her hands on her face, unable to decide if she would laugh or cry. She had never seen a blue horse before.

"You don't blame me, do you? I only did it because—"

"No!" Will said to him suddenly, too loud,

pitching the cloth against the wall.

Tess reached out a hand to catch his sleeve as he strode toward the door. "Will!" she called, and hurried after him, Cedric right behind her.

In the time it took to cross the frozen yard to the cottage, Will's temper had cooled somewhat. He was still rankled, but no longer to the point of doing violence. He did need a way into Westminster Hall, though he hadn't planned on so colorful an entrance.

The troupe was gathered round the makeshift table, eating a stew of dried cooked beans and sausage. They all looked up from their bowls. Botte smiled, leaning back on the bench, and ran a hand through his receding red-blond hair. "It's only draper's dye," he said with a snort of laughter.

"*Eh bien,* the guildmaster was most insistent. They make the dye, you see. It is their device, so how better to show—"

"You might have asked me first."

"We didn't know you'd get so hot about it," Tom added. "Elsewise we'd have rented a horse from old tightskins"—this was a joking reference to the proprietor of the tavern. "Besides, you and the *demoiselle*'ll get a share," Tom reminded him, going on to say what choice pickings it would be.

Botte's gaze followed Will to the table. Tess came from the hearth with a bowl of food and set it before him. When Tom paused for breath, Botte said, "Elgar tells me you took work on a butcher's cart today, one that hauls victuals to the palace. You must've had some plans of your own?"

Will tasted the beans and sausage. He could hardly reveal his true motives or his mission. Instead he said, "I thought I'd have a try at honest work, that's all."

Botte shook his head, resignedly. "I'm beginning to think there's no hope for you. However," he grinned, motioning with his hands, "Tom and I are a bit less honest and considerably more foresighted. Gather round, all of you an' listen, so everyone knows their part." Slowly and carefully Botte explained each detail of the well-honed scheme. They had gleaned most of their information from the guildmaster. Not only was he a pompous fellow and proud of his station in life, but he also loved the sound of his own voice and he had unwittingly supplied Botte and Tom with a wealth of useful details concerning the pageant, the great hall, and the guards.

"Once we're in the great hall," Botte concluded, "we work our way through the right side of the crowd, then back through the left. When the chapel bells sound matins, we meet before the east gate. We'll wait till the half-bell sounds, and not a heartbeat longer. So don't be late!"

Botte went on to tell that he'd got passage on a French currack, a trading boat. "She leaves with the morning tide, and is bound for Calais," he said. Giving Tess and Will a fatherly nod, he remarked, "There's still time to change your mind. You and the *demoiselle* can come with us. You can even bring that damn horse you're so fond of. Well, what say you, Growl?"

Will pushed the bowl aside and smiled. "It's tempting, but I've got scores to settle here, and vows to keep."

Botte shrugged, and, looking round, said, "Just remember, all of you, keep sharp and to your business an' we'll be long away before anyone's the wiser."

As the troupe dressed for their nightly performance, Will's thoughts were centered on the pageant, Westminster Hall, and how he could incorporate his plans into Botte's larcenous schemes. The more he thought of it, the more hopeless it all seemed, to mention nothing of the danger.

Later, in the tavern, the jongleurs' act was cut short by a fight. The disagreement began halfway through the juggling routine, when a slaughterhouse worker, a massive fellow—as most in that line of work tended to be—grabbed a dockworker, shook the pence from his jupe, and threw him into the street.

Elgar, Noam, and Cedric had fifteen brightly colored balls dancing on the smoky, rancid air of the tavern when the dockworker returned with a bloody nose and four brawny friends. They stormed the door, squealing like Scots, wreaking havoc on the tavern and all within. Flailing arms filled the air, curses rang out amid the solid crack of furniture. Trenchers and bowls collided into the smoke-blackened walls, and screams split the night.

The troupe made a hasty exit through the kitchen, with Fleur and Tess first out the door. In full retreat, Elgar, Noam, and Cedric abandoned their balls in midair. Botte lost a dagged sleeve and most of his magic tricks in a tussle with a drunken brawler. Momentarily trapped in the forest of legs, Luigi was kneed in the jaw. And one obstinate dockworker cracked a bench over Growl's broad back. The man's face turned blank as a sheet when the bear shook its head, reared up, and roundly slugged him.

Will trotted through the kitchen, laughing. He was overtaken at the door by a tavern girl who came screaming from the melee, her clothes in shreds. She did not hesitate or even blink when the muzzled bear stepped gallantly aside and let her pass.

Early the next morning, a hammering on the cottage's warped door roused the jongleurs. Noam slept closest to the door. He crawled from his pallet, pulling the blanket with him, and staggered to the door. He hung there, half-naked, pushing his greasy blond hair from his eyes. It took a moment before he recognized the guildmaster and two others. Their arms were laden with articles, and they shifted from one foot to the other.

"Mon dieu," Fleur screeched. "It is yet night. Who is it? Tell them to go away!"

Botte swayed awake, grumbling, "Shut up, my dove." He reached for his hosen.

Will dragged a shirt across his shoulders. Tess, moving beside him, quickly tied a scarf about her head and wrapped herself in the shawl. The fire in the hearth had died to ash. The hard-packed dirt floor of the cottage was cold as stone.

Upon entering, the guildmaster and his two associates exchanged glances, looking about with curious eyes as by twos and threes people appeared from the disorder of props and garish costumes. Stilts leaned against the walls, and huge masks made of stiffened, painted cloth peered out from amid other, stranger oddities.

The guildmaster proudly unfolded six blue velvet cloaks, woad blue, of course, to be worn in the pageant. There was a gown as well, complete with a fashionable over-tunic. Both were of white velvet and sewn with brilliants. The gown, the guildmaster said, had been worn for several years by an apprentice. "He's grown a beard since then," the guildmaster explained. "We need a proper Woad Goddess, and since we're a richer guild this year," he bragged, "we can afford a real girl. Now this," he said, opening a willow box, "is most significant. It must be worn by the young woman during the pageant."

It was a wreath of holly, and as the guildmaster pointed out, blessed, and dedicated to their saint. "You must wear it when you present our gift to the king," he told Tess in a resolute voice.

Several hours of frantic activity followed the guildmaster's visit. The gown's small fitted waist was hopelessly tight for Tess. Fortunately, the scalloped over-tunic covered it, and Fleur simply opened the gown's side seams. Attired in the altered gown, and over-tunic—with its intricate cut-outs and dazzling brilliants—and topped with the flowing blue velvet cape, Tess appeared as lissome as before.

In the stable, where Navet was being harnessed, and the cart draped with streamers of blue silk, Will surveyed the other horses stabled there. There were five palfreys boarded by the prelate of a nearby church. One, a chestnut mare—a flashy bit of horseflesh with a blazed face, honey-colored mane, and a long, luxuriant tail—was exactly what he had in mind. Will only hoped he would be gone before the bobtailed mare's owner discovered the theft.

"*Magnifique!*" Fleur exclaimed. "Oh, it is splendid. Look," she giggled, angling a mirror for Tess to see. It was true, Tess was astounded by her newfound thick blond braids that gleamed beneath the wreath of holly.

As they prepared to leave, the plan was gone over carefully once more. Botte, Tom, and Fleur would board the currack that afternoon and wait. The boys, Luigi, Tess, and Growl the bear would make the journey to the palace. At matins, they would meet and leave by the east gate. They would travel together as far as the embankment where the trading boats were moored. The boys and Luigi would fall out there, and Growl and Tess would go on their way with the cart. Simple. Will hoped that it would be, though he had no idea how he would deliver the message, or if the earl of Warwick would even be present. What concerned him even more, was that his uncle had not arrived. There were but five days remaining until the barons convened.

The goodbyes were not so simple, particularly for Tess and Fleur. The two shared tears and hugs. They had become quite fond of one another and it was sad to see them say farewell, for both knew they would most probably never meet again.

They set off towards the guildhouses, where the pageant was to form. No sooner had they pulled from the stable yard, than they were aware of the city's festive mood. The streets were filled with people, many of them in costume. In contrast to the high spirits of the populace, the day was dirty grey and the damp chill of the breeze promised rain.

On they went, threading their way through the narrow, filthy, crowded streets. Cedric, Noam and Elgar were three gigantic angels armed with swords and shields, bearing banners emblazoned with the likeness of a patron saint and emblems of the guild. A blue horse pulled a garlanded, silk-draped, cart driven by a dwarf in fool's cap, and in the rear of the open cart, a huge brown bear sat on his haunches and leered at the passing panorama, while a girl wearing a glittering gown and a holly wreath on her head waved to one and all.

Before the guildhall there was such a tumult, one could hardly hear the shouted words of the mayor and the other speakers. Much confusion followed as the line of parade was assigned. Guildsmen, hired jongleurs, actors and musicians cursed and harangued, vying for the best positions.

Tess noticed that some of the props and costumes were crude and haphazard, but the richer guilds had fine attire and, in some cases, three or four festively decorated carts.

Following a blessing by the bishop, there was a rude blaring of trumpets and a ruffle of kettle drums. The procession began. Hundreds of wealthy merchants, together with the mayor and his council, led the immense parade.

The richer guilds came first, with the lesser joining in behind. Each group was marked by their bright colors and preceded by their banner which bore a likeness of their patron saint and the symbol of their guild. Some participants wore masks; some chose not to. The wealthier guilds often hired entertainers to brave the cold in skimpy costumes and walk the distance to the palace, while they wrapped themselves in fur cloaks and rode on fine palfreys. The lesser guildsmen, like poor men everywhere, were left to walk in the cold and to carry their own banners.

All along the route, houses and windows of buildings were hung with colorful lengths of silks and brocades. Banners fluttered from the rooftops and there were such crowds of people that it seemed to Tess that all the world had come to watch and cheer. As far as Tess could see, the procession stretched before her, snaking through the dreary afternoon like a brightly colored dragon.

As they passed the Eleanor Cross at the juncture of Charing Road, Tess felt a drop of rain. In the misting grey afternoon, the monument was a mournful sight. Tess had been told that there were twelve such crosses. All built at the behest of the first King Edward for his beloved Queen Eleanor. The solemn line of crosses marked the course of her funeral cortege from Lincoln to Westminster, one before each church where her coffin had lain. Tess thought it a sad story, as disturbing as her first glimpse of Westminster. The palace, viewed through the crazed fretwork of barren branches, appeared sinister, like a beast that lies in wait. It was immense, a mountain of grey stone that seemed to rise from the very depths of the river.

Tess had not felt afraid until that moment.

The palace gates were draped with banners. Amid the flaunted colors and teeming crowds, torches blazed in the drizzling rain.

The parade snaked through the palace gates, winding before the great hall. King Edward and his council came out, braving the weather, to gaze down from a parapet of the central tower. Slowly, the king raised his hands in acknowledgment of his great city's guilds.

Tess noticed the pretty woman beside the king. She was almost certain it was the same woman who had sent a page to her with a gold piece at Sandal Castle. She was even more beautifully dressed than at Sandal, for on this occasion she wore a gown of golden cloth set with jewels. From a distance and with the torchlight playing on it, the gown was the color of the sun in all its splendor. Her tall, hennin headdress was also of purest gold and shimmered, glancing in the torchlight with the slightest movement of her head. She seemed a fairy queen, regaled with gold and jewels. Tess heard others in the crowd say as much, and call her their new queen.

It began to rain. In the courtyard, all the pageant members were forced to queue up in the order of their entry. Immediately before the woad dyers' guild was a guild of fishmongers, whose members were dressed as huge gudgeons, complete with embroidered fins and gills, and when they walked, their scaled tails bounced along the cobblestones.

The forecourt of the palace and the smaller courts nearby overflowed with horses, carts, and noisy revelers. Confusion reigned, and the noise was such that the heralds and their trumpets could hardly be heard above the clamor.

When the doors of the great hall were opened, the tradesmen proceeded, guild by guild, down its exceptional length, past the assembled guests, to bow before the king and lay their gifts on a long, cloth-draped table.

Fires blazed in the hall's enormous hearths, and torches lined the walls. There was such crowding that it was difficult to move at all, and in a short time the press of people became so great that the hall could not contain them, and the huge doors were left open to the rain and chill of the December dusk.

High tables had been set for the king and his court, the archbishop and other powerful ecclesiastics. A second lower dais was set for lesser nobles and lesser churchmen, and below these the tables of the merchant class. An army of servants milled by the passages to the kitchens, awaiting their call, while others served wine from ewers to the guests, and liveried servants passed through the throng with trays of comfits and dried, sugared fruit.

The resonant voices of the heralds rang out, presenting each guild by turn—armorers, braziers, wax chandlers, pewters, brewers, mercers, drapers, dyers, salters, ironmongers, and bakers. Each guild had chosen one person to present their gift to the king, two if the gift was weighty.

As Tess approached King Edward, she felt a twinge of nerves, a fluttering in her breast. Will, lumbering beside her, saw the distorted image of Richard Neville, Earl of Warwick, through the bear's glass eyes. He was standing apart from the other members of the council, talking intently with two younger nobles.

Tess and he would pass directly before them as they turned from the king to place the guild's offering on the table. It would be now or not at all, Will realized. He must think of some way to gain Warwick's attention, only his and no other's.

Will knew the sheriff's lieutenant was surely present, no doubt the sheriff as well. He might not have another opportunity to come so close to Warwick. Months of carrying the message with the sole intent of delivering it to this man now hung in the balance. Henry's faith in Warwick weighed against Will's better judgment.

Will had known Warwick only as an enemy, a scourge to the Lancastrians. He wanted to believe that Warwick would give them refuge, or at the very least that no harm would come to Tess. But there was no time for assurances, no time to bargain; and Will knew if he were to deliver the message, it must be now.

The folded length of blue velvet Tess carried in her arms quivered and quaked before her eyes. She was very nervous, and her face felt afire as she curtsied low before the king and the splendidly gowned Elizabeth Woodville, who was seated at his side.

Such niceties were not required of bears, and Will was free to observe the earl of Warwick. The two men he had been talking with moved off into the crowd. He stood alone.

As Tess raised her head, Elizabeth Woodville smiled at her, a smile of recognition. It pleased Tess to think that she had remembered her from Sandal. Tess returned her smile, thinking she must surely be as kind as she was lovely.

Tess moved toward the table, searching for an open place to lay the gift. As they passed, Will looked up at Warwick, whose eyes were set on something in the distance. Will said, "I am sent by Henry Lancaster, anointed king of England."

Warwick turned his head, looking round, glancing behind him. He murmured something Will could not make out for the thickness of the hide. It would have been funny had it not been so deadly serious.

Becoming bolder, Will raised up heavily on his hind legs. The startled Warwick turned abruptly, taking a step backwards. Will repeated the phrase. This time Warwick understood, for his eyes jerked open as if he'd been struck with a whip.

The bear's sudden movement caused a stir in the crowd. Tess turned at the sound of gasps, dropping her gift atop another. She thought she heard Will's voice. She saw the look on the face of the man who stood before him and reasoned the message was meant for him. But there was no way Will could have passed the missive to him, she thought.

For a single terrible moment Tess did not know what to do, her heart heaved and she lurched forward to catch the leather collar. The bear went down on all fours. Tess tore her gaze from the man's small hard eyes and, stumbling a little as she descended the dais, led the bear away.

In only a few steps they were swallowed up by the crowd, and it seemed they moved hardly at all. Tess clung to the leather collar. It was as if all certainty had deserted her limbs; she was shaking from head to foot.

Cedric appeared before them in the throng. He had removed his mask, but was still wearing the woad-blue cape. He raised a hand in a cheery salute as he maneuvered through the crowd. In only a moment he was beside them.

"I want you to go with him," Will said. He was suddenly afraid for her, no longer trusting Warwick. There had been something in his manner, in his eyes. The small, bright eyes, like the eyes of a wild animal ready to spring. "Go with Cedric, leave me here."

Tess wanted to tell him to be silent, that someone would hear, but all she could say was, "No. I have come this far with you. I will not leave you now."

The words had hardly left her lips when two young men dressed as squires pushed from the crowd, and bade Tess and the bear follow them.

They had not noticed Cedric. He melted into the throng, watching after them. Something was wrong—he sensed it, though he did not know what. Music and caroling began from somewhere up above, one of the choir lofts perhaps—a latin hymn, whose words Cedric did not understand.

Earlier that evening, as the lengthy guildsmen's procession before the king was just beginning, John Croaker saw a page standing by a table where wine was being served from a silver ewer. He motioned for the boy to fetch him a cup. The page returned carrying two cups of wine—with Oliver Neville at his heels.

"So here you are, you little swine," Neville boomed, swatting the sheriff soundly on the shoulder. He took the wine from the page and shoved one cup into Croaker's hand. "What do you think of her?" Oliver asked.

The pewter cup was cold in John Croaker's hand. "The Woodville woman?" he asked, even though he knew perfectly well to whom Oliver

Neville was referring.

"Our queen," Oliver reminded him with a sly smile. "Cousin Richard has been gnashing his teeth all day. For a moment this afternoon, I thought he was going to fall on the floor and chew on the carpets." Neville was full of gossip—he was as bad as an old woman.

John Croaker had not been present at the meeting between the king and his council. But he had heard what had passed between Edward and his mentor, Richard Neville, the Earl of Warwick. As the sheriff well knew, Warwick's pride was every bit as great as his overweening ambition. Croaker felt certain that Edward's announcement of his secret marriage to Elizabeth Woodville—who was in effect what amounted to a commoner—must have dealt Warwick a deep wound, particularly after Warwick had bargained so long with King Louis of France for the hand of Bona of Savoy. It was a slap in the face and not the first time of late that Edward had deliberately defied his mentor. Bit by bit, Edward was excluding Warwick, distancing him from power.

Warwick had taken each blow with cold control, outwardly at least. He would have his revenge, the sheriff was certain of that. Henry Lancaster was the weapon Warwick needed to thrust Edward from the throne.

Oliver was still gossiping, some rubbish about the Rivers family, the kinsmen of the queen. All at once, he looked at the sheriff and said, "You should dress better, more color. You're as drab as a crow. Doesn't it depress you, wearing black? Ah, there is Cousin Simon. I must go and speak to him," he said as he moved off, picking his way through the crush.

John Croaker turned the pewter cup in his hand, admiring its etched design, the coat of arms of York. He was thinking he must decide on a coat of arms. He tasted the wine. It was French and quite good. He let it roll over his tongue and held it a moment to savor the taste before he swallowed.

As arranged, his men were all in position. He did not expect the messenger to show himself until the day the barons convened, five days hence, but it would be a useful exercise for his men.

He raised himself on the balls of his feet, attempting to look over the crowd. Among the milling throng, he could no longer see Damon Swift, Lewis, or the horseboy.

John Croaker wandered back toward the tables, threading his way through the crowded hall, observing the robes and jewels of the ladies. He was certain many of the gowns had cost a king's ransom, for they were truly masterpieces of the embroiderer's and goldsmith's art. Tall hennin headdresses sailed past far above his head, and at every turn he saw men in doublets of velvet sewn with jewels and trimmed in fur, wearing golden chains about their necks, and weighty rings on their fingers.

Nearer the tables, he noticed Warwick standing with the other members of the king's council. The king had placed him at the far end of the line, and he stood nearest the table where the gifts were being laid, one by one, by the representatives of the guilds after they had dutifully made their obeisance to the king.

The sheriff saw the bear rise up on its hind legs. He thought Warwick's startled expression amusing, for a bear was prominent on the earl's coat of arms.

Meanwhile, Damon Swift wove a path toward one of the colonnaded entrances, where a number of passageways intersected the great hall. Moving through the crowd, he met a group of young ladies-in-waiting.

He smiled and bowed his head. One woman particularly caught his eye. She was fair and blue-eyed, and she reminded him of the girl in Northampton. His gaze momentarily lingered on the pale flesh of her throat. As if she had read his thoughts, the corners of her lips dropped and she quickly looked away.

When he at last found Lewis, he was haranguing the horseboy over some matter and Swift asked, shortly, "What is it? What's the matter with him?"

"A witch!" Lewis snorted. "He said he saw a

witch, and now he won't come out from behind the columns."

Damon Swift gave a wry smile. "Perchance she was seated beside the king," he chuckled. King Edward's secret marriage to Elizabeth Woodville was the gossip of the day. Many said she had bewitched him, for why else should he marry a penniless widow. Swift regarded the horseboy with an expression of impatience. "Come, out with you. Be quick about it."

The boy shook his head obstinately, refusing to come from the safety of the columns. "I don't want her to look at me," he whined. "She's got the evil eye."

"Don't be an ass," Swift snapped, reaching for the boy's shoulder to drag him out.

But the horseboy dodged back, clearly terrified. "No, she's there! She's a witch. I know she is. I saw her change a bear into a man."

Swift laughed despite his annoyance. "You saw her do what?"

"I did. I swear I did. She turned a bear into a man and then she screwed him!"

Lewis made a strangling sound. He could not speak for laughing.

Swift's jaw stiffened; he was no longer laughing. A cold logic surfaced and he demanded, "Where did you see her a accomplish this feat? You have been under guard the entire time. Why did your guards not witness this spectacle?"

366

"Aye," Lewis cackled. "I'd have given one of my nuts to see it!"

Swift silenced him with a glance. "Well?" he prompted the horseboy.

The youthful face was white with fear, and the boy's Adam's apple bobbed up and down with each word. "At Sandal," he stammered. "The guards was drunk. I followed her into the woods, an' I saw her. I saw what she did. I swear it."

Lewis was still laughing. Swift told him to shut up and, turning to the horseboy, asked, "At Sandal?"

The horseboy nodded. He was trembling.

Swift whirled round abruptly, catching a glimpse of the girl and the bear as they descended the dais into the crush of people. Again the horseboy's words ran through his mind. *She turned the bear into a man.* A man. . . . Had that been the answer all along? Was that the means by which the messenger had vanished so completely? Was there a man inside the bearskin?

Swift grabbed Lewis by the arm, shoving him forward. "Alert the men," he ordered. "I want the girl and the bear. Do it quietly."

Lewis stared at him. "What? You don't believe—"

"Do it now!" Swift commanded, and motioning to another of his men standing nearby, he instructed, "Do not let this boy out of your sight." Swift clamped a hand on the boy's shoulder and fixed him in a formulated stare. "If you are lying to me," Swift breathed, "I will kill you. I promise you." He did not wait to hear the horseboy's blubbering reply, but dashed off, signaling to several other men standing by the tables to follow.

Tess clung to the bear's collar. Her legs felt stiff, paralyzed with fear and suddenly unwilling to do her bidding. It was only with the greatest effort that she managed to put one foot before the other and leave the relative safety of the hall, the sound of laughter and conversations, behind.

The taller of the two young squires led the way; the other followed, lagging some distance back, at a casual pace. They walked through a series of dimly lit smaller chambers into a large vaulted vestibule, bright with torchlight, from which six passages channeled into the vast depths of the palace.

Only two of the passages flickered with the feeble light of wall sconces; the others were in total darkness. The young man in the lead chose the first. After only a short distance the passage turned sharply right.

No one spoke. The distant drone of voices and music could still be heard above the scraping sound of their shoes and the clicking of the bear's claws on the stone floor. Presently, they came to a steep flight of stairs.

John Croaker's eyes roved wildly over the crowd. At last he saw Damon Swift and plunged through the thronging mob.

"Thank God, I've found you!" John Croaker exclaimed. He could hardly speak for panting.

"Milord, they are here!" Swift announced, his voice slurred with excitement. "It is the girl and the trained bear. I am certain of it! They were seen journeying here."

Croaker shook his head, his face was red with exertion. "No!" He swore and tugged at Swift's arm. He knew all of that, he had just spoken to Warwick. "Call off your men. Send them back to the hall. All must appear normal."

"Milord." Swift's voice rose sharply. "The bear is the messenger. I am certain of it!"

"Yes, yes. I know all that. Now do as I say. Call them off. And Swift, bring four crossbowmen, trustworthy ones, and meet me in my suite. Also, tell Lewis to collect twenty men and have them ready to ride in an hour. Go! Quickly!"

Swift sprinted off, his sword slapping against his boot. The sheriff leaned for a moment against the passage wall. Away from the heat of the hall, it was bitter cold and his rapid breaths made frosty puffs of steam. When he had gained his second wind, he set off, walking quickly.

Twice, the young man walking before Tess and Will glanced back—once at the sound of heavy footsteps, which sounded as if they came from above, and again when a door closed behind them.

They continued on through a bewildering maze

of passages, where torches, placed in brackets on the stone walls, lit the way. Will had lived at court, for a time, but he had never fully explored the palace's labyrinth of passageways. At least not to the extent that he knew where he was at the moment, aside from a general notion that they were walking east toward the rear of the palace, toward the river.

Will lumbered along on all fours, his view of the passageway made grotesque by the distortion of the glass eyes and the flickering torchlight. Several times he glanced at Tess.

Her face was stiff, pale with tension, unexpectedly beautiful in the harsh dancing light. He was suddenly filled with remorse. Why had he not married her two years before? Why had he been such a fool? Why could he not have been satisfied?

At their approach, a door opened silently. A pool of yellow light spilled into the passageway. An old servant with a smooth pate and droopy jowls stepped into the light, and nodded to the man leading the way.

At the door the two young men turned away, walking back in the direction they had come. Will and Tess entered the chamber alone. The old servant closed the door behind them as soundlessly as he had opened it. Will heard the metal bar slide into place, though, and Tess glanced nervously over her shoulder at the sound.

Just inside the door, they passed before a huge freestanding stained-glass window which was encased in a rectangular framework of heavy wood, and had been placed before one of the chamber's two windows. The glow of the wall sconces and the leaping flames in the hearth were reflected in its vivid colors. It was fine, but oddly out of place, like something one might find in a chapel. It lent the room a bizarre appearance. There was an alcove to one side of the room and two door arches. The rooms beyond were in darkness.

The earl of Warwick awaited them before the blazing hearth. In his velvet doublet sewn with jewels, his fingers dripping rubies, he was the picture of a wealthy nobleman. For a moment he said nothing; he simply stared. All at once he smiled, almost eagerly, and said, "I applaud your ingenuity. Or have I only imagined that the bear spoke to me?"

The old servant took up a position near the hearth. Apparently Warwick trusted him.

"You have not imagined it, milord," Will said, rising to his feet, and stretching his aching spine.

Tess immediately set her fingers to unhooking the clasps. Her hands were numb from the cold of the passageways and she fumbled for some moments with the slender wires.

Warwick signaled to the old servant and he disappeared through the door arch nearest the alcove. "There is a legend, perhaps you have heard it, in

371

which God grants the beasts of the earth the power of speech for an hour at Christ-tide." He watched with obvious interest as a young man emerged from the bear's skin. "You were most convincing."

With his head free, Will breathed in several long draughts of air. Warwick was little changed from what Will remembered. He was not a tall man, neither was he young; Will thought him surely near to fifty. His beard, which was trimmed to a precise point, was touched with grey, as was his close-clipped curling hair. Aside from his rich attire and his rather small, coldly calculating eyes, there was nothing about him — certainly not his pleasant manner and clean, even features — that would betray his lust for power or his ambitious greed.

Apparently Warwick had sent the old servant for drink. After a few moments he returned balancing a tray of wine cups.

"Accept my hospitality," Warwick offered. "You deserve a cup of wine for your performance."

Will's throat was painfully dry, but he declined. His glance said as much to Tess.

Warwick's eyebrows rose. "Do you think I would poison you?" he laughed, lifting a cup from the tray and taking a drink before remarking, "Lack of trust is what has set England against herself."

Will did not rise to the bait. He felt suddenly irritated, foolish. The powerful sense of dislike he had always felt toward the man returned unbidden. Working his arms free, Will drew the missive from where he had secreted it in the padding of the bearskin. He wanted only to deliver the message and be gone.

Warwick's jeweled hand grasped the leather packet. He set the pewter cup aside on the mantelpiece and attacked the packet with a badgerlike intensity. Having no luck using his thumbnail to pry open the waxseal of the leather packet, he sent the old servant to fetch a knife.

Tess's gaze roved over the chamber, but no matter where she looked, her eyes invariably returned to the oddness of the window. Truly the chamber was finer than anything she had ever known, but compared to the grandeur she had witnessed in the hall, it seemed shoddy, not elegant enough for a noble who glittered with jewels, a member of the king's council. Will had come to a similar conclusion. It was a disturbing thought.

Having succeeded in opening the packet, Warwick laid the knife aside on the mantelpiece and angled the missive toward the firelight. He read it avidly, his eyes devouring the words.

Suddenly he looked up, thrusting the paper at Will, demanding, "This is no message. It is naught but a rambling." He halted, pressed a smile upon his lips, and said, "It is a prayer, nothing more?"

"Yes," Will agreed. "The missive was meant only as proof that the words I give you are those of

Henry Lancaster."

"Words?" he asked, knowing Henry was at times strange—more truthfully, demented.

"Yes, milord." Will felt the blood rushing to his face. He had not been prepared for the awkward, foolish feeling of a little boy who is made to recite something. He took a deep breath, and said, "King Henry bids you, 'Freedom is neither a grave nor a prison. Come to Banbury Cross when the Christ's moon is risen.'"

"He awaits me there?" Warwick smiled. He was well-aware of Henry's foolish love of words. Henry was a fool. But at the moment a very valuable one.

"Yes, milord. At the church of All Hallows."

Warwick made a silent mirthful sound. "I am certain Henry and I will have much to discuss." He flashed them a sleek smile and, tossing the missive into the flames, took up the fire iron, rapping it sharply against one of the pair of large andirons. Sparks danced in the blackness of the hearth.

Will addressed him. "If that is all, milord, we will go."

For a moment there was only the crackling hiss of the fire. Will thought he heard a movement from beyond the nearest door arch, the creaking of a floor board, a shuffling of feet. He reasoned it was the old servant, for he no longer saw him.

Warwick replaced the fire iron. "No," he said. "I

am afraid that will not be possible." In the hearth, the missive curled to black ash.

At the sound of Tess's sharply indrawn breath, Will's gaze riveted upon the door arch. John Croaker stepped from the shadows, followed by Damon Swift and four sturdy crossbowmen.

Concealed in the darkness of the adjoining room, they had heard everything. John Croaker threw Will and Tess a gloating look. He thrust his lower lip forward and smiled. Turning to Warwick, he said, "Who could have foretold that Henry would seal his own fate?"

"Yes," Warwick remarked, a sleek smile of victory upon his lips. "We could have all spared ourselves a good deal of trouble."

But Will's eyes were on John Croaker. Will knew now with certainty that his and Tess's fate was sealed. They would be killed.

The old servant came wearing a cloak and a bag cap. On his arm were his master's cloak, fur hat and gloves.

Damon Swift and the crossbowmen moved into the room, taking up positions behind and to either side of Will and Tess.

"You spoke to me of trust," Will mocked. "Your words speak of good, but your deeds still speak of treachery!"

Warwick settled his fur hat upon his head. He smiled, mildly. "A regrettable situation, yes." The servant placed the cloak on his shoulders and passed his gloves to him.

"Allow her to leave, at least." Will's voice was edged with desperation. "She had no part in this."

"That is a lie," Swift interjected.

Warwick sent Swift a furious glance. "Be silent, young man! I do not wish to hear your comments."

Swift said no more, but the harsh censure caused a muscle in his jaw to twitch.

Warwick's eyes settled again on Will, his glance grazing the girl's pale, pretty face. "Ah," he said, "A pity. But she knows what you know, and quite frankly, you both know too much. You would warn Henry, and that would never do. No, there is too much at risk," he concluded, almost apologetically. At this point the earl of Warwick could afford no miscalculations. He was determined to oust the ungrateful Edward from the throne. His avowed intent was to replace him with the weak-minded Henry so that he, the earl of Warwick, would in truth hold the reins of power.

Warwick and the old servant walked toward the door. Before the gaudy colors of the stained-glass window, he paused, addressing John Croaker. "I will leave at once with a company of men for Banbury. Kill them. Do it quickly. I want there to be no trace. Then follow me at all speed with a troop of your most trustworthy men."

At the sound of footsteps, Cedric flattened himself to the wall. The torches lighting the passageway went no further than the central door of the suite. It was utterly black where he stood, molded to the corner of a smaller side passage.

He heard the door open and, peering cautiously from his hiding place, he saw a noble in a swirling cloak stride off down the passage. A servant trundled after him. Cedric felt certain it was the old man who had admitted Will and Tess, for he moved with the same arthritic gait.

Cedric waited a moment longer in the darkness, thinking. That meant there was the sheriff, his lieutenant with the square-cut hair, and four crossbowmen. Six men total. It was impossible. There was nothing he could do. There was no time to get the others, and he doubted they would come in any case, not armed with only knives to fight against six men armed with swords and crossbows.

He should go, he decided. But no sooner had he made up his mind to leave, than he realized he could not. He must try. Making his way to the smaller doorway, the one he had seen the sheriff and his men enter earlier, he hovered there in the shadows.

Pinpricks of fear raced up his arm as he reached for the latch. He tried it, gently. It moved. He heard voices within, but he could not make out what was being said. Inside, he moved stealthily through the dark. The voices were quite distinct now.

"Take them to the cellars and kill them there.

Throw the bodies in the river. Swift, I want no screams."

"Through several yards of earth and stone?" Swift protested. The sheriff sent him an ugly look. Swift shrugged, and smiled unpleasantly, remarking, "A tongue is easily removed."

"An hour," Croaker warned him. "No more. We must ride out yet tonight. First though, I will have the bearskin for a trophy. Do you recall the ridiculous banker?" he asked, directing his remark to Swift. "I shall have a good bit more than an arm," he boasted.

A good bit more, indeed, John Croaker thought with satisfaction. For his services, Warwick had promised him the title of earl and the Catesby estates. He would soon have his rewards.

Swift smiled, but he was not amused. The sheriff's stupid whim was cutting into his time—time that he needed to properly punish the pair before him.

"Remove the skin," Swift ordered. "Be quick about it!"

Will could now see all of the men, save the one directly behind him. He glanced from Swift to the sheriff, who lounged casually with an arm on the mantelpiece. The knife Warwick had used to open the missive was also there, just beyond the sheriff's elbow.

Will looked back to Swift, and said simply, "No."

Swift lunged forward and struck him across the face with the back of his hand. "Take it off," he repeated savagely.

"No," Will said, playing for time. He could feel the blood trickling from his lip.

His refusal seemed to madden Swift, whose yellow eyes narrowed menacingly. "Shall I hit her, then?" Swift threatened.

He will do it, Will thought, only to then realize, with an awful sinking of the heart, that it was nothing compared to what Swift had in mind for her. "All right," he said, and with slow deliberate movements he began to shed the bearskin.

Tess attempted to help him with trembling hands, understanding from their exchanged glances, go slow, go slow. For the longer it took, the longer they would have to live, to think of a way to save themselves.

Twice Will staggered as he removed the skin. Each time he gained a step nearer John Croaker standing before the hearth. Without the bearskin, Will was cold; his only clothing was Milo's thin linen hosen, and he stood there barefoot on the icy floor.

Swift's yellow eyes followed Tess's every movement as she stooped to gather up the skin. Will crouched beside her. Their hands touched; their eyes met. A ghost of a smile touched her lips and the look in her eyes all but stopped his heart. He could not let this happen to her; he had to do something. Do it now, before it was too late.

From his crouched position, he could see every man in the room. He could also quite plainly see John Croaker's long-toed *poulaines* and a portion of his legs in the black hosen. He was now within striking distance. He rose up slowly, his muscles bunched to lunge.

Tess read his intention in the sudden darting glance, and she waited, an almost hysterical terror stealing over her. She was not exactly sure of what happened next or of the order in which it occurred. A loud crash sounded from beyond the darkened door arch. And in the same instant Will was dragging John Croaker backwards, with an arm twisted grotesquely behind him, his wrist jammed to his shoulder blade, and his ugly face contorted with pain and fury.

In his other hand Will held the knife poised at the sheriff's throat. Tess, sensing Swift's movement behind her, scrambled away toward Will.

"Keep behind me," he told her, not taking his eyes from the men facing off at him.

"Will?" a voice called from the dark of the door arch.

"Cedric?"

Cedric's peaky face appeared from the shadows. He looked about with a dazed expression. In the darkness he had inadvertently overturned an empty wine ewer.

The crossbowmen could not decide where to aim

their weapons, and alternated between Will and the boy who moved cautiously into the room.

"Go and see if there is anyone in the passage," Will told Cedric, who slipped across the room, past the crossbowmen like a shadow.

After a moment, his reply came back. "No."

"Go with him," Will said, glancing to Tess. This time she did not protest.

Aside from their clipped monosyllabic exchanges, a chilling silence had descended upon the chamber—particularly between the sheriff and his men. There was only the sound of their rasping breaths.

"Lay down your weapons," Will told them. The crossbows concerned him—the short, lethal, steel darts.

Swift's face remained impassive. The crossbowmen did not move to comply.

"Tell them to lay down their weapons," Will growled into Croaker's ear.

A muscle in Croaker's jaw twitched, but he remained silent.

It was obvious what would happen to the sheriff if they attempted to interfere. It was even more keenly obvious to John Croaker, who finally shrieked, "Do as he asks!"

Once the crossbows were laid out on the chamber floor, Will began to move toward the door, dragging the sheriff along with him.

Swift moved forward, swaying like a dog at the

end of its chain. His nostrils flared with an animal-like ferocity, and he snarled, "You cannot escape, you are trapped, all of you."

Will made no response. He merely dragged the sheriff another step toward the door. They were before the window now. Will was conscious of every sound, every movement—aware of the strange empty feeling in his chest, the uneven beating of his heart, and the cloying sweet odor of the oil the sheriff had lavished on his hair.

Perhaps Will had been expecting it, for when Swift lunged at him, he sent the sheriff hurtling into him with a mighty thrust of his arm. The resulting collision sent both the sheriff and Swift sprawling across the floor. The crossbowmen scrambled for their weapons. Swift, dragging himself from the floor, screamed, "Kill him!"

Will charged toward the door. He heard the thrum of the crossbows. Involuntarily his muscles braced for the tearing impact. Instead, it seemed the air around him exploded in a million sparkling particles of glass. A haze of tinkling sound brushed over him, pecking harmlessly against his bare flesh as he lunged through the door. Behind him he heard a full, deep roaring bellow, followed by cursing, shouting, and the trample of feet.

At the entrance to the darkened passage, Tess and Cedric were waiting. Will dashed toward them. He grabbed Tess's hand, and the three of them ran for their lives.

From the side passage they entered a larger passageway lit by torches. The sound of running feet seemed to come from all directions, but after a time it became fainter. They had encountered no one thus far, but where the passages were lit, there was the very real danger that they would. When they came to the last of the torches, Will took it down to light their way.

They had left their cart by the east gate. None of them had any notion of the time, they had lost all sense of it, and it was possible that Elgar, Noam, and Luigi had already left. Even so, the gate was there, and through the gate lay freedom. But which way was east?

It seemed they had gone deeper into the palace, for they came upon no windows, and the stale air smelled of dust and neglect. Will reasoned that they were in the oldest section of the palace, and if they could continue on to the end, then work their way forward, it was possible they could find themselves near the chapel, and the east gate. It was a slim hope, but all they had.

Presently they found a long slitted window open to the elements. They could distinguish nothing below, though, and learned only that the night was utterly black and that it was snowing.

The flickering torch eventually sputtered and went out, but not before they saw a larger passage. They hoped it would lead to a staircase, for all agreed they had climbed two flights of stairs to reach the sheriff's suite.

They now had to depend on touch to find their way. Brushing one hand against the wall, and with the other stretched before him, Will made his way along the passage — Tess and Cedric following him. After about twenty paces, he felt the passage turn right, another six paces brought him up against a solid wall. He swore a silent oath, and retraced their steps. By now his feet were so cold he could hardly feel them.

He was not desperate, until he heard voices and running footsteps. He started back down the other side of the passage. But Tess tugged at his arm, whispering, "This way, I felt a draft of air. I am certain."

"They're coming from that direction," Cedric said.

"Ten paces," Will promised, counting them off mentally as he felt his way along. He had only gone five when he felt a slight, very cold breeze. Cedric noticed it, too.

After only a few more steps, they discovered the alcove and the window. It was a tall window, of the old style, with a wide embrasure. Snow drifted on the icy air, and the moon was hidden by the clouds. Even so, the spire of the chapel stood out blacker than the night. They appeared to be directly above the sacristy, and not as high off the ground as Will had first thought.

Will leaned from the window. He could make

out the dim shape of a roof about eight or ten feet below. The voices and footsteps were definitely closer, and coming toward them.

"I can do it," Cedric said.

"No, I'll go first. I need you here to pass Tess down."

Tess begged him, "Will, no." But when the voices behind them became louder, she realized there was no other way.

Will climbed into the embrasure. Looking down, it occurred to him that the roof was most likely of slate and the sudden impact of his body might easily shatter the surface and send him off in an avalanche of broken tiles. He hesitated, deciding finally there was nothing else he could do.

Clinging to the embrasure, Will lowered himself slowly. He hung in midair a moment, then let go. He had misjudged the distance to the roof, and the impact took his breath away. The tiles did not shatter, though the noise was appalling and he thought someone must have surely heard. The roof sloped and he had to clutch at it to keep from rolling. He pulled himself to his feet and, gaining his balance, motioned for Tess.

Tess and Cedric had knotted their woad-blue cloaks together, tying one end under her arms. It took every bit of Tess's courage to climb into the embrasure. Slowly, she lowered herself. She closed her eyes, but it did not help, for when she released the embrasure, with only the cloak to cling to, she felt as if she had swallowed her heart.

Will caught her, folding her in his arms. He motioned to Cedric, who sent the cloak floating down, before lowering himself from the window and dropping to the roof beside them.

Moving cautiously across the roof, they made their way to a still-lower roof and from there to the ground.

They found themselves in a small, very dark courtyard. Judging from the clamor beyond the walls, the festivities had not yet ended. Only after a futile search for a gate did they discover that the courtyard was blind. The only way out, was through a door that led into the chapel.

Will was weighing the dangers of scaling the walls, when voices sounded above them. From where they stood, deep in the shadows, they could make out heads peering from the window they had exited only a short time before. They seemed to be arguing among themselves. After a few moments the heads vanished and the voices died away.

The door was clearly the only way out. A pale thread of light shone beneath it. Will reasoned it was the sacristy. He had no sooner put his thought to words, then the bells began to toll. The Mass was beginning, logically the sacristy would be empty. At least Will hoped it would be.

Will felt for the latch. It rose with a faint click.

He pushed, easing himself past the door, then motioned to Tess and Cedric to follow.

Rummaging through the room, they donned the hooded robes of the order. Will would have liked to find a pair of boots, but he was not so fortunate.

Beyond the sacristy door, a line of brethren sang a Latin chant as they filed toward the choir. Will, Tess, and Cedric fell into their queue, following along. When the line of brethren turned to ascend the stairs, the trio walked swiftly out a side door into the night. Snow swirled in their faces; it fell heavier now, clinging to their eyelashes, the barren branches, and dead clumps of grass.

In the huge courtyard, people milled about, and a snarl of carts began to move toward the gates. Cartmen and guildsmen harangued and argued, and drunken brawls broke out as the exodus from the palace began.

Will had given up hope of locating the cart. But as he, Tess, and Cedric hurried toward the gate, he sighted Navet and the blue streamers. Luigi was driving the cart, while Elgar and Noam stood in the open bed, leaning out precariously as if they searched for faces among the throng of people.

Pressing their way forward, Will, Tess and Cedric hurried after the cart. Cedric reached it first. Will boosted Tess up to him, then hauled himself aboard the jolting cart.

The east gate, white with quickly gathering snow, remained the final obstacle to their freedom. But as they drew even with its massive stones, no guards stepped out to challenge them. The iron portcullis was raised and set in place, and if there were guards, they were nowhere in sight.

Chapter Nineteen

"You idiot! You bloody, stupid idiot!"

The words struck Damon Swift like stones. He had ceased to attempt to defend his actions. The sheriff, he imagined, would soon weary of his tirade. Meanwhile, time, precious time, was slipping away; and the messenger was free, as free as the running fox. There was no doubt he would go to warn Henry, and with all speed.

When the sheriff fell silent, Swift turned contritely and said, "Milord, a window can be repaired. The damage this man is capable of inflicting upon all our futures cannot be measured."

"Shut up, you fool!" He was right, of course, though John Croaker felt no less inclined to forgive his stupidity. "Go and collect the men," he commanded. "Go on. Get out. I expect to be riding at dawn."

The woad-blue streamers snapped in the icy

breeze as the cart swayed along, keeping pace with the mass of humanity. All along the route, people trudged or rode in carts, dragging their masks, talking loudly and laughing. The glow of their torches lit the Eleanor Cross as the homeward-bound procession snaked toward London. Torches flared and bobbed in the darkness, illuminating the whirling snow with trailing clouds of sparks.

Snowflakes caught on Tess's lashes, glistened on the bridge of her nose, and cobwebbed against the lopsided holly wreath. Her cheeks were as red as apples, and tears spilled from her blue eyes. Yet she could not stop laughing. They all laughed, even Will with his great bare feet. They laughed because they were alive and free and jouncing through the snow.

At the embankment, Luigi drew up on the reins, halting the horse. The bells on his fool's cap tinkled in the wind. "Here, we say farewell," he announced. But Elgar and Noam had already taken their leave and were hopping from the cart. Cedric moved into the seat to take the reins.

Tess leaned forward and touched the little man's shoulder, as Will wished him a safe journey and gave him a hand-down from the cart.

"Cedric," he called, taking a step backwards on his short legs.

"I ain't going."

"But why?" The boys moved slowly down the whitened embankment, waiting, shuffling their feet.

Cedric glanced back, looking almost apologetic. "I don't like boats. They scare me."

With a shrug of his little shoulders, Luigi turned to Tess. "We will miss your fair smile," he said, jauntily tossing her a kiss. Then he turned away, hurrying through the snow to follow the shadowy figures down the embankment.

Cedric made a clucking sound. The gelding's ears twitched, and the cart jerked into motion.

"What will you do?" Tess asked Cedric. "Where can you go?" Her brows knitted with concern, and she glanced at Will.

Cedric's eyes were set on the horses' ears. "Me, eh, I might become honest . . . take some decent work."

"I've need of a squire," Will suggested.

Cedric looked back over his shoulder, his face aglow. "Do you mean it?"

"Of course. But I warn you, I intend to live a quiet life."

Cedric gave a little laugh. "I won't complain," he said. He grinned at Tess, and jiggled the reins, hurrying Navet.

Snowflakes swirled in the darkness. Near the tavern, they discovered that the narrow streets were hopelessly tangled with revelers and carts. Still garbed in the robes they had taken from the sacristy, they unhitched Navet and went on foot, leading the gelding through the alleyways and stable lots.

The boot-marked slush of the tavern yard was also crowded with carts and people going back and forth. The latrines were located to one side of the smaller of the two stables, and the sewage ran unchecked into an open ditch. They were cautious where they stepped. At that time of year there was no stench to warn a person of the ditch—either that, or the insides of their noses were too stunned by the cold to recognize it.

The sounds of the tavern filtered through the snowy lot. Will sent Cedric to the stable with Navet. "He's hungry, but don't give him much," Will cautioned, adding, "See if the stableman's about, first."

Cedric nodded. He knew what to do. He knew all the locks and how to open them when the stableman wasn't around.

Will and Tess entered the ramshackle cottage. In the dark, the dirt-floored structure appeared picked clean, bare to the walls. After a fumbling search for the dented oil lamp, and repeated efforts to strike a flint, they finally got a light and spied a small bundle tucked behind the door.

The bundle contained Will's leather *jaque,* shirt and hosen, Tess's dress, and the little christening gown that Fleur had so lovingly fashioned. Will's boots were not in the bundle. He searched for a moment, before stripping off the sacristy robe and quickly donning his own clothing.

By the feeble light of the lamp, Tess ran her

numbed fingers over the silk and intricate lace of the gown. There were tears in her eyes. After a moment, she held up the tiny gown for Will to see. "Fleur did not forget," she said.

"No," he agreed, stuffing his shirt into his hosen. "Though I would rather she had left my boots." He pulled the rough, woolen robe back on over his clothing. He was certain that Tom had taken the boots, recalling that the soldiers had stolen all his, save the shabby pair he'd been wearing.

Will strode round the room once more, considering the improbability of acquiring a pair of boots, a pair that fit. His feet were not small. He would have to think of something quickly; his toes were already beyond feeling.

"Perhaps they are here somewhere," Tess suggested, scanning the room half-heartedly. Will did not answer; he was already at the door. Tess stuffed the little silken christening gown inside her sacristy robe and ran after him.

Cedric looked again from the stable door. At last he saw Will and Tess coming from the cottage, walking swiftly through the swirling snowflakes. When they reached him, he said, "The stableman's in there." Cedric inclined his head toward the rear of the low-beamed stable, where the tack was kept. "I didn't see nobody else," he added, advising them with a sly-lipped smile, "He's drunk."

Will returned the smile, thinking that in such a

state the old weasel might be a bit more reasonable. "Did you find two more horses—ones that can run?"

Cedric gave a quick nod. "I pinched a saddle for your gelding, too."

A loud snoring greeted Will as he entered the stableman's quarters. The tiny cubicle stank of sour wine and sweat. At a glance Will saw that the old man was indeed drunk, dead drunk. His mouth gaped open, and the bare feet protruding from the moth-eaten blanket were callused and large, possibly larger than his own.

Will looked around for the old man's boots. He saw them at the foot of the straw-stuffed pallet, slouched one against the other. They were badly worn and had a rank, pungent odor about them, one not entirely due to horse turds. He sat down on the straw pallet, shoving the old man's legs aside with his hip, and pulled on the boots. They were a bit too wide, but blessedly warm. Will would have left him money for the horses and the boots, but he had no coin to spare. "You'll get your reward in heaven, my friend," Will remarked to the snoring drunk as he ducked beneath the doorway.

Among them they had only a single gold coin, the one Elizabeth Woodville had given to Tess at Sandal, and that she kept secreted in her slipper. She would have need of the gold piece, for Will intended to send her and Cedric north from London by the drovers' road to Malvern. Will knew there was a tavern there. They could wait several days. If he did not come after the third day, it would be safer for them to continue north to Lambsdale. The sheriff would have no cause to search for them there.

In the stable, Will hurriedly explained his plan to Tess and Cedric. The crux of it was that he would have to move quickly if he were to overtake Warwick and warn King Henry. "You could not keep pace," he said to Tess.

"I will not be sent away!" Her blue eyes flared with determination. "No." She was adamant.

"You cannot ride at such a speed. It would kill you and the babe."

"No," she insisted. "I am not so large as that. I have climbed from roofs; I have run after you; I have followed you all this way, and I will not leave you now!"

Her earnest eyes were as blue as a summer's day. What would he ever do without her? And worse still, what if there were only himself to blame for losing her? "Follow me to a grave—is that what you want?" He grasped her small shoulders, attempting to reason with her. "They will not stop hunting me until I am dead. They cannot allow me to reach Banbury."

"If you leave me, I will follow you."

"I am not deserting you."

"Yes," she cried. "You are. That is what you are

saying."

He gave her an agonized look, suspecting that she would do just as she threatened. Would she be any safer on the drovers' road? He no longer knew the answer. Defeated, he let out his breath with a hiss. Without another word, he boosted her into the saddle.

The trio rode through the snowy night and into a glittering morning, where the trees and brush were bathed in a crystal light. A realm of cold and lifeless beauty unfolded before them. Snow crunched beneath their horses' hooves, and with the breeze came the tinkling sound of ice in the branches.

By afternoon the wind had risen, bringing mottled clouds to close the skies and hide the sun. They stopped only long enough to rest their steaming horses.

On they rode, leaning forward against the squalls of wind, their fingers tingling from the cold. Late in the day they stopped at a tavern. They amazed all within; none had ever before seen a blue horse.

"We are jongleurs," Cedric told them. He could not resist further astounding the simple folk with his juggling of cups, trenchers, and whatever else they provided.

Lifting Tess from her horse, Will asked for the hundredth time, or so it seemed to Tess, if she were feeling well.

"I am not sick," she protested, her cheeks and

nose rosy from the cold. "Do you think I will break?"

He marveled at her. In truth, she seemed no worse for any of it, no worse than he or Cedric.

From the tavernkeeper they learned that a noble and a large force of his armed retainers had passed through the village but several hours before.

Over cups of watered-down ale, cheese, and bread that was surely a week old, the tavernkeeper told the travelers of Stone Bridge. "It's the only way to cross the river. I wouldn't trust the ice."

"There be a bridge at Claxton," an old peddler seated by the hearth spoke out. " 'Tis a shorter route to Banbury, but the road's your own to make." For the price of a pot of ale he gladly gave them directions.

He had not lied about the road; they made it where they could. The forest was thick, deep now with snow, and the stinging wind whipped at their robes and sent ice crystals to sparkle in the air.

It was near dark when they came from the woods into open pasture land. In the creeping blue cold of evening, the trio paused on a hillock to rest their horses. Will rode ahead a short distance, and, standing in his stirrups, sighted the river. He saw no bridge. They had passed it by or not yet come upon it. He was considering this when, from the tail of his vision, he saw a flurry of riders through the barren branches, twenty or more, riding as if the devil were chasing them.

John Croaker? It seemed likely. Will himself had learned of the bridge for the price of some ale; and the tavernkeeper and his patrons would have been more than eager to tell another traveler of a painted horse they'd seen, and a boy who juggled cups and bowls.

Putting his leg to Navet's side, he turned the gelding and galloped back to where Tess and Cedric waited.

Riding three abreast, they plunged down the hill, their horses bracing their forelegs against the steep slope. The lowland meadows beside the river were thick with snow, and with objects which were only half-seen — windfalls of branches and rotting stumps.

Soon all beneath the shining hilltops was lost to the dark of evening. Only when they reached the broad smooth sheen of the river did they again see the riders. They themselves had been sighted too, for they heard the hue and cry at their backs.

If the bridge was nearby, they did not see it, and there was no time to search it out, for the horsemen were bearing down on them.

At the edge of the river, Will reined in Navet. Tess galloped up on the bobtailed chestnut mare. Cedric, on a bay, jostled into them. They were trapped with the frozen river before them and John Croaker at their backs.

With his eyes stinging from the cold, John Croaker pressed ahead, shouting to his men, "Take them alive!"

Damon Swift, riding close at his side, called out, "The girl is mine," but the wind stole his words away. He leaned forward, spurring his horse on, a savage thrill of victory coursing through his breast. Nothing now could keep him from exacting his revenge. There would be no escape for her this time.

Will tossed a quick glance over his shoulder and saw them hurtling forward, their horses kicking up a spume of snow. The blood sang in his ears, and through his pounding pulse he heard John Croaker's roaring bellow. There was nowhere to go, only the river.

In desperation, Will swung Navet toward the ice. Tess and Cedric followed, their horses skidding. They slid down the bank, galloping full stride across the ice with the crash and hammer of hoofbeats at their backs.

A dark swift line swept past Tess. She felt her mare shift sideways. A crack like a stroke of lightning snapped the air, and then she heard the deep grating rumble of the ice. The ice was moving, shifting, breaking all around them, chasing them across the deep, black water. The wild beating of her heart seemed to suffocate her, and when she screamed no sound came out. Her little mare flattened back her ears and plunged on, gamely keeping pace.

In another stride they would clear the ice. Behind them they heard high-pitched screams of men and horses, but they did not look back. They sent their horses lunging up the bank, struggling over the frozen ground.

Only then did they pause to look back, but all they saw was the deep black water, the churning ice.

Chapter Twenty

They set their horses toward Banbury. They had no time to spare, for there was still Warwick, and he would surely cross at Stone Bridge by dawn.

The Eleanor Cross with its mantle of snow stood before the church. They clattered past a low stone wall and into the churchyard. On either side were the graves of the faithful, and beyond, the square Norman tower of All Hallows.

A tall, spare-looking man came from the chapter-house door with a lantern in his hand. Snow glistened in the halo of light, and the crunch of his footfalls echoed across the courtyard.

Will twitched at the reins and walked his horse toward the figure, thinking there was something in his manner, his stride.

"Hamo!" Will called, not believing it was he. Will slid from his saddle.

"Young William, my God it is *you!*" Hamo exclaimed, setting down the lantern to embrace him.

"My uncle, he is here? The king? Roger Percy also?"

Hamo answered, "Yes, all of them."

"The king must go quickly. Warwick is just at my heels. It is a trap."

"I will go and warn them." Hamo went striding back to the chapter-house door, leaving the lantern to light the snow.

Will lifted Tess from her horse, folding her in his arms. Dropping his head close to hers, he murmured, "How goes it?"

She pressed her hand into his. Her fingers had no feeling. She smiled quickly up at him. "All is well," she said.

The darkened church came to life as lights appeared. A boy, roused from his sleep, came squint-eyed to take the horses.

With a clatter, the chapter-house door flew open. Thurstan Hartley strode into the courtyard, braving the cold in only his robe. "William! Thank God!" he said, clasping his nephew in a fierce hug.

"Am I to be forgiven, Uncle?"

"You have never been otherwise. Come, bring your companions inside where it is warm."

Once inside, by the glow of the newly stoked hearth fire, Will took Tess's hand and drew her forward. Self-consciously, she pushed the cowled hood from her head revealing the circlet of holly leaves and smiled, uncertainly.

"My God, is that not Adam Shaw's granddaughter? What other surprises have you brought for me in the middle of the night?"

"No others that we may discuss now, except Cedric, my squire."

Roger Percy appeared in the doorway, his face cramped with the familiar, weary smile he always wore.

"Roger," Will said in greeting. "The king?" he asked.

"Yes, the horses are being saddled. But he will not leave until he has spoken with you."

Will crossed the room with Tess in tow. At the door arch Roger touched his arm. "He will not remember you, so you are warned."

They found Henry kneeling at the altar rail. The Mass had ended. The monks had risen from their prayers, and their feet shuffled on the cold flagstones of the church. A monk, with a tonsured head, appeared with a golden candle extinguisher. Wisps of fragrant white smoke curled into the air.

Outside, the day had dawned. A gray light poured through the tall gothic windows, along with drafts of cold air.

Roger Percy touched the king's shoulder. "Milord, I have brought the young messenger."

Henry moved stiffly, old before his time, his flesh as fragile as paper where it was drawn over his features. He smiled gently, and said, "There is no need for you to kneel before me. Who are these children, Roger?"

"I am your messenger, milord," Will responded. "Do you not recall, the abbey at Hexham?"

"Oh, yes," he said. "That is why I have come here, to pray for peace." His pale eyes wandered to Roger Percy. "Roger says I must go. Peace must wait for another day." He smiled wanly at the fair young girl with the freckled face and, looking to Will, asked, "Is this your wife?"

"She is soon to be, milord. As soon as I might marry her."

"Then it shall be now." He seemed delighted by the prospect and sent Roger Percy, in spite of his protests, to fetch the priest.

The sunrise lit the stained-glass windows as the priest hurriedly put on his garments while anxious moments passed.

Will took Tess's hands and touched his lips to her forehead. In the cool light, her skin was as pale as cream. She was simply beautiful and good. It seemed he had always loved her, never knowing it, never realizing she had been there, wide-eyed with wonderment, waiting for him like a golden summer morning. Now that he had found her, he would never let her go. Before the king and those assembled, the priest quickly muttered the words.

Tess did not mind. In the rough woolen robe she stood there. She thought she must surely be sparkling, for with her hands in Will's she had everything she had wished for, as though somehow, she had known by premonition. It had not been wrong, she thought, so wildly to wish for something, to wish for love and find it in his arms and in his heart.

The words were said. And when the priest came to it, there was no ring to bless. King Henry hesitated not at all. Twisting a golden band from his finger, he passed it to the priest. Only when the last words were spoken was a harried Roger Percy able to lure him from the nave.

King Henry, muffled in a tattered cape, rode off with Roger Percy and his knights. Within the hour, Warwick and his forces blustered into All Hallows' snowy forecourt. They found only the priests, the penitent Lord Devrel, his nephew and wife, and half a dozen of the old earl's retainers.

Warwick recognized the young couple at once. He gave no sign of it, though, aside from regarding them with a look of slight surprise. He said not a word to Will. No words were needed, for the look that passed between them was filled with malice.

Warwick was wise enough to know that it would profit him nothing to arrest them. It was Henry he wanted. He certainly did not wish to drag Will Hartley before King Edward and in doing so involve himself in treason. Not yet, at any rate. He would not risk alerting Edward of his intentions to place Henry on the throne, particularly before he had the means to implement them.

There would be another day. Roger Percy could not elude him forever.

So Warwick returned to London empty-handed. It was there, in his splendid solar at Westminster, that word reached him of the sheriff's unfortunate fate.

Three days hence at Westminster, Thurstan Hartley and his nephew William rode with the barons to the cathedral. Edward had promised clemency to all who came at Christ-tide, knelt down, and swore fealty to him.

Like the other rebel barons, they had swallowed their pride and, in the interests of their family and their lands, gone to make their promises to the Yorkist king.

Edward came before them wearing a crown, like Caesar in glory. In an aside to one of his councillors, Edward noted, "All the sheep have returned to the fold."

Warwick, who was among the councillors, remarked cynically, "You may find a few wolves among them, sire."

Edward smiled, though there was no warmth in his expression. Glancing at his former mentor, he said, "I have no fear of wolves, Warwick."

As the ceremony proceeded, Will knelt down beside his uncle and the other barons. He swore by God's Holy Gospel that he, William Hartley, would faithfully keep the laws, treaties, and agreements of Edward, by the grace of God, King of England.

Even as Will said the words, he knew there was and could never be any loyalty in his heart for Edward of York. There had been a lifetime of turmoil between them, between York and Lancaster, too many lies, deceits and treacheries.

Undoubtedly his father and his brothers would have rejected his actions as cowardly, but he had seen the truth for what it was, and it was senseless to go on . . . since more blood would be spilt. He was anxious to be done with it, to return to his lands, to hold his wife in his arms, and to live his life.

Epilogue

Will Hartley left his horse before the hall with trailing reins. He rushed inside, dragging the scent of the cold spring day with him, taking the steps by twos and threes.

His Aunt Maud was giving instructions to a woman servant outside the lying-in chamber. She looked up to see her nephew top the stairs at full stride. "Where do you think you are going?" she asked, startled by his sudden appearance.

Will would have answered, but he heard a scream and, though he could not see her, he knew that it was Tess.

Maud plucked at his sleeve, protesting, "You cannot go in there." She had never heard of such a thing. It was indecent. It simply was not done. She would have told him so in no uncertain terms had she had the chance. But he swept past her into the room, leaving her to sputter and fluster after him.

Will did not know what to expect, certainly not a roomful of chattering women and Tess lying on the bed spraddle-legged and moaning.

A fire blazed in the hearth, and the sweltering heat combined with the doughy mingling of blood and female scent all but took Will's breath away.

Tess cried out again. Her pains came close together now, harder, sharper. Bertrade leaned over the bed to comfort her. Through a haze of pain, Tess saw the midwife's sweaty face. Again the woman shoved against her knees, encouraging her.

Sybelle, Tess's sister, sat at the beside, and Bertrade clutched Tess's hand. The two women looked up at Will's approach, and quickly drew a sheet over Tess. The midwife frowned and pushed aside the concealing sheet. " 'Tis no time for modesty," she snapped indignantly. "How am I expected to see through a sheet?"

Will hesitated. He felt suddenly like a ghost among the living, unwelcome and unneeded. But Sybelle moved aside. Will crouched at the beside, balanced on his heels. He lifted Tess's limp hand from the sheets and pressed it to his lips. Her fingers were cold as ice.

"Do you know how much I love you?" he murmured in her ear. Tess turned her head at the sound of his voice, and made a valiant effort to smile. She glimpsed his face an instant only. Another searing pain tore through her abdomen.

Tess squeezed tight her eyes, enduring it, fighting back the urge to scream. Bertrade saw the color drain from Will's face, and eased Tess's hand from his.

Will was grateful that she had. He weaved to his feet and stepped aside, light-headed, woozy as a drunk. It was the heat of the room he told himself. His knees felt about to buckle.

Another convulsion of pain gripped Tess. The pressure was unendurable. She screamed. A flurry of activity erupted around the bed. The midwife hovered over Tess, speaking in a crooning voice. All at once she shouted, "Here, it's coming!"

Will saw the tiny, wet head emerge, the rush of blood upon the sheets; and he, who had hacked through flesh and bone, and survived the worst of battle, suddenly could not decide if he would faint or vomit. He turned away, waiting for his head and his stomach to settle. He heard the infant squall.

"You have a daughter," someone said. Will could not bring himself to look — not yet.

Only when Tess called to him did he come on shaky legs to view his daughter. As Will crossed the chamber, Sybelle smiled and touched his arm encouragingly. She was so pleased for her sister.

At the bed, Bertrade fussed over Tess, plumping a pillow behind her shoulders so she might hold the babe. Tess was exhausted. Even so, she beamed with happiness and pride. The ordeal was ended, and she had a perfect, lovely babe to hold and love.

Tess raised her head, smiling at her husband.

"Oh, look, Will, isn't she beautiful?"

The sight of Tess with the babe cradled in her arms made Will's breath catch in his throat. For a moment words eluded him. In truth, the infant's face was red and wrinkled, though he could hardly tell what the truth was. "Yes," he agreed, and reached to touch his daughter's tiny hand, never doubting for a moment that she would grow to be a beauty.

PASSION BLAZES IN A ZEBRA HEARTFIRE!

COLORADO MOONFIRE (3730, $4.25/$5.50)
by Charlotte Hubbard

Lila O'Riley left Ireland, determined to make her own way in America. Finding work and saving pennies presented no problem for the independent lass; locating love was another story. Then one hot night, Lila meets Marshal Barry Thompson. Sparks fly between the fiery beauty and the lawman. Lila learns that America is the promised land, indeed!

MIDNIGHT LOVESTORM (3705, $4.25/$5.50)
by Linda Windsor

Dr. Catalina McCulloch was eager to begin her practice in Los Reyes, California. On her trip from East Texas, the train is robbed by the notorious, masked bandit known as Archangel. Before making his escape, the thief grabs Cat, kisses her fervently, and steals her heart. Even at the risk of losing her standing in the community, Cat must find her mysterious lover once again. No matter what the future might bring . . .

MOUNTAIN ECSTASY (3729, $4.25/$5.50)
by Linda Sandifer

As a divorced woman, Hattie Longmore knew that she faced prejudice. Hoping to escape wagging tongues, she traveled to her brother's Idaho ranch, only to learn of his murder from long, lean Jim Rider. Hattie seeks comfort in Rider's powerful arms, but she soon discovers that this strong cowboy has one weakness . . . marriage. Trying to lasso this wandering man's heart is a challenge that Hattie enthusiastically undertakes.

RENEGADE BRIDE (3813, $4.25/$5.50)
by Barbara Ankrum

In her heart, Mariah Parsons always believed that she would marry the man who had given her her first kiss at age sixteen. Four years later, she is actually on her way West to begin her life with him . . . and she meets Creed Deveraux. Creed is a rough-and-tumble bounty hunter with a masculine swagger and a powerful magnetism. Mariah finds herself drawn to this bold wilderness man, and their passion is as unbridled as the Montana landscape.

ROYAL ECSTASY (3861, $4.25/$5.50)
by Robin Gideon

The name Princess Jade Crosse has become hated throughout the kingdom. After her husband's death, her "advisors" have punished and taxed the commoners with relentless glee. Sir Lyon Beauchane has sworn to stop this evil tyrant and her cruel ways. Scaling the castle wall, he meets this "wicked" woman face to face . . . and is overpowered by love. Beauchane learns the truth behind Jade's imprisonment. Together they struggle to free Jade from her jailors and from her inhibitions.

DISCOVER DEANA JAMES!

CAPTIVE ANGEL (2524, $4.50/$5.50)
Abandoned, penniless, and suddenly responsible for the biggest
tobacco plantation in Colleton County, distraught Caroline Gil-
lard had no time to dissolve into tears. By day the willowy red-
head labored to exhaustion beside her slaves . . . but each night
left her restless with longing for her wayward husband. She'd
make the sea captain regret his betrayal until he begged her to
take him back!

MASQUE OF SAPPHIRE (2885, $4.50/$5.50)
Judith Talbot-Harrow left England with a heavy heart. She was
going to America to join a father she despised and a sister she
distrusted. She was certainly in no mood to put up with the in-
sulting actions of the arrogant Yankee privateer who boarded her
ship, ransacked her things, then "apologized" with an indecent,
brazen kiss! She vowed that someday he'd pay dearly for the lib-
erties he had taken and the desires he had awakened.

SPEAK ONLY LOVE (3439, $4.95/$5.95)
Long ago, the shock of her mother's death had robbed Vivian
Marleigh of the power of speech. Now she was being forced to
marry a bitter man with brandy on his breath. But she could not
say what was in her heart. It was up to the viscount to spark the
fires that would melt her icy reserve.

WILD TEXAS HEART (3205, $4.95/$5.95)
Fan Breckenridge was terrified when the stranger found her near-
naked and shivering beneath the Texas stars. Unable to remember
who she was or what had happened, all she had in the world was
the deed to a patch of land that might yield oil . . . and the fierce
loving of this wildcatter who called himself Irons.

*Available wherever paperbacks are sold, or order direct from the
Publisher. Send cover price plus 50¢ per copy for mailing and
handling to Zebra Books, Dept. 4343, 475 Park Avenue South,
New York, N.Y. 10016. Residents of New York and Tennessee
must include sales tax. DO NOT SEND CASH. For a free Zebra/
Pinnacle catalog please write to the above address.*

EVERY DAY WILL FEEL LIKE FEBRUARY 14TH!

Zebra Historical Romances
by Terri Valentine